Elusive Flame

Kathleen E. Woodiwiss

Elusive Flame

WHEELER
PUBLISHING, INC.
ROCKLAND, MA

★ AN AMERICAN COMPANY ★

Published in Large Print by arrangement with Avon Books, Inc., in the United States and Canada.

Wheeler Large Print Book Series.

Set in 16 pt Plantin.

Library of Congress Cataloging-in-Publication Data

Woodiwiss, Kathleen E.
    Elusive flame / Kathleen E. Woodiwiss.
        p. (large print) cm.(Wheeler large print book series)
    ISBN 1-56895-692-4 (hardcover)
    1.   Large type books. I. Title. II. Series
[PS3573.0625E48   1998b]
813'.54—dc21

98-44847
CIP

Elusive Flame

CHAPTER 1

October 24, 1825
London, England

Cerynise Edlyn Kendall stood at the lofty windows of the front parlor and, through a wealth of tears, gloomily observed the people scurrying along the lane traversing Berkeley Square. They seemed in urgent haste to find shelter before the gathering clouds sent a torrent of rain down upon them. The chilling gusts that accompanied the glowering sky buffeted both young and old, male and female, puckishly snatching cloaks and redingotes of passersby who were put to task keeping top hats, fashionable bonnets or their flyaway wraps in place. Cheeks and noses were brightened to a reddish hue, and shivers came from those more lightly clad. For the most part, the city's inhabitants were making their way with varying degrees of eagerness or resignation to family and homes or to more lonely existences. They gave little heed to the comfort awaiting them or, for that matter, how fragile life really was.

A large porcelain clock, artfully adorned with figurines, delicately chimed the fourth hour on the marble mantel in the parlor. Cerynise clenched her slender hands together in the gently gathered fullness of her skirt, burrowing them into the stiff, black taffeta as she struggled valiantly against an encroaching grief. As the tinkling of the timepiece quieted, she stilled the urge to glance over her shoulder

1

with the same expectancy that had become ingrained by the ritual of tea of which she and her guardian, Lydia Winthrop, had partaken daily for the last five years. The suddenness of the woman's death had stunned Cerynise, and even now, she found it difficult to accept. Lydia had seemed so vivacious and energetic for a woman approaching seventy. Even on the night of her death, her wit and humor had nigh sparkled in contrast to the dour sullenness of her great-nephew, who had come to call upon her that evening. Yet, however much Cerynise wished otherwise, Lydia was dead and buried. Only yesterday Cerynise had stared fixedly at the mahogany casket while final prayers were being spoken for the repose of the woman's soul. To her wearied mind, it now seemed an eternity had passed since a handful of dirt, signifying man's return to ashes and dust, was scattered over the descending coffin. That kind, loving woman whom Cerynise had come to love as her protectress, confidante, surrogate parent and dearest friend was now forever gone from her sight and company.

Despite Cerynise's efforts to banish her sorrow, soft lips trembled back from fine, white teeth as a new rush of tears welled up to blur the thickly fringed hazel eyes. Never again would the two of them enjoy delightful little chitchats over brimming cups and crumpets or sit together in the evening before a cheery, heartwarming fire while Cerynise read aloud to the elder from a treasured book of verse or fiction. The sitting room would no longer be imbued with the lilting strains of melodies which Cerynise had sung while Lydia played the pianoforte. Neither would they traverse a bustling strand together nor share their thoughts while strolling along the banks of the Serpentine in Hyde Park, nor would they simply enjoy the presence of the other in the peace and serenity of the glade. Forever gone would be her guardian's gentle support, which, despite the obstacles of society, had bolstered a young girl's dream of becoming a great painter, to the extent that exhibits had been held and paintings had been sold for goodly sums to wealthy patrons, albeit under an element of secrecy with only the initials CK hinting of the artist's identity. Even now, as poignant memories brought ever-freshening waves of grief sweeping over her, Cerynise could almost imagine the tall, slender, black-garbed silhouette of the elder standing a short distance behind and to the right of her easel as she had oftentimes done while Cerynise painted and, in her rather husky voice, reminding her ward to always be true to herself no matter what.

Cerynise's despair and loneliness were more than she seemed capable of bearing at the moment. She felt completely drained and weak. It was not at all surprising to her that the room seemed to tilt unnaturally, leaving her swaying on her feet and blinking against an encroaching dizziness. In desperation she clutched the window frame for support and rested her brow against the cool, dark wood until gradually the feeling subsided. She had eaten very little since Lydia's death, managing to down nothing more than a few sips of broth and a dry wedge of toast. What sleep she had finally gleaned in her bedchamber upstairs wasn't worth noting. Still, she doubted her ability to find ease from her sorrow even now, though she knew that Lydia wouldn't have wanted her to be unduly distressed by her untimely departure. The elder had once offered a world of comfort and compassion to a frightened twelve-year-old girl who, at the time, had just lost her parents in a devastating storm that had sent a large tree crashing down upon their home. Cerynise had blamed herself for not being there to save them, but Lydia, who had grown up in the area and been childhood friends with Cerynise's grandmother, whose own death had preceded her daughter's by several years, had gently led the girl to understand that she, too, would have been killed had she not been away attending a young lady's academy. No matter the hardships one had to face, the elder had counseled her solicitously, life had to go on. Lydia would have expected her to remember that now.

Yet it was so terribly hard, Cerynise groaned inwardly. If Lydia had been ill even one day of those five years or if there had been some kind of warning, then the whole household would have been better prepared, but as much as it might have forewarned her, Cerynise would never have wished a long, debilitating illness on the elder. No, if the hand of death could not have been stayed, then the fact that Lydia had succumbed in such seemingly good health was truly a blessing, however much it had shocked the young woman who had loved her in life and now grieved her passing.

Raindrops began to pelt the windows and trickle down the glass in quickening runnels, drawing Cerynise's thoughts back to the present. With a storm closing in upon the city, the street was now nearly devoid of pedestrians. Only a few hastened by to find shelter. Carriages continued to pass, their drivers hunched deep in their dapper liveries as they squinted against the droplets.

Soft footfalls came into the parlor, and Cerynise glanced around to meet the reddened eyes of the parlor maid who, like the other members of the household staff, was sorely lamenting the demise of her mistress.

"Yer pardon, Miss Cerynise," the servant murmured, "I was wonderin' if ye'd be wantin' tea now that ye're back?"

Cerynise had no interest in taking sustenance, but the tea would perchance warm her after her graveside visit. She had gotten so chilled to the bone from the unseasonably cold weather presently thwarting them that she could only foresee it as a dreadful harbinger of what the approaching winter would be like.

"Tea will be fine, Bridget. Thank you." Her syllables were softened by a subtle drawl characteristic of her Carolina birthplace which her sojourn in England had barely changed.

5

Amid a profusion of other studies, her tutors had diligently sought to instruct her in proper English diction and etiquette, but having considered none of them as wise or as brilliant as her own studious parents, Cerynise had enjoyed frustrating their efforts to correct her speech like some precocious child who was wont to tease her elders. Though she could assume a stiltedly refined speech that could fool the keenest ears when it met her mood, she had stubbornly refused to become a foreigner to her homeland, for she had made up her mind even before departing the Carolinas that someday she would return.

The maid bobbed a curtsy and hurried away, relieved to have something to occupy her, for the house had grown somber and deathly still in the last few days, as if it too mourned the loss of its mistress. At times, Bridget could almost imagine she could hear the uniquely rasping voice that had, for some years now, filled her life with cheer and kindness.

A tea cart, laden with a silver tea service and Meissen china, was soon pushed into the parlor. Accompanying the steeped brew was a plate of scones adorned with creamy butter and a crystal server of strawberry preserves to tempt the palate.

With a pensive sigh Cerynise left the window and took a seat on one of a pair of matching settees that faced each other before the fireplace. Bridget rolled the cart near and, with another polite bob, took her leave. Cerynise's hands trembled as she lifted the teapot, filled a cup, and added cream and sugar, a small concession which she had made to English custom, but one she particularly enjoyed. She considered the scones, having every intention of eating one, but after taking the bread onto her plate, it suddenly lost its appeal. She could do nothing more than stare at it. Between resolution and actual compliance, there loomed a chasm that, for the life of her, she couldn't seem to cross.

I'll eat it later, Cerynise promised herself and, with a shudder of distaste, set the plate aside. Lifting the cup, she tasted the concoction, hoping it would calm her stomach as well as her nerves. It wasn't long before she found herself at the windows again, sipping the tea as she looked out upon the elegant Mayfair district in which they lived. Beyond the limitations of her view, the world seemed so vast and untamable that the enormity of her sense of loss gave her cause to wonder how she could wisely make the best of her circumstances now that she was alone and no more than ten and seven years of age.

Cerynise closed her eyes against the dull ache that had been brewing in her head since her return home, no doubt caused by tension and endless hours without sleep. The pain in her temples progressed into a constant throbbing until it seemed that every hairpin in her hair had no other purpose but to intensify her discomfort. Setting the teacup aside, she grew more purposeful and began to search out the offending pins, freeing them from the intricately coiled knot on top of her head and raking her fingers through her hair until the thick, softly curling tresses tumbled in free abandon over her shoulders and down her back. The torment persisted with unrelenting vengeance, seeming to pierce her brain until Cerynise felt compelled to seek another form of relief. She began to massage her scalp, giving little heed to how she ruffled the pale-streaked tawny mane that adorned it or, for that matter, that she was in the formal parlor, where proper dress was usually the rule. Only servants were in the house, and although Lydia's great-nephew was inclined to drop in unannounced at odd and sundry times, he hadn't seen fit to come to the funeral. In fact, the last time he had visited, he had been so vexed with the elder when he left that he had raged at her and vowed that he wouldn't be back for a fortnight. That had been a mere three days ago.

The pounding ache in her head began to ease to a more tolerable level, allowing Cerynise to think more clearly about her future. She began to pace restlessly about the parlor as she tried to put her life into clear perspective. She had one remaining relative, and that was an uncle living in Charleston. He had been a bachelor all of his life, having preferred his books and studies over marriage and a family, yet Cerynise suffered no uncertainty that he would welcome her back with open arms.

Prior to her departure, he had assured her that, had he not doubted his ability to nurture her as a knowledgeable parent and teach her all that a woman should know, he would never have let her go, but after carefully considering the advantages she would reap living with the older woman, he had acquiesced to Lydia's suggestion and, with brimming tears, had urged his niece to go to England, study art and languages, learn everything that an elegant lady should be cognizant of, and then come back a polished gem. However far away, Sterling Kendall was her one sure haven.

At least, she wouldn't have to worry about money for a while, Cerynise mused with a measure of relief. With what her paintings had already gained in coin, she could live very comfortably while she created others. Charleston had its own share of wealthy planters and merchants, many of whom were avid collectors of art. Still, they might not be as enthusiastic about her work if they were to learn that the artist was hardly more than an unknown, and a girl to boot. To be reasonably successful there, it seemed advisable for her to find another representative who'd be willing to sell her paintings without lifting the cloak of mystery from her identity. Considering what she had already earned, she didn't think it would be too difficult to interest an enterprising art dealer in performing such a service.

Cerynise halted her pacing abruptly, momentarily startled by the reflection the long gilded mirror hanging in the entrance hall cast back at her. Her disheveled appearance was certainly

9

unexpected here in the front parlor, but what she found even more amazing was the fact that, with her long, softly variegated hair curling wildly about her shoulders, she looked closely akin to a wild-haired Gypsy girl, albeit a well-garbed one.

Her head tilted aslant on a gracefully long neck as she perused herself with critical detachment, wondering if her uncle would find her changed much after her lengthy absence. When he had watched her sail away, she had been nothing more than a scrawny girl painfully conscious of her height. Now she was a woman fully grown, still taller by a few degrees than a fair share of her gender, and although slender, she was well curved enough to have attracted a small following of young gallants who had begun to pester Lydia about the details of her coming out. With her recent lack of nourishment, her thickly fringed hazel eyes looked enormous beneath sweeping brows that angled upward in soft brown slashes. Her cheekbones were exquisitely high and perhaps, at the moment, more pronounced than usual, lending a slight hollowness beneath. Her nose was straight, slim, and fairly decent from her perspective, but little color remained in the soft lips that curved unsmilingly back at her.

Except for a tiny frothing of scalloped white lace overflowing the high, pleated ruffle at her neck and more of the same at her wrists, she was clothed entirely in black. Her fashionable spencer jacket of velvet, trimmed with black braid swirled military-fashion over her bosom, ended just above the waist. Her sleeves were puffed at the shoulders. Otherwise they were closely fitted, ending at the wrists with the black pleats lined with the same costly white lace. Her skirt bore festoons of decorative braid above the hem, the length of which was stylishly short, at least enough to display trim, stockinged ankles and flat slippers.

Wry amusement traced Cerynise's lips as she finished assessing her image. She was sure that Lydia would have approved of her letting down her reserve as well as her hair in the front parlor. Although the elder had been every bit a lady, she had nevertheless been sensible enough to know when to observe proprieties and when to ignore them in deference to common sense and simple honesty. Cerynise couldn't imagine herself having garnered much wisdom from all the tidbits of advice the woman had sown over the years if she hadn't allowed that valuable grain of logic to take firm root.

Sounds of a carriage rattling to a halt in front of the Winthrop residence were immediately followed by a loud clapping of the front door knocker. The insistent rapping seemed to echo throughout the manse as the butler traversed the hall with his usual unhurried gait. As he did so, Cerynise hastily gathered her hair back into some semblance of restraint and secured the knot at her nape with hairpins. It certainly wouldn't do for a genteel lady to greet guests looking like a hoyden.

11

A noisy clamor, liberally punctuated with feminine giggles, arose in the entrance hall, evidencing the disorderly entrance of the new arrivals. Before Cerynise could investigate, two men burst through the arched doorway of the parlor, followed by a harassed butler, who seemed rather appalled by their effrontery.

"I'm dreadfully sorry, miss," Jasper apologized, his aging face etched with concern. "I would have announced the presence of Mr. Winthrop and Mr. Rudd, but they gave me no chance."

"No need to fret, Jasper. It's quite all right," Cerynise assured him. She moved forward with well-feigned serenity, taking care to hide her trembling hands in the folds of her skirt. She knew Lydia's nephew better than she cared to, despite the fact that whenever Alistair Winthrop had visited her guardian he had always demanded a private audience. He was tall and lank, seeming rather disjointed in his gangling limberness. His black hair had been slicked back from his face, and sidewhiskers accentuated his gaunt features. In profile his thin nose seemed to slope in its descent, just barely protruding a degree or two beyond his sharply jutting chin. He was not a handsome man by any means, but he had obviously spent a goodly amount of coin on his personage, for he was garbed in a flamboyant fashion completely devoid of prudence.

His companion, Howard Rudd, was equal to him in height, but the man's ponderous belly seemed to blaze a trail before him. His bulbous nose was darkened with broken veins, and a small purplish birthmark marred his left cheek. Although Cerynise hadn't seen the barrister in two or three years, she distinctly recalled him slyly fingering every treasured piece within reach while awaiting admittance into Lydia's private chambers. The gleam that had burned in his eyes during those times had seemed to betray a covetousness that had often caused her to wonder if he would make off with anything of value. Cerynise found it difficult to imagine that Lydia had continued to rely upon the man after such a lengthy absence, for it had been apparent from the fumes which had long ago enveloped him and were even now apparent that Howard Rudd was prone to liberally indulge in strong libations.

"Mr. Winthrop has always been welcome here, Jasper," Cerynise began demurely, directing her attention to the butler. Lydia had always made a point of receiving her nephew with polite deference even when his arrival had proven an intrusion during the dinner hour or when guests were being entertained. The elder would have expected her charge to do the same. "And, of course, Mr. Rudd..."

Harsh, derisive laughter interrupted, and Cerynise faced Alistair, somewhat surprised by his rudeness. His strange way of walking had oftentimes made her wonder if the man had a rigid bone in his body, and she found herself again pondering his disconnected stride as he swaggered toward her with dark eyes glittering malevolently.

"How gracious of you, Miss Kendall," he sneered, his wide mouth seeming as unmanageable as his body. "How very, very considerate you are."

Cerynise tried to brace herself for what would follow, for she sensed it wouldn't be enjoyable. Her meetings with the man had entailed nothing more lasting than passing each other in rooms or hallways. Nevertheless she had formed a rather low opinion of Alistair Winthrop. During her brief glimpses into his behavior, he had proven himself to be a conceited braggart, who seemed to think he had some claim to fame because he was the great-nephew of an enormously wealthy woman, even if it was only by marriage. Cerynise had oft suspected him to be a wastrel, but more than that, he had never shown the slightest regard for his aunt. Though Lydia had always remained mute about his reasons for calling, Alistair had usually left counting his new assets or else striding irately out berating her so-called closefisted stinginess, which he had done at the conclusion of his last visit. His name-calling had strengthened Cerynise's aversion to the man, to the degree that she now considered it a true test of her acting skills to be able to maintain a gracious poise in his presence.

Alistair waved a pale, hairy hand in the lawyer's direction as he paced in front of her. Loudly he commanded, "Tell her!"

Howard Rudd wiped the back of his own hand across his ever-drooling lips and stepped forward to comply. Before he could do so, a lewdly garbed young woman came flouncing into the parlor, streaming a brightly hued feather boa out behind her. Her bosom and hips were amply displayed, the first by a plunging neckline, the latter by the tightness of her gown. Her hair was piled high on her head in a mass of bright golden ringlets, a shade that might have been extremely difficult to find in nature. Black kohl lined her brown eyes, and a beauty patch dotted her right cheekbone above a heavy deposit of rouge, which, Cerynise surmised, closely matched the reddish tint that presently marred the whiteness of Alistair's collar.

The woman wiggled up against her escort with a nervous little giggle. "Oh, Al, please don't be mean ta me an' make me wait in the hall anymore," she crooned. Pursing her mouth in an exaggerated pout, she fluttered overlong lashes at him and stroked a hand caressingly over his waistcoat. "I ain't ne'er been in a house what's as grand as this, but I knows good manners when I sees 'em. Why, the servants ain't offered me a chair or a sip o' tea since we come in. Can't I please, please stay in here with ye? I simply can't bear ta be alone in that big ol' hall. It gives me the creeps, thinkin' yer poor ol' aunt might've keeled o'er dead in there."

Alistair snarled in exasperation and threw off her hand. "Oh, all right, Sybil! But mind

15

you, you're to keep still, understand? I want none of your caterwauling."

"I hear ye, Al," she replied with another nervous twitter.

Jasper sniffed and, dragging his gaze from the offending creature, lifted his beaked nose with lofty dignity as he gained Alistair's glowering glare. Even so, he ignored the man and directed his query to his late proprietor's ward. "Your pardon, miss, but should I stay?"

"Go!" Alistair barked, waving the butler away. "None of this concerns you!"

Jasper proved immobile until Cerynise inclined her head in a stilted nod, giving him leave to retire to another part of the house.

Alistair glared after the departing servant as if seriously tempted to chide him for an offense, but he dismissed the incident for more important matters and returned his attention to the counselor. "Continue, Mr. Rudd."

The barrister drew himself up to his full height and, capturing Cerynise's gaze, conveyed a concern apparently intended to emphasize the gravity of the moment. "Miss Kendall, you must be aware that I've had the honor of serving as Mrs. Winthrop's solicitor for several years. It was I who drew up her last will and testament. I have it here with me."

Cerynise gave him the same wary attention one might lend a snake threatening to strike as the man removed a sheaf of parchments from an inner pocket of his tailcoat and, with pompous ceremony, broke the seal. As hard

16

it was for her to fathom Lydia's own continuing loyalty to Howard Rudd, he was here and
obviously in possession of legal documents.
Slowly she sank back into the nearest chair,
her thoughts congealing. "Do you intend to
read Mrs. Winthrop's will now?"

"Has to be done," Howard answered.
"That's the thing." Still, he looked to Alistair
for confirmation.

"Get on with it," Alistair snapped, spreading
his coattails fastidiously and lowering himself
into a large armchair on the opposite side of
the table from Cerynise. He gave the young
woman a smug smile and began to toy with one
of a pair of Meissen figurines that resided
there.

Sybil wasn't at all pleased by the attention
her lover was bestowing upon the young lady
and promptly deposited her ample rump on
the wooden arm of his chair. Her eyes cast an
icy glare toward the one sitting beyond the table
as she wrapped a possessive arm around Alistair's bony shoulders. He had failed to mention that his aunt's ward was so fetching, yet
she vividly recalled his arguments against her
accompanying him. The memory of those
angry protests confirmed in her mind that
he hadn't wanted her to come along simply
because he had planned on doing things to the
girl that he normally did with her in the privacy of his flat...and his bed

Howard Rudd cleared his throat, feeling
sorely in need of a beverage to lubricate his
vocal cords, but he knew that Alistair wouldn't

17

tolerate him taking another sip until their business was concluded. He unrolled parchments festooned with beribboned seals and scanned them. "Goes on a bit, it does. Small amounts to this one and that, mainly servants, distant kin, nothing of any significance. What really matters is that Mrs. Winthrop has left the bulk of her estate, including this house, its contents, and all of her assets, to her only kin, her nephew, Mr. Alistair Wakefield Winthrop. He is to take immediate possession."

"Immediate?" Cerynise gasped. There had never been any reason to discuss such matters with her guardian, but she had always understood that Lydia cared for her deeply and would have allowed her time to prepare for a more orderly transition to other quarters or climes before handing over the house to another. Having been no relation to the woman, Cerynise hadn't expected anything beyond that simple courtesy. Truly, it was impossible for her to imagine the elder being so callous and unconcerned about her ward that she would have overlooked the need for that small provision.

"Would you mind if I looked at the will?" she asked, hating the small tremor in her voice. She rose expectantly, holding out a hand to receive the papers.

Rudd hesitated, glancing toward Alistair for direction, and received a curt nod that casually authorized him to pass the document to the girl. Though Cerynise was no expert on such matters, she carefully inspected the pages of closely written script. To an unpracticed eye, the will appeared authentic. There was absolutely no question that Lydia's initials verified each page of the text and that her signature elegantly embellished the last.

Distantly Cerynise was aware of the lawyer twitching uneasily as she perused the pages, and finally, when his patience wore thin, he stretched forth a hand to take them from her, motivating her to quickly skim downward. It was then that her eyes caught on the date beside Lydia's signature, and with a start of surprise, she looked up at the man.

"But this was written six years ago."

"That's right," Rudd replied, snatching the testament from her and rolling it up. "Nothing wrong with that. Plenty of people take care of such matters long before there's a need. Very sensible of them."

"But that was before my parents were killed and Lydia became my guardian. Under the circumstances, it seems that she would have rewritten her will—"

"To include you?" Alistair interrupted caustically. With an angry snort, he launched himself from his chair, nearly dumping Sybil onto the floor, and began prowling about the spacious room like some animal of prey, touching each piece of furniture, every costly knickknack, even the heavy damask draperies, as if driven by a compulsion to mark each article as his own. "That's what you mean, isn't it, Miss Kendall? You think my aunt should've left you something."

19

Though her animosity toward the man rose up within her like the taste of bitter gall, Cerynise forced herself to speak with carefully measured calm. "I believe your aunt was very methodical about her business affairs and, since that seemed her nature, I can't help but believe that she would've taken the initiative to revise her will whenever a situation of any importance changed around her. At the very least, she would have allowed me time to make arrangements for my departure before giving everything over into your possession."

"Well, she didn't!" Alistair declared hotly, thrusting his upper torso forward with an emphatic, angry movement. "She did enough for you while she was alive, and she damn well knew it! Letting you stay here all these years, catering to your every whim, clothing you in the best, putting out good money to sponsor those absurd exhibits for your paintings...Why, you should go down on your knees and thank heaven for my aunt's generosity instead of whining that you weren't given more time to waste my inheritance."

Cerynise gasped, highly offended by his words. "I certainly didn't expect to fall heir to any portion of her assets, Mr. Winthrop," she explained crisply. "I merely meant that it seems odd that your aunt made no mention of me at all, despite the fact that I'm still underage. She *was* my legal guardian, or have you forgotten?"

Alistair smirked. "Perhaps dear Auntie thought she'd be done with you long before she passed on. She probably meant to marry you off to some wealthy gentleman and arrange for you to become someone else's responsibility. I'm sure with her stamina, she really wasn't expecting to die so soon."

The hazel eyes blazed with fire behind silken black lashes. "If you had known your aunt at all, Mr. Winthrop," Cerynise gritted out, "you'd understand that Lydia sincerely cared for people and didn't brush them carelessly aside just to be rid of them."

"It doesn't matter what you think!" Alistair barked, tightening his grip on a delicate porcelain shepherdess. Cerynise fully expected to see the fragile piece break in his hand as he gestured with it to stress his assertions. "All that matters is the will! You heard what was decreed. I'm master here now, and what I say is law in this house!"

An elated titter erupted from Sybil, and she clapped her hands in eager delight, like a child enthralled with a puppet show. "That's telling her, Al! Just oo' does 'at chit think she is, anyway?"

"Obviously Miss Kendall thinks she's a lady of consequence," Alistair mocked, setting aside the shepherdess and advancing upon Cerynise with gleaming black eyes.

Instinctively Cerynise backed away. She didn't know the man well enough to make any clear judgment as to what he might be capable of doing if angered, but she was certain he was no gentleman and would likely become violent if vexed. To her dismay, the settee halted her retreat, and she was forced to stand and meet his wildly gleaming eyes as he smirked at her.

Recognizing her fear, Alistair felt a surge of power. "But Miss Kendall is wrong again," he said almost softly. "She's no one at all, just a little beggar who has been coddling up to my aunt all these years for the purpose of extracting whatever favors she could from the old woman, like this gown she's wearing."

Reaching out, he grasped hold of the white lace lining the high ruff and gave it a jerk, wrenching a startled gasp from the girl as he ripped it free.

"Take your hands off me!" Cerynise cried, her rage kindling her courage as she flung away his arm. "You may own this house, sir, but you most certainly do not own me!"

Alistair's lips angled upward in a confident leer as his dark eyes dipped caressingly to her bosom. She was, after all, such a tempting little thing. It would be a shame not to taste her. "That can change, my pretty little peach."

"Al?" Sybil was instantly alert to his prurient imagination. She wasn't at all acceptive to the notion that she might have to share him with a young wench who made her feel like a dumpy toad, for there was always the chance that he'd come to prefer the fresher tidbit over the one that had grown stale from use. It wasn't that she cared for the roué overmuch. She was far more interested in how rich he was going to be. She pranced across the room

22

and, with a little wiggle, wedged herself between the dueling glares of the two who stood toe to toe. She snuggled up against Alistair, reminding him of her generous curves. "Don't bother yerself with that scrawny li'l milkweed, lovey," she cooed, her bright red lips curving invitingly. "Yer Sybil is here just itchin' ta make ye happy."

Alistair chortled vindictively as he thought of a way to repay Cerynise for her haughty disfavor. Slipping an arm around his mistress, he smiled down into her heavily painted eyes. "How would you like some new clothes, Sybil?"

Her elated squeal would have been answer enough. "Oh, Al, do ye mean ye're gonna buy me some?"

His bony shoulders slipped upward in a blasé shrug. "Why should I buy you any when there's a whole wardrobe awaiting you upstairs in my lady Cerynise's chambers?"

Sybil's face crumpled in disappointment. "But, Al! We ain't the same size," she complained. She couldn't bring herself to openly admit that nearly everything about the younger woman, except her height, was either slimmer or smaller. "She's too tall for li'l ol' me."

"Well, find her room upstairs and see what fits," Alistair urged. "Surely, with what my aunt spent on the chit, there has to be something in her chambers you can wear. Now go!"

Accepting this logic, Sybil fairly twittered in glee as she flew out of the room. Her high heels clattered on the stairs, echoing throughout the house until the sound of doors being opened and slammed finally ended in an ecstatic screech.

Alistair was rather pleased with himself for having conceived of the idea. That fact was blatant on his face as he faced Cerynise. "Why, I do believe Sybil has found your bedchamber, m'lady."

Cerynise gave him a coolly disdaining smile, the sort a mother might bestow upon a naughty child, deftly squelching his cocky arrogance. "When Sybil is done, may I be allowed to pack my belongings and leave? I'm sure I'll be able to find a room at an inn until I can secure passage to the Carolinas."

"You have no belongings!" Alistair railed. "Everything in this house is mine!"

"I beg to differ," Cerynise replied stiffly, lifting her chin in growing obstinance. For all that she had led a sheltered life under Lydia's supervision, she wasn't without experience dealing with bullies. Her beloved father had been a schoolmaster, and while sitting in on more than a few of his classes, she had confronted a goodly share of immature males who had thought they could run roughshod over anyone younger, smaller, or weaker than themselves. Many had been spoiled by affluent parents and were wont to play mean, vicious pranks. Alistair Winthrop was definitely of that class. "My paintings are certainly my own and so is the money I earned from those that were sold."

Rudd interjected with the confidence of an

24

attorney who had recited his arguments well in advance. "When you painted, young lady, you used materials that were purchased by Mrs. Winthrop. She enlisted the aid of an instructor to teach you all the nuances of that field, and no doubt paid a hefty price for his service. In short, you were living under her roof, she was your guardian, and you were underage. It was she who arranged to exhibit your paintings, argued for the best price, and banked the resulting funds. Why, the paintings weren't even signed with your name, merely CK. I know, because the exhibitors refused to shed any light upon the artist's identity when I went to see them, saying only that Mrs. Winthrop had arranged for everything." He paused briefly to wipe his glistening brow before he summed up his arguments. "Therefore, the actual owner of the paintings, as well as any profits from them, was none other than Mrs. Winthrop."

Cerynise flushed in rising indignation. Regrettably, the man was right about everything but the last. It had been her talent that had merged the colored paints into realistic scenes of people going about their daily affairs in seascapes, landscapes and interiors. Oils and canvas were only that until an artist made something of them. Lydia had been mindful of the fact that the work of a mere girl would never have been taken seriously by wealthy patrons and had insisted that Cerynise's identity remain a carefully kept secret. That had been her *only* reason for keeping everyone in the dark.

25

"Lydia was merely holding that money for me," Cerynise declared hotly, but even to her own ears, her defense sounded feeble. "There was no reason for a separate account, and if I hope to sail home to Charleston, I'll need the funds to buy passage on the next available ship."

"It wouldn't have mattered if there had been a separate account," Alistair retorted. "My aunt was your guardian. Everything you have belonged to her...." He smiled tauntingly. "And now it belongs to me."

"Oh, look at this!" Sybil squealed in delight, racing back into the room. She was wrapped in an evening cloak of heavy pink moiré silk, richly embroidered with garlands of rosebuds around the edges of the deep hood and the front opening. "Ain't it a beauty?" Though she was in danger of tripping over the hem, Sybil whirled around to show off her new acquisition. She only wished that she would have been able to fit into the matching gown, but that had been impossible. "There's a whole dressin' room full o' all kinds o' pretty things. Why, I ne'er in all me born days seen the like. Bonnets! Slippers! Gowns galore! Pretty li'l lacy things ta wear underneath." She tossed a laughing warble over her shoulder as she preened for Cerynise's benefit. "How do I look in my new cloak?"

Cerynise couldn't resist giving the rude hussy a suggestion. "Perhaps you'll be able to patch the seams on the gown once you let them out."

"Al!" Sybil cried, stamping her foot in outrage. "Ye gonna let her talk ta me like that?"

Alistair was decidedly guilty of having entertained similar thoughts after observing the plump strumpet prancing around in front of them. Her bright lips and rouge seemed to overwhelm the delicately hued garment, and as much as he had wanted to exact revenge on the girl for being so uppity, he was of a mind to suspect that, without major alterations, only her cloaks and outerwear could be utilized by Sybil.

His dark eyes wandered back to the prim beauty and casually caressed the soft, enticing curves that the mourning garb gently molded. Her back was straight, her head elevated, conveying an undaunted pride. She looked for all the world like a pale-haired goddess, and as much as he might have wished otherwise, it was a hard fact that Sybil suffered badly in comparison.

Cerynise's nape prickled as she felt the weight of Alistair's stare, and she peered up at him in sudden wariness. His wide lips twisted upward in a confident one-sided grin that made her skin crawl. Even before he paced forward with his strange disconnected gait, she had begun to suspect that his thoughts were not the sort a proper lady would invite.

"You needn't distress yourself overmuch, Cerynise," Alistair cajoled, reaching behind her head and freeing the thick knot of hair that she had hastily secured. "I can let you stay here in some capacity. I'm sure we'll be able to work

27

something out between us. Perhaps we'll even become intimate friends." Despite the coldness in the hazel eyes that watched him intently, he swept the curling length forward, allowing it to veil a rounded breast before his hand stroked downward over its silken strands.

Cerynise's outrage reached its zenith, and with a snarl she raised both arms and shoved him away from her with all of her might. "You disgusting viper! Do you actually think I would consider being on intimate terms with you? You dare come here, prancing about like some handsome lordling who deserves all of this? Why, you're nothing but a worm crawling out of your dark, dank hole to eat the flesh of poor innocents! I'll rot before I stay here under your authority!"

Alistair's eyes flared at her insults, and his face darkened to an ugly, mottled red as he hauled back an arm to strike. "I'll teach you who is lord here!"

Howard leapt forward with a startled gasp and grasped his companion's wrist. "Mark the girl, and she'll have something to show the authorities when she goes to complain," he cautioned anxiously. "Best to send her on her way without causing a stir, don't you think?"

Alistair gave no indication that he had even heard the solicitor as his whole body shook with rage. It was a long moment before he regained some measure of control over himself and jerked free of Rudd. *"Get out, bitch!"* he bellowed. "You're not worth the trouble it would take to teach you some manners!"

28

Cerynise could scarcely breathe as she whispered, "Most willingly. I'll pack a few things and then be gone—"

"*No, you won't!*" Alistair barked. "*You're going now!*"

Seizing hold of her arm, he whisked her out into the main hall. Jasper was there, having kept a distant vigil. The butler glanced from one to the other in blank astonishment before he ventured haltingly, "Sir, I beg you..."

"I'm master here now!" Alistair asserted at the servant's attempt to intrude. "If anyone disputes that, then he can go the way of this baggage." Yanking open the door, he hauled Cerynise around and shoved her out of the portal with enough force to send her stumbling down the granite steps. He held the door aside in open invitation as his words further assailed the butler. "But consider well before you do! Positions are damn hard to come by, and not one of you will receive a reference!"

The dark eyes turned their blazing fury upon Cerynise, who blinked back at him against the driving rain. "Now get out of my sight while you still can, chit! Or I'll have you arrested! Or better yet, sent to the madhouse!"

"Don't think he can't do it!" Rudd interjected, peering around the edge of the door. "He's a man of property now, respected and all. You're no one. Unless you want to find yourself in Bedlam, you'd better be off." In the next instant the solicitor gasped in surprise and yanked his head back out of harm's way as Alistair clasped the heavy portal and slammed it shut with a loud crack of finality.

Cerynise huddled against the crisp wind and wrapped her arms about herself as she sought to find some meager warmth and protection from the elements. Here she was, literally thrown out of the only home she had known for the last five years and threatened with worse consequences if she remained. As cold as it was and without a wrap to ease her misery, she'd likely suffer frostbite before she reached a place of shelter. Having taken her art seriously, she had never spared the time to culture close friendships with women her own age. Most had been far more interested in attracting husbands than she had been. As for Lydia's friends, they were much older and probably incapable of coping with the sort of violence that Cerynise had just experienced. And who could actually say what Alistair Winthrop might be tempted to do if anyone intervened in her behalf. After her insult, she had glimpsed a wrath that had given her cause to fear the man. During that moment he had actually seemed to waver on the border of insanity. Whoever helped her would likely elicit similar reactions and no doubt severe repercussions. As much as she yearned for solace from an acquaintance, Cerynise couldn't imagine involving anyone who would be susceptible.

Alistair might well have crossed over into an area of madness already...one had to consider that possibility. Yet, in this matter, he had the law on his side. As Lydia's heir, he had

30

every right to dispose of the Winthrop property in any manner he saw fit, including laying out a list of those who could or could not reside under his roof.

Dismally Cerynise stared up at the house, but her vision was now impeded by a mixture of tears and rain. Her grief over Lydia's passing, coupled with her recent lack of nourishment and sleep, left her exhausted and little prepared for what would undoubtedly be a long walk through the city.

"Better get started," she gritted dismally through lips already stiff from the cold. Unable to control her shivering, she began trudging down the street, knowing where she must go. With the rain and the deepening cold, it would be difficult, yet she had no other choice.

She had progressed only a short distance when the sound of running footfalls made her turn and look behind her. Bridget was clearly out of breath by the time she reached Cerynise. Before leaving the house, the parlor maid had paused long enough to sweep a heavy shawl around her. In her arms she carried her own woolen cloak, which she wrapped around the shivering girl.

"Oh, mum, this is terrible," she fussed amid her weeping. Lifting a trembling hand, she wiped at the wetness trailing down her cheeks. "I could hardly believe it, ye bein' set out o' Mrs. Winthrop's house without so much as a place ta go. Mr. Alistair can't really do that, can he, mum?"

"I'm-m afraid h-he can, Bridget. Mrs.

31

Winthrop's will gives him that right." Cerynise touched the maid's hand gently with icy fingers. The raindrops falling on her face seemed just as frigid. "Y-you must go b-back. No one c-can afford to be dismissed w-without references. Now here...t-take your cloak...and g-go..."

She tried to drag the garment from her shoulders, but the maid shook her head. "Nay, mum. 'Tis yours now, as sorry as it be. Mrs. Winthrop gave me one o' hers last Michaelmas. So's ye see, mum, I've got a much finer one ta replace this ol' rag."

"Are y-you s-sure?" Cerynise queried, unable to stop her teeth from chattering.

"Aye, mum," Bridget affirmed, nodding with unswerving conviction. "I might not be able ta leave Mr. Winthrop's employ, but at least I can send ye away knowin' I've done the best I can for ye."

"Thank y-you, Bridget. You're a dear friend," Cerynise whispered, her eyes once again filling with moisture. "I shan't forget you."

Hastily the servant informed her, "Right after Mr. Jasper o'erheard what Mr. Winthrop was plannin' ta do, he set us ta movin' yer paintin's ta the storeroom below the stairs. He said he didn't care that he'd be lyin' ta the scoundrel, he was goin' ta tell Mr. Winthrop the paintin's were sent ta some gallery or another, an' that we don't know which one. Ye've gots ta find a way ta get 'em back, mum. Ye've just gotta."

"All of y-you could b-be t-taking an awful chance," Cerynise stuttered, deeply moved by

32

the loyalty of the staff. "Y-you mustn't endanger y-yourselves t-trying to s-save them. I-I'm going to the d-docks...t-to...obtain p-passage t-to Charleston, s-so I might n-never return f-for them."

"All's the same, mum, we'll keep 'em hidden for ye. 'Twill be our own revenge for what Mr. Winthrop did ta ye."

"G-go back n-now," Cerynise implored, giving the serving girl a gentle push toward the house, "before Mr. Winthrop sees you out h-here talking to me."

A sob crumpled the maid's countenance, and in a sudden show of affection, she flung her arms around Cerynise. "Bless ye, mum!" After a moment she sniffed and retreated to meet the other's gaze through swimming tears. "Ye've always been the soul o' kindness ta us. We'll count the days till that rascally Mr. Winthrop gets what he deserves."

Weeping bitterly, Bridget tore herself away and raced back toward the house, her black skirts flapping wetly around her legs, her small feet sending geysers of water splashing upward as she crossed ever-deepening puddles.

Cerynise pulled the woolen hood over her head and huddled deep within the garment, seeking as much protection from the pelting rain as the garment could afford. Beneath it she was already soaked, and with the intensity of the howling wind and the slashing downpour, the cloak would only serve to lessen her discomfort rather than banishing it altogether. Even so, she was grateful for the gift as she made her way along the street, for even in so short a time it seemed that the air had gotten colder.

It was some moments before Cerynise realized that a curious numbness had settled down within her after her confrontation with Alistair. To some degree it cushioned the harshness of her plight, for she no longer dwelt on how cold and miserable she'd be without warm clothing and food. Instead, she kept telling herself over and over again that she could walk as far as she had to. All she had to do was put one foot in front of the other. Encouraging herself with that simple bit of logic, she eventually found herself near the bridge that crossed over the Thames into the district of Southwark.

The storm had gathered over the city, deepening the twilight into a brooding darkness, but in the strange eerie gloom, she could still make out several ships proceeding upriver where they would at some point along the wharves drop anchor. Her eyes flitted toward the distant banks in search of the taller masts which clearly distinguished the seagoing vessels from the smaller fishing boats. Whenever her family had visited her uncle at his house near the waterfront in Charleston, she had been given ample opportunity as a child to view the various sailing vessels gliding through the waters toward the southern port. While Uncle Sterling had fished nearby, she had perched on the wharf with sketchbook in hand, drawing

34

contentedly as he talked to her about the different sailing ships and taught her how to recognize one type from another. She still remembered much of what she had learned from him.

Memories of that distant city flowed like a deep, surging river through her mind, and in a space of a few heartbeats Cerynise could almost hear the trilling birds nesting in ancient live oaks beside her family's home, the drone of insects on sultry summer nights, and feel the soft flutter of Spanish moss against her face as she raced through the woods with the joyful exuberance of a child, and ever so much more. She could even imagine that she caught a whiff of honeysuckle and could taste the sweetness of pralines melting on her tongue. However brief those recollections were, she was pierced by a longing so profound that it was all she could do not to cry out in anguish.

Here she was, nearly frozen, exhaustion and grief enfolding her like a sodden blanket, her thin fingers rigid from the numbing cold, having no ken how she would ever obtain passage home now that she was bereft of funds. What sea captain looking at her now would permit her on his ship, much less allow her to sail on it? It seemed a farfetched idea even to her, but she knew that somehow-...some way...she must go home.

Obeying a desire so powerful that she could not curb it, Cerynise began making her way across the bridge. Rain had collected in the depressions between the cobblestones, but by now her slippers were so thoroughly soaked it no longer mattered. All she had to do was put one foot in front of the other, she reminded herself, and eventually she would reach her destination.

The fetid stench of the river intensified as she entered the borough of Southwark. She kept close to the river, walking relentlessly onward until through the deep, storm-bound shadows she could make out the lofty masts of larger sailing ships off in the distance. Heartened by the sight, Cerynise quickened her pace, painful though it was to walk with toes aching from the cold. She knew deep down that it was foolish for her to wander this area alone. In the security of Lydia's coach, she had passed through the district enough to have become cognizant of a bolder type of women who, along many of the streets and byways, openly offered their bodies to sailors or any man who'd pay out a few coins to be entertained in bed. Cerynise knew that she was seriously tempting fate, for she could be accosted, perhaps even mistaken for a female of loose virtue. But she pushed that cautioning logic aside, regarding it as a luxury she could ill afford.

The warehouses and shuttered tenements that she passed were dark. It was, after all, a place where every candle or ounce of oil was considered precious. The poor would understand her present plight, but they could not help her. It was up to her to find a way to go home. And find it she would!

Cerynise had no real sense of just how far

36

she had come. Her steps had begun to drag wearily as she wove an unsteady path along the bank, but when her foot suddenly caught on something that felt amazingly human, she peered into the shadows beneath an over-turned dinghy that had been hefted across two planks.

"What the bloody hell are ye doin'?" a slurred voice snarled from under the craft. "Can't ye watch where ye goin'!"

Cerynise tried to focus on the small, wiry form that crawled out from under the boat. "Y-your pardon," she stammered, wondering if it was fear or cold impeding her tongue. "I d-didn't realize y-you were t-there, sir."

"Well, I was, see," the little man retorted peevishly, staggering to his feet. He was shorter than Cerynise, completely bald, ancient if he was a day, and had not a tooth in his head. Yet, for all of that, he was garbed as a seaman.

"W-what w-were you doing d-down there?" Cerynise managed to ask.

The tar fixed his gaze upon her in some exas-peration and flipped the hood of his slicker over his head as he hunched within the garment. "If'n ye *must* know, girlie, I was catchin' a li'l snooze whilst I was waitin' for me cap'n ta go back ta our ship."

"I'm-m terribly s-sorry for d-disturbing you, sir. I d-didn't s-see you in the d-dark," she answered as graciously as her clattering teeth would allow. Despite the man's irasci-bility, she hoped he might be persuaded to help her. At the moment, he seemed her best

37

chance of getting the information she needed. "I d-didn't h-hurt you, did I?"

"Hurt me? Ol' Moon, here?" the sailor asked incredulously. Thrusting out his scrawny chest, he hitched up his britches as if tempted to strut for her benefit. "Girlie, it'd take a whale ta hurt ol' Moon."

"I'm-m r-relieved to k-know that."

Much placated by her cordiality, Moon eyed the girl more closely. In spite of her stuttering tongue, she spoke like some of the rich class who came to the ship to which he was assigned to make inquiries about the quality of accommodations. Usually, after viewing them, they went in search of another one. But a blind man could see that this slender slip was several leagues above the sort of women who normally roamed the docks looking for men to entertain. "What cha doin' out here in the rain all by yer lonesome? 'Taint no fit place for a nice li'l girlie like ye."

"I-I need passage h-home m-most desperately, and I was t-trying to f-find a ship that w-would be s-sailing fairly s-soon to t-the Carolinas. W-would you happen to k-know of such a vessel?"

"The *Mirage,* for one," the toothless one replied without hesitation. "She be sailin' under the command o' Cap'n Sullivan. I'm his cabin boy."

"And w-where m-may I find th-this Captain S-Sullivan?"

Moon twisted slightly and jabbed a thumb

toward a tavern from whence a wedge of light streamed into the misty darkness. "The cap'n's takin' vittles at that there alehouse."

A mixture of relief and trepidation washed over Cerynise as she saw where he pointed. She was greatly heartened that her search would be shortened, but dreadfully afraid of entering such a place, for she was not so naive as to believe that sailors only wanted to imbibe in strong libations after reaching port. They would be looking for more lively entertainment, the kind that Sybil was probably well versed in providing. "I d-don't s-suppose you w-would consider taking me to see h-him, w-would you?"

Moon cocked his head thoughtfully as he considered her bedraggled appearance. He wouldn't normally have bothered himself for a stranger, but this young girl had evidently fallen on hard times and was suffering severely from the miserable conditions. Then, too, she had a gentleness about her that quickened a long-dormant gallantry within him. "I su'-pose I could, seein's as how ye're gonna freeze ta death if'n ye stay out here much longer."

"A-aren't you c-cold, too?"

Moon rubbed a crooked forefinger beneath his hooked nose and snickered. "Not with me innards feelin' all nice an' warm from rum." Leaning close enough to taint the air that she breathed with a strong aroma of the brew, he beckoned with a sweep of his arm. "This way, girlie."

Cerynise stumbled along behind him as he

tottered unsteadily toward the beacon of light. Upon entering the tavern, she stayed just inside the door while Moon made his way toward the back of the crowded establishment. The din that filled the place made her cringe. Sailors were shouting for service, banging their tankards insistently upon heavily planked tables, while others were talking at the top of their voices in an attempt to be heard over the discord. A few were guffawing uproariously as they made a game of pinching or slapping the bottoms of every serving girl who passed. A small handful of others were muttering in low tones as they idly caressed the strumpets who had nestled near. Carefully averting her eyes from the latter, Cerynise scanned the crowded room for Moon.

The tar was leaning over the hefty shoulder of a man who sat at a table wolfing down food, and though she saw Moon's lips moving, she couldn't hear a word he said above the noise. Cerynise could only assume that it was none other than Captain Sullivan to whom he was speaking. The man was well past two score years with an unruly thatch of graying hair, bushy side-whiskers and a chin stubbled by bristles. He not only resembled a pirate, he seemed as prosperous as one as he flashed a weighty purse and silently bade a serving wench to fetch another pitcher of ale for the men at his table. Finally he glanced around at the tar and inclined his head in a brief nod.

Moon came scurrying back to Cerynise

with a broad, toothless grin. "The cap'n'll hear what ye has ta say now, girlie."

Barely had Cerynise entered the human maze through which the tar had passed ahead of her than a hand reached out to seize her. With a gasp she managed to sidestep the seaman who grinned back at her with teeth blackened with rot.

"Eh, mates, what's this the rain's washed in?" he cried with a chortle, bringing his companions' attention to bear upon her. "A drowned rat, if'n I e'er saw one."

"Gor! Don't look like no rat ta me!" another exclaimed lustily as he caught her cloak and whipped it free of her shoulders, in the process breaking one of the ties that secured it. His eyes steadily brightened into a leer as they swept the soaked gown she wore beneath. "A bit soppin', al'right, but a real looker, she be!"

"Keep yer foul hands ta yerself, ye horny toad!" Moon snarled, stepping back to cuff the man. "Don't ye knows a liedy when ye sees one?"

"A liedy?" the tar repeated with a sharp hoot of disbelief. "In here? Oo's ye tryin' ta bamboozle, Moon?"

"Ne'er ye mind!" the ancient tar snarled, snatching the lady's cloak from the man. "I can sees for meself ye ain't ne'er eyed a liedy afore in yer whole bloomin' life an' wouldn't knows one if she stuck ye in the eye!"

The resulting laughter of those sitting near enough to overhear the insult made her erstwhile admirer glower in bruised resentment.

41

"Oh, I seen 'em al'right, but their sort ain't o' a mind ta be seen in a place like this."

"Well, ye're seein' one in here now," Moon retorted.

"A bitch, more'n likely," the sailor grumbled and, having issued that slur, turned his back upon the pair.

Lanterns flickered dully at the edge of Cerynise's blurring vision. She blinked several times as an invading weakness threatened to undermine her resolve. Only by sheer dint of will did she manage to make her way to Captain Sullivan's table. Moon hurriedly swept around a chair for her to sit beside his captain, and she gratefully accepted his provision, for she seriously doubted that she could have stood much longer on her own.

"Moon says ye're wantin' passage on me ship," Captain Sullivan began, his keen dark eyes sweeping slowly downward from the long hair that hung in wet strands around her face until they reached the muddied hem of her gown. As pretty as she was and as costly as her drenched garb might have been, the girl looked much the worse for wear. Tucking his tongue thoughtfully in his cheek, he met the hazel eyes that were now dull from fatigue. "Can ye pay?"

Cerynise could hardly admit her poverty, but neither could she lie. " 'Twould be foolish for me to seek passage on a ship if I couldn't pay for it in some fashion."

"And that would be?"

Cerynise braced herself, knowing only too

well how irrational her proposal might seem to a captain of a ship. "My uncle, Mr. Sterling Kendall, will give you the funds upon my arrival in Charleston...."

For a moment Captain Sullivan stared at her as if convinced that she had taken leave of her senses. Then abruptly he slapped the flat of his hand upon the table and began to guffaw in rampant amusement, making her cringe with dread and embarrassment. He left no doubt that he considered her offer absurd. Finally he calmed and peered at her askance with merriment still lighting his ruddy face. "Now let me see if I understands ye, miss. Ye say yer uncle will pay once the voyage is done?"

Cerynise inclined her head ever so slightly, fully aware of the untenable position into which she had been thrust. "I realize that it would be rather unorthodox—"

" 'Tis balmy, that's what it be!" he barked suddenly, jolting a start from her. "Either ye're a blisterin' fool or ye take me for one, girlie."

"Neither, Captain Sullivan," she replied carefully and looked at him through welling tears. Though exhaustion muted her tone, she was nevertheless grateful that her tongue wasn't thwarted by the cold at the moment. "I assure you that I'm in full command of my senses, but after the recent death of my guardian, I find myself thrust from her home by the people who have inherited her property. In their endeavor to take my every possession from me, they've left me nothing with which to barter. I'm now a veritable pauper as of a

43

few hours ago." She paused briefly, realizing she had been reduced to begging. "Believe me, sir, if I thought I could persuade you to take pity on me, I would gladly promise you twice the fee a passenger might normally pay for passage on your packet if you'd just accept that my uncle will give you the funds. He's the only one I can rely upon."

The dark eyes raked over her again, this time with some evidence of sympathy. "Ye must understand, miss, that I'm obligated to account for all the fees I take in. Me shipping company requires it." Then he added with some reluctance, "Yer uncle could be dead, for all ye know, miss, and who, then, would pay for your passage? 'Twould have ta come out o' me own purse if'n ye couldn't pay."

"I understand, Captain Sullivan," she murmured dolefully, rising from her chair on limbs that threatened to give way beneath her. "I'm sorry to have bothered ye."

"Beggin' yer pardon, Cap'n," Moon interjected, leaning near Sullivan's shoulder again. The tar was amazed at his own growing desire to help the girl. "What 'bout the *Audacious*? Cap'n Birmin'ham don't answer ta no man but hisself, sir. He could take her, if'n he be o' a mind ta."

"Aye," Captain Sullivan agreed, stroking a hand thoughtfully over his bristly chin. "He owns his own ship...but as far as I knows, he's never taken on any passengers."

Cerynise passed a hand over her brow, wondering if she had heard the men cor-

44

rectly. She felt so weak that she couldn't be sure just how perceptive she was or if her words were even coherent as her tongue began to trip over her words again. "Y-you did s-say Birmingham, d-didn't you?"

Captain Sullivan looked at her curiously. "Do ye know Captain Birmingham, miss?"

"If he is p-part of the Birmingham family who l-lives near Charleston, th-then I do," she said haltingly.

" 'Tis Beauregard Birmingham who captains the *Audacious* we're speakin' of," the captain explained. "Do ye know him?"

Her energy was swiftly ebbing, leaving her hardly enough reserve to answer the man. "Before my father's death...he ran a private school...for the offspring of the planters and merchants who lived in that area." She hated her lagging speech, which was becoming more pronounced. "At one time...Beauregard Birmingham was one of his students. We were acquainted with his family...and that of his uncle, Jeffrey Birmingham."

"Perhaps if Cap'n Birmingham remembers ye well enough, he might take pity on ye," Captain Sullivan mused aloud, continuing to stroke his bewhiskered chin. He caught his cabin boy's gaze and jerked his head toward the door. "Give the lady safe escort ta the *Audacious*, Moon, an' tell Cap'n Birmingham he owes me one. I'll collect in a tankard o' ale when next we meet."

"Aye, Cap'n." The toothless grin was nearly as broad as the seaman's face. " 'Twill be a pleasure ta hie meself o'er there with the liedy an' take a close look-see at that there ship o' his afore we set sail."

Full darkness had descended by the time Moon led Cerynise from the tavern, but the winds had died down. Tendrils of fog had begun to whisper over the banks of the river and slide insidiously over land as distant clanks and strange dragging sounds echoed eerily from the mists that hung over the water. Moon made his way through the night as if by rote, pausing now and then to give her a chance to catch up. Cerynise could see nothing in the gloom that closed in around them. She was hesitant of her footing, for her legs felt stiff and leaden beneath her. She was so thoroughly chilled and fatigued, it took determination to remember her resolve and drag her sodden slippers across the cobblestones. She staggered ever onward in spite of the difficulty of remaining upright and on her feet. Finally she could see the lofty masts of a ship rising above the swirling mass of vapors.

Moon glanced over his shoulder as he pointed toward the craft. "Bet ye've ne'er been on a ship like that there one o' Cap'n Birmin'ham's. A bloomin' merchant frigate, she be! There ain't many ta be seen like her, 'at's for sure. An' can ye believe, girlie? He paid for it hisself with all 'em furs an' jewels an' things what he brought back from Russia several years ago. From what I hears, he's been back ta the Baltic and Saint Petersburg this time, too, he has, an' is carryin' twice as many treasures 'an before. 'Tis even rumored he talked the cap'n of an East India Company ship inta swappin' some silks an' pearls an' jade an' stuff for some o' the rich booty he was carryin'. Now he's here takin' on more treasures ta tempt the merchants in Charl'ton, as if he ain't gots enough ta entice 'em already. Why, a man'd be a fool ta carry passengers when he's gots treasures like that fillin' his holds. But let's hope the cap'n will be o' a different mind wit' ye, girlie."

Cerynise was unable to utter a reply. They were nearing a ship that rested against the quay. It was a proud, three-masted vessel, so huge it seemed to dwarf everything around it. But at the moment she couldn't be awed by anything. Her strength had vanished, her senses dulled, her wits long fled. Each step was an agonizing exertion that she could no longer force her shaking limbs to perform. All she wanted to do was curl up somewhere, close her eyes, and sleep.

Moon paused at the bottom of the gangplank and called to the watch on duty for permission to come aboard, but his voice sounded hollow and distant to Cerynise. Vaguely she was aware of her legs slowly crumpling beneath her and her body tilting back ever so slightly, as if time had ceased to be. Her head bumped almost gently against the cobblestones, but a dull ache began to throb there. Then a craggy voice cried out in alarm, and an eternity later, strong arms lifted her up against a stalwart chest. In the next moments the heavy mists seemed

47

to swirl around her, closing in upon her like a dank tomb, choking off her breath and pulling her down into a dark abyss as a numbing, uncaring oblivion swept over her.

CHAPTER 2

Cerynise struggled to find a shadowed haven from the radiance filling her world. The light was bright and obtrusive in its boldness, intruding into the nebulous haze that seemed to surround her. Squeezing her eyes tightly shut, she sought to banish the glare into the nether realm, for surely it was a torment born of hell. Alas, it remained undiminished beyond her protesting lids. Finally she yielded a cautious peek through silken lashes and found the culprit to be the morning sun, shining through the expanse of windows somewhere behind her left shoulder and reflecting off an oval mirror fixed atop a shaving stand located across the room. Had they been of steel, the brilliant shafts radiating into her face might have pierced her brain.

All around the shimmering oval aura, indistinct shapes remained darkly aloof and pensively silent in their distant detachment. Some were far too large and bulky to claim human form, and yet, hard as she struggled, she could not lay face or body to others that seemed of more manly dimensions. Or was it only her imagination that made her think that she was not entirely alone?

48

Cerynise realized with some relief that she was no longer plagued by a feeling of discomfort. Indeed, she was warm and cozy in a bed, her body encased in clean-smelling sheets and a feather comforter, her hair dry with curling strands partially masking her face, and her toes no longer pained by the cold. If not for the penetrating ball of brightness shining between her narrowed eyelids, demanding that she pay heed, she might have still been slumbering in peaceful contentment.

A soft sigh slipped from her lips as she rolled away from the offending light. The goose down pillow beneath her head was a bit firmer than she was accustomed to, and with a balled-up fist, she punched it into some semblance of comfort, eliciting a strangely masculine essence that bestirred her senses like a warm caress. She rubbed her nose against the downy softness, deliberately extracting fleeting whiffs of the scent, and in quixotic reflection, licked a tongue languidly over smiling lips as several delicious fantasies swept through her mind. It was momentarily delightful to imagine that she had been carried off by a handsome sultan who, after claiming her, had banished his harem to the four corners of the earth, proving himself totally smitten by his love for her. Just as captivating was an illusion of a swashbuckler, handsome and daring enough to carry her off to his ship, where he promised to lay the world at her feet.

A slight shifting of her bed and a subtle creaking, similar to that which the masts of a ship might make, brought Cerynise's eyes flying open in sudden alarm as she realized she was not housed on solid ground. The paneled wall that met her astounded gaze seemed unusually close. She reached out a hand to touch it, trying to bring it in line with what was familiar to her, but as her fingers lightly traced the delicate molding, she became aware that her world was once again swaying incongruously to all that seemed right and customary in her life. Her hand flew to her mouth, smothering a gasp that was more mental than actual. She was definitely on a ship, she concluded, but whose?

Her ears caught a sound, and as she listened, her apprehension mounted. A faint scratching, like a quill on parchment, came from behind her.

As her thoughts became fraught with growing anxiety, her hand moved to her throat. Abruptly her eyes widened as she realized the slender column was no longer bedecked in a stiff ruffle. Her heart began to hammer as she slipped an arm first beneath the feather tick and then the sheet that covered her. Her fingers swept hurriedly downward, appraising her state of attire, and brushed a naked breast. In rising astonishment she continued her examination and found her hips and thighs equally devoid of clothing.

Her panic was too great! Twisting around, Cerynise gathered the covers up high beneath her chin and came upright in the bed to escape the reflected sunlight as she searched for the other occupant of the cabin, for she had no doubt now that there was another in the room. It didn't much matter to her at the moment whether he was a swashbuckler or a sultan. The man was definitely a cad for having stripped her naked! And heaven only knew what else he had done!

Cerynise saw the man immediately. He was sitting at a desk with a quill in hand, making notes in a ledger that lay open before him. At her movement he dragged his gaze from the book and lent her his undivided attention. She found herself meeting eyes of deep sapphire blue in a face warmly bronzed by the sun. His black hair was wont to curl ever so slightly and was just long enough at the nape to brush the open collar of a shirt that appeared no less than dazzling white in the morning light.

"I'm glad to see that you're alive." His voice was deep and imbued with warmth and humor. "You were sleeping so soundly, I was beginning to wonder if you would ever wake. As it is, you've slept the night and most of the morning through."

"Where are my clothes?" Cerynise blurted the question out in a rush, stricken with horror at the evidence surrounding her.

"You took a bad chill, Cerynise, and your clothes were too wet to leave on you. I had my cabin boy wash and dry your undergarments, but I fear your gown has been ruined beyond repair."

Her mind raced. He had called her by name, and yet he was a stranger to her. "Do I know you?"

A smile tugged at his lips as he laid the quill across the ledger and rose from his chair. Though she pressed back warily against the wall behind her, he came forward with eyes glowing with amusement. Bracing an arm across the upper frame of the bunk, he leaned forward slightly and stretched out his other hand to capture a long, silken tress that had tumbled forward over the quilt.

"Though Moon was informative about your father, I've never known but one in my entire life who had this particular shade of hair. She was a young girl who sometimes sat in her father's classes, taking notes as if she were every bit as old and advanced as the rest of his students. Whenever I'd tweak her nose, she be inclined to stick her tongue out at me and declare me a hopeless tease. Still, she seemed disposed to follow at my heels whenever she could...."

Cerynise's mind flew. There was only one of her father's students whom she had ever looked up to with such devotion. He had left Charleston at the age of ten and six to find his future on sailing ships, but whenever he had returned to home port, he had always brought back gifts for her that he handed out during his visits with her father. "Beau?"

"The same, my girl." Stepping back, Captain Beauregard Birmingham clicked his heels and swept an arm before his chest in a debonair bow. "A pleasure to see you again, Cerynise."

"You've changed," she breathed in awe. Indeed, he was very much a man now, and more handsome than she had once dared to imagine he would become. He was taller, heavier, with shoulders wide enough to make his waist and hips seem as narrow as any woman's. In all, he was every bit the princely vision she had thought him to be when she had tagged along behind him yearning for a glance, a smile or a wink, any kind of recognition that would assure her that he was just as taken with her as she was with him.

"So have you," he murmured, his lips curving into a lopsided smile as his blue eyes twinkled back at her. "You've become quite a woman, Cerynise...a *very beautiful* young woman."

Cerynise could feel the heat rising to her scalp. Though unspoken, the insinuation was there, burning to be probed. "W-who undressed me?"

Beau's gaze never wavered. "I fear I would have shirked my responsibilities as captain of this vessel had I let some member of my crew perform the service. And since I was once your protector when other boys were wont to badger you, I couldn't very well allow any harm to come to you now."

Cerynise groaned in abject misery. "Please tell me you kept your eyes closed."

Beau met her searching gaze with an amused smile, momentarily awed by her eyes as they caught a shaft of light from the mirror. For the moment, they looked similar to dark green crystals, but he knew from experience gained years ago that they could change color in a shifting light or with the donning of another color. With some difficulty he dragged his mind to full attention. He knew she was upset and pondered how he might soothe her shock. "If it would make you feel any better..."

Cerynise glared up at him accusingly. "Are you going to tell me a lie, Beau Birmingham?"

His knuckle pressed against smiling lips as he struggled to contain his laughter. "My only concern was for your state of health, Cerynise," he assured her, making every effort to present a gallant mien. "You were nigh frozen, and I feared for your life. You had to be warmed, which would have been difficult to do with all of your clothes on. They were thoroughly soaked. Believe me, I'm no lecher...."

She groaned, thoroughly humiliated. "Neither are you blind!"

"Nay, I'm not blind," he admitted with a chuckle. "And though under different circumstances I would have been pleasured by the sight of your perfection, I was deeply concerned for your welfare, Cerynise." Having been delayed by an autumn ice storm in Russia several years ago, he had seen firsthand the ravages frostbite and shock could reap upon an unsuspecting man, even to the point of death. But he carefully avoided mentioning that, after stripping away her clothing, he had placed her in a tub of comfortably steaming

54

water and left her to soak for some moments while he tried to spoon warm brandy between her blue lips. Failing for the most part in that endeavor, he had taken her to his bed and briskly toweled her body dry before gathering a blanket around her and holding her against his own warmth. She would never have understood the feelings that had washed through him when finally her trauma began to ebb and she nestled close against him. Even so simple a thing as her breath tickling his throat had been startling in its effect on him, and he had realized that he wouldn't be able to trust himself with her if she accompanied him to Charleston. She was far too tempting for a man who'd been too busy trying to convince the local shipping authorities that he hadn't broken any of their asinine laws with his weaving in and out of ports. An hour or two in the arms of a winsome wench might have done much to ease his manly vexation. At least, it would have made it easier for him to be around this one.

Cerynise turned her face toward the wall, allowing a lengthy silence to pass between them. Though the arguments were there to give testament to the appropriateness of his action, she was nevertheless mortified by the idea that he had been so bold with her.

"Would you like something to eat?" Beau asked, wisely changing the subject. "I was hoping you'd wake so we could dine together and perhaps talk a bit. The last time I saw you was at your parents' funeral, shortly after I returned from a voyage. Before I knew what was happening, Mrs. Winthrop was whisking you away in a carriage. I didn't even have a chance to offer my condolences. Then your uncle told me that you and the widow were making haste to catch a ship bound for England." He paused briefly before continuing in somber tones. "Last night Moon informed me that you've been left very much out on the street by the Winthrop heirs and are wanting to go home. And that you're hoping I will take you."

Cerynise faced him again, anxious to know his answer. "Will you?"

Beau sighed heavily, knowing he dare not. As lovely and womanly as she had become, he knew he'd find it difficult to conduct himself with the sort of gallantry his mother might expect of him. He wished that he could still think of her as that scrawny little girl whose tongue had been as keen as her wit, but after viewing her in the altogether, he'd never again be able to return to that former way of thinking. She was very much a lady now, and the consequences of dallying with sweet innocents ensconced on his ship could affect his life in a most permanent fashion. At the very least, there would be hell to pay when he arrived home. "This is a merchant ship, Cerynise. There are no suitable accommodations for passengers." He stretched the truth only by a slim margin, for the cabins had been filled to the hilt with the more precious cargo he was carrying. "I will, however, arrange for Captain Sullivan to see you safely home on the *Mirage*. He'll be sailing before the week is out, but I'll probably be leaving a bit sooner. Until I do, I give you leave to stay here and use my cabin."

Disappointment overshadowed the surging hope that had first arisen within Cerynise. "I tried to explain to Captain Sullivan that Uncle Sterling would pay for my passage after I arrived," she murmured dejectedly. "But he said his shipping company would expect an accounting."

"You needn't concern yourself about the fee," Beau assured her. "I've already told Moon to make all the necessary arrangements for you. I'm sure you'll have nothing to worry about with him watching over you. That old man is tenacious when his loyalties take root. I learned that when we sailed together years ago." Beau leaned his head aslant as he looked down at her. "I rather gathered he now thinks of himself as your private paladin. He was nearly beside himself with worry after you passed out."

"I couldn't have made it this far without him," Cerynise acknowledged quietly.

Beau stepped to one of two tall lockers neatly recessed in the wall at the far end of his bunk and pulled out a gentleman's robe. Draping the garment over his arm, he paused beside a chair and gathered up a bundle of folded clothes that had been left there. Cerynise recognized them as the undergarments she had been wearing beneath her gown. Yet even at first glance she could tell that they had been badly stained with dark splotches.

57

"What happened to my clothes?"

"I'm afraid your gown faded on them after you got drenched in the rain," Beau replied, handing the undergarments to her. "No one on the *Audacious* knew what to do to whiten such frilly things."

"And my gown? Where is it?"

"The velvet was still damp as of a few moments ago, but even dry, I doubt that you'd find it serviceable." He shrugged his shoulders at the sudden confusion she displayed. "A child might."

"You mean it has shrunk in size?"

"Precisely." Beau brushed the back of his hand across the robe draped over his arm. "For the moment this is the best I can offer as a replacement. I'll try to find something more conventional for you to wear later this afternoon. Perhaps tomorrow I'll have more time to purchase a gown for you. While you're dressing, I'll inform my chef that we'd like to eat."

With that, he quit the cabin, allowing Cerynise the privacy she needed to collect her scattered thoughts. Struck by an awareness that she was now occupying the domain of a man with whom she had been infatuated since childhood, she rose from the bunk and looked around with a feeling of reverence as she slipped into the oversized garment he had left with her. A faint essence of a manly cologne claimed her attention, tantalizing her with images of one Beauregard Birmingham. The scent was subtle yet strangely stimulating to her womanly senses. Indeed, she found it rather amazing that she could be moved to such a degree by the presence of one whom she hadn't seen since her departure from her parents' funeral. Fearing at the time that she would never see him again, she had strained to watch him from the windows of the carriage. After a lengthy absence, his appearance had been well worth noting even then. It had certainly held her attention until they were out of sight, and thereafter she had suffered a deep regret that he hadn't arrived in time to talk with her. But now, in his manly maturity, he was no less than magnificent.

An unquenchable grin flitted across Cerynise's lips as an unusual blissful feeling filled her nigh to overflowing. With eyes glowing, she considered the tasteful interior and the fine furnishings that contributed to its masculine appeal. The quarters were like the man himself, handsome, polished, distinguished, yet comfortably open to the world and its adventures, like the spacious expanse of small-paned windows located above the stern gallery. The massive desk, hand-tooled with a leather top and solidly made of mahogany, was the most impressive piece in the room. Beau had looked quite imposing behind it, she had thought. For a moment she snuggled back into the leather confines of the chair and found to her surprise that only her toes reached the floor. The way he had loomed over the bunk, she could surmise that he had reached a height easily equal to his sire, a man whom she remembered standing at least a head taller than most women and a fair number of men as well.

Curiously Cerynise scanned the titles of books through the glass doors of a pair of bookcases located on either side of the windows and to her amazement found a fine collection of biographies, poems and fiction mixed in with those immediately more pertinent to sailing and navigation. Her lips curved in a smile, and she shook her head in wonder at the man. What had once seemed a bland indifference toward classical literature on his part as a student had undoubtedly been well contrived for the benefit of his male companions, who might have supposed that such inclinations were evidences of weaknesses in the male species, in spite of the fact that Beau had always ridden, raced, and swam better than most of them. It seemed her father was right after all, for he had always claimed the lad was far more mentally astute than he had cared to let on.

Across the room, a table and four chairs resided beneath a hanging lantern. Several low, curved-top chests sat here and there, no doubt containing the captain's possessions. The shaving stand, upon which the sun had lit earlier, stood beside a paneled opening that had been left slightly ajar. Within the cabinet she glimpsed an oval tub hanging on a peg and tucked almost out of sight. Moving near, she smiled as she imagined the long-legged man trying to bathe with some comfort in such a compact receptacle. Then her eyes caught on a long tawny strand of hair that had been snared on the rim, and her breath was snatched inward with a shocked gasp, for she suffered no uncertainty that it was her own.

"He *bathed* me?" she cried in an astounded whisper. Full comprehension was only a fleeting breath away. "Good heavens, he bathed me! He *bathed* me!"

Her astonishment knew no end. The idea that Beau Birmingham had taken such liberties with her heightened her coloring to a vivid scarlet. She wanted to moan, weep in misery or do something to find relief for the overwhelming embarrassment that swept through her.

Opening the robe, Cerynise stared down at her naked body as if she had never seen it before. Indeed, she felt somehow foreign to it now that she knew that Beau had gazed upon it, too. Her breasts were full and delicately hued, her waist slender, her hips and thighs smooth and sleek. Had he been her husband, she would have gladly yielded him all the sights she had to offer, but since he was the one whose memory had never failed to quicken the beat of her heart all these many years, Cerynise could only wonder what he had thought about while he bathed her. He had meant it for her good, she assured herself, but had there been something about the incident that he had tried to hide from her? Was that why he hadn't told her that he had bathed her? Or had he only meant to save her the anguish of humiliation that she was now suffering?

For the time being, Cerynise shunned the idea of wearing a corset, but she hurriedly donned the rest of her undergarments. Over them she wrapped the oversize robe around her and folded back the sleeves, trying not to think of how Beau's long, lean fingers might have stumbled on the tiny buttons that had fastened her camisole between her breasts. A man would have had difficulty with anything so small. Or had he casually dismissed her nakedness and performed his charitable deed without dwelling on the fact that she was a woman now?

Cerynise faced the small mirror above his shaving stand and, managing to blank her mind for the present, proceeded to brush her teeth with a forefinger and a small amount of salt that she had found in a silver box wedged firmly in a groove on the table. She combed her fingers through her hair, raking out most of the snarls, and tore a bit of lace from the hem of her petticoat to tie it with. Deeming herself decidedly pale, she pinched her cheeks and bit her lips to bring forth a brighter hue. As she surveyed the results, it dawned on her that she had never taken such care to look her best when she had foreseen the likelihood of passing one of three young swains who, after taking close account of her customary strolls with Lydia through Hyde Park, had often waited for her somewhere along the path with the hope of gaining an introduction from her guardian. Lydia, however, had taken mischievous delight in thwarting their attempts, having been dedicated to the idea that her ward would become a famous artist or, at the very least, marry into the nobility.

A light rap of knuckles came upon the door. "Are you decent, Cerynise?" Beau called through the wood. "May I come in?"

"Yes, of course," she answered quickly, making sure the collar of his robe was tucked securely around her neck. Her attempt at modesty, Cerynise thought wryly, was like closing the gate after the sheep had fled. It hardly served much purpose after Beau had seen her without a stitch of clothing.

Upon entering, Beau stood aside as he held the door open to admit a small, energetic, black-haired man with sparkling black eyes and a small black mustache that curved like a cherubic bow above his upper lip. The curled ends extended upward in a cheery smile.

"Zee mademoiselle iz about to taste zee finest cuisine she has ever sampled in her life. Philippe has cooked zee food 'specially for her...." the man announced. Then he paused in acute surprise as his eyes finally lit on her. Suddenly a-smile with appreciation for her beauty, he pressed a hand to his chest as he sought to make amends. "Mademoiselle, you must forgive *le capitaine* for not pre-senting us. I am Philippe Monét, *Capitaine* Birmingham's chef de la cuisine." Turning his hand with an elegant flourish, he halted any further introductions. "And you are zee Made-moiselle Kendall, whom *le capitaine* failed to mention is zee most ravishing creature in all zee world."

Cerynise laughed with pleasure at the light-hearted exuberance of the wiry, little man, but when she glanced toward Beau whose brow had become slightly quirked, she had the distinct impression that he had grown rather perturbed with the chef. The reason was a mystery to her. Did he resent being chided for his failure to make a mannerly introduction? Or was he totally unappreciative of the fact that his cook was gushing over a guest with so much enthusiasm?

Unable to find any definite justification for his displeasure, Cerynise faced the chef and replied graciously, *"Enchanté de faire votre connaissance, Monsieur Monét."*

Philippe's mustache twitched with unquenchable delight as he heard his native tongue spoken with such elegance. It was obvious the lady had been schooled by an articulate Frenchman to pronounce the words so divinely. Eagerly Philippe began spouting off a stream of fluid French, but Beau quickly held up a hand to halt his verbosity. "Please! Converse in English for us poor unfortunates who are not fluent in a variety of languages."

"Excusez-moi, Capitaine..." the cook began.

"Philippe, if you please!" Beau rebuked impatiently, his eyebrow now sharply peaked.

"Your pardon, Capitaine," the smaller man humbly apologized. "I fear I forgot myself when zee mademoiselle answered me in my own language."

"Control yourself, if you can," Beau urged aridly. "I know Miss Kendall is beautiful,

Philippe, but she is my guest, and I would prefer that she not be embarrassed by your ardor."

"Oh, Capitaine, I would not wish zhat for zee world," Philippe declared, wringing his hands fretfully as he faced Cerynise.

"Then would you mind serving us our meal before it's too cold to eat?" Beau implored curtly before the man had time to launch into another apology.

"Of course, Capitaine." Blushing lightly at his captain's reprimand, Philippe responded with a clipped bow and promptly clapped his hands.

Immediately a freckle-faced boy, who had been waiting patiently beyond the threshold, carried a large tray laden with their morning meal through the doorway. When the youth saw Cerynise, he displayed none of the cook's jubilance, but halted awkwardly in mid-stride, unable to say a word. His jaw slowly descended as he stared agog.

"This is Billy Todd," Beau announced, having been chided for his lack of etiquette enough for one day. "He's my cabin boy and a good sort who generally does his job"—he dropped a hand on the back of the boy's neck as he continued—"at least when he remembers to keep his eyes in his head and his chin above his shoulders."

Billy's cheeks took on a speckled ruby hue. "Sorry, sir, miss...ma'am...mum..."

"Miss will do," Beau informed him bluntly. He had never seen members of his crew so affected by a pretty face before. But then, he had to remember that he hadn't been exactly clearheaded either when he had held the girl snuggled within his arms. "Now put the tray down, Billy, before you spill something."

"Aye, sir," the cabin boy replied, complying with great dispatch.

Philippe assisted the youth, and in no time the small table was laden with a rather lavish meal of smoked salmon, crepes with caviar, vegetable ribbons lightly sautéed in lemon butter and, waiting to be enjoyed afterwards, a lime soufflé chilled on ice. The latter was considered a rarity for sea voyages, but from Russia, they had brought back a small amount of ice packed in sawdust. Soon the chef and the cabin boy retreated, leaving Beau to assist Cerynise into a chair on his left.

"For a man who travels across vast oceans, Captain, you seem to enjoy the best that life can offer," Cerynise commented, surveying the elegantly presented dishes.

"You needn't be so formal, Cerynise," he chided with a grin, lifting his gaze briefly to hers. "You've called me Beau for as long as I can remember. I give you leave to continue."

At that precise moment Cerynise became convinced that there were no eyes in all the world bluer than the ones which now smiled at her. As a child she had once found herself staring into his mother's eyes, thinking how beautiful they were. Then later, she had realized they were the same color as Beau's. Staring into those darkly translucent depths now, it was easy for her to imagine a woman being swept away by admiration for him without a single word being uttered.

Cerynise mentally shook off the spell he unwittingly cast and scolded herself for acting as addled as a dazzled schoolgirl. "Moon mentioned something about you traveling to Russia."

"Some of the fare we now have sitting before us came from there."

"It must have been exciting for you to go there, but it seems so far away."

"Not nearly as far as you might think, Cerynise. In fact, it's rather a short jaunt in comparison to sailing around Cape Horn on a voyage to China. Even that will soon be shortened once they perfect the sailing ships they've begun to make. Clippers, they're called, and beauties they are. Being heavily sparred to bear a greater width of canvas and with their hulls as sharp as a razor, they'll slice through the ocean in no time."

"It sounds like you're married to the sea," Cerynise replied rather wistfully.

"Not really," Beau answered. "I want a home and family just like the next man, but I've yet to find a woman who can steal my heart from the sea. Perhaps in another ten years I'll be ready to give up sailing, for I seriously doubt it will come any time soon."

"Stealing your heart will be a difficult task for any woman to accomplish, I think," Cerynise mused aloud. A pause in their conversation allowed her a moment to sample a crepe. She found it so delectable that she promptly forgot the drift of their discussion and rolled her eyes skyward in sheer delight. "Oh, Beau, the crepes are wonderful! Truly, I've never tasted anything so heavenly."

A soft chuckle accompanied Beau's reply. "I'd say that it was the caviar if I wasn't aware of the talent of a certain chef in my employ. Philippe is so accomplished, I fear I'll be losing him one day to someone who'll promise him a kingdom if he would but go and cook for them. He's been with me for three years now and takes over my kitchen in Charleston whenever we're at home."

"Do you have a house there?" she queried in surprise. "I'd have thought with being gone so much that it would be easier for you to stay with your parents while you're there."

"I enjoy my privacy too much to roost in the wings of Harthaven while my ship is in home port," he explained, tossing her another grin as he flaked off a piece of salmon with his fork. "Besides, when my father and I are in the same house together for too long, we begin to act like a pair of stallions fenced in the same paddock."

The idea of the Birmingham men snorting and stamping about within the confining walls of a house wrenched giggles from Cerynise. Her hilarity was such that a piece of crepe which she had been in the process of swallowing got caught in her throat. She choked and promptly began coughing, trying to dislodge it.

"Now I've done it," Beau declared, rising to his feet. He caught her hand, bidding her to stand as he stepped close behind her. Much to her astonishment, he slipped his arms about her slender waist. "Now bend over as far as you can go, and try to relax and cough it out."

Hanging her upper torso downward over his forearms as he squeezed her ribcage with sharp, quick jerks was the most undignified position that she could have ever been in as far as Cerynise was concerned. She felt very much like an awkward goose of a girl, which some boys had been wont to call her years ago. The long robe only made her more clumsy, for in her attempt to keep her backside a respectable distance from her host, her foot got tangled in the dragging hem and she stumbled backward, falling literally into Beau's lap as he dipped his knees to catch her. For a moment his arm clasped her tightly to him, and she felt secure, but as she pulled away from his stabling grasp and tried to stand, her foot slipped once more on the robe and she went flying, this time in a lateral direction. Beau flung an arm outward to catch her, but while drawing her back he lost his balance. In the next moment they both sprawled backward, he to the floor and she on top of him.

Cerynise's breath rushed forcefully outward in surprise as she fell, and whatever small particle had hitherto been lodged in her throat came free. Although relieved, she didn't think anything could assuage her embarrassment over her own awkwardness. She could feel her face flaming hotly as she struggled to sit up. Her every thought was on making good her escape, for she was sure by now that Beau was mentally questioning her propensity for calamity, and she didn't want to lend further weight to any suspicion of that sort. Too late she realized that in her effort to get up, she was now straddling his loins, albeit from a rearward perspective. The swiftly growing firmness beneath her buttocks made her eyes widen. Hot coals might have had the same effect. Scrambling to her feet, she kept her back deliberately presented to the man upon whom she had landed and made a pretense of straightening the wayward robe as she waited for her hot cheeks to cool.

Beau pushed himself to his feet. He had known well enough that he was in dire need of a woman in his bed, but he hadn't realized to what extent until Cerynise Kendall had come aboard his ship. Her womanly softness pressing down upon his loins had ignited a fuse that had proven far too explosive for a display of coolheaded logic. The fact that he greatly desired to have his way with her this very moment was reason enough to hasten her departure to the *Mirage*. It didn't matter that she had always been the little girl following at his heels. She was very much a woman now, too beautiful for his peace of mind. He couldn't trust himself around her, no matter how much he had respected her parents.

Beau collected his aplomb by gritted-teeth

tenacity and, after a moment, was able to gain control of his goading lusts. Returning to the table, he seated himself once more, but he noticed that a deeper blush had invaded his companion's cheeks and could well assume the reason. He had no idea what Cerynise had learned about men while living in an aging widow's staid and sterile house, but he could imagine that her knowledge was sorely lacking in that area. If she stayed around him very long, however, that was bound to change. She'd soon come to realize that he wasn't made of stone. Indeed, he could foresee their relationship coming down to a simple test of endurance, with one of them definitely being pressed to the limit.

Silence prevailed between them as they finished the meal. Beau's appetite for food had waned with the blunt realization of his own craving for carnal appeasement. He couldn't very well take his guest to bed, as much as he might have reveled in the experience with such a fresh subject. Neither could he throw her out of his hungering sight without decent apparel. The only choice that remained was for him to leave the ship. Perhaps when he had the time, he could search out a wench who might satisfy his manly needs. Only then would he be able to act the gentleman in this one's presence.

Later that afternoon, Billy Todd rapped his knuckles lightly against the captain's cabin door and called through the wood, "Miss, are ye awake?"

"Yes, Billy, just a moment please." Cerynise clutched the robe closer around her neck and lifted its long skirt as she hurried to answer the summons. She greeted the boy with a smile, but it was no brighter than his. "What is it, Billy?"

Billy held forth a small bundle of clothing. "Yer pardon, miss, but the cap'n said ye were in need of somethin' ta wear for the time bein', an' what with me bein' the smallest seaman aboard, he asked if'n I'd be willin' ta share with ye for a spell." Seeing her eyes widen in sudden dismay, the lad rushed on to plead, "Please don't think me forward, miss. The cap'n said ye might be wantin' ta wear somethin' 'sides that there robe o' his, seein' as how it's so big an' all." His eyes passed quickly over the length to the slender bare feet and trim ankles showing beneath the raised hem, which dropped abruptly at his inspection. Billy's freckled cheeks flushed darkly, and in some confusion, he pressed the garments into her hands. "They be clean, miss. I washed 'em meself."

"Oh, I have no doubt they are, Billy," Cerynise assured him, worrying far more about the propriety of a woman wearing a boy's clothing. "And it's very kind of you to offer, but I wouldn't want to put you out."

The look of adoration that briefly swept his face conveyed a willingness to do much more if she but asked him. "Please take 'em, miss," he cajoled, "else the cap'n'll wonder if I even offered 'em ta ye."

Cerynise laughed, brightening the lad's countenance. "In that case, I think I'd better. I wouldn't want you to get into any trouble on my account."

"Anything else ye need, miss, ye be sure an' let me know." Blushing even more fiercely, he added, "I'd be only too glad ta see ta yer wishes."

"Thank you, Billy. I'll let you know if I should think of anything," she replied, and then directly began to wonder if she would have time to try on the clothes before Beau returned to his cabin. "Will the captain be on deck for a while longer?"

"Oh, no, miss. The cap'n left ta visit some friends o' his 'bout an hour ago, but he said for me ta tell ye he'd be comin' back ta have dinner with ye later this evenin'. Till then, he asked if'n ye wouldn't mind stayin' in his cabin..." Billy sensed that she was waiting for him to continue and, with a lame shrug, explained, "Seein's as how the men might gawk an' forget 'bout their duties if'n ye come up on deck."

"The captain bade you to tell me that?" Cerynise queried in surprise.

Billy winced in chagrin and seemed suddenly unsure of himself. "Well, maybe the last part wasn't meant for yer ears. Ye won't tell him I said that, will ye?"

Cerynise shook her head and smiled. "No, Billy, 'twill be our secret."

The cabin boy sighed in relief. "We ain't ne'er had a woman on board longer'n a couple o' hours, miss, so ye can expect our manners ta be a bit raw."

"If the other seamen are as gallant as you, Billy, then I have no doubt the *Audacious* is manned by a crew of gentlemen." Her smile widened, bringing a glow to his cheeks and a buoyant grin to his lips. She guessed the lad to be only a few years her junior, and although life at sea could sometimes be terribly harsh on the young, in Billy's case it was obvious that he had landed on his feet. Though as lean as a reed, he looked well nourished, clean and happy, all indications of the integrity of the man who captained the ship upon which he sailed.

"I'd best get back ta work now, miss. If'n ye need anythin', just ring the bell what's outside the door an' I'll come runnin'."

Soon after the portal had closed behind the boy, Cerynise examined the garments and gingerly tried them on. As slender as she was, she was not without womanly curves, which posed a problem in putting on the narrow duck trousers that were similar in shade to the sails. They had to be worked up over her pantalettes, for there was no way she would consider wearing the rough cloth next to her skin. She'd surely be chafed raw. After buttoning them, she adjusted the small mirror on the shaving stand and considered the results, turning this way and that to view every angle. The front was vulgar enough to brighten her cheeks, but when she caught sight of her backside, she gasped in astonishment, for the pants showed nearly every detail, cleaving to her buttocks like a second skin and snuggling into the cleft between. Even without Beau's request, Cerynise knew it would have taken a team of stout drays to drag her up on deck. Wearing such indecent garb around seamen would be an open invitation for them to do more than just gape.

The tail of the shirt was long enough to cover her hips, allowing her to wear the ducks with some measure of modesty, but the fabric was soft after many washings. Seeing how it clung to her breasts, Cerynise quickly dispensed with the notion of wearing a corset, which would have pressed her bosom close to overflowing the top of her camisole with no doubt imprudent results. Even the most casual glance into the neck of the garment would convince the viewer of her lack of modesty.

Despite her qualms about wearing Billy's clothes, Cerynise decided there was no harm in making use of them while Beau was away and she had the cabin to herself. The long robe hindered her movements and was so wide across the shoulders that it was forever falling open to her waist. Still, if Billy or someone else came in, she'd have to seek the enveloping folds of the larger garment to hide what the lad's clothing readily displayed.

Billy Todd returned a couple of hours later to inquire whether she was hungry or not. Cerynise declined his pleas to eat, telling him that she preferred to rest instead. She still felt drained from the events of the past week,

75

and she could think of no better succor for her physical and mental well-being than sleep and relaxation.

Folding down the coverlet on Beau's bunk, she laid the robe on the mattress near the wall where it would be easily accessible if there came a need while she napped. She snuggled beneath the comforter and closed her eyes, thankful for the hospitality her host had extended to her.

The realization of Beau's absence began to settle down upon Cerynise as she stuffed his pillow beneath her head and became aware once more of the elusive scent of the man. It came as something of a shock to her that she was just as susceptible to his absence as she was to his presence. The woman she had become was hardly much different from the youngling she had once been. Long ago she had pined her heart away after Beau had gone to sea, but now, with only a short interval since his departure, she found herself eagerly anticipating his return. Considering their lengthy separation over the last five years and the voyages that had kept him away prior to her taking residence in England, Cerynise could find no cause for the hollow feeling that now plagued her in his absence. It seemed far-fetched to think that one man could move her to such extremes, yet when she compared the joy she had experienced over their reunion to the strange, inexplicable yearning that presently thwarted her mood, what else could she lay it to?

With the exception of another brief visit from Billy Todd in the middle of the afternoon, when he had brought her tea and crumpets, the hours passed slowly in the solitude of the cabin. Soon after the tea tray was taken away, Cerynise strolled to the gallery windows and curled up on the padded seats cushioning the storage compartments that had been built underneath. She was enthralled with the activity along the wharf and would have enjoyed painting the ever-changing scenes and the variety of people whom she could see through the small panes of glass. The sounds that flowed from the quay were muted by the transparent barrier, but not so much that she couldn't hear them altogether. Finely garbed gentlemen rubbed shoulders with swarthy seamen, while plump merchants tried to shoo off ragged urchins who wouldn't desist their pleading until a handful of coins was tossed in their direction. Fishwives strolled along with baskets balanced on ample hips, hawking their wares. Other vendors wheeled carts laden with vegetables, fruit, eggs, and all manner of fresh foods. Cerynise saw Monsieur Philippe bustling out to greet several, and on occasion, a sailor had to be called to help carry back the abundant purchases.

As twilight approached, the activity on the quay diminished, but a different sort of peddler became more prevalent. The gaudy garb and heavily painted faces of the harlots clearly marked their profession even before they began to call out to passing sailors or to the men on the *Audacious*. They were not above displaying a goodly length of thigh or lowering their blouses to a greater depth to entice customers. Some even went so far as to show off swelling mounds with vividly rouged nipples. Cerynise felt her own face flaming at their wantonness, and yet, after her own recent experience with being destitute, she couldn't help but sympathize with their plight, though she thought she'd rather be dead than exist by selling her body to strangers.

A carriage rumbled to a halt in an open space nearby, and Cerynise's heart leapt with excitement as she saw Beau alight. He paused at the door of the conveyance to gather what he had taken with him, laying a pair of long guns over his arm and then slinging a burlap bag over his shoulder. As he paid the driver, several of the strumpets pranced forward. When he turned, he was immediately beset by a variety of invitations, the boldest being a pretty wench who rubbed herself against him in a provocative manner as her hand dipped downward to boldly explore his loins. Beau seemed unabashed by her inspection as he casually scanned her and then the others who were vying for his attention, but when the winsome harlot stood on her tiptoes and tried to extract a kiss from his lips, he turned his face aside with a chuckle and shook his head. Waving the strumpets off with a smile, he strode toward the ship, leaving the comely one pouting with arms akimbo.

Cerynise eased her constricted breath out

in a long sigh of relief, knowing how distressed she would have been if Beau had taken one of the women under his arm and escorted her to some temporary haven. Indeed, she probably would have sulked more than the harlot.

It had always been Beau for whom her heart had awakened whenever he had come into a classroom or ridden near. Cerynise listened just as intently for his footfalls to approach the cabin door. After a moment she heard the floor creak just beyond the portal. Then a light knock accompanied the announcement "Cerynise, it's Beau. Can I come in?"

"Yes," she called, somewhat surprised by the nervous catch in her voice. Then, because she couldn't bear to have him realized that she had witnessed his encounter with the strumpet, she fled the gallery. Espying the robe on the far side of the bunk, she suddenly recalled her need for its protective covering and scurried to fetch the velvet armor, but not quickly enough to avoid being caught in a most unladylike position.

Beau swung open the door and then halted abruptly as he stepped within, for he found himself confronting a very fetching derriere clothed in ducks and stuck up in the air like a flag of truce. He would have gladly accepted the young lady's surrender almost on any terms, yet he was prone to wonder if he was having another lewd fantasy involving her. He found his brain as well as his breathing ensnared, and it came as no surprise to him that she had acutely awakened his manly cravings when none of the harlots had succeeded.

Cerynise backed off the bunk and nearly made her admirer groan with the sharp hunger she evoked within him. He was certain he had never seen anything quite as stimulating as those snugly bound crevices, for the tight trousers hardly left anything to his imagination. Where his eyes were fastened was unmistakably where he wanted to be.

Turning quickly aside as she got to her feet, Beau made a pretense of washing his face and hands at the shaving stand. The cold water helped to some degree to cool his imagination, but it was a lengthy moment before he managed to regain control of himself and face the girl in any guise of control. He almost breathed a sigh of relief when he saw her attired in his robe again. At least with her in that all-consuming garment, he could look at her without fearing that in the very next moment he might forget all logic and sweep her down upon his bed.

Cerynise dared a small, timid smile. "Billy's clothes are surprisingly comfortable."

Beau could have cursed himself for having thought of the idea, which had come to him after breakfast. She had looked too damned appealing and accessible in his robe. Were she garbed as a boy, he had thought, he'd be able to ignore her better, but the lad's breeches had deftly conspired to make her look all the more feminine and desirable. She was a child-woman of such beguiling beauty, he seriously doubted that he'd ever be stricken with such ravenous cravings while looking upon another, at least not until he managed to thrust this one's image far into the realm of forgetfulness. Her hip-length hair swirled in shimmering tawny waves around her slender form, while her widened eyes, soft as the deep glen of a wooded copse, stared back at him in indecision. " 'Tis best that you don't let any of my men see you in Billy's clothing. The sight might prove too much for them."

The intense scowl creasing Beau's brows made Cerynise almost quail. She was unable to discern the cause of his anger and ventured forthrightly, "I sense that you are displeased because I'm wearing them. And yet Billy said you wanted me—"

"*Displeased* hardly describes what I'm battling now, Cerynise," Beau interrupted, striding across the room to put his desk safely between them. He faced the stern windows and frantically sought to divert his thoughts toward a different path. He cast a searching glance about, skimming the cushions that he never took time to sit upon. His eyes paused as he noticed a slight depression similar to the breadth of Cerynise's slender hips near the far side of the bench. When he glanced outward toward the dock, he saw the young strumpet awaiting a customer near the spot where he had left her. Beau had no need to ask what his guest had witnessed, for it was evident to him where she had been ensconced just prior to his coming aboard.

Beau turned his attention upon Cerynise, wondering if she might have been offended by the fact that he had allowed the wench to fondle him. No doubt to an innocent it might have seemed a rousing caress, but at the time, he had reluctantly had his mind on seeing Cerynise again and hadn't been the least bit interested in taking the harlot up on her offer.

Beau found Cerynise watching him with equal alertness. "Philippe has dinner prepared. Are you hungry?"

"Immensely!" She managed a grin despite her misgivings. "Are you?"

"Starved," Beau replied, making an attempt to chuckle. He strode back through the door, rang the bell which Billy had told her about earlier, and then returned to his desk. While the cabin boy and the chef laid out the food on the table, Beau made notations in his ledger and sorted receipts. Philippe and Billy were both quietly restrained, as if they, too, sensed their captain's dark mood, and with no more than a murmur the two made their departure. Cerynise approached the table, and in quick response Beau unfolded his long form from behind his desk, crossed the meager distance between them, and pulled out a chair for her. Graciously she accepted his assistance and folded her hands demurely in her lap to hide their trembling as he took a seat.

In silence he poured her a goblet of wine, and she, in turn, addressed her attention to arranging food on his plate. Though the cuisine was just as delectable as it had been earlier that morning, Cerynise found that she had lost her appetite, for it was impossible for her to ignore the captain's brooding vexation.

There was definitely a strange unreality about sitting at a table with the man. She had imagined this moment for so many years that it might have become a trifle hackneyed after their lengthy separation...*except* that nothing about Beau Birmingham would ever seem trite or insincere to her. If he had been a god, she could not have adored him any more than she did now or had done during all the years she had known him. Even if they went their separate ways and married others, he would always remain her champion on a white charger.

"I'm sure Billy informed you that I wanted you to stay in my cabin," Beau said after an uncomfortable silence. "Were you able to enjoy the afternoon in spite of that?"

"I rested for most of the afternoon," she replied. "I couldn't seem to sleep after Mrs. Winthrop's death...it came so abruptly...and the suddenness of it was...well...rather devastating." Cerynise took a tiny sip of the wine, hoping it would lend her courage, and wondered if she had been as timid and fearful of the younger Beau Birmingham as she was of the man. She lifted her eyes to him. "Did you have a pleasurable day?"

"Actually, I did. I went hunting, which I haven't been able to do much lately. I enjoy the sport while I'm in the Carolinas, but it's not always easy to do in other parts of the world."

"I've missed not being home," she murmured, reminiscing.

"Your uncle has certainly missed not seeing you these last few years," Beau surmised. "I've visited him from time to time when I've been in home port, but most of our discussions have been about you."

Cerynise groaned softly. "I'm sure you couldn't have found that very entertaining."

"Your uncle and I have been laboring under the misconception that you were nothing more than a child. He'll no doubt be amazed when he sees you."

"My uncle was in good health when you last saw him?" she queried hopefully.

"As hardy as he has always been."

She smiled in relief at the news. "Captain Sullivan suggested that Uncle Sterling may have died, and I began to worry that it was true."

Beau thought he needed to caution her about sailing on the *Mirage* and tried to do so without frightening her. "If you can at all manage it, Cerynise, try to stay in your cabin as much as possible during your voyage home. Captain Sullivan doesn't always know what his crew is up to, so it may be best if you just keep out of sight. Moon is to be trusted and will see to your needs."

"You won't change your mind about taking me home?"

Beau sighed, knowing his limitations only too well. "I fear not, Cerynise."

That was all he said, and that was all he needed to say for her to accept his answer as final. Abruptly she changed the subject, for the thought of leaving him left her despondent. "If I use your cabin tonight, where will you sleep?"

"I'll string a hammock in my mate's quarters. Mr. Oaks sleeps so soundly he won't even know I'm there."

"I fear that my presence aboard your ship is putting you to a great deal of bother, Beau."

"You're a friend. What are friends for if they cannot help one another?"

Beau arose soon after the meal was concluded and took his leave, barely managing a smile for her. Cerynise quietly waited while Billy cleared the table, and then upon his departure, she braided her hair, doffed her clothes, and washed her chemise and pantalettes. Sliding naked into a bed was something that she had never done before. It seemed totally wicked, yet she didn't have enough clothes to spare any to sleep in. She was totally surprised to find a rather thrilling experience awaiting her as she slid between the bedclothes. With the elusive scent of Beau drifting through her senses and the sheets caressing the soft peaks of her breasts, she could almost imagine him as her phantom lover. The idea aroused sensations she had never encountered before. They were quite titilating. Indeed, there flourished a strange yearning in her woman's body that led her to stroke her breasts inquisitively while illusions of Beau hovered near.

She imagined her hand caressing him much as the harlot had done and wondered what she would find if she were ever so bold.

Stirring as it was, her fantasy gave her no ease, for it awakened a sharp hunger within her that made her toss and turn in discontent. Whatever she craved was not something she was cognizant of, but she had no doubt that Beau would have the answer. Someday, perhaps, he would instruct her as her husband....

"Foolishness," she hissed in the dark, growing angry with herself. Beau didn't even want to let her sail with him! How much less motivated would he be to take her to wife?

CHAPTER 3

Alistair Wakefield Winthrop woke from a port-induced slumber to the harsh reality of a pounding head, a reeling stomach, and a mouth that tasted like the leavings of a passing horse. He rolled in the bed, came up against the leaden bulk of his mistress and then groaned. The sight of Sybil's bloated face smeared with kohl and lip rouge hardly improved his disposition. He reversed his direction, left the bed and, holding his head as if leery of it toppling off, staggered stiltedly across the room to the garderobe. He just managed to reach the indoor convenience before his stomach rebelled and followed its natural course.

Some moments later, Alistair emerged and

donned his trousers and shirt. He couldn't steady his fingers long enough to button the latter garment and, with a muttered curse, left it hanging open as he stumbled from the bedroom. Pausing on the landing above the stairs, he shielded his eyes from the light streaming in from the back windows and fumbled like a blind man toward the stairs. He gripped the balustrade with whitened knuckles and made his descent one jolting step at a time, arriving on the lower floor after a painstaking interval of time.

The door of the dining room stood open, allowing him to see the housemaid who was setting out dishes under the close supervision of the dreaded Jasper. From beneath drooping lids, Alistair's bloodshot eyes swept the spacious area. Nowhere could he see evidence of tea being brewed.

His hackles rose in indignation. No matter how high in the hierarchy of servants Jasper might have ranked, his living depended no less than the others' on his master's goodwill. The butler had obviously forgotten his tenuous position, but Alistair was determined to bring the man up short with a reminder. He'd be damned before he'd put up with any long-nosed arrogance from an arrogant lackey!

"What's to be said of the way a house is run when the squire has to come in search of his own tea?" Alistair demanded sharply.

The clatter of silverware falling on the table affirmed that the housemaid had been duly startled. She gaped at Alistair, looking suitably alarmed. Jasper scarcely blinked an eye.

Alistair silently fumed. *That ol' sod is a cold one, curse his frigid heart!*

"I regret the inconvenience, sir," Jasper apologized stoically. "If you would like to establish a regular schedule, I can assure you that it will be scrupulously respected forthwith."

"Get that clabber out of here!" Alistair railed, waving a hand in the general direction of the covered dishes now arraying the table. "Just get me a cup of tea, *if* that wouldn't put you to *too* much bother!"

"No bother at all, sir," Jasper replied blandly and, with a flick of his fingers, directed the housemaid to the task of clearing away the dishes. The butler brought the tea himself and placed it at the end of the table where Alistair was now seated with his elbows braced on the polished surface and his head resting in his palms. Though no sound was made, the master started suddenly in surprise, having dozed off.

"Oh, it's you." Alistair sighed in relief. He blinked his eyes, banishing the vision that had haunted him for the briefest moment. Shakily he raised the cup to his mouth, trying not to slosh the contents over the rim. His failure was keenly felt each and every time a scalding droplet plummeted to his lap and rapidly soaked into his trousers. No doubt his thighs would be liberally speckled with blisters by the time he managed to get enough tea into his system for his brain to start functioning.

"Mr. Rudd is here, sir," Jasper announced in a solemn tone. "Shall I show him in?"

"Might as well," Alistair muttered ungraciously. A moment later he frowned sharply as Rudd came stumbling through the dining room door. The man's clothing was wrinkled, his eyes as bleary as his host's. Above all of that, he seemed terribly distressed. *The sot!* Alistair mentally sneered, unaware that his own appearance closely mirrored the discombobulated demeanor of his companion. "I thought you were going home to sleep after you left here last night."

"Did eventually," Howard Rudd mumbled, holding up a hand to shade his eyes from the light streaming in through the windows. He gestured feebly toward the drapes. "Close those damned things!"

Obediently Jasper darkened the room and quietly placed a cup of tea before the barrister as the latter slid into a chair on Alistair's right.

"Send him away," Rudd muttered in low tones, gesturing in the general direction of the butler's back. "Got to talk to you in private."

A needling apprehension prickled Alistair's nape. He snapped his fingers, wincing at the pain evoked by the action, but having gained Jasper's attention, he pointed toward the door.

Rudd listened to the butler's footsteps fading toward another section of the house and finally took a deep breath, as if he were about to plunge into a dismal, dank pool. "Now, I don't think there's anything to be concerned about. Want to make that clear right from the start...."

A sickening dread crept up from the depths of Alistair's dark soul. All along he had feared something would go wrong; now apparently it had. "Spit it out, man!"

"Problem is I can't find Mrs. Winthrop's legal papers, deed to the house, list of investments and bank accounts, things like that. The papers ought to be in the house, but I've looked everywhere that I can think of, and so far nothing has turned up."

"They have to be here!" Alistair insisted. Bracing his hands against the table, he pushed himself to his feet and walked to the windows on limbs that seemed ready to slither out from under him. "She lived well enough on the annual proceeds. Why, there must've been at least thirty thousand pounds a year that came to her from her assets."

Rudd was suitably reverent at the mention of such an impressive sum, an amount exceedingly far beyond his own circumstance. "Always very prudent with her investments, she was, at least while I was still her solicitor. No reason to believe that has changed in the years following my last official visit here."

"Then where in the hell are her records?" Alistair demanded, ready to fly into a rage. How could he have possibly come so far only to be thwarted still? He snarled in frustration and then hotly asserted, "I'm rich, dammit! Richer than some of those titled highbrows! Nobody's going to keep that money from me. Nobody!"

"Easy now," Rudd cautioned. "No sense getting yourself overwrought. Not good for the humors, you know. The records must be somewhere. If we have to, we'll tear this house apart—"

"No!" Alistair broke in sharply, drawing a startled look from Rudd. After a brief pause, he continued in a calmer voice. "We'll search around, all right, but we'll have to be discreet about it. I won't have the servants bruiting this about. It might raise questions."

Rudd's face had taken on a slightly greenish tinge, which darkened perceptibly as he stared at Alistair in growing apprehension. Then his eyes narrowed suspiciously. "What sort of questions?"

"Never mind what kind! Just do as I say! The old biddy held the purse strings while she was alive, making me plead for every pound, but she won't hinder me from her grave. I'll have it all, I will!"

"Might I venture a suggestion?"

"What?"

"Perhaps Miss Kendall might know where the records are kept."

The glower that Alistair gave him sent a chill racing down Rudd's spine. The barrister snatched up a brandy snifter, filled it to the brim and proceeded to drain it in three large gulps.

"Miss Kendall is not here," Alistair reminded him acidly. "If you recall, I sent her away."

Rudd's head bobbed agreeably. "Aye, that's

right. But now I'm thinking she might—"

"*Why didn't you think on it yesterday before I threw her out into the street?*" Alistair roared.

Rudd flinched as each word slammed into him with brutal force. "Didn't occur to me that there'd be a problem. If we could find her, we might..."

Alistair approached close enough to sneer into the lawyer's face. "Do you seriously think I want to alert Cerynise Kendall to the fact that I haven't a ken where Lydia's financial records are? Isn't that situation a tad strange for an heir to be in?"

"Well, yes," Rudd conceded, "but I really don't see what she can make of it all. And even if she did make something of it, what matter? She's hardly in a position to cause any—"

Alistair grew adamant. "*She's out of this! Gone! And she'll stay that way!*" His red-rimmed eyes flashed sullenly. "With any luck, some hardworking cutthroat will rid the world of her ere long, *if* it hasn't happened already."

Rudd reached for the brandy bottle again, but Alistair snatched it away. Then, with a crook of his finger, he motioned for the man to follow him. Rudd did so, albeit with lagging step.

"I'll give the servants the day off in honor of their beloved employer's passing," Alistair confided, wrapping an arm around the solicitor's neck. "While they're gone, we'll search this house room by room. If those papers are here, then we'll damn well find them."

A carriage drew to a halt near the area of the quay where the *Audacious* was tethered to the dock by her bow-fast and stern-fast lines. The stoic-faced Jasper stepped out and, after bidding the driver to unload the trunk from the boot, turned to help Bridget descend to the cobblestone wharf. Together they bundled up an assortment of valises, satchels, a wooden case and an easel before following several merchants across the gangplank.

"Is there a Mistress Kendall aboard?" Jasper asked the first seaman he came to. "We were told by Captain Sullivan that the lady whom we desire to see is here on board the *Audacious*. Have we been misinformed?"

Stephen Oaks was the first mate on the frigate, and hardly anything transpired without his knowledge. "The lady is here, as I've been told by my captain," he replied politely. "Do you have business with her?"

"We've brought a few o' the liedy's belongin's," Bridget explained, dimpling beneath the mate's smile. "She'll be needin' 'em for sure if she's ta set sail from England."

"If you'll give me your names, then I'll inform the captain that you're here."

In a moment Beau appeared and questioned the pair briefly before venturing down to his cabin. He had shared his mate's quarters during the night, but he had found little rest in the hammock while images of Cerynise in all manner of disarray flitted through his mind. He could only wonder if seeing her in

93

actuality would be any worse than confronting her in his imagination.

Beau tapped on the cabin door, heard what sounded like muffled scrambling, and waited in the lengthy silence that followed. The portal was finally snatched open, and he found himself staring into the flushed, utterly beautiful visage of a woman who had been caught unprepared for visitors. He espied the reason, which she was trying desperately to hide behind her back. Undoubtedly she had washed her undergarments, spread them around the cabin to dry and, at his knock, had seized them up again. Now she was making every effort to keep the apparel out of sight while she clutched the lapels of his robe together in some embarrassment. She had good reason to be disconcerted, Beau decided, for the velvet cloth molded her unfettered breasts sublimely.

"There are two servants on deck who've come from the Winthrop house with some of your possessions," he announced, and repeated the names that he had been given. "Shall I have them come down to the cabin?"

"Oh, certainly!" Cerynise replied eagerly, and then reddened profusely as she recalled her state of dishabille. "But give me a moment, will you?"

Beau threw a thumb over his shoulder to indicate the bell behind him. "Ring it when you're ready, and I'll send them down."

"Thank you."

Beau hoped sincerely that her own clothes

would be less disruptive to the coolheaded poise he was striving hard to maintain. "My men will bring down your trunks and things once your company leaves. I'm sure you'll be delighted to have something other than my robe to wear."

"It's a nice robe," Cerynise murmured with a smile, running a hand over the sleeve.

His eyes flicked down her slender form, admiring all that the garment contained. Now that he had seen her in all of her naked glory, he was hard-pressed to see anything but what he wanted to see. "I rather fancy the way it looks on you. It certainly never looked as nice on me."

Cerynise could feel her cheeks warming from the pleasure of his compliment. "You're being most gallant, sir, in view of my poverty."

"If others looked as delectable in their poverty as you do, my girl, I'm sure they wouldn't mind it so much." Taking a blue frock coat from the recessed closet, he gave her a wink reminiscent of those he had once bestowed upon her in years gone by. "I'll send down your guests."

When Bridget came through the cabin door a few moments later and saw Cerynise, she gave a glad cry and rushed forward to give the girl an exuberant hug. "Oh, mum, we were so worried about ye, an' here ye are, looking so grand."

"But why are you both here?" Cerynise asked worriedly. "Mr. Winthrop hasn't dismissed you, has he?"

"Only for the day, miss. We'll have to be back

in the morning," Jasper explained. "Mr. Winthrop said he had some business to take care of and didn't want servants underfoot disturbing him."

Cerynise breathed a sigh of relief. "Oh, thank goodness. I was afraid I had been the cause of you both being let go."

"We brought your easel, miss. Mr. Oaks said that he'd send it down shortly," the butler informed her. A smile sorely tested the stiff muscles of his face as he swept a small wooden coffer from behind his back. "And I believe these are your paints, are they not?"

"Oh, yes!" Cerynise cried, gathering the chest to her with a joyful laugh. "But how in the world did you ever manage to sneak them out of the house?"

"We did it early this mornin', mum, whilst Mr. Winthrop an' Miss Sybil were still asleep," Bridget confessed proudly. "We didn't have any idea, then, that he'd be sendin' us away for the day, but here we are, for yerself ta see, mum. We didn't dare bring everythin' o' yers, ye understand, just a few gowns an' things what wouldn't be readily missed. We moved yer paintin's up ta the closet in the attic. Ye knows the one what's behind all 'em crates. Unless Mr. Winthrop knows o' it, it don't seem likely he'll be a-findin' it any time soon, even if he goes up there. If'n ye can leave the name o' a place where ye'll be after ye gets ta the Carolinas, then we'll try an' send them ta ye."

"I'll ask Captain Birmingham if he can loan me enough to pay for the shipment. I wouldn't want any of you to be put out by the expense."

" 'Twould help, mum," Bridget agreed. "For the most part, we've decided ta seek employment elsewhere. Mrs. Winthrop had friends what can vouch for us, an' all o' us know we'd be better off workin' for someone else."

"But once you leave," Cerynise said worriedly, "won't Sybil realize that some of my clothes have been taken and accuse you or some of the other servants of stealing them?"

Bridget tossed her head in flippant disregard for what the trollop might think. "I doubt Miss Sybil'll even notice they're missin', mum. She certainly can't wear 'em. The ones we brought were at the bottom o' a huge pile she left on the bloomin' floor after riflin' through yer wardrobes and chest o' drawers. Most likely she's already forgot they were even there."

"You've taken an awful chance bringing them to me," Cerynise surmised, but a glowing smile assured them of her gratitude. "I don't know how I can thank you enough."

"Just knowing that they've been given to their rightful owner will be our reward, miss," Jasper assured her. "We wouldn't have felt right without making some attempt to help you." He chuckled, displaying a rarely glimpsed humor. "Why, Mrs. Winthrop would have come back to haunt us if we hadn't tried."

"You're both dear, dear friends," Cerynise averred, taking each by the hand. "I shall miss you terribly."

"You were the apple of Mrs. Winthrop's eye,

the child she never had," Jasper murmured gently. "Bridget and I have come to think of you as her adopted daughter. We'll grieve in your absence."

The parlor maid took a deep breath to halt the sadness welling up within her and, blinking away blurring tears, glanced about the cabin to redirect her thoughts to something less emotional. "Have ye e'er seen anythin' what looked this grand, mum?" she asked in a thick tone and then corrected herself. "I mean, besides Mrs. Winthrop's home, o' course. I've ne'er been on a ship afore an' always imagined they'd smell a bit like fish or somethin'. Little did I think that ye'd be able ta find passage home on such a fine ship when ye hadn't a farthin' ta yer name."

"Captain Birmingham is an old acquaintance," Cerynise stated carefully, preferring not to explain that she wouldn't be returning to the Carolinas on his ship. "Years ago he was one of my father's students. The most promising, I might add, despite his reluctance to settle down to his studies. 'Twas truly my good fortune that he was in port."

"Oh, he's a real looker, al'right, mum," Bridget eagerly expounded. "Then, there was the nicest Mr. Oaks what greeted us..."

The delicate clearing of Jasper's throat was enough to remind the parlor maid that she had forgotten herself. The butler squeezed Cerynise's hand. "We should be going now, miss. I hope you'll take care of yourself and write to let us know how you're getting on."

"I shall," Cerynise pledged, her eyes misting. "Just as soon as I reach Charleston."

"Very good, miss," the man murmured. "We shall both look forward to receiving your communiqué."

"Bridget, would you ask Captain Birmingham to come down to his cabin for a moment," she bade the maid. "I'll see if I can get enough funds for you to ship my paintings without delay."

The maid was suddenly a-smile at the idea of seeing the first mate again. "Right away, mum."

A moment later Beau returned to find Jasper waiting stoically in the corridor leading to his cabin. He had no time to question the man before Jasper swung the door open for him.

"The lady wishes to speak with you, sir," the butler announced.

Cerynise turned as she heard Beau enter and, with a hopeful smile, went to meet him. "Jasper and the other servants have hidden my paintings in Mrs. Winthrop's house and would like to send them to me, but I don't have a single coin to my name. I was wondering if I could beg a loan..."

"What will they need?" he asked, going to his desk and opening a drawer.

"Ten pounds at the most I would imagine. There's quite a number of paintings, and since I've sold others for a goodly sum, some as high as ten thousand pounds, I think I'll be able to sell the rest in the Carolinas and repay you double the amount you loan me."

99

"You've sold them for how much?" Beau questioned incredulously.

Cerynise lifted her shoulders in a hesitant shrug, fearful that he might think her boastful. "Ten thousand pounds."

"And this Alistair Winthrop, whom you told me about, tried to claim them as his?"

She was confused by his rising ire. "Yes."

"Then the man's a first-rate thief," Beau stated sharply. "The paintings are obviously yours and no one else's."

"Mr. Winthrop and his lawyer, Mr. Rudd, refused to consider that possibility since Mrs. Winthrop bought the paints, paid for the art lessons, and arranged for the exhibits."

He snorted, irritated with such asinine logic. "And what would she have had if you hadn't painted them?"

"Nothing much beyond canvas and oil paints," Cerynise answered simply.

"Exactly."

She smiled, her heart warmed by his conclusion. "I tried to explain that to the two, but they were intent upon stripping me of my every possession. Truly, I'd have gladly yielded them generous rents for the past five years I lived in the Winthrop house. Even deducting that from what I had already earned from my paintings, I'd have had a tidy sum left over. Unfortunately Alistair has claimed the funds as his own."

"Perhaps I should find you a lawyer of your own," Beau suggested. "I'm sure you'd have good cause to attach a lien against the inheritance."

100

"I'd rather go home," she murmured quietly. "I've missed it so."

Beau counted out a pile of coins and dropped them in a pouch, which he then pressed into her hand. "For good measure, I think we should give Jasper fifteen, for the shipment and for their trouble. Is that sufficient?"

"Oh, yes, Beau. Thank you!" She had the greatest desire to throw her arms around his neck and kiss him for his generosity, but that wouldn't have been at all proper.

"It's probably better if I don't meet Alistair Winthrop," Beau mused aloud, curbing a grin. "I'd be tempted to blacken the man's eyes."

Upon leaving his quarters and closing the door behind him, he paused to speak in muted tones with Jasper. At the servant's eager nod, he withdrew a purse from the pouch on his belt and, after handing it to the man, shook hands with him. They parted, and as Beau crossed to the companionway, Jasper returned to the cabin.

Cerynise handed the butler the small bag of coins that she had been given. "Whatever you do, be careful," she urged. "I don't want Mr. Winthrop to get wind of what you're doing and have you thrown into prison. If you're caught taking the paintings from his house, he'll have good cause to set the law nipping at your heels."

Jasper's stiff features began to shine with amusement. "He'd have to catch me at it first, miss, but with the late hours he keeps at night and his tardy departures from bed in the morning, I rather suspect that won't happen. Besides, the way Mr. Winthrop and Miss Sybil snore, we could steal the house out from under them, and they wouldn't even know it. I think, miss, you'll be rather amazed at what we'll be able to transport to the Carolinas."

Soon after the two servants' departure, Billy carried down the easel and several smaller satchels. He was closely followed by a brawny sailor who toted her largest trunk on his shoulder. As the huge tar took his leave, the cabin boy paused at the door. "The cap'n told me ta tell ye, miss, that he'll be away for the night, so ye'll be able ta stay in his cabin without bein' disturbed. He also told me ta make sure ye had everythin' ye might want or need."

Cerynise was curious to know what could occupy a captain for a whole evening besides the harlots who roamed the docks. She wasn't at all pleased by the premise that he might be in some other woman's arms while he was away, but she could hardly express her disappointment, no matter how much she felt it. Bravely she offered a smile for Billy's sake. "I suppose I could do with a bit of privacy."

"Then you'll be havin' it right enough, miss," the lad assured her with a ready grin.

Soon after the cabin boy had taken his leave, Cerynise sorted through the clothes in the trunk and the assortment of satchels just to see what Bridget had managed to bring her. She was thrilled to find her best gowns, evening wear, and several day dresses tightly packed in the trunk. The valises were filled with shoes, nightgowns, chemises, silk stockings, and other accouterments that a well-garbed lady had need of. Indeed, what had been brought was much more than Cerynise could have dared hope for considering the difficulty of trying to sneak her possessions past Alistair. Bridget had managed to supply her with at least half her wardrobe, a feat that nearly boggled her mind. She had no doubt that she'd now be able to garb herself in a manner that hopefully would claim the captain's attention and perhaps inspire him to let her sail on his ship.

"It has to be here!" Alistair insisted. He was slouched behind the desk in the library. Rudd, however, had slumped to the floor in roweling defeat several hours earlier.

"Isn't here," the solicitor sighed in a wearied daze. He shook his head in stunned disbelief as he glanced around at the countless stacks of documents strewn around him. In all of it, there hadn't even been the tiniest bit of information that could have helped them. "Not here or anyplace else in the house."

Howard Rudd was pale, bleary-eyed, and thoroughly exhausted. He was still in the grip of the same fierce anxiety that had goaded Alistair, but his tension had become more evident. He had developed a repetitive twitch on one side of his face, and his lips were so thinly drawn they looked bloodless.

"It has to be here," Alistair repeated almost numbly. "There has to be some record of where the old bitch stashed her money."

Rudd scrubbed a hand over his face and expelled another laborious breath. "There isn't. Outsmarted you, she did." He raised an arm that felt weighted by heavy iron bands and swept it lamely about the room. "You've got to face it! There's nothing here. All of this paper, all of these correspondences and household accounts go back for years, and there's not a single hint of where she might have put her money. She has hidden it too well." He hauled himself to his knees and, from there, managed to stand upright, albeit with a great deal of difficulty. "The only thing I have any certainty about right now is the fact that there's not one farthing left in any of the accounts or investments to which I was privy years ago. Wiped clean, every one of them."

"Damn the shrew!" Alistair railed. "She can't get away with this! She just can't!"

"She has," Rudd replied bluntly, exhaustion robbing him of any semblance of prudent discretion. "Not a bloody thing you can do about it either. At the very least we'd need several more months to search out all of the places where she might have kept the funds. Why, we'd be lucky to find even half of them."

"I can't wait that long!" Alistair snarled. "The creditors are at my throat now. I'd be in debtor's prison now if not for the fact that I'm the old hag's heir."

"We could tell them that her affairs were left

104

in some disorder," Rudd suggested wearily. "Won't that buy you some time?"

"Aye! Time for all and sundry creditors to start wondering if something has gone awry!" He glared at Rudd. "You knew all of this needed to be handled quietly *and* quickly. Why didn't you tell me that you didn't know where her money was to be found?"

Rudd's face darkened at the condemning tone in the other's voice. "Don't try blaming me for this!" He reached for the brandy decanter, found it empty, and slammed it down again on the sideboard. "I played straight and told you that I hadn't handled Lydia's affairs for some years now. How could I have possibly known what she did in that time?" He bent a dark scowl upon Alistair. "And we both know what that means. She could have done *any-thing* with her blooming fortune!"

Silence reigned as the men glowered at each other.

Rudd threw up a hand in defeat. "Perhaps we should stop for tonight, begin again with a clear head in the morning."

"When was the last time you had a clear head?" Alistair derided, but he, too, was ready to call it a day. He fell back in his chair, surveying the mess that their search had produced. It was the same almost throughout the whole house. The whole day long they had rummaged through everything that they could lay hand to and had found nothing. Wardrobes had been turned out, drawers emptied, even mattresses upended. The servants would be

105

returning on the morrow, and after one look at the disaster that had been heaped upon the house, they'd likely guess that something was amiss.

Alistair winced as a sudden, terrifying vision of himself locked away in prison flashed before his mind's eye. Filthy, hungry, exhausted, totally at the mercy of guards who had none. It was a scene that had haunted him much too often of late and, with it, had always come a sharp feeling of queasiness.

He forced himself to think of other matters and realized that he hadn't eaten for the better part of a day. He scowled, fixing his gaze upon Rudd. "Go find Sybil and tell her to cook us something to eat." As the attorney passed through the door, he called after him, "And it had better be edible or she'll feel the back of my hand. That bitch is as worthless as the rest of them."

"I'll see what I can do to help her," Rudd mumbled, preferring that option to trying to down anything the wench could come up with. He had tasted her cooking before and had regretted it for days.

Rudd had been gone for several moments when a distant rap of the front door knocker reached Alistair in the library. Immobilized by fretful worry, he made no attempt to answer the summons until it sounded again. Only then did he realize that with the servants gone and Rudd and Sybil in the kitchen, he would have to go to the door himself. Cursing sourly beneath his breath, he rose on stiffened limbs and picked his way through the stacks of papers littering the library. As he entered the entry hall, the mantel clock chimed the ninth hour in the parlor.

Damnable late hour for someone to be calling. Unless, he thought with a small surge of hope, *Cerynise has decided to come crawling back. If only she has!* He certainly wouldn't let the comely little bitch out of his grip again, at least not until he had wrung every bit of information that she possessed from her.

His heart plunged into despair when he saw a man of middling years with gray hair, a neatly trimmed mustache, and wire-rimmed spectacles standing before the threshold. The visitor was garbed in a neat, sedate style that, if anything, marked him as a member of the professional class. Having expected to be admitted by a servant, the visitor looked back at the rumpled, bewhiskered Alistair with a fair amount of surprise.

"Your pardon for the late hour, sir, but might I ask if Miss Kendall is in?"

"Miss Kendall?" Alistair was instantly suspicious. The fellow was hardly a suitor, and as far as Alistair knew, all of her kin were far across the ocean. Curiosity got the better of him, and with a gracious smile, Alistair stepped aside to allow the man to enter.

"You're here to see Cerynise, Mr....?"

"Forgive me, sir. My name is Thomas Ely. I was Mrs. Winthrop's solicitor. My deepest condolences on her passing." He frowned slightly as if trying to place Alistair. "Are you a relative, sir?"

"A relative..." Even as Alistair's tongue stumbled on the word, his mind raced on in a frenzy. Not for an instant did he doubt Mr. Ely's claim. Nor was he surprised by the barrister's presence. Throughout the whole miserable day, the foreboding suspicion that something had gone amiss had steadily grown stronger. Rudd had touched on it when he had said that Lydia could have done *anything*. They had both known all along that there might be a new will. Ely's presence all but confirmed that theory.

"I'm Mrs. Winthrop's great-nephew," Alistair informed the man as he steered him into the parlor, the only room in the house that was still intact. Solicitously he conveyed his appreciation. " 'Tis good of you to come so soon."

"Oh, but I haven't," Ely replied, looking confused and a bit wary at the same time. "That is, I didn't learn of Mrs. Winthrop's death until I read of it in the notices today. Frankly, I was surprised that I wasn't informed immediately."

"Dear Cerynise didn't notify you?" Alistair asked in carefully contrived surprise. His mind had begun to work with icy clarity, and he felt amazingly calm, not at all nervous or anxious as he had been for some days now. He had been waiting for the ax to fall. Now that it had, he was keenly attentive to the possibilities opening up to him.

"No, I'm afraid she didn't," Ely confirmed. At Alistair's invitation, he took a seat on one of the settees. "I must say, I was quite shocked to hear of Mrs. Winthrop's demise. I saw her scarcely a week ago and she seemed in excellent health for a woman of her years."

"Her passing was very sudden," Alistair agreed, managing to convey some sadness. "A terrible loss for us all."

Ely's expression was noncommittal. "If I might speak with Miss Kendall..."

"Yes, of course...certainly. If you'll excuse me a moment, I'll see where she may be. We're positively at a loss without the servants. They've been given the day off to mourn. So it may take me a moment."

"I'll gladly wait," Mr. Ely assured him.

Leaving the parlor and crossing the entrance hall, Alistair entered the dining room and then bolted through the pantry toward the kitchen. He encountered Rudd coming out the door.

"Sybil doesn't know how to cook," Rudd complained. "And I'm hardly able to do much better myself. She suggested that we should go out to an inn for supper."

Alistair seized the man's lapels and snatched him forward until Rudd's eyes crossed in an attempt to meet the piercing gaze that bore into him. "Never mind about that now. A Mr. Thomas Ely has come to call. Is that name familiar to you?"

Rudd blanched. "He's a barrister in the City, well-respected chap, from what I understand."

"He was also Lydia's *solicitor,* or so he informs me. Now he wishes to speak with

Miss Kendall. Do you know what that means?"

A whimpering sound emerged from the depths of Rudd's throat. "We're undone. What are we to do?"

His trepidation amused Alistair. It was so gratifying to be in control when others were falling apart. It was only further proof (as if he needed any) of his own superiority. "Be quiet, you imbecile! We're not undone. Do you understand? This is only a minor problem, one I can handle alone. Just make sure that Sybil stays in the kitchens or we *will* be undone."

Rudd responded with a convulsive nod and turned about as if he walked on stilts. Alistair paused to smooth his hair back and straighten his shoulders. Pinning a puzzled smile on his face, he crossed the hall and entered the parlor.

"My apologies, Mr. Ely. Apparently I've been misinformed. Miss Kendall has gone out to visit friends this evening."

The solicitor looked appropriately surprised. "Gone out? While she's in mourning?"

Alistair sighed, as if understandably distressed. "Miss Kendall is very young, Mr. Ely, and I'm afraid Aunt Lydia was inclined to indulge the girl overmuch. I'm sure Miss Kendall means no disrespect."

"All the same, I really don't see how she could under the circumstances." Abruptly recalling himself, Ely cleared his throat and began to rise. "In that case, I shall return in the morning. May I assume that Miss Kendall will be available to receive me by then?"

"I would expect so. However, if you'd be kind enough to tell me the nature of your business with her, I shall inform her of your expected return upon her arrival home."

"My business with Miss Kendall is private, sir. Again let me apologize for disturbing you so late. I bid you good evening."

"In that case there's no need for you to return on the morrow."

Ely sank back to the settee in astonishment. "I assure you, sir, there is every reason..."

"Which you say you cannot reveal to me, but when Miss Kendall is underage and residing under my roof, I'm naturally responsible for any guests she might receive and the reasons for doing so."

"Your roof?" Before he could consider the knowledge he revealed, Mr. Ely pointed out the error in the other man's thinking. "You're mistaken, sir. This is now Miss Kendall's residence"

Alistair went deathly still except for his racing thoughts. Keeping his voice low and calm, he probed, "Ah, then should I take it that Aunt Lydia did as I suggested?"

"As you suggested, sir?"

"Well, yes, of course." Alistair feigned a surprise no actor could have managed. " 'Twas I who advised Aunt Lydia to leave her property to Miss Kendall. After all, the girl is alone in the world, having lost both her parents at a tragically young age. Aunt Lydia was her guardian for at least five years and had grown very attached to her."

111

"I was certainly aware of the depth of devotion Mrs. Winthrop felt for her ward, but I had no idea you—" Ely broke off, not at all certain about the situation. He looked at Alistair narrowly. "Frankly, sir, such generosity is unheard of nowadays."

"Ah, but you see I've always subscribed to the notion that money is the root of all evil. Don't you agree?"

"Or at least the love of it, I suppose," Ely mused aloud. "Certainly in my time I've seen a great many evils done with greed as the motive."

"Exactly so, sir. However, for the girl's sake, I do hope dear Aunt Lydia's affairs were left in proper order. That was the case, wasn't it? Aunt Lydia was such a stickler for details and clarity."

"Oh, most definitely. Everything is in excellent order. As a matter of fact, I have here"—the solicitor withdrew a folded paper from his pocket—"a detailed and comprehensive list of Mrs. Winthrop's holdings. I'll begin notifying the banks and investment firms of the change of ownership on the morrow. As for the will itself..." He glanced over the document perfunctorily. "It couldn't be simpler. Aside from a few bequests to long-term servants, Miss Kendall inherits everything."

"Everything?" Alistair repeated softly, having no strength in his voice.

Ely nodded. "Exactly. As I said, it couldn't be simpler."

"How very wise of dear Aunt Lydia to keep things so straightforward," Alistair remarked tightly. "Why, I've often heard of wills that required the attention of numerous solicitors and documents passed from hand to hand among the partners of an entire firm with each making his own refinements."

The other man smiled ruefully. He, too, could see the absurdity of such tangled situations even though he had to acknowledge they did occur. "I can assure you, sir, nothing of the sort will happen in this case. On the contrary, Mrs. Winthrop spoke only with me about this matter. I handled everything from start to finish."

"I'm sure she greatly appreciated your service," Alistair murmured as his hand closed on the bronze statue of a dancer that graced one of the small tables near the settee. It looked like the sort of thing that was worth a lot of money, but at the moment it held a different value for him. "Confidentiality is such an important part of the relationship between solicitor and client."

" 'Tis indeed. Why, I've ofttimes had to explain to my dear wife that I cannot possibly discuss—"

Alistair pivoted with the dancer gripped in his hand. Ely had only a scant second to see the blow coming. Even so, his reflexes were good for a man of his years. He threw up an arm in a desperate attempt to block the blow, but he failed. The heavy bronze smashed into his forehead with a sickening thud. Behind the wire-rimmed spectacles, his eyes rolled back in his head as he slowly toppled aside where he lay unmoving.

Alistair's breathing was more rapid than usual, but not excessively so as he observed the trickle of blood that ran across Ely's brow. When it threatened to stain the settee, he yanked a silk afghan from a nearby chair and wrapped it about the lawyer's head. Then he dragged the man from the couch, tugged him across the rug to the bare floor, and continued through the entrance hall toward the back stairs.

Rudd stuck his head out of the kitchen door and glanced around, having heard a sound that had struck him as odd. He gasped sharply in shock as he espied Alistair towing the body, and immediately a sickening dread filled him. If anyone could rail in a whisper, then he did exactly that as he demanded, "What have you done?"

Alistair was tempted to chuckle as he noted the lawyer's ashen face and the horrified expression that had frozen his features. "Go to the parlor," he instructed without pausing in his labors. "There are papers on the floor. Pick them up and bring them along."

Rudd stammered, "Wh-what are you going to do?"

"What in hell do you think I'm going to do? Leave the corpse in the parlor until the servants return? Or allow Sybil to see it and leave here screaming? The hell I will!" Alistair declared. *Really, was it too much to ask that he not be saddled with a dunderhead at such a time?* "We've got to get rid of him, of course. Dear Auntie wrote a new will leaving everything to

114

Cerynise. Mr. Ely, here, was thoughtful enough to bring it along with him, as well as a current list of all of Lydia's holdings."

Dazed, Rudd shook his head lamely. "That's terrible...wonderful...It will help us track down all the money, but it isn't yours. It's—"

"Mine!" Alistair claimed emphatically. He was half crouched over Ely as he pulled him along, but he paused and raised his head to look at Rudd with a wickedly feral smile. " 'Tis all mine. The little bitch will never see one farthing of it. Now be a sensible fellow and do as I say."

Without bothering to look up again to see if Rudd obeyed, Alistair resumed his task, dragging Mr. Ely down the passage leading to the small, walled garden behind the house. From there, a door draped in ivy led out onto a small lane that ran alongside the house. If memory served him well enough, there was usually a handcart in a small shed at the end of the garden.

Rudd joined him at the storehouse a few moments later, looking decidedly grayer in the moonlight. Alistair snatched the papers that he clutched from him and tucked the bundle within his own waist shirt.

"Help me lift him," Alistair urged, gesturing to the body.

Rudd grimaced at the notion. "Are you sure he's dead?"

"Of course, I'm sure," Alistair snapped. "What do you think I am? A dimwit?"

Gingerly Rudd took hold of the man's legs

and together they swung the body into the cart.

"Step out beyond the gate and take a look down the lane to see if anybody is out there," Alistair directed. "We can't take any chances with a full moon."

Once again Rudd obeyed and returned with assurances that he hadn't caught a glimpse of anyone either near or far. "Where are we taking him?"

"The river," Alistair answered bluntly. "Now go get three of those old cloaks hanging near the servants' entrance."

Rudd felt on the verge of throwing up what little he had on his stomach. He didn't like what he was having to do, but neither could he find it in himself to depart the premises. Mrs. Winthrop had been a *very* wealthy woman, and if he could, he wanted to share some portion of the sizable inheritance that would presumably be forthcoming. He just hoped they'd live that long.

Upon the lawyer's return, Alistair noticed that the man looked unusually pale and haggard even in the moonlight. "What's the matter with you?" he hissed caustically. "A body might guess from the way you're carrying on that you'd just seen me kill your own sweet mother."

Dutifully slipping into one of the black shrouds, Rudd raised dull, worried eyes to his partner-in-crime and mumbled gloomily, "I've never done anything like this before...."

Alistair sneered in contempt as he draped a cloak over the body and proceeded to wrap another around himself. "Perhaps not, but you think nothing of stealing the last crumb out of a widow's mouth and leaving her to die in poverty."

"I never knowingly killed anyone!" Rudd argued in defense of himself as they maneuvered the handcart into the lane.

"Well, you never knowingly killed this one either," Alistair mocked, turning his wide mouth into a derisive smirk. "Can't you realize what a stroke of luck this is?"

"Wouldn't necessarily call killing a man *luck*."

"With naught but one blow and no mess left behind? If that isn't luck, my friend, what is it?"

"Cold-blooded murder, I'd say."

"Bah! You're squeamish!" Alistair accused, and tossed his head. "You'll reap almost as much from this as I will, and then you can drown your conscience in as much brandy as you please."

"Wish I had a drink now."

"Later! We've got work to do now!"

Rudd couldn't answer. He was gasping for breath as he pushed the handcart toward the river. Following the narrow lanes that ran behind the row of houses, they reached the Thames without setting foot on a major street. They saw no one and, as far as could be reckoned, were seen by no one. It was a convenient hour for dumping a corpse. Proper ladies and gentlemen would be retiring for the night. Their servants would be finishing up with their chores and doing the same.

The mists rising off the river and the darkness enveloping the city combined to obscure the pair and their burden from even a casual glance cast from a back window. When they finally left the shelter of the lanes and ventured across the Strand, their good fortune held firm. Only a few carriages were passing, the windows shuttered against the night chill, the drivers slouched in their redingotes.

"Quickly now," Alistair implored as they reached the water steps near the bridge. "Let's dump him and get out of here."

Rudd took hold of the front of the cart while Alistair held up the back. With nary a thump, they lifted it down the steps. At the bottom, Alistair paused to indulge himself in a moment of victory. Then, with a little smile of satisfaction, he tilted the cart and dumped the body into the black water. The faint splash could hardly be heard above the gentle lapping of the river against the bridge pilings. As they watched, all that remained of Thomas Ely floated away on the fast-moving current.

Half an hour later, the handcart had been returned to its accustomed place, and Rudd was seated in the library in front of a fire. Since his return, the level of brandy in the decanter sitting near his elbow had rapidly diminished. Sybil had been put to work straightening up the clutter that had been left after their frenzied search, and though she had balked, all that had been required to silence her grumbling was a threatening glower from Alistair.

Alistair had joined Rudd in the library, but

he hadn't needed any strong fortification of spirits. It was enough for him to pore over the papers that Thomas Ely had thoughtfully brought to the house. A warm glow of satisfaction filled him. Everything he had ever wanted was within his grasp. He could now live as he had always wanted to. He would have his heart's desire. Nothing and no one would ever stand in his way again. His ambitions and smile were totally unrestrained. Indeed, he felt better than he had in years. He was powerful, secure, happy! People spoke so harshly about the foul deed of murder, but they were ignorant of the marvelous sense of serenity it could impart. He was just turning that thought over in his mind and relishing it when his eye drifted to the bottom of the final page of Lydia's will, the one which he was about to consign to the cheerful flames. There, in neat copperplate, three words leapt out at him:

Copy to File.

His throat clenched, smothering a scream of pure rage. His mouth opened and closed but no sound emerged. Rudd remained oblivious as he gulped his brandy, but he started abruptly when Alistair's fist began hammering the desktop.

Rudd looked around with brows elevated to a lofty level. "Have you taken leave of your senses?"

Heat suffused Alistair's face as he crumpled the will in one hand. His eyes were hard chips of obsidian lit by raging fury. "There's a copy of the will!"

"Of course, there's a copy. You really didn't think Mr. Ely brought the only one in existence, did you?"

"Forgive me," Alistair rejoined scathingly. "Not being one of your blood-sucking peers, I was unfamiliar with common legal practices."

"I could have told you there was a copy, perhaps even more than one." Rudd's eyes narrowed owlishly. "What are you going to do about it?"

What indeed? Alistair sat back in the chair, finally releasing his tenacious grip on the bundle of papers. He forced himself to breathe deeply and steadily. The pleasant satisfaction he had felt moments ago had faded. He made no attempt to recapture it. But the calm he had felt after killing Ely reasserted itself. He allowed it to wash over him like a soothing tide.

"We'll have to find Cerynise now."

Rudd sighed heavily. "Had a feeling you'd say that."

"Since you've anticipated my needs, suppose you tell me how to go about fulfilling them."

"She said she was going to find passage to the Carolinas," Rudd mused aloud. "We can probably find her near the wharf looking for a ship to take her home."

Alistair's jaw slowly lowered as he stared across the room at the barrister. At times it amazed him just how astute Rudd really was.

The heavier man hoisted himself out of the settee. "Don't know how she'll pay for the fare, though, seeing as how you left her with only the clothes on her back."

"She's a woman. She'll find a way," Alistair sneered. "She was too hoity-toity to consider servicing my needs, but she'll damn well belly up to a sot what'll give her passage home."

"Don't intend to start looking for her tonight, do you?" Rudd asked, weaving his way toward the desk.

Alistair raised his eyes in disgust to his companion. "You're drunk again!"

Rudd smiled blandly. "Drowning my conscience, as you prescribed, Dr. Winthrop."

"We'll start our search in the morning," Alistair muttered, having no other choice. It was doubtful that any of the seafaring captains would enjoy being disturbed from their duties or pleasures at this time of night. "See if there are any ships going to...where was it?"

"Charleston...in the Carolinas," Rudd reminded him.

"Oh, yes...Charleston...the Carolinas. If anyone has seen her on the docks, 'tis likely they won't forget a tempting little morsel like Miss Kendall."

"Perhaps she's been abducted and is earning her keep in the brothels," Rudd suggested. "I could start my search there. That should occupy me for a time."

Alistair laughed mirthlessly. "But I doubt the harlots would be entertained. No, we'll begin our search on the dock in the morning."

If the solicitor was inclined to argue, Alis-

121

tair's malevolent grin quickly dissuaded him. This was, after all, the man whom Rudd had watched turning out the body of his victim into the Thames without so much as a blink. Rudd wasn't about to cross him now or even in the future. He had a nightmarish aversion to his carcass being pulled apart by greedy little fish.

CHAPTER 4

Billy Todd frowned as he glanced down at the breakfast tray that he had brought to the captain's cabin an hour earlier and had just now returned to fetch. "Aren't ye feelin' well, miss?"

"Oh, yes, very fine," Cerynise readily assured him, unwilling to confess her inability to sleep during the night and elicit questions that she'd prefer not to answer. "I feel better than I have in some days now."

"Then might ye be likin' some other kind o' vittles?"

Cerynise smiled and shook her head. Billy was being very thoughtful and going out of his way to see to her comfort, no doubt on the captain's orders. "I'm just not hungry this morning, that's all."

"Mr. Monét does it up fine, as ye can see, miss, but if there be anything else ye'd rather have, I'd only be too glad ta fetch it for ye."

Cerynise was put to task to imagine what else could have tempted her pallet more than the meal he had brought, for it had looked even more delectable than her first sampling of Philippe's extraordinary cuisine. But the reason for Beau's departure had remained obscure to her during a restless night of tossing and turning, and she hadn't felt at all like eating when her every thought was fraught with worry that her presence aboard ship had somehow motivated him to seek lodging elsewhere. She certainly hadn't wanted to impose upon his gentlemanly forbearance or be an encumbrance of any kind. Then, too, the memory of the harlot fondling him had set her imagination sharply awry and the burgeoning suspicion that the two had gone off together seriously thwarted her serenity. What that doleful conjecture had evoked within her could have been likened to a prisoner being hauled by weighty chains down steep dungeon steps. No matter how much she had struggled to overcome an encroaching dejection, she had felt her spirits descending precipitously into a gloomy pit.

"Fruit and tea will be enough this morning, Billy," she insisted. "Really."

The cabin boy gave her a shy grin. "The rest makes ye feel like a Christmas goose, eh, miss?"

Cerynise was surprised by his conclusion and lamely confessed, "I hate eating alone, Billy, but most of all, I fear I've displaced the captain from his quarters."

The boy brightened at once. "Then ye'll be happy ta know the cap'n is back, miss. Arrived a good hour ago, he did."

She might have found his news infinitely more comforting had Beau made some effort to come to his cabin, bid her morning tidings or even ask how she had fared throughout the night, but he hadn't. Such simple etiquette might have done much to convey some small concern for her well-being, and she could only assume that he had no interest in carrying on their friendship and would likely be relieved when she was gone.

Cerynise couldn't bear the thought of being slighted by Beau and grew increasingly anxious to be on her way before she actually became cognizant of his disregard. "Then I shall make haste to pack up my possessions and ready myself for the move to Captain Sullivan's ship. I'm sure Captain Birmingham would enjoy having some privacy after being away all night."

Billy wisely assumed an amenable mask. The captain was *not* in the best of moods, and the lad could only guess that whatever the man had gone searching for, he hadn't found it to his liking. "No need ta hurry yerself, miss. The last time I saw the cap'n, he was talkin' with the mate 'bout the crated furniture what's being brought aboard."

"Furniture?"

"Aye, miss. The cap'n will be shippin' a load o' it back wit' us. All 'em wealthy folk livin' in Charl'ton like the idea o' gettin' furniture from the old country. Usually they're the first ta come aboard after the *Audacious* arrives in port."

124

"Captain Birmingham seems to be a very enterprising man," Cerynise mused aloud. She could readily understand how he might be so occupied with business that he had little time to spare for cultivating friendships or affections.

Billy wasn't quite sure what the word *enterprising* meant and could only assume that it had something to do with being resourceful. If so, then *enterprising* described his captain exactly. "I best be on me way, miss. The cap'n is wantin' his breakfast in Mr. Oaks's quarters, an' I'll be hearin' 'bout it from him if'n I don't have it there in short order."

"Mr. Oaks's quarters?" Cerynise's brows gathered. If Beau had returned an hour ago, then he could just as well have joined her for breakfast instead of eating a solitary meal in the mate's cabin. It was becoming increasingly evident that he was making every attempt to keep his distance from her.

"Aye, miss. The cap'n didn't want ta disturb ye." After a moment of uncomfortable silence, the youth added his own conjecture, "I guess 'cause o' ye an' him not bein' married an' all."

"Oh." What more could she say? The youth's statement only solidified her belief that the captain was trying to avoid her.

An hour later, Cerynise felt quite civilized garbed in a pale peach gown. Tiny tucks were sewn in multiple *V*'s down the front of her short-waisted bodice, and a stiffly pleated, silkier fabric served as a ruff of sorts. Satiny thread

125

of the same hue finished the edge of the fabric, causing the pleats to flare charmingly outward from beneath her jaw like the petals of a flower. The sleeves were long and generously puffed at the tops, but closely fitted otherwise, ending at the wrists with a scalloped treatment of flaring pleats. A trio of pleated flounces, as long as her forearm, cascaded in tiers down the skirt.

Cerynise had brushed her long hair until it gleamed, tied it securely near her crown, and swept the entire length several times around the top of her head, creating a simple but charming coiffure. She touched a bit of jasmine-scented toilet water behind each ear and donned a pair of slippers over pale-hued stockings. Then she sat down to await Beau Birmingham's return to his cabin or perhaps an order instructing her to prepare herself for the trip to the *Mirage.*

Cerynise sighed. She wasn't necessarily thrilled with the idea of sailing home aboard Captain Sullivan's ship, but Beau had proven adamant about his inability to take her with him. She wouldn't plead with the man. Considering his recent efforts to keep his distance, to do so would only bring her shame.

A knock on the cabin door came sooner than she had anticipated. Nervously smoothing her hair and gown, she crossed the room, hoping that Beau had come at last, but a man, perhaps a score and five, with fair hair and a narrow, fine-boned face stood before the threshold. When his gray eyes fell on her, he stared at her as if all reason had fled. Then, with a start, he recalled his manners and snatched off the cap that he wore, blushing as he did so. "Your pardon, miss, but the captain asked me to escort you up on deck."

Cerynise had no doubt that the man was a member of the crew, but she was at a loss for a name, for she had never seen him before. "And you are?"

The color in the man's cheeks deepened to a ruddy hue as he realized his blunder. "Your pardon again, miss. I'm the mate, Stephen Oaks."

"And did the captain say why he wanted me to come up on deck?" she inquired. "Will he be taking me to the *Mirage* now?"

The mate was a bit stymied by her question. "He didn't say, miss, only that you're to come on deck."

A frown flitted across Cerynise's features. Having sent his lackey to fetch her, Beau Birmingham was undoubtedly hoping to get rid of her posthaste and without any effort on his part. No preamble, no discussion. She would be off of his ship before she could blink. Truly, if the man had *ever* learned any manners, he certainly wasn't trotting them out on her behalf.

"The captain is rather rushed right now, miss, what with the loading and all," Oaks explained. "But he thought of you just the same and wondered if you might be liking a bit of fresh air and sunshine."

Cerynise didn't appreciate being kept in

the dark about her departure and tried once again. "Do you happen to know *when* the captain is planning on taking me to the *Mirage*? Or has he directed someone else to escort me?"

Stephen Oaks was no less perplexed. "As far as I know, miss, the captain didn't mention anything about you leaving. I'm sure he would have said something to me if he had planned on being away again for any length of time...seeing as how we're trying to finish up with the loading so we can set sail in the next day or two. Why don't you come on deck and talk to him yourself, miss? He can tell you better than I what he has in mind."

Cerynise realized she was being beguiled into obeying, but she had no wish to decline the summons. Having been secluded in the cabin for more hours than she cared to count, she was more than willing to venture out. She paused to wrap a handsome cashmere shawl of peach and olive-green paisley about her shoulders and then followed as the mate led the way along the corridor and up the companionway.

A soft breeze wafted across the deck of the ship, blending the salty tang of the sea with the earthy scents of the city and the cobblestone quay against which the ship nestled. No clouds hindered the morning light, and the sun's rays were bright and clean, bouncing off the water in radiating shards as if they were being poured through a crystal. Small prismatic spots of light dappled the deck, creating a shimmering display that nigh bedazzled Cerynise. For a moment she stood transfixed, soaking in the scene with an artist's delight, wishing she could unpack her paints and put every minute detail on canvas before this mystical ambience was forever lost.

"Have you ever seen anything so beautiful?" she breathed in awe.

The mate cocked a brow wonderingly as he glanced around, for he had no idea what the lady was talking about. He drew his own conclusions. "Aye, miss, the *Audacious* is a real beauty, that she is."

Cerynise smiled at his limited vision and made an effort to reach out with her own. The ship was certainly one a sailor could be proud of. Even to a novice it was readily apparent that it would remain so for some time, for it was being maintained in good order.

At present, men swarmed the deck and the adjacent pier as they labored to transfer the cargo onto the ship. A large wooden crate was hoisted aloft and, before long, laboriously lowered through the open hatch to the hold below. Barely had it settled into place and the ropes been wrenched free before another was being securely lashed and sent on its way from the quay.

"Is that the crated furniture Billy spoke of?" Cerynise asked the mate, who was also observing the proceedings.

"Aye, miss," Mr. Oaks replied. "Breakfronts, armoires, beds and the like are what we'll be hauling back to Charleston this time.

I'm sure we could finance a whole voyage with just the furniture we bring back. The captain likes to glean the very best from every port we enter."

"Billy said your docking is well-anticipated," she murmured distractedly as she shaded her eyes and scanned the deck for Beau, much as she had done as a girl.

"Aye, miss. Captain Birmingham has gained quite a reputation for his excellent taste in merchandise. The Charleston merchants would love to get their hands on the treasures he brings back so they could make a nice profit reselling them, but the bulk of the furniture is usually sold to private collectors who rush to meet our ship as soon as we dock. They wrangle over the pieces and try to outdo each other by offering the best price, leaving the captain nothing to do but accept the most generous proposal."

"If the furniture he brings back is as fine as what he has in his cabin, I can understand why there is such a demand for it."

"Aye," Stephen Oaks agreed and then tipped his hat to her again. "Now, miss, if you'll pardon me, I need to get back to work."

"Of course."

Cerynise's sweeping gaze ended on the forecastle, for it was there she found Beau. He was garbed casually in a white, full-sleeved shirt and long, slender trousers that accentuated the muscular trimness of his hips. The shirt lay open to the middle of his muscular chest, revealing sun-bronzed skin and a light furring of black. No doubt he had brushed his thick mane back from his face during an earlier morning grooming, but curling wisps now tumbled carelessly onto his brow. He was wont to comb his fingers absently through those shining, coal-black locks as he argued with another man who was older, shorter, and nattily garbed. Cerynise guessed the stranger to be a merchant, but whatever his profession, it was apparent from the quality of his clothes that he was immensely successful at what he did. It was equally evident that Beau could stand on his own in his dealings with the man. Throughout their conversation Beau remained unyielding, firmly holding his position by shaking his head until his companion finally threw up his hands in exasperation. Then Beau smiled as he handed the man a receipt to sign, counted out a sizable sum from a purse he wore on his belt, and gave it over into the waiting hand of the other. A handshake ended the agreement, and the stranger beamed as he clamped his hat upon his head and took his leave, obviously satisfied that whatever bargain they had struck had been fair for them both.

His business concluded, Beau glanced toward the companionway, wondering what was keeping Mr. Oaks. It wasn't that he needed the man for anything at that particular moment; he only wanted to see if he had brought Cerynise up from his cabin yet. He finally espied the mate approaching the forecastle through a maze of laboring men, but it was the bit of color behind Mr. Oaks that soon drew Beau's eye, assuring him that his young guest was now gracing the deck of his ship with her uncommon beauty. That small wedge of pleated flounce, barely visible behind his second-in-command, held his gaze ensnared, but it was hardly enough.

Purposefully Beau strolled to a spot near the upper rail where he could view Cerynise without hindrance. It was a sight that nearly caused his heart to lurch in admiration. In some amazement he realized that he was no less affected by the way she looked in her ladylike finery than he had been when she had worn Billy's ducks. Since she had come aboard the *Audacious*, he had been unable to thrust her from his mind. Indeed, his difficulty in finding a wench equally as winsome had caused him to regret ever seeing her again, for he had returned to his ship no better off than when he had left. And now, what nearly tore him apart inside was the fact that she looked simply delicious. For someone who had always been like an older brother to the girl, he was being brought up short by his growing infatuation with her.

"I brought Miss Kendall on deck, Captain," Oaks informed him, as if there had been any need.

"I noticed." Beau cast a quick glance around to gauge the reaction of his crew. Basically most of the sailors had one eye on the girl and the other on what they were doing. "And so have the men, 'twould seem."

Stephen Oaks cleared his throat, repressing

the urge to look back at her himself. "Miss Kendall was wondering if you'll be taking her to the *Mirage* any time soon, sir. If you ask me, it seems a bloody shame to let her sail on that old washtub when we could just as well empty out a cabin and take her home in fine style. Besides, I've seen that scurvy lot of Sullivan's in the alehouses, and I'm of a mind to think that they can't be trusted with a lady, much less one as comely as Miss Kendall."

Beau settled a chilly stare upon his second-in-command. It certainly didn't help that he, too, was cognizant of the flaws associated with that particular ship, its skipper and crew, but he was crushingly aware of his own limitations. Having two genteel sisters and a mother who was the very epitome of a lady, he knew only too well the difference between gently bred women and the trollops from whom he sought easement for his manly needs and disposition. Having failed during the previous night to find comfort in the arms of the latter, he knew he'd have to face three months or more of acute torture if he allowed the most lovely, gracious and utterly tempting Cerynise Kendall to accompany them on their voyage home.

"Are you suggesting, Mr. Oaks, that I allow her to disrupt my whole crew for the duration of the voyage home? 'Twould be lucky if any of us reached safe port the way we're wont to ogle her. Myself included."

The mate looked back at his captain in sharp suspicion. "I take it you didn't find what you went searching for last night."

133

"Hell!" Beau muttered disagreeably. "I might as well have been a damned eunuch. After being around Miss Kendall, bedding a whore would've been the same as trying to down hardtack after feasting on Philippe's fare. The idea left me...shall we say...*uninspired*."

Oaks curbed a smile. "I rather gathered as much, the way you came back snorting like a rutting stag."

"And you think she'd be safer here than on Sullivan's ship?" Beau asked curtly, fixing an incredulous squint upon the mate. "Hell, the way she looks now, I might as well forget I'm captain of this damned frigate."

"Perhaps you'd be more comfortable if I escorted Miss Kendall back to your cabin."

"*No!*" Beau barked.

Once again Oaks fought to squelch his amusement. "But I thought only to ease your pli—"

"*Don't think!*" Beau advised tersely with an angry slash of his hand. "I'm not in the mood for any of your coolheaded logic, Mr. Oaks. If you must know, I happen to enjoy watching the lady, and with my men observing us both, it may well be the only way I can safely indulge that propensity."

"Perhaps if you'd allow her to sail with us, Miss Kendall would be content to remain in her cabin for most of the voyage...."

Beau scoffed at the idea. "Being kept a prisoner doesn't strike me as a situation suitable for *any* woman."

"Then you're willing to subject her to the

dangers that Captain Sullivan's crew might force upon her."

"That's merely a conjecture, Mr. Oaks. On the *Audacious* 'twould be a certainty." Beau waved a hand, dismissing his first officer. "We've work to do. We'd better get on with it."

"Aye, Captain."

Clasping his hands behind his back, Beau strode down to the main deck and crossed to the rail to see how the work was progressing on the quay. Noticing fibers snapping apart in a rope that a handful of crewmen were straining against in order to steady a large crate presently being hoisted toward the deck, he thrust out an arm to bring the bosun's attention to bear upon the cable. "Watch that guy, Mr. McDurmett. There's a bad flaw in it."

A tall, sandy-haired man with a weathered face glanced up to inspect the cordage and, upon seeing the difficulty, gave his superior a casual salute. "Aye, Cap'n. I'll take care of it right away, sir."

No sooner had Beau turned from the rail than an audible snap was heard and the stabling line whipped free. Startled cries erupted from the loading crew, who spilled backward to the dock. From another sector came warning shouts as the now-spinning, armoire-sized crate swung forward toward the ship. Beau whirled and, catching a glimpse of a lofty shadow rapidly approaching, glanced up with a start. The heavy box passed overhead with the stabling rope whipping wildly behind. Beau

135

hardly paused. Leaping upward, he seized the guy, only to realize that the weight of one man wasn't enough to halt the ponderous load. The crate never paused as it sailed toward the crowded deck, hauling him along with it.

The shouts had drawn Cerynise's attention to bear upon the dangerously careening crate, but when she espied Beau dangling under it, her heart was stricken by fear. The risk of the weighty thing plummeting to the deck and crushing him beneath it was too great for her peace of mind. Clasping a hand over her mouth to smother a frightened scream, she watched in paralyzed awe as he began clambering up the rope.

The powerful muscles of his back and shoulders bulged as Beau swung intentionally outward away from the crate. Upon the return, he reversed his direction, extending his legs toward the load. He hit the cumbersome dervish with feet braced wide apart, stabilizing it enough to allow Oaks and several others to seize the rope. As they did, Beau clasped hold of the box and, climbing upon it, released the guy, giving his men full control of it as they sought to bring the wayward load in line. Gradually the crate slowed its swaying, and a command sounded to start lowering it into the hold. Beau jumped free and landed on his feet on the far side of the hatch. Then he turned, dusting off his hands as if concluding an everyday occurrence. Only then did Cerynise find her breath, which had been frozen in a hard lump in her throat.

When the crate came to rest on the lower deck, an audible sigh slipped from the crew. They soon broke into relieved laughter and engaged each other in a flurry of back-slapping as they showed their appreciation for a disaster successfully averted. Beau gave no evidence of begrudging his men this familiarity, but it was not long before he gave a signal for the loading to resume.

Stephen Oaks lifted his cap and wiped his forehead in relief as he came back to Cerynise. "Bit close, that one."

Cerynise's heart still felt a bit wobbly in its rhythm. The only thing she could think of at the moment was what might have happened if the crate had come loose and plummeted down upon Beau. The vision of him lying lifeless beneath the cumbersome box made her shudder. Weakly she murmured, " 'Tis fortunate Captain Birmingham is so perceptive."

"Aye, 'tis that, miss," Mr. Oaks eagerly agreed. "There isn't much that gets past him. He always seems to be a step ahead of the rest of us. Why, he's just as quick of mind as he is of foot."

Cerynise was too deeply shaken by the incident to make further comment on Beau's feat. The fact that he had ignored the danger to himself in his quest to subdue the crate was perhaps all well and good. But as far as she was concerned, she had serious doubts that she'd ever be able to watch another heroic, life-threatening deed of his without fainting dead away.

137

Some moments passed before the tingling fright that had assailed Cerynise ebbed to a more tolerable level. Once again she found her gaze drawn to Beau. With unwilling fascination, she observed him as he moved with comfortable ease among his men and the constant stream of visitors. Wherever he was needed, he was there, listening, observing, directing or explaining. At times, he stood back in an attitude of approval as he watched his men performing their tasks adeptly, but whenever a need arose, he stepped in, giving curt orders here, suggestions there. Cerynise could fully understand why he was always speedily obeyed. The merest thought of those eyes, which seemed to flame with a blue fire of their own, staring at her in cool displeasure was enough to make her tremble. Yet there was nothing dictatorial or arrogant about his manner. He simply exuded confidence and a firm command that other men were bound to follow.

A growing desire to sketch Beau amid the activity of the ship and the ruddy, weathered faces of his men began to flourish. If she could have foreseen the possibility of completing even a rough sketch before she had to leave, she would have asked Mr. Oaks to find her a place on deck where she'd be able to draw without hindering their work. But it seemed the only one who could give her a definite answer about her departure was Beau, and she couldn't work up enough courage to approach him while he was absorbed in his work.

Several moments elapsed before a carriage veered onto the dock, passing close enough to a six-in-hand to make the lead pair of drays bolt upright. Behind them, the other four steeds grew skittish and shied away. Turning the air nigh blue with loud curses, the teamster sawed frantically on the reins as he tried to bring his animals in line. His huge steeds calmed to some degree, allowing him to rail obscenities and shake a clenched fist at the other driver, who seemed to deliberately ignore the disturbance he had caused.

The new arrival continued on a destructive path, sending startled peddlers scattering in screaming panic and eliciting outraged screeches as other vendors saw their baskets of produce flying helter-skelter. A young boy, after surveying the squashed remains of his vegetables, picked up a tomato and flung it against the conveyance, leaving a reddened blotch adhering to its black door.

Finally the carriage came to a halt near a stack of crates that had been heaped up beyond the gangplank of the *Audacious*. Immediately the carriage door was flung open, and two men moved simultaneously to make their descent. For a moment they struggled to squeeze past each other and succeeded only in drawing derisive hoots from the vendors. Finally, the rounder of the two relented and sat back, allowing his companion to precede him. That worthy stepped to the ground just as the squashed tomato slid from the door and plopped onto the top of his shoe. Feeling a sudden splat, the man cast a curious glance downward. The slow turning of wide, flaccid lips conveyed the depth of his disgust. He kicked the seedy pulp off and then, glowering toward the chortling peddlers, flipped a coin to the coachman, who immediately raised an angry protest. When his demands were ignored in lofty arrogance, the driver swore and began to rein his horses about, causing the remaining occupant to hastily execute an escape from the turning coach. His ungainly departure left him teetering on the ground with arms flailing wildly as he struggled to regain his footing. His lank-bodied, black-haired companion muttered a curse and relented enough to toss another coin to the driver. Evidently it was enough to mollify him this time, for a self-satisfied smirk compressed one side of his rough-featured face. With an air of one who had all the time in the world, he folded his arms across his chest and relaxed back upon the seat to await the pair.

The reckless arrival of the carriage had alerted nearly everybody aboard the *Audacious*, including Mr. Oaks, who eyed the two passengers curiously as they strode toward the gangplank. If they were merchants at all, then they were none he had been made aware of. Even so, he went to meet them.

Cerynise followed more slowly, at least until she was able to see the men clearly. Then she gasped in shock, recognizing Alistair Winthrop and Howard Rudd. "Oh, my..."

Stephen Oaks recognized the anguish in

140

the lady's tone and, glancing back, grew concerned at her sudden pallor. "Is something wrong, miss?" he asked, returning to her side. "Here, you'd better sit down." Without waiting for a reply, he guided her solicitously to several smaller crates and held her hand as she sank listlessly to one of the wooden boxes. "I'll go and fetch the captain...."

It was too late. Alistair Winthrop and Howard Rudd were already coming up the plank, demanding to see the one in charge. Cerynise watched in mute horror as Beau turned to face them. Frowning in bemusement, he approached them.

"May I help you?"

"You certainly may!" Alistair answered haughtily. "We're looking for a runaway girl, and from what we've learned from Captain Sullivan down the river a piece, she's here on your ship."

"A runaway girl?" Beau cocked a curious brow as he sized up the pair. He quickly decided he didn't like what he saw *or* smelt. They both reeked of stale brandy or some other strong intoxicant. "I'm not aware that we have a runaway girl aboard the *Audacious*. You must be mistaken."

"Oh, you have her all right," Alistair insisted, his lips turning in a sneer as his dark eyes glinted with anger. "And I'm going to find her! Even if I have to search this damned barge to the depths of her stinking hold."

The cruel talons of dread clawed at Cerynise. She had no idea what the two men were about, but she could only assume that after kicking her out of the Winthrop house, they needed her to return for some malicious purpose of their own. Perhaps they had even found out about all of the clothes and things that Bridget and Jasper had managed to bring to her and intended to accuse her of thievery. She had come so close to leaving England. Another few days and she would have been sailing home.

"Do you have names?" Beau queried brusquely, surreptitiously flicking a hand toward Oaks, who promptly motioned several sailors to form a human wall in front of Cerynise.

"Alistair Winthrop," that one announced.

"Howard Rudd, Solicitor," the other volunteered apprehensively, noticing at least half a dozen tars edging closer.

"Well, Alistair Winthrop and Howard Rudd, Solicitor," Beau replied tartly, "this happens to be *my* ship, and anyone who thinks they can search it without my permission is in danger of being thrown into the river headfirst. Now, suppose you tell me what this is all about, and *perhaps* I might consider delaying your icy dip."

Rudd bobbed his head in eager agreement. "Must explain."

Alistair cast a livid glare over his shoulder at his companion, who seemed suddenly afflicted by a nervous rolling of his eyes and a sharp twitch that made his head jerk in the same direction. The warning signals fairly flew over Alistair's own head, for he was far more intent upon getting what he wanted from this uncouth Yankee. "We've come for Miss Cerynise Kendall, and we have every reason to believe that she has acquired passage on this vessel since Captain Sullivan has vigorously denied that she has done so on his."

Beau was totally unmoved by the man's statement. "Why do you wish to see Miss Kendall?"

"She was a ward of the Winthrop estate and, as such, has become my responsibility."

"You don't say." Beau's eyes were as cold as his terse smile. "Well, I have it on good authority that Miss Kendall is from the Carolinas and not an English subject. Therefore I fail to see how you can make any legal claim to her."

Alistair curled his lips in an angry sneer as he tossed another glance behind him at the mutely pleading Rudd. Jerking his sleeve away from the solicitor's persistent plucking, he sighed sharply in exasperation before he fixed his gaze again upon the captain. "Obviously you didn't hear me. Miss Kendall hasn't yet come of an age whereby she can make lawful decisions on her own. She was a legal ward of my late aunt until the elder's recent death. Now she has become mine, and I'm duty-bound to provide for her care."

"From what I hear, you threw her out into the street," Beau countered. "That's hardly an act of solicitude."

Alistair scoffed in rampant distaste. "I'm sure

143

the chit gave you quite a tale to win your sympathy, Captain, but that will hardly dissuade me from complying with the wishes of my aunt. Now where is the girl?"

Cerynise pushed herself upright on legs that felt far too weak to carry her across the deck. She silently shushed Mr. Oaks's protests with a finger across her lips, and then moved forward through the bulwark of broad-shouldered sailors to join the three men who stood near the rail.

"I'm here, Alistair," she announced with a heavy sigh. "What do you want?"

The man quickly whirled at the sound of her voice, but his jaw sagged slowly a-slack as his gaze swept her. He had expected to find a bedraggled, wretchedly miserable girl, but she was just as well groomed and beautiful as ever. Obviously the captain had already extended a goodly amount of coin on her to garb her so well. Perhaps he had even been reimbursed for his generosity. Tossing a virgin upon her back and instructing her in some of the finer pleasures of life was a feast some men only had illusions of, himself included.

Alistair forced a gentle smile despite the resentment that began to roil within him at his supposition. "Why, to take you home, of course."

"I no longer have a home here in England," Cerynise replied icily. "You made that perfectly clear when you threw me out."

"Tsk, tsk! How you do run on, Cerynise." He feigned a laugh as he waved a thin hand in the air to dismiss her claims. "If you're not careful, dear child, you'll make the captain think that I'm an ogre or something far worse."

"Strange," Beau pondered aloud. "I was just thinking that very same thing."

Alistair suddenly grew wary, for the man's eyes flashed with a chilling blue light that was, at the very least, threatening. "The girl has no business being here, Captain," he assured his host hurriedly. "I shall remove her forthwith." He reached out to take hold of Cerynise's wrist, wrenching a startled gasp from her. In the next moment he found his own wrist seized by the captain. Alistair's voice reached a high octave as he demanded, "What is the meaning of this?"

"I'll explain very simply," Beau offered almost pleasantly. "I'm not letting you take Cerynise until she assures me herself that she wants to go. And I really don't think she does. Do you understand?"

"This is an outrage! You can't do this!" Alistair cried, snatching free of the other's steely grasp.

Beau's soft chuckle was totally lacking in humor. "Can't I?" Then he looked toward the lady. "Cerynise, do you wish to leave with this *gentleman*?" The emphasis he placed upon the last word came through clearly as an insult.

She shook her head, unable to take her gaze from Alistair's rapidly darkening face. "It's not true what he said. I'm not his ward. I saw Mrs. Winthrop's will myself. There was no mention of any guardianship being transferred to him."

" 'Twas in a codicil we found later," Alistair explained, removing a piece of parchment from his coat and snapping it open in front of Beau's face. "Read it for yourself, Captain. I have legal ownership of this girl. She must obey me."

The muscles in Beau's lean cheeks tightened progressively until they fairly snapped. "Guardianship is hardly the same as ownership, Mr. Winthrop. Perhaps you need to consider the difference. As for this..." He flicked his fingers contemptuously against the paper. "This could be anything, a forgery for all I know."

Alistair sputtered in indignation. "I'm a man of wealth and position, sir! The law will affirm that I have a valid right to remove this girl from your ship. Indeed, you'd be well advised not to trouble yourself in this matter any longer, for I assure you that I can bring the law down upon this measly little ship and prevent you from *ever* leaving port. *Now!* If you don't want things to go badly for you, you'd better comply with my wishes posthaste."

Rudd nodded from behind Alistair's shoulder, as if affirming the fact that the captain would suffer dire consequences. But for the sake of caution, he tried once again to redirect Alistair's attention to the hulking sailors who were closing in around them.

Beau arched an eyebrow in sharp derision. "Badly for me? You threw Cerynise out to fend

146

for herself on the streets, a girl whom you now claim is your ward, and *you* caution *me* about the law?"

"Lies!" Alistair railed. "All lies! Cerynise is obviously saying that because she wants to stay here with you. Perhaps you've given the girl more attention than can possibly be deemed appropriate and have whispered sweet, little promises of empty adoration in her ears until she's now reeling with empty-headed pash and is so bedazzled she's willing to sail to the far ends of the earth with her noble captain." Alistair cast a scathing glance down the long masculine form, and his pliable lips twisted downward in sharp disdain. "No doubt she's already allowed you to mount her like some horny stag."

Cerynise gasped at the insult, but Beau proved more physical. He hauled back a fist and sent it flying toward the other man's face. Alistair saw the blow coming and tried to duck, but he was not entirely successful. Beau's hard knuckles caught him on the cheekbone, sending him sprawling backwards into Rudd, who nearly collapsed in surprise. The lawyer sputtered in confusion as he hefted his companion to his feet again.

"You dare accost me!" Alistair cried indignantly, clasping a hand over his throbbing cheek. "I'll have you arrested!"

He tried again to take hold of Cerynise, but she jerked away and skittered behind Beau who stepped forward menacingly to confront Alistair. "Get off this ship before I throttle you, you scurvy lump of dung."

147

Alistair's eyes flared at the slur, and he raised a clenched fist to shake it at Beau. "I'll make you sorry you ever laid eyes on Cerynise Kendall."

"I doubt that," Beau scoffed. Raising a hand, he beckoned the waiting sailors forward. "Throw this offal overboard."

Glancing askance at the burly sailors, Rudd began to tug desperately at Alistair's elbow. "Better go now! Better go now...."

"You'll regret this!" Alistair warned at the top of his lungs as he backed toward the gangplank. "When I return, I'll bring the authorities with me and see you arrested for molesting my ward. I'll have a watch set this very morning to prevent you from leaving port while Cerynise is aboard your ship. If you dare make a run for it, I'll have you hauled back in chains and charged with kidnapping. You'll spend the rest of your sorry life rotting in prison!"

Beau paced forward, and Rudd frantically yanked on Alistair's arm as he hissed some worthy advice: "Don't rile him any more than he is already, else he'll come after us! We'll let the authorities deal with him!"

Alistair was hardly subdued. Even as Rudd towed him toward the safety of the dock, he shouted irate curses at the captain. Getting him into the carriage proved just as difficult, for he was still intent upon venting his tirade. His enraged screeches could even be heard above the clatter of hooves as the conveyance rumbled away.

In the wake of its passage, silence reigned

for barely a moment. Then a dog barked, a horse whinnied, and a vendor cried out the prices of his wares. On board the *Audacious,* the sailors returned to their duties, but now sly winks were being exchanged among them, murmured comments made, and bets taken.

"I'm dreadfully sorry, Beau," Cerynise apologized as he stepped back to her. She spread her hands, unable to understand why Alistair had been so adamant that she leave with him. "I never expected *anyone* to protest my departure, certainly not after being thrown out of the Winthrop house. Under the circumstances, I think it would be best if you had someone escort me to Captain Sullivan's ship before Alistair sets up a guard to patrol the area around your ship."

Beau shook his head. "That's impossible now."

Cerynise realized it would have been difficult to find a man who wasn't busy and tried to think of a way she could get her baggage over to the *Mirage* herself. "Then if you'd tell me how to find Captain Sullivan's ship, perhaps Moon will be willing to come back and fetch my things."

Once again Beau bluntly negated the idea. "I won't allow it."

Cerynise stammered in confusion. "W-won't allow what, Captain? I don't understand. If you can't spare any of your men to serve as my escort, why won't you allow Moon to come back for my baggage?"

Beau crossed his arms in some vexation as

he stared down at her. "*Because*, Miss Kendall, if you try to leave the country on the *Mirage*, you'll never make it beyond these docks. Alistair Winthrop will find you, and knowing Captain Sullivan as I do, he'll not be inclined to argue with the authorities."

"Then what am I to do?" she queried dismally.

The magnificent brows gathered in a contemplative scowl. "Just how desperate are you to reach the Carolinas?"

"Most desperate," she averred.

Beau stroked his chin thoughtfully. "Alistair poses a problem that could prove almost insurmountable if he truly has been named your guardian. Even if the codicil is a forgery, the authorities will give him the benefit of the doubt...at least for a time."

"You said 'almost,' Captain." Cerynise looked at him closely. "As long as there's some chance of defeating Alistair's purposes in taking me back, I'm willing to hear any suggestions you might have."

"Aye, but you may not like what I have to say. Yet I can think of no other way at present to nullify Alistair's immediate claims to you."

"Say what's on your mind, Captain," she urged. "I'm listening."

Beau's mouth quirked thoughtfully as he continued to stare at her in silence. He would likely shock her to her senses, perhaps send her fleeing back to the Winthrop house.

Being the recipient of his intense gaze, Cerynise grew increasingly uneasy. She could only believe that whatever Beau was about to recommend was something so immensely odious he was reluctant to explain. "I really wish you wouldn't do that."

Beau blinked in confusion. "Do what, my dear?"

The endearment brought a blush of pleasure to her cheeks, making her drop her head in an attempt to hide it. "Stare at me so intently. It makes me feel as if you're dissecting me like some fledgling physician with his first corpse."

Beau winced sharply, making much of his repugnance. "I shall strive most heartily to improve my manners, my dear."

There it was again! Enchanting words from princely lips!

Cerynise released her breath in short, shallow drafts as she sought to to steady herself. His eyes might well have worked their magic on her, but his words had the same effect as honeyed mead, leaving her more than a little intoxicated.

She cleared her throat, taking firm control of herself. Even so, her eyelids fluttered with uncertainty as she lifted her gaze to meet those smiling sapphire orbs. "It seems that I'm being left in needless suspense, sir," she prodded with a faltering sigh. "Won't you *please* tell me what you have in mind?"

"Forgive me for the delay, Cerynise." His wide shoulders lifted in a casual shrug. "Since the idea has only just come to me, I must pause a moment and consider the possible repercussions that may occur because of it."

Chewing thoughtfully on a corner of his bottom lip, he pivoted sharply and strode to the rail. For a length of several moments, he stared off beyond the docks toward the city as he considered what he owed this girl by way of his friendship.

His father, Brandon Birmingham, had once stood near this very same place decades ago, viewing this identical city from his own vessel. The elder Birmingham had faced many of the same challenges his son had often confronted as a ship's captain, and with a parent's concern for his only male offspring, Brandon had sought to share the wisdom he had gleaned from his own experiences. He had taught his son not merely with words but through example. Above all, he had shown him the true meaning of duty and honor.

A man's rightful claim to being a gentleman was not something one could inherit, like a title, his father had once counseled. It came through careful instruction from one who knew the depth and scope of its inner workings. Brandon's father had once taught him, and in turn, he was duty bound to teach his own son. Compassion, fairness, valor, honor, and integrity were a few of the characteristics a man could lay claim to as a gentleman. Certainly one had a responsibility to protect members of his own household from the harsh cruelties of the world, but such an obligation also extended to friends and those poor unfortunates who had neither. Noblesse oblige, more or less. Except that his family was not of noble birth, at least none that had ever made a difference in their lives. Still, the weight of responsibility had to be carried gallantly, no matter how it might weigh heavily upon a man at times. Oppression could come in a variety of forms, physical mistreatment being the most obvious. Beau's face darkened as he remembered Cerynise's condition when he had lifted her in his arms and carried her aboard the *Audacious*. It enraged him to think of Alistair Winthrop gaining control of her and resorting to other measures of subjugation. But there were other kinds of persecution that were not readily apparent, such as the whispered conjectures, the gossip, and subtle innuendoes that could destroy a reputation and inflict a lifetime of damage.

Alistair Winthrop appeared to be a desperate man. Beau did not doubt that for an instant. Certainly, while the man was able to make legal claim to Cerynise, however false it might be, he could prevent her from escaping to the Carolinas. Beau could think of only one possible arrangement that could hold sway over a guardian's rights and be adequate enough to protect her from Winthrop and the danger the man represented, even in a court of law.

The silence dragged on until Cerynise thought she couldn't bear it another moment. If Beau was tormenting her for some sadistic pleasure, then he was being completely thorough in that endeavor.

Beau clasped his hands behind his back as he returned to Cerynise. He smiled briefly. " 'Twould seem there are no alternatives, my dear. Your friend, Alistair, leaves us little choice if you are indeed intent upon going home."

"I am," she affirmed once again.

"Then, my dear, we must be married posthaste."

Cerynise stared at him, wondering if she had heard him correctly. "Excuse me?"

"You heard me correctly. 'Tis the only available solution for us both. As things stand now, Winthrop will have little difficulty convincing the authorities to turn you over to him. I'm a foreigner in this country, and I've angered port officials who seem jealous of my ability to whisk in and out of this country with relative ease. 'Tis not uncommon for them to resent Yankees. And if I try to leave with you, I'm sure they'll attempt to seize my ship and cast me into prison. As my wife, you'll be under my protection, and I can almost promise you that no magistrate is going to step between a husband and his wife."

How strange the things she noticed now that the world had gone out of kilter with the universe. The man standing in front of her was so tall, her head barely touched the top of his shoulders, and there was the nicest little scar on his chin....

Having gained no response, Beau probed for an answer. "Do you understand, Cerynise?"

"Of course," she breathed. "You want to marry me, you said." The thought of being his wife filled her with many contradictory emotions...shock, fear, and a burgeoning excitement she didn't dare consider at the present moment.

"Actually, that's not quite what I said," Beau corrected carefully.

Her gaze flicked up, revealing her confusion.

As much as he yearned to make love to her, Beau refused to commit himself to a long-term union from which he'd be unable to walk away. He enjoyed sailing too much, and if he continued roaming the world after taking on the responsibilities of a wife and offspring, he'd be doing them a grave disservice, for he would never be around to nurture them or when they truly needed him. Indeed, the way he flitted from continent to island or elsewhere, he'd probably spend just enough time at home to see the child he had sired from a previous visit and to get his wife pregnant again. He had seen it happen much too often in the lives of other captains and seamen to doubt that it would be any different for him.

Beau explained with painstaking clarity, lest Cerynise suffer any doubt about what he was proposing. "Once we arrive in Charleston, we can have the marriage annulled, and then we'll be free to go our separate ways. By then, you'll be at home where you want to be, and I won't have my ship confined on the wrong side of the Atlantic while I wrestle with the courts."

"There's no need for you to do anything so drastic, Beau," Cerynise murmured in quiet dignity. He made it bitingly clear that he really didn't want her for a wife. He was only being chivalrous, helping her out of a predicament, nothing more. She hadn't really thought him to be serious. Well, not for more than an instant perhaps. "You can simply sail away."

"Without you?" Beau was astounded at her suggestion. "I wouldn't do that, Cerynise. I'd never forgive myself, most certainly not after seeing what you'd have to confront with Alistair Winthrop as your guardian. Call it a debt that I owe your father for not giving up on me when I could just as well have gone the way of some of my friends, who laughed at his efforts to make them study. Your father's visits to my parents brought about the results he desired in keeping my mind fixed on what was important rather than on the frivolous enjoyments a lad is wont to seek after. I owe him much more than I can ever repay."

Cerynise stared at him, thinking of that tall, handsome lad with short, loosely curling black locks and jet-lashed blue eyes with whom she had always been enamored. She recalled the times when he had lifted her astride his horse in front of him to give her lessons and, over a season, had gently coaxed her out of her fear of riding. Then there was that singular afternoon many years ago when she had been playing by herself near the schoolhouse and several boys, after leaving class, had started pestering her, yanking her pigtails, snapping her with pebbles launched from peashooters, and doing everything they could

156

to make her supremely miserable. Beau had heard her outraged cries upon his departure from school and had come running to box the ears of her tormentors, gaining for himself a harsh reprimand and extra homework as a penalty from her father, who after hearing her story later that evening had traveled to Harthaven to humbly apologize to the lad and thank him for defending his daughter.

Beau was now the one growing impatient for an answer and wondered if the girl had fallen into a daze. He didn't know what percentage of women swooned after receiving a proposal of marriage, but she had never impressed him as the type. "Blast it, Cerynise, it's not as if I'm asking you to swear fealty to me or..."

"Oh, but you are," she pointed out, not unreasonably she thought.

Beau seemed taken aback. "All right, perhaps I am, but we both know it will only be a temporary situation. As soon as the voyage is over, then we can sever the marriage, and that will be the end of it."

He made it sound so simple, Cerynise mused distantly. A marriage of convenience to be followed by a prompt annulment. A legal technicality. A way out of their situation. Nothing more. Nothing really at all.

But she knew it wasn't quite that easy, at least not with her. To claim Beau Birmingham as her husband had been a long-held dream born a decade ago in the mind of a child. She smiled wistfully. Strange how enduring that fantasy had been. She still yearned for it even now.

Cerynise looked up into eyes that were a deeper, truer blue than the sky overhead. He was the boy she had once known, and yet he really wasn't. He was a man full grown, with a mind of his own, and he was offering to give her the protection of his name when she most desperately needed it. His very presence made her feel utterly safe. Yet, at the same time, she was aware of a poignant disquiet growing within her, which made her almost fearful. If she fell more deeply in love with her prince, what would happen to her heart once their marriage was dissolved? Would she be able to bear the abject loneliness that would descend upon her once they were separated? Would he even care what she might suffer when they went their separate ways?

Beau saw nothing in Cerynise's face that gave any hint of her acceptance of his plan. Indeed, she seemed almost apprehensive, as if fearful of what their marriage might lead to. He could only imagine that with the lack of space aboard ship she might be afraid of sharing his quarters and of what might follow. Making love to her was not something he could promise would never happen; he was too damned aware of his own needs to do an irrational thing like that. Three months could seem like an eternity when one was bound up in oaths of abstinence. He was no monk by any means, nor a gentleman to that degree, nor would he commit himself to her in that way. His mating instincts were too strong to be ignored even now. What torment would he devise for himself if he foolishly spilled such gallant covenants only to regret them later? The way he was feeling presently, *later* could mean only a matter of moments from now. Still, he relented enough to suggest, "For the time being, think of it as a...a titular arrangement, if you must. Beyond that, I can only pledge that I won't force you to do anything with which you're not in complete agreement."

Cerynise closed her eyes, trying to mentally sort out what he had just said to her. He wasn't necessary vowing not to touch her...or was he? What else could one possibly imagine about *a titular arrangement*?

"Is my proposal something you can accept?" Beau pressed after another lengthy wait.

Cerynise opened her eyes and, in a small voice, stated her decision. "It seems to be the only option I have to be free of Alistair."

Beau had no doubt that any suitor who had hopes of gaining her for a wife either now or in the future would have a hard time calmly accepting what she was agreeing to at this very moment. Since they were destined to be confined aboard a ship for the length of three months, give or take a week or two, any swain would naturally wonder what the two of them had done together to while away so much time in a temporary marriage. No one could predict what their relationship would bear. But when Beau tried to determine what his own reactions would be if some swain pressed him to sign annulment papers after the voyage, an odd sense of vexation rose up within him, as if he'd actually resent being prodded into signing away his rights to a woman who nearly took his breath away. It was uppermost in his mind that he desired her, no doubt more than any woman he had ever known, but he also wanted to be free of the chains that could forever bind him to land.

"I sense that you're troubled over the necessity of making this decision..."

Cerynise halted his words with a small shake of her head. "I'd prefer not to discuss this matter any further, Beau, if you don't mind. I've made my decision, and I can only urge you to proceed as quickly as possible ere we find our plans set awry."

"I'll make the arrangements," Beau informed her, slipping a hand beneath her arm and turning her toward the companionway. "But I'm sure before the afternoon is well spent, the nuptials will be concluded."

He escorted her back to his cabin and, after a short time, sent Billy Todd to her with instructions to be useful in whatever way she deemed fit. Beau had informed the lad what would take place before the day was out, and as a result, Billy was terribly flustered. He was inclined to stare at Cerynise as a ruddy hue ebbed and flowed into his cheeks. Every seaman aboard the *Audacious* had been aware of the captain's reluctance to marry for some years now, and to hear that he was giving up his freedom had come as something of a shock to all of them. It didn't matter that the girl was more winsome than any Billy had personally seen; he was still flabbergasted by the alacrity with which his captain was advancing to make her his own.

"Cap'n says...the two o' ye—" Billy broke off and simply gaped at her, finding his tongue tied by his awkward attempt to make conversation.

"Said what, Billy?"

He waved a hand in mute apology, but as she continued to await his answer, he hurried to give an excuse. "I forgot, miss."

" 'Tis quite all right, Billy," Cerynise soothed, subduing a dejected sigh. "I'm not very mindful of anything right now either." Perhaps it was just as well that she had someone else to reassure. Trying to ease the lad's abashment diverted her thoughts from what she was actually committing herself to. Marriage with a man whom she all but idolized? What could be so distressing about that?

The years she had spent in England had eventually led her to dismiss her long-savored dream in which she would become Beau's wife as nothing more than a girlish fantasy. It had definitely not seemed conceivable. Thereafter she had thought about marriage with only passing interest. She had simply assumed that one day she'd marry and, in a vague sort of way, had looked forward to doing so. Yet she had also been content to have the fulfillment of that premise floating off in the distant future somewhere. Painting became the focal point of her attention, and it had taken over her interests so completely that it had left her with little inclination for daydreaming about the faceless, unknown male who would one day become her husband.

Except that he was no longer faceless now, and he really wasn't going to be her husband, at least not in the way that Lydia had delicately tried to explain shortly after Cerynise had crossed the threshold into budding maturity. Beau would merely be doing her a favor, rather like the *parfait, gentil* knight of Chaucer would do, she as the damsel in distress and he as a chivalrous knight riding to her rescue.

A vision of Beau outfitted in shining armor and racing to her aid on a gleaming white charger was wonderful to behold in her mind, even if it did seem a bit absurd. She was sure that Beau would absolutely abhor being in armor, preferring as he did the casual comfort of a shirt and finely tailored trousers. He rode remarkably well, as she recalled, but she entertained serious doubts that he'd approve of any horse being festooned with plumes and embroidered reins. Still, she might have found it pleasurable had he consented to kissing her hand....

Ah, yes, she mused in sublime pleasure. That would be absolutely perfect to start off with. The farfetched idea drew a giggle from her, but she choked it off, realizing that Billy Todd was still in the room, laying out the captain's clothes.

"Miss?" He looked around nervously. "Are you all right?"

Cerynise gave the cabin boy a bright smile, trying to dispell any notion that she was ailing or afflicted in any manner. "I'm sorry, Billy. My imagination has a tendency to run away with me at times."

The cabin boy reddened as he realized that she might well be thinking of the evening to come when she and the captain would be alone together in the cabin. "I can see where it might have cause today, miss."

Scarcely an hour after Billy had taken the captain's clothes and left her to her solitude, Cerynise was once again interrupted. This time it was Stephen Oaks whom she ushered in. He seemed almost as stunned as Billy and, for a moment, wavered between shock and amusement. The latter finally won out.

"I guess 'tis true what they say," he mused aloud. "If you sail the seven seas long enough, you'll eventually see everything."

"Is this wedding so remarkable, Mr. Oaks?" Cerynise inquired, trying to curb her irritation. She didn't need to be reminded of how startling the impending nuptials might seem to the crew, but it certainly wasn't *that* outlandish for a man and a woman to suddenly decide to wed. "People get married every day."

"Aye, miss, but they're not the captain. I'd never have thought that he'd consent to tying himself down to any lady by wedding—" The mate broke off, immediately aware of having gone too far. "I beg your pardon, miss. I didn't mean...that is, there is nothing wrong with you marrying the captain, not at all. 'Tis a grand idea, in fact. The perfect solution, as it be."

Cerynise's brows lifted to a lofty level. "Solution? Do you mean you know—"

Mr. Oaks held up a hand, forestalling her. "All I meant, miss, is that the crew was betting the captain wouldn't let that sod, Winthrop, take you. We had no doubt that he'd find a way ta keep you safe. The only question we couldn't answer accurately was just how he was going ta do it." The mate grinned broadly. "Of course, most of the men didn't realize he'd go this far. They were thinking perhaps a few shots would be fired, and there'd be a run for the open sea, that sort of thing. Nothing like this, though."

Cerynise stared at him in amazement. "You thought the captain would set you to flight along the Thames, fighting your way out like...like a band of *pirates*...all because of me?"

Mr. Oaks responded with a casual shrug. "It happens, miss. From time to time, there's a difference of opinion that can't be easily or peaceably settled. Why, in Barcelona last year, we—" The mate caught himself abruptly and changed the subject. "The point is, miss, I know the captain better than anybody on board. It didn't seem likely he'd do anything to endanger you, so there wasn't a lot of choices to be had. Besides, he's not exactly the

164

most ordinary bloke I've ever come across. Likes to do the unexpected, he does." Oaks chortled and patted the purse he wore on his belt. "At least, it was unexpected to most of the lads."

Cerynise's jaw sagged as the realization dawned. Then she snapped her mouth closed in an angry huff. "Do you mean, Mr. Oaks, that you actually wagered on the outcome of our set-to with Mr. Winthrop?"

Stephen Oaks looked suddenly sheepish. "Aye, miss."

"I hope you will enjoy your winnings, Mr. Oaks," she replied as graciously as she could manage at the moment. Indeed, she was rather surprised at how steady her voice sounded in her own ears. "Now, if you don't mind, I would like a few moments to myself before—"

It was impossible for Oaks to ignore her irritation. "I'm sorry, miss. Sometimes my mouth runs ahead of my wits."

" 'Tis a folly some people must cope with," she replied pithily. "However, if you'll excuse me...."

Mr. Oaks looked acutely repentant as he twisted his cap between his hands. "That's actually what I came to tell you, miss. 'Tis time."

She gasped in shock. "Already?"

The mate gave her a nod. "Aye, miss. There's a rector right here in Southwark who owes the captain a favor or two. He came straightaway when he was sent for. He and the captain are on deck waiting for you now."

Cerynise was astounded. The time had come upon her in such a rush that she wasn't at all sure she was mentally prepared to face the nuptials. "Surely there are formalities, permission to be obtained, and other things...."

"You'll have to ask the captain about all of that, miss. Now, if you don't mind, I've been sent to escort you to the quarterdeck."

Cerynise meekly followed the mate, once again watching one foot being placed before the other as she ascended the companionway. She could see this thing through, she told herself, and get beyond it without feeling any remorse because it was only a farce. The real difficulty would come later, when she had to sign her name to the annulment papers and watch Beau Birmingham sail out of her life.

The loading of the cargo had stopped, and the entire crew had gathered. Most were on the main deck. Others had climbed into the ratlines for a better view. The men fell silent when she emerged, and their eyes slowly followed as she climbed to the upper deck. She was dimly aware of a slight figure of a man standing beside Beau, but she barely noticed him, for her attention was completely focused on the powerful, compelling individual who was about to become her husband.

Beau was handsomely garbed in a darkly subdued navy-and-gray plaid frock coat, white shirt and cravat, high-buttoned waistcoat that matched the gray in his coat, and darker gray trousers with straps fastened beneath black ankle-boots. The sight of him made her heart flutter nervously, for he was quite distinguished looking in his dapper attire. Looking at him made her wish that she had been fore-warned about his decision to dress for the occasion. Smoothing her hair was the best she could do as Mr. Oaks escorted her to the deck.

Beau smiled into her eyes and, reaching out to take her hand, pulled her against him. The unease that Cerynise had felt over her appearance dissipated. It was as if spring had come once more to the land. Her would-be husband slid an arm around her waist and pressed his lips against the hair above her temples. "You look lovelier than any bride I've ever seen, my dear."

Cerynise braced a trembling hand against his waistcoat to keep herself from falling forward against him, for the sturdy arm encompassing her pulled her much too close for what seemed suitable for an *in name only* arrangement. If Beau didn't yet realize how susceptible she was to his sweet words, cajoling looks and to his very presence, she most certainly did. She knew exactly why her heart raced out of control above the confines of her corset.

"May I return similar compliments to the groom, sir?" Cerynise breathed, hoping he couldn't detect the nervous quaver in her voice. "Your appearance has far-exceeded my expectations. Indeed, I feel put out with myself for not having taken more time with my own preparations."

"Your worries are groundless, my dear." Beau leaned down to nuzzle her hair again, stirring forth a tantalizing scent that flicked across his senses, awakening him to the realization that she was not only beautiful, but utterly feminine as well. It wasn't a compliment he casually bestowed upon all women, but it was unquestionably true in this case. "You smell nice, too."

At the moment, it didn't matter to Cerynise that she felt wonderfully suffocated by his presence or that her cheeks were glowing warmly. She could only assume that his wooing was contrived for the rector or perhaps for the pleasure of his crew. She could hear many of them encouraging their captain amid the running banter of their cohorts. That fact didn't concern her overly much. What really mattered was the astonishing sense of contentment that she felt in his embrace, as if she had always belonged there. But then, she had always dreamed she would.

A thin, gray-haired, middle-aged man with kindly gray eyes stepped near. From the rough appearance of his hands, Cerynise quickly surmised that he had been tilling soil prior to his arrival, no doubt readying it for the winter ahead. Although he had obviously made some effort to wash, his deeply calloused hands still bore traces of dirt in the cracks of his hardened skin and beneath his ragged nails. His frayed waistcoat was only partially fastened, his stock ill tied and askew, and his cheeks bristly from a recent growth of whiskers, all evidence of a man who had hastened to answer an urgent summons and one who had difficulty making ends meet. Yet, in spite of his rather poor and disheveled appearance, Cerynise felt immediately at ease in his presence, for she sensed him to be a gentle and kindhearted man.

"You are Miss Kendall?" he queried with a friendly smile.

"Yes, sir."

"And you are entering into this marriage of your own free will, without coercion of any sort?"

The question was unexpected, and she glanced up at Beau in some surprise. He squeezed her hand reassuringly. "Mr. Carmichael doesn't concern himself with formalities overmuch, my dear, but he must confirm, for his own peace of mind, that both parties have come willingly to a decision to marry. Did you of your own free will agree to marry me?"

Though Beau presented the question, Cerynise turned her gaze to the clergyman and answered in a softly hushed tone. "I am consenting, sir."

The warmth of Beau's hand replaced the coldness that had threatened to engulf her only moments ago when she had climbed to the quarterdeck. She entwined her fingers through his and held on tightly.

"Dearly beloved, we are gathered here in the sight of God to join this man and this woman in Holy Matrimony...."

CHAPTER 5

Gazing into her eyes, Beau murmured the words that bound them together. "I take thee, Cerynise Edlyn Kendall, to be my lawfully wedded wife...."

The words, quietly uttered, reverberated through Cerynise's heart. She seriously doubted that she had ever heard anything that touched her so completely as his promises to love, honor and cherish. With all of her being, she wanted the words to mean something to him, too, and fervently hoped he wasn't merely murmuring them for the sake of gallantry. She could feel her eyes misting as she began to repeat her own vows, and she lowered her gaze to the strong, lean hands that held hers in a gentle grasp. "I take thee, Beauregard Grant Birmingham, to be my lawfully wedded husband...."

Some moments later, Mr. Carmichael inquired, "Who has the ring?"

Cerynise held her breath, for she had forgotten that small detail and was sure that Beau had also. She expected to hear some excuse as to his reason for not having one and was immensely surprised when he began to work a small band of gold off his little finger. Smoothly slipping the ring past the slender knuckle of her third finger, he repeated the words the rector spoke. "With this ring, I thee wed...."

The older man finally concluded the ceremony. "I now pronounce you man and wife."

He gave a nod to Beau. "You may kiss the bride now."

Suddenly there was a loud chorus of voices shouting encouragement. "Aye, Cap'n. Kiss her! Show us how it's done!"

Cerynise blushed to the roots of her hair and would have turned away for fear of being coolly rebuffed. A small gasp of surprise escaped her as Beau tightened his arm about her waist and pulled her completely around until they were facing his crew. Raising his free arm, he motioned for silence.

"All right, me hearties," he cried with a jovial chortle. "If you want an exhibition, I'll give you one, but mark my words well. I'll not instruct you again. Learn now or never!"

Hearty laughter, heavily mingled with applause, drowned the beat of Cerynise's heart as Beau settled his arms close around her. She felt awkward, not knowing what to do with her own arms, and finally slid them behind his neck as she lifted her gaze to his. Slanting its way across his handsome lips was a rather wickedly wayward grin reminiscent of a smile the younger Beau Birmingham had always worn during his teasing moods. Cerynise could almost see the puckish little demon perched upon his shoulder, but all reason fled as his face descended and hovered close above her own.

"Bear with my kiss, madam," he whispered, his breath warm upon her mouth. "My men would be disappointed if I were remiss in giving you one."

Suddenly his lips were moving over hers in a warmly seductive kiss that bestirred some strange, unexplainable pleasure in the pit of her womanly being. It was a heady brew that sapped the strength from her limbs and made her head swim and her heart race wildly out of control. She felt herself being turned and lowered over the arm braced beneath the small of her back. The position no doubt allowed his men full advantage of the view. From there, the kiss advanced rapidly, startling her virginal senses as his tongue silkily plied her mouth and greedily consumed the sweet nectar of her timid response. Cerynise had never imagined such a shocking thing could happen in a kiss and didn't know how to gracefully respond except to allow him full access. Then, too, she wasn't exactly sure whether it was the proper way to kiss or not, considering it was her first one. Still, she was sharply skeptical that so thorough a kiss was needful for the benefit of his crew. Yet, considering their agreement, she could envision it as being the only one she would ever receive from Beau Birmingham, and that single worry took away any desire to resist. *If* she had to settle for a sterile relationship with her new husband, then she would garner every delectable memory she could store away in her heart before their marriage was terminated.

Without her being aware of it, her arms tightened around his neck, causing loud applause and wildly exaggerated crooning and heavy sighs to erupt from his men. Amid the din, the subtle coughing of the pastor almost went unnoticed except for Cerynise, who abruptly came to her senses. Moving her hands forward over Beau's shoulders, she gave him a gentle push as she turned her face aside.

"Beau, please...."

He straightened, pulling her up with him, and faced his men. Cerynise could feel her face burning as he clasped her close against his side. Indeed, she doubted the whalebone corset she wore cinched her waist as tightly. Immediately there arose a deafening cacophony of whistles, shouts of approval, and thunderous applause. Beau laughed and gave them a jaunty bow, and Cerynise sank into a deep curtsy, feeling pleasantly obliged to follow his example.

Beau waved an arm again to silence the uproar. "All right, you lovesick sea wolves, you've had your spectacle for the day. What say you for bringing up a keg or two to celebrate?"

Cerynise clamped her hands over her ears and winced in pain at the noise that his suggestion had invited. She could feel Beau's laughter against her midriff far better than she could hear it. Several of his men dashed off to fulfill his behest, and soon a barrel of rum was spiked, a spigot attached, and brimming cups passed around.

Mr. Carmichael had readied the papers for them to sign and patiently awaited their attention.

Beau was the first to notice the man's patient smile and escorted his young bride to the small table that had been set up for the clergyman's benefit. The elder dipped a quill into the inkwell and handed it to Beau.

"Captain, if you would sign on the bottom line," he urged, directing Beau's attention to identical places on the two official-looking documents laid out side by side on the table. "I thought it would be best to have you sign two copies, one for the church registry here, and the other for you to take to your home port in case there should be inquiries into the legality of your marriage there."

"Of course," Beau agreed, scratching out his name in a graceful flourish.

"And now you, Mrs. Birmingham," Mr. Carmichael coaxed.

Mrs. Birmingham. The full enormity of what she had just vowed flooded through Cerynise, setting her to trembling.

Beau passed the quill to her and promptly caught it again as it slipped from her shaking fingers. He returned it to her, this time curling his hand around her own until she held the quill securely within her grasp, but one glance at her pale cheeks gave him cause to think that she might faint. Clasping an arm close around her waist again, he leaned near to whisper, "Not much longer, Cerynise."

She saw the table swirling crazily before her eyes and, smothering a moan, averted her face from the sight. For a brief moment, she dared to lean into the manly form that lent her

174

support. He held her in silence, unruffled by her reaction. Gradually her reeling world subsided, and she straightened, inhaled deeply, and then plunged into the task of signing her new name. It looked strange there on the white parchment, an oddity that had no real substance.

Mr. Carmichael signed his name, applied wax and stamped it with a church seal to attest to the authenticity of the papers. Then he applied sand to the signatures, blew it off, and carefully handed a copy to Beau. "For your records, Captain."

Mr. Oaks had joined them only a moment before and had remained at a respectful distance until Beau faced him. Without a word, the mate handed over two weighty purses to his superior, who in turn passed them on to the rector.

"And this, Parson, is for your orphanage."

Sudden tears brightened the cleric's eyes as he met Beau's smiling gaze. He opened a trembling mouth several times to convey his gratitude, but the words were repeatedly choked by his swelling emotion. Finally, with face crumpling, he nodded vigorously. Beau gently laid a hand upon the man's shoulder and escorted him to the gangplank. They parted with a fierce handshake, and then, after a final wave of farewell, Beau turned and made his way back to his bride.

The tears that filmed her eyes amazed him, and a small frown crossed his brow as he drew his own conclusions. "Regrets so soon, Cerynise?"

She shook her head. "Nay, Captain. I was just a bit overwhelmed by what you did for Mr. Carmichael."

Beau casually brushed aside any praise for his benevolence. "My gift is hardly worthy of the man. He and his wife have taken it upon themselves to establish a safe haven for the orphaned children of this city, at least as many as they can find. He's like your father in many respects, carrying a burden for the young and their future in this world. Mr. Carmichael works and scrimps to put food in their mouths and a little joy in their hearts."

Mr. Oaks had stepped away a moment and now came back bearing a cup of rum for Beau. He grinned as his superior sampled a draught. "Congratulations, Captain. It isn't often a man can find such a beautiful lady to take as his bride. You're to be envied."

More like pitied! Beau mused. Jumping from the roasting pot into the fire was certainly not a logical thing for any man to do, but he'd done just that to save a friend from certain disaster. The fact that that friend was now a woman whom he desperately yearned to savor posed a difficulty he was not at all sure he could surmount, either now or later. But at least with the way things stood now, if he passed beyond that thin barrier, no one would accuse him of taking license with an innocent virgin.

Billy Todd scurried up to the quarterdeck to announce, "Mr. Monét has yer meal prepared in the cabin, sir, an' a right fine one it is, too."

"Thank you, Billy." Beau faced his bride. "Would you care to dine, my dear?"

Cerynise realized with some astonishment that she was starving and eagerly nodded.

A smile flicked across Beau's lips before he faced his second-in-command. "Take over for me, Mr. Oaks. I shall be dining with my wife if you should have need of me."

Oaks gave him an eloquent wink and grinned. "Aye, sir."

Cerynise turned to make her way to the companionway but gasped in sudden astonishment as she felt herself being swept up in her husband's arms. "What are you doing?"

"Carrying my new bride to my cabin," Beau answered with a chortle, having gained another loud ovation from his crew. "My men expect it, my dear."

"I hope they don't expect too much," Cerynise quipped, showing a small dimple on the right side of her mouth as she smiled and looped her arms about his neck. What she said wasn't necessarily the truth, but she enjoyed teasing him nevertheless.

As they descended the shadowed stairway, she could feel his eyes scanning her face from very close range. He finally broached what was on his mind. "I gather, then, that you didn't particularly relish my kiss."

The impish sprite who was wont to appear from time to time pondered his question in a guise of perplexity. " 'Twas most illuminating, sir. I've never been kissed exactly like that before."

"Have you *ever* been kissed before?" Beau asked dryly.

"Now, sir, if I were to answer your question, I'd be giving away secrets I'd rather not confess."

They came to his cabin door, and after lifting the latch, Beau pushed the door open with a shoulder and swept her through. "What confidences can long remain untold between a husband and his wife? A couple usually share the most intimate of secrets."

"Are we to be intimate, then?"

Beau kicked the door closed behind him and grinned down at his bride as he continued to hold her within his arms. He had the greatest temptation to kiss her again just the way he had done on deck, yet he was intrigued by her inquiry. He knew that she referred to something entirely different than what he had in mind. *Intimate friends* was a fair distance in meaning from *being* intimate, but he countered with a question more pertinent to the easing of his tension. "Would you like to become intimate, my dear?"

The realization of what he meant dawned on Cerynise, and beneath his closely attentive stare, a vivid hue suffused her cheeks. Even so, she kept her composure well enough to sweetly ask in return, "Would you like to stay married, sir?"

Beau wasn't at all sure how he could answer that truthfully without destroying the moment. For her benefit he seemed to ponder her question. "It all depends on how well we get along in our intimacy."

Cerynise nodded understandingly. He wanted to be intimate, but he had no desire to have his freedom curtailed for the rest of his life. "I'm sure our dispositions will be tested enough during the voyage for us to ascertain our compatibility without physical union, Captain, so if you're making overtures to your bride, perhaps you should consider that I will not accept them without a lasting commitment."

Beau sighed. "I thought you'd say that."

"Disappointed, Captain?" she asked with feigned concern.

"I think you're a little minx," he remarked, withdrawing his arm from beneath her knees and letting her feet slide to the floor. In spite of the bulk of their clothing, the effect of their bodies sliding together created a sharp longing that only intensified Beau's concern as to how he'd be able to cope with the tensions of withholding himself from her in the weeks and months to come. And then, strangely, there was that other thing. Only a moment ago he had longed to kiss her, and that temptation had not ebbed in the least. He yearned fervently to part those soft, comely lips with a kiss that would demonstrate all the passion of a newly spoused husband. Yet he found the enticement immensely unsettling, for it contradicted his normal mode of thinking. For a man who had refrained from kissing harlots even in the frenzied heat of passion, the irrepressible urge was something he had never before encountered. Kissing was unnecessary with strumpets, he had reasoned long ago, deeming it far too personal a practice to share his mouth with them. And no matter how intimate fornicating was, as a seaman and a bachelor intent upon remaining single he had found it necessary to ease his temperament as well as his manly needs in such a manner.

Beau had a sudden image of himself as some bewitched inamorato who slavered in fiendish lust for her kisses and her body, and no matter how outrageous he wanted to consider that notion, he perceived a small measure of truth was to be found in it nevertheless. He could hardly deny the fact that he was hungry for them both.

Catching Cerynise's hand, he whirled her gently away from him, allowing himself time to turn away to the washstand before she could stop spinning. Washing his hands, he stated gruffly over his shoulder, "Our wedding feast is awaiting us, madam. 'Twill be cold if we delay much longer."

Cerynise withdrew her shawl and waited timidly as Beau stripped down to his shirt and trousers. He tossed aside the cravat and, with one hand, unfastened his shirt as he approached the table. Refusing to look at her, he drew out a chair for her as he tried to take control of his wanton thoughts. Every time he glanced at her lately, it seemed that he was confronted by an unquenchable urge to take possession of her. The kiss he had given her up on deck had lit a fire in his blood, and he knew henceforth that it would be doubly hard for him to control those insatiable longings.

Settling down into his own chair, Beau opened the wine and poured two goblets nigh to brimming as she, in wifely duty, ladled the bouillabaisse into their bowls. They ate in silence for a while, each mulling over separate predicaments. The idea of going to bed with Beau as his wife would have been the culmination of past dreams, yet Cerynise knew she could not in all wisdom take such a risk, perhaps getting with child and then being cast aside like something worthless.

Beau, on the other hand, was fully cognizant of the commitments that he'd have to make to claim Cerynise's virginity. His bride had come back into his life only a few days ago. After so short a period together, how could he dare make judgments that would bind him to her for a lifetime? He had to have time to get to know her! And she, him! And if he took her under her conditions, then he'd definitely be saying farewell to sailing, and that idea was not particularly to his liking.

Cerynise was anxious to hear about Charleston, and though Beau hadn't been there in some months, his news of home and acquaintances was far fresher than hers. "Do you remember Mr. Downs, how he used to come to the schoolhouse and fuss about the boys racing through his garden after they left class? Do you suppose he's still living?"

"Aye. Now his grandchildren are trampling it underfoot." Beau chuckled. "But the old man is infinitely more tolerant of them."

"I always thought he was a cantankerous old man, but I don't imagine that was really true. In fact, I'd probably be just as angry if someone destroyed what I'd worked so hard to create. I'd like to see Mr. Downs, if only for the memories I have of home and my father's school."

"Perhaps we could take a drive out there in my carriage after we reach Charleston," Beau suggested.

A soft smile accompanied her answer. "I'd like that, Beau. I have many memories of you when we were children....Well, actually when I was a child and you a growing youth eight years older."

"You'll certainly bedazzle all of your old neighbors. They're probably still thinking of you as that spindly little girl with enormous eyes and braided pigtails."

Cerynise giggled. "Please, Beau, don't remind me how horrible I looked then."

"You err, madam, if you remember yourself as being homely. You couldn't have been when you now look like a graceful swan."

"Please!" she begged again through her laughter. "You'll feed my vanity with such wonderful flattery."

He gave her a crooked smile as he refilled her goblet. "Do you think I lie?"

"I know you're not a liar, Beau. I remember too well the many times you'd admit the truth to my father even though it might have meant harsh discipline. I can only think that that kind of honesty has carried over into your maturity.

182

My father was so desperate to keep you from killing yourself on that stallion you used to ride. If you didn't finish your lessons, he usually took that opportunity to make you stay after school, just so he wouldn't have to worry about you getting on that animal."

"My father finally had to put ol' Sawney down after he went blind. I'm sure it was from all of those thorn trees he was inclined to take me through. At times, he just got it in his head that he didn't want to be ridden and would try to get rid of me any way he could."

"Oh, I can remember one of those times very distinctly, and listening to you only affirms the fact that my father had cause to worry."

"Aye, he did, but I was determined to master that ol' brute. In the process, I nearly killed myself."

"I'm glad you didn't," she murmured.

Her soft gaze and warm smile were what a man could dream of in a lonely port far away and yearn for through months on end. How could he take her truly to wife and then be able to leave her?

At the conclusion of the meal, Beau pulled out a pair of trousers, the kind that he usually wore when he worked. Unfastening the more costly ones that presently clothed him, he cast a glance toward Cerynise as he warned, "You might want to turn away if you have any reservations about watching a man change his clothes. I need to go back on deck, and I'm sure as hell not going to run to another cabin every time I lower my pants. My men would

183

certainly think that odd, considering our newly wedded state."

Cerynise coolly presented her back. "Have you become angry with me again because I rejected your proposal of intimacy? Or do you usually snarl at all the women you marry?"

Beau laughed shortly. Having already come firmly to the awareness that being within close proximity of his wife aroused every mating instinct he was capable of feeling, he was not in the best of moods. When he saw no hope of her yielding to anything else he had in mind, how could he even think of being gracious. "If you're going to be my wife even for a few weeks, my dear, you're going to have to get used to my cursing, if that's what you mean. Sailors are prone to say what's on their minds without giving thought of a woman being within earshot."

"So, are you going to instruct me in your seaman's vernacular?" In the lengthy silence that followed, her teeth tugged nervously at her bottom lip as Cerynise awaited his reaction to her gentle goading. She had challenged him often as a child; how could she stop now?

Beau slowly perused the stiffly erect form of his young wife as he stripped off his shirt and trousers. Of course, she had no concept of the pain it caused him to curb his male instincts and refrain from seeking appeasement with her. Nor did he have any idea if telling her the truth would help his circumstances, but he was not above trying. "What I'd really like to do, my dear, is to instruct you in something far more pleasurable. Since you're not in favor, you can expect me to be a little on edge when I'm around you. A man can hardly look at a beautiful woman without imagining her naked in his arms. In your case, I need not wonder. It has dwelt on my mind since your first night here in my cabin."

"When you bathed me, you mean?" she prodded.

Beau nearly dropped his jaw in surprise. She was carefully keeping her gaze fastened on the far wall, he supposed, but he sensed that she was just itching to savor his shocked expression. "How did you know?"

"I saw a long hair on your tub which looked very much like mine."

Beau buttoned his trousers as he approached her. "I had to do something, Cerynise. You were chilled all the way through, and I didn't want you to catch your death. In recent years I've seen a man succumb to the frigid weather after he tried to return to our ship from shore leave. You were so cold, I was afraid you wouldn't make it through."

"Is it safe to turn around now?"

"Aye."

Deliberately Cerynise faced him and immediately felt heat flooding upward from her neck to the crown of her head. He was naked from the waist up, and the sight of those wide square shoulders and the hard muscular chest narrowing to a taut waist made her breath wane in awe.

"You're n-not dressed," she stuttered in confusion, discomfited by the sight of such manly grace and beauty.

Noticing the scarlet blush imbuing her cheeks, Beau settled a curious stare upon her as he approached. "Haven't you ever seen a man without a shirt before?"

"Perhaps when I was a child, but only my father." She focused her gaze elsewhere. "Beyond that, I can't remember."

"Look at me, Cerynise." When she refused, Beau caught her hand and clasped it to his chest, holding it firmly there against her efforts to draw away. "You see? I'm flesh and blood. Nothing to be ashamed of."

Her eyes lifted hesitantly, meeting those of indigo blue. They seemed to burn with a fire of their own, fanning a flaming heat deep within her. "My encounters with half-naked men are a rarity I cannot deny." She passed her gaze shyly over the muscular expanse. "But if I were to guess, I would say that you come close to being perfect."

Beau chuckled softly. "Eh, now? Look who's giving pretty compliments."

" 'Tis true," she sighed, her mouth quivering upward in a tentative smile.

He moved her hand upward near his heart, over a male nipple, slowly across his chest and then downward to the top of his trousers, all the while watching her eyes growing increasingly limpid with what he could only imagine was desire. He stepped near enough to touch her with that bare expanse and tilted his head aslant as he slowly lowered his lips towards hers. He saw her mouth part to welcome his. It was all the excuse he needed. Suddenly she was in his arms, and he was crushing her hard against him. He explored her mouth with heady delight, his kisses attesting to his ravenous greed. Behind her back, his fingers began to pluck apart the fasteners, deftly loosening the placket of her gown down to her hips until he was able to sweep it forward over her shoulders and arms. The garment slid past her petticoat with a gentle swishing rustle as he drew away to indulge his gaze. Her diaphanous-clad bosom rose tautly above her corset, awakening a memory of when he had hurriedly stripped away her wet clothing. At the time, he had been far too anxious about her condition to indulge his manly appreciation for her feminine form. It was only later, after he had become confident that she would revive, that his memory had taunted him with visions of the soaked chemise clinging to her round breasts and lithe form, whetting his hunger no small degree. It was no different now.

Beau smiled down into those darkly translucent orbs that eyed him almost warily, conveying her timidity and uncertainty. Beneath his lengthy stare, she made an effort to cover her breasts, causing him to shake his head.

"Let me look at you," he urged softly, gathering her hands into his. He brushed fleeting kisses upward from her wrist to a fair shoulder, drawing soft, wavering sighs from her lips. His own traced her silken skin in a slow descent until they reached the tantalizing fullness pressed brazenly above the lace of her camisole. He saw her eyelids flutter as he caressed the swelling mounds with warm kisses, coming nigh to the clothed peaks but prudently avoiding them for the moment. His playful dallying reversed itself, sliding upward along her throat. Then he straightened to his full height and, watching her face carefully, lowered his mouth toward hers. He saw no sign of resistance in the offing. His tongue coyly teased hers until she joined the playful merging, awakening his delight as she flicked her own shyly across his mouth. His kisses grew more dedicated to strengthening her response, delving deeply, drawing her tongue inward, and nearly devouring her lips in a tantalizing frenzy as his mouth covered hers.

Cerynise felt as if her whole being would melt, but her heart began to drum a faster rhythm as he pulled back to allow his fingers to leisurely stroke along the top of her chemise, working the undergarment downward provocatively until the uppermost part of a delicate pink sphere peeked up at him above the lace. Fascinated by its softness, he rubbed the silken texture gently with a fingertip, causing the beat of her heart to race in quickening excitement as his stroking caresses began to move infinitesimally lower. A sharp catch in Cerynise's breath accompanied the moment the tiny nodule thrust into view, for his thumb was instantly there, gently brushing across it and then moving around the pink flesh that encircled it.

The gratification Beau felt for having come so far without being halted brought an accompanying sigh from his own lips. His head dipped downward, and her breath was snatched inward in a sudden gasp of surprise as his open mouth claimed her nipple. A flaming fire began languidly stroking across the pliant crest, awakening an insatiable hunger deep within her, until a muted moan was wrenched from her lips. Her head fell back in ecstasy as she yielded herself completely to the sensual delight that he awakened within her. Vaguely she was aware of her corset being loosened behind her back, and then her petticoat accompanying its descent to the floor.

Her hair was plucked free and fell in shimmering waves over her shoulders. His hand followed its silky, cascading length down her back until it reached her pantalettes. It slipped inside, moving over her naked buttocks, stroking the delectable fullness until Cerynise felt driven to press herself tightly to the hardness beneath his trousers. Then, of a sudden, she was being lifted up into his arms. In three long strides, Beau was at his bunk, laying her upon it, and jerking down the covers beneath her. He swept the last of her clothing from her, and then stood back to doff his trousers, making no effort to turn away. Cerynise's eyes widened at his bold manly display, but in the next moment he was pressing alongside, kissing her face, her breasts, and nibbling at her waist and hips.

"I want you," he murmured huskily, sliding

his hand downward over her body and then sweeping it upward again between her thighs. Cerynise started in surprise at his intrusion and tried to roll away, but with soothing words and sultry kisses he cajoled her to relax until she opened herself to him. He was infinitely gentle as he searched her womanly softness, and before long her senses were reeling in ecstasy. Strange fires were lit and began to flare upward from her loins, making her writhe as the sweeping sensations began to course through her body.

Cerynise felt driven to roll on her side and face him. Soon their lips and tongues were blended in a wild exchange of fevered kisses. Fairly besotted by them, she pressed close to his muscular form and lifted a slender thigh over his hip. The fiery blade pressed forward to caress the moist womanly softness until the slow, teasing strokes along the outer fringes evoked sensations that caused them both to gasp in sensual delight. Awakened to an unbridled brazenness, Cerynise began to caress and kiss her husband's tautly muscled chest. Her fingers fluttered shyly over small hard nipples and around the male breasts. In the next moment Beau was catching her hand and moving it downward over his chest until he closed it around the hard shaft, drawing a startled gasp from her. He murmured near her ear as he caressed her face with kisses, and she timidly complied with his instructions until she was snatching his breath. The thrill of pleasing him augmented her nerve, and she became bolder, appeasing her own curiosity while driving him to heights that Beau had never known were possible to obtain before entry. Perhaps there was something to be said after all about making love to a wife instead of a well-versed woman of the world.

An urgent knock sounded on the door, drawing a startled gasp from Cerynise and a sharp groan from Beau. He passed a hand across his brow, silently cursing the one who had been callous enough to intrude upon them at this most untimely moment.

"What do you want?" he snarled, rising up on an elbow and casting a glare toward the portal.

"Sorry, Cap'n," Billy Todd called contritely through the barrier. "Mr. Oaks sent me down ta tell ye there be a man from the magistrate's office what's come aboard ta see yer papers an' check yer shippin' dates. He says till ye've settled yer dispute with Mr. Winthrop, he an' his men'll be keepin' a close eye on the *Audacious* ta make sure ye don't try ta skedaddle."

Beau was sure he could have committed mayhem upon Alistair Winthrop right then and there if the man had been within reach. "I'll bring the papers up in a moment."

Cerynise drew the sheet up to cover herself as Beau heaved a laborious sigh and swung his long legs over the side of the bunk. He sat there in deep frustration with an elbow braced on a knee and his forehead propped against his hand. He couldn't believe that he had come so far to be forestalled at the very threshold of pleasure.

Turning on the bed to face Cerynise, he kissed her with undiminished passion. "Wait for me here," he whispered against her lips and then smiled down into her eyes. "I'll come back as soon as I can."

Cerynise searched his face, not knowing what to say. The knock on the door had done more than startle her. It had awakened her to the realization of what she had nearly given him. He had, after all, made no pledge for the future, and although they were married now, he would undoubtedly want his freedom upon their arrival home. And if he asked for it, she entertained no doubt that she'd give it to him, for she would never dream of holding him against his will, no matter how deeply she might be hurt.

Better to keep him at arm's length, prudence whispered. *Then you needn't worry that he'll leave you with child.*

Cerynise felt rather brazen watching her new husband dress, but if there was nothing more to be gained from their marriage than these small, intimate moments, then she would reap as many as she could before she closed the door in his face. That was coming soon enough.

CHAPTER 6

"What do you mean, you're not going to bed with me?" Beau railed at his young wife. "You were there just a little while ago. So what has changed since I went on deck?"

Cerynise had winced at each word he had shouted and couldn't help but tremble before his glowering stare. She had anticipated his rage when she stated her position, but she hadn't imagined that it would come in such thunderous tones. "Will you please lower your voice, Beau," she begged. "You'll have the whole ship knowing our business."

In a vivid display of temper, Beau snarled and sent his log sailing across the cabin. It hit the corner of the locker, sending sheaves of papers flying helter-skelter before it plummeted to the floor. "I don't give a damn if the whole world hears us, madam. All I want to know is what happened to make you change your mind while I was up on deck talking to that dolt of a constable!"

"If you'll lower your voice, I'll tell you," Cerynise quietly assured him. "But if you continue shouting at me, I'll leave this ship and let you sail to the Carolinas without me."

Beau snorted cantankerously and stalked to his locker, where he knelt and began gathering up his receipts and documents. When he had left the cabin some moments earlier, he had felt as if his entrails were being drawn out through his belly, so caught up in the heat of passion had he been. To say that he was now acutely disappointed with his wife's declaration would have vastly understated his distress.

"I know that you don't really wish to be married, Beau," Cerynise began nervously and abruptly quailed at the glare he tossed at her over his shoulder. Gathering her courage, she forced herself to continue, but now there was definitely a shakiness in her voice that she could not subdue. "If I allowed you to have your way with me and, as a result, got with child, your freedom would be jeopardized. I don't ever want you to feel as if you're tied to me simply because you may be pressed to do the right thing by your offspring. Therefore, if you're still willing to take me to Charleston, I believe it would be better for us both if there was some distance between us. If I could have another cabin..."

Beau had the greatest desire to throw his log again in roweling frustration, this time to the opposite side of his cabin, but he restrained the urge to vent his wrath upon the already battered book. Instead, he unleashed it upon his winsome bride. "Damnation, woman! Didn't I tell you before there's not one left in this whole ship that isn't stored neck-deep with cargo?"

Cerynise wrung her hands, knowing she wouldn't be able to resist him if he plied her again with his persuasive wooing. He could steal her will away with no more than a soft, nuzzling kiss. "I'll need only enough space on the floor to spread a blanket and a place to wash and dress."

Beau mumbled a foul curse, and then, without saying a word, he marched to the cabin door, yanked it open and roared through the passageway, "Oaks!"

From there, he went to his desk and slammed the log down flat on top of it. His eyes seething with fury, he gave her a withering glare that clearly conveyed his rampant disgust with the situation in which he found himself. Then he began to pace about with fists tightly clenched, his wrists folded one over the other behind his back as he awaited his second-in-command.

Cerynise watched him warily. In the nine years he had been on his own, Beau Birmingham had changed in ways she was just beginning to fully comprehend. Only the superficial traces of the boy whom she had remembered so well now remained. He was a more determined man than she might have once imagined he would become, one who had only to glance at her to make her keenly aware of his ire. He had grown accustomed to his authority and to issuing orders that were readily obeyed. By agreeing to marry him, she had entered an area under his control. As her husband, he had an absolute right to keep her ensconced in his cabin and make love to her if he so desired. Except that she had balked, and now he was having to deal with something that closely resembled mutiny in the ranks.

Footsteps swiftly descending the companionway brought their attention to bear upon the open portal, where a brief moment later the panting first mate appeared.

"You bellowed, Captain?" Stephen Oaks asked with a jocular grin.

"Aye!" Beau answered caustically. "Set some hands to removing the cargo from the cabin next door."

Oaks seemed suddenly dumbfounded. "Where shall I put it, sir?"

"Anywhere!" Beau growled, throwing up a hand in a gesture of impatience and irritation. "Preferably in the other cabins if there's room."

Stephen Oaks was still perplexed as he inclined his head toward the accommodations next door. "What do you want done with this one once it's cleaned out?"

"Outfit it for my lady's comfort...."

"Your lady...?" Oaks's jaw sagged as he glanced from one to the other in confusion. "You mean...your...your wife, sir?"

"Is there *another* lady on board?" Beau questioned sardonically, settling his fists on his narrow hips. *"Of course, I mean my wife!"*

Oaks was sure his hearing would never be the same. "But I...I thought—"

"Don't think, dammit! Just do as you're told!"

"Aye, Captain." Looking extremely nervous and befuddled, the mate stumbled from the cabin with admirable speed, managing enough presence of mind to close the door gently behind him.

Cerynise almost felt sorry for the man, except that she was far more worried about herself and what might be forthcoming from her husband. She waited in trepidation as Beau pivoted about and stalked to the gallery windows, as if he couldn't bear to look upon her another moment. Gazing out upon the river, he clamped his hands behind him again and stood with his long, darkly garbed legs splayed in a rigid stance, his polished boots planted firmly apart as Cerynise quietly began packing her belongings for her move to another cabin. She started as Beau's voice broke the silence.

"You can't tell me you didn't enjoy it, too," he challenged without turning. "You would have let me make love to you if not for the intrusion."

Cerynise knew only too well that he was right, but she held her tongue, seeing no advantage in discussing how completely she had been swept away by his ardor.

"What didn't you like about it?" Beau continued stoically. "Were you averse to touching me?"

Cerynise opened her mouth to deny the possibility and then clamped it closed, realizing she would only be giving him incentive to press for her submission if she let him know how thoroughly she had enjoyed caressing him.

"You refuse to say anything about what happened between us?" he rumbled.

"I dare not," she meekly replied, facing his stalwart back. "I can only say that I found no displeasure in what we did together. It was quite delightful, in fact, but we both know the consequences I would eventually reap by allowing you to have your way with me. Until

I'm certain there is no doubt in your mind about wanting me as your wife, not only now but in the years to come, then 'tis best I withhold myself from you until our marriage is annulled."

"So, you lay your trap for me like all the other women who wheedle men into marriage," Beau accused snidely. "You give me a little tidbit to savor and thereafter dangle the sweetmeat on a string before me until I am besieged with anguish and finally consent to yield you everything you want if you would but give me what I seek in return."

Cerynise could feel her temper rising at his callous conclusion. "Sir, may I remind you that marriage was your solution to leaving London with me *and* your ship." She glowered as he faced her and continued on, her temper undiminished. "A titular arrangement was *your* idea, sir, but now you whine and bemoan the fact that I hold you to your proposal. Don't give me any of your sniveling excuses about how difficult it may be for a man to be around a woman. That's the price you'll have to pay for wanting to return to your bachelor status once we reach Charleston! I haven't asked you for anything more than what you've already given, and I urge you to be gentleman enough to do the same."

With one last scowling glance, she strode to the door, yanked it open and made her departure in a decided huff.

"Dammit, Cerynise, come back here!"

Ignoring his gruff command, she seized her skirts and fairly flew along the corridor and up the stairs. She could hear his rumbling curses and his running footfalls in hot pursuit, but they only served to put wings to her feet.

She was breathless and flushed by the time she neared the last step. One glimpse at her gained the curious attention of nearly everybody within close proximity of the companionway, but what Cerynise hadn't expected was a pair of young, stylishly garbed gentlemen who were just crossing in front of the stairs as she bolted to the deck. Their resulting collision caused her to reel haphazardly, prompting one of the gallants to gasp and grab her arm in an attempt to halt her fall. At once, the man found his own wrist seized in a steely grasp.

"Take your hands off my wife!" Beau commanded, having leapt up the stairs three at a time in his haste to catch her. The jealous rage he had felt at seeing another man touch his wife nearly caused him to launch a fist into that one's face.

"Your pardon, sir," the gentleman apologized hurriedly as he loosened his grip on the lady and stepped back. "She seemed in danger of falling. Otherwise, I would never have been so bold."

Mollified, Beau bestowed a stiff smile upon the man. It was the best he could manage at the moment, for he was still enraged with Cerynise for having fled. He caught her hand, and because he promptly sensed from the icy look she tossed him that she was determined to reclaim her freedom, he tucked the captured hand out of sight behind his back, where he held it firmly. Directing his gaze toward the man, Beau finally managed a verbal response. "I'm sure my wife is grateful for your assistance, sir. Thank you, gentlemen. Now, if you will excuse us, we were discussing a matter of grave importance...."

"Are you the captain?" the second gentleman asked, seeming suddenly hopeful.

Beau gave the man a stilted nod. "Yes."

The two strangers exchanged relieved smiles before the second one spoke again. "Your mate said you were indisposed, Captain, but we've traveled some distance to discuss a matter which should be of great interest to you. We have in our possession some rare artifacts which a merchant, who knows you, said might intrigue you since you're a collector of beautiful art."

"Just what are these rare artifacts?"

"Paintings, sir," the first gentleman answered. "We've brought one with us so you can see the quality we're talking about. Might you be interested in looking at it, sir?"

Beau could have chosen a better time than the present to give his attention to what they had brought, especially since Cerynise was still trying to get free of him, albeit surreptitiously, but he gave his consent, tenaciously hanging on to the slender wrist. In a moment the second gentleman, who had hastened to leave the ship, came back carrying a framed canvas wrapped in a soft cloth.

"Wait until you see this, Captain," the first one said with a buoyant smile as he glanced at Beau. He awaited the unwrapping of the piece with close attention and then, as his companion turned the painting toward the captain, he swept his hand in a flamboyant flourish before it. "Have you ever seen anything so magnificent, sir?"

Cerynise gasped, recognizing one of her own paintings. It was a scene of a woman carrying a child and a basket of food to her working husband, who was holding his arms out to take the curly-headed youngster. Seeing it again under such circumstances, Cerynise had the greatest desire to laugh. Although the two men were oblivious to the compliment they had given her by claiming it was a rare artifact of highest quality, she squelched her amusement and leaned near Beau to murmur. "Dearest," she cooed for the benefit of the two, "could I speak with you in private for just a moment, if you wouldn't mind?"

Beau was confused by her endearment, but he made their excuses. In presenting his back to the men, he was forced to free his wife's hand but he was instantly gratified when she slipped it demurely into the bend of his arm. After moving away a significant space to where they could talk privately, he faced her. "What is it, Cerynise?"

"Beau, I really think those men are trying to dupe you."

He frowned in bemusement. "What makes you say that? The painting is very fine. It has a quality about it that I rarely see...such as the masters have painted in the past."

Cerynise beamed brightly as she gazed up into his face. "Thank you."

The truth struck Beau, but his amazement was swiftly compounded by his admiration of the piece. "You painted *that?*"

She responded with an eager nod. "Aye, and it sold for nearly five thousand pounds."

"I never dreamed you could paint that well," Beau admitted, feeling in great awe of her talent. He slashed his hand as if to negate his statement. "What I mean is that after you told me what your paintings usually sold for, I was expecting something far more commendable than my first notions of your ability, but I *never* expected talent worthy of a Rembrandt."

"Oh, Beau, what a lovely compliment." She smiled gently and lightly caressed his hand, all thoughts of anger expelled from her mind and spirit. "That's the nicest compliment I've ever, *ever* had."

" 'Tis simple truth, my dear girl."

Cerynise coyly played with a button on his shirt, causing his heart to lurch rather strangely in his chest. "Then you'll tell those two you're onto their schemes and that they'd better fly before you throw them overboard like you threatened to do with Alistair?"

Beau raised a hand invitingly toward the companionway. "Why don't you await me in my cabin, my dear? I don't wish you to hear our discussion. It may well burn your ears."

"Yes, of course," she replied, feeling immensely sorry for the men all of a sudden.

Beau waited until he heard the cabin door close behind her before approaching the two. "Gentlemen, I'm very interested in this painting you've brought and am wondering if you may have others painted by the same artist."

"I fear not, sir. This one was so rare, we feel enormously privileged that it came into our possession by the passing of an uncle. But we have others which are just as valuable."

"I'm not interested in any others. Just this one. How much will you take for it?"

"Seeing as how it's so exceptional, we'll have to have at least twenty thousand pounds for it."

"I'll give you seven, not a farthing more."

The first man was set to dicker. "I don't know, sir...."

Beau started to turn aside, and after a quick exchange of anxiously querying glances between the two, the second hastened to speak. "*However*, Captain, we seem to be in a desperate bind at this time...."

"The painting isn't stolen, is it?" Beau pressed, settling a suspicious gaze upon the men.

"Oh, no, sir! Absolutely not!" the first declared. And then his cheeks darkened in chagrin as he confessed, "Truth be, sir, we've been cast out of our family home after our tailors presented our father a bill for our clothing. He said unless we learned to control our spending, we'll never see a shilling of our inheritance. In the meantime, our tailors are threatening us with dire consequences if we don't pay them. We'll take the seven. It won't be enough to settle our debts, but it will placate our tailors until we manage to sell the other paintings."

"How did you come by this one?"

"My mother recently purchased it, along with others of rare quality. She intended to add them to her collection, but when my father forbade her to give us coin, she gifted us with her paintings instead."

Satisfied that the pair were telling the truth, Beau gave them a clipped nod. "I'll have my mate fetch the money for you and a receipt for you to sign."

The two smiled and waited patiently as Beau moved away to talk to Oaks. "I need you to go down to my cabin and beg admittance from my wife, at least long enough for you to fetch the strongbox and a receipt. If she should ask...which I doubt that she will...tell her some merchants have come aboard to collect what is due them. Count out seven thousand pounds, make the receipt out for that sum, and then return here."

Stephen Oaks had been admiring the painting as his captain gave instructions and couldn't resist an inquiry. "A new acquisition, Captain?" He smiled as he drew Beau's gaze to the painting. " 'Tis a beauty, sir."

"So is the one who painted it."

Oaks looked at him in surprise. "You mean...?"

"My wife," Beau answered, allowing a

spartan smile to curve his lips. "But it's not for her. 'Twill be a Christmas gift for my parents."

"A very nice one, 'twill be, sir."

"Aye, I'm sure of that, but I'd prefer that you not speak of this matter to my wife."

"I'm swore to secrecy, Captain," Oaks declared, clasping a hand to his breast.

"Good, now get along with you."

Stephen had gone only a few paces when he paused and half turned with another question. "Do you still want the men to clear out the cabin near yours, sir?"

His brows gathering in dark gloom, Beau faced away. "Aye, Mr. Oaks. 'Twould seem my wife would like more privacy than my cabin affords."

The mate heaved a sigh, wondering if the lady knew what she was asking of her husband. Or if she had any indication what she would be subjecting the crew to while their captain was so out of sorts. " 'Tis a pity, sir, to be sure."

"Aye, Mr. Oaks, that it is."

Some time later Cerynise entered the small cabin that she had been given and nearly shuddered as she glanced around the gloomy interior. Blank, windowless walls seemed to close in around her from all four sides in the narrow room, which she roughly estimated was less than a quarter of the size of Beau's cabin. The only relief came from the door, but only because she had left it ajar. She had no doubt that with her abnormal dread of being closeted in tiny, cramped spaces she'd suffer exceedingly during the voyage home.

A bunk occupied one end, but it was much smaller than the captain's and, instead of a soft feather comforter, rough woolen blankets had been tucked in around the mattress. She ran a hand musefully over the pillowcases and sheets, smelling their clean but bland odor, and felt an inexplicable melancholy invading the area very near her heart. She quickly blinked away a start of tears and took a deep breath to fortify herself before considering the rest of the meager furnishings. A washstand with pitcher and basin resided beneath a small mirror hanging on the wall. A tiny table and a single chair near the bed would have to suffice for any meals she would partake of in the cabin. Other than that, a battered sea chest, butted up against the wall, left little space for her to move around.

"Is it to your liking, my dear?"

The familiar voice wrenched a start from her, and when she faced Beau in trembling disquiet, she found him standing in the doorway with a shoulder braced against the doorjamb. Her chin lifted in obstinate pride as she contemplated the complacent smile that lightly touched his handsome lips.

" 'Twill do," she replied stiltedly.

He tilted his dark head at a curious angle as his eyes probed the unwavering dark greenish orbs that stared back at him with cool indifference. "Are you sure?"

Cerynise nodded stoically. "I'll have my

privacy and now I won't have to worry about intruding upon yours. Considering all of that, why shouldn't it suffice?"

The wide shoulders lifted briefly in a casual shrug. "Oh, I'm sure it would serve the needs of any other passenger, but I seem to remember from years back that you had a fear of being shut up in anything small and airless. I especially recall when some of my classmates sought to play a prank on you and locked you in that old trunk in your father's barn. When I followed your screams and finally let you out, you were in such a panic you locked your arms around my neck and nearly strangled me before I could get you calmed down."

Every instinct within Cerynise rallied to take offense at the supposition that he had deliberately chosen this cabin for no other purpose than to see her completely miserable. "The Beasley boys were a mean, rowdy bunch, as I remember. They always did take delight in playing on others' fears." She fixed Beau with a coolly querying gaze. "Was that your intent as well, Captain?"

"You said that all you'd need would be a small space to sleep," he reminded her. "Considering the cargo I'm taking back to Charleston, this was the best I could offer you. The other cabins *are* larger, but after making room for you, they're now stacked to the ceiling. This was the *only* cabin I could spare."

"Could or wanted?"

Beau was not above laying out her options. "If you don't like the accommodations, madam, you can give up this nonsense and come back to my cabin. I've told you before I don't normally take passengers aboard my ship. You're the exception, and I'm sure as hell not going to throw my cargo overboard so you can have a cabin that suits your personal requirements."

Cerynise felt her own ire rising at his terseness. "If you think I'm going to crawl back to your cabin, Beau Birmingham, and beg you to let me stay, then you'll be disappointed to know that I'll rot in here before I do."

Beau fleered at her stubborn declaration. "Suit yourself, my dear, but if you should decide differently, my cabin door will always be open to you *even* if you don't beg me to take you in."

Stephen Oaks descended the companionway and, upon espying his captain in the corridor, hurried to join him at the door. When he caught sight of Cerynise standing in the tiny cabin, he swept off his cap and, with a ready smile, inquired, "Would you be liking your baggage carried in now, Mrs. Birmingham?"

"Whenever it's convenient, Mr. Oaks," she said solemnly. "There's no rush."

The mate grinned at her for so long Beau grew perturbed. "Was there anything else you wanted to ask my wife, *Mr. Oaks*?"

"Well, actually there was," the mate replied, ignoring the peevish frown that presently resided on the captain's face. "Seeing as how these quarters are unfit for a lady, I was going to suggest that your wife use my cabin. I'm sure she'll be far more comfortable in mine on the voyage home."

"And where will you bunk?" Beau asked acidly, resenting the man's interference.

"I'll be perfectly happy slinging a hammock with the crew," Stephen answered amiably. "Truth be, I've missed the camaraderie below deck since I've been advanced to my present position."

"That's the price of being first mate," Beau reminded him curtly. "Your authority over them must be maintained. I simply cannot allow it."

"Then I can bunk here in this cabin," Oaks offered, turning a boyish grin upon Cerynise again.

"Your kindness is appreciated, Mr. Oaks," she assured him graciously. "But I couldn't possibly put you out of your own quarters."

The mate sighed as if disappointed. "A pity my cabin will go unused then," he rejoined. "You see, I'm quite resolved on the matter, Mrs. Birmingham, and until we see the port of Charleston, I'll not set foot across the threshold except to remove my belongings...should you have a change of heart, that is. 'Tis entirely up to you whether you use it or not, but it shall be available."

"Damnation!" Beau growled.

Cerynise glanced up at her husband to find a glowering scowl the likes of which might have come nigh to frightening the devil himself. Of a sudden her lips curved upward winsomely in a delightfully triumphant smile, and with an elegant nod, she accepted the mate's offer.

"Well, seeing as how your cabin will go vacant, Mr. Oaks, I can hardly refuse." And then, because her husband folded his arms across his chest in an overt display of agitation, she sweetly praised the mate. " 'Tis rare to find a gentleman gallant enough to give up his own quarters for a lady. If I had my way, your chivalry would serve as a standard for other officers of your rank, but alas, few are inclined to put themselves out on another's behalf."

Beau cleared his throat sharply, knowing full well that his wife was directing her barbs toward him. Even as a child, she had always had a skill for stinging ripostes that, like a whip, could flay a boy's hide. They were both older now, but behind that sweet, beautiful exterior of a genteel woman lurked an impish vixen who was every bit a match for the beast in him.

"My cabin is this way, Mrs. Birmingham," Mr. Oaks readily informed her, sweeping his hand outward.

Upon passing Beau, Cerynise set the spurs firmly by displaying a brightly buoyant smile and evidencing her elation by a little skipping dance. What was left for Beau to do but follow in her wake? He did so mutely, watching her skirts swaying jauntily ahead of him.

Oaks led the procession down the passageway toward the captain's cabin, but prior to reaching it, he paused beside the door that led to his own. Suddenly remembering the cluttered state in which he had left his quarters, he reddened in chagrin and begged, "If you'd give me a few moments to tidy up...."

"By all means," Cerynise responded, reluctantly stepping back in the corridor with Beau.

"If you can tear yourself away from your champion, madam," her husband said broodingly, "I'll take you up on deck, where we can perhaps discuss this matter in some semblance of mutual courtesy." It didn't seem at all likely that she'd yield to any of his demands to return to his cabin for a talk.

The offer sounded far too grudging to suit Cerynise. Deliberately lending the wall her undivided attention, she moved her slender shoulders upward in an abbreviated shrug. "I would be loathed to inconvenience you, sir."

Beau's breath hissed outward in a cynical snort. "I fear you've inconvenienced me more than you can possibly imagine, madam."

"Then I shan't trouble you any further, Captain. I'm perfectly willing to wait here." And then, because she simply could not help herself, she added loftily, "Perhaps Mr. Oaks will be kind enough to escort me on deck later should I find myself inclined to take a breath of fresh air."

Beau leaned a shoulder against the paneled wall buttressing her rigid back and pointedly questioned, "Do you enjoy deliberately provoking me or does it come naturally?"

Cerynise lifted an astonished stare to meet his. "Me? Provoking?" She laughed lightly, banishing the idea with a fluttering sweep of dainty fingers. "I could take lessons from you, Captain, have no doubt."

Focusing her gaze on the far wall again, Cerynise promised herself that she would ignore that tall, powerful figure standing so close beside her. It proved far more difficult than she had imagined. She couldn't breathe without feeling his presence with every heightened sense of womanly perception in her possession. If she allowed herself, she'd yield herself to those provocatively stirring memories that he had created when his large hands had moved boldly over her naked body, rousing sensations that even now sent a hotness gushing into her cheeks. If silence was the only way to quell the turbulent emotions he had unleashed within her, then by heavens, she would never utter another word.

Beau could hardly harness his longing to trace a finger around a dainty ear and the stubborn set of her jaw. The temptation was far too potent for him to pass off lightly. He bent near, indulging himself in her delicate fragrance, and considered the wisdom of using a different tactic. "Did I tell you, Cerynise, how utterly beautiful you are when you're lying all warm with desire in my arms?" he whispered. "You're like a strong wine that has gone to my head, and despite my attempts to subdue such tantalizing visions, I cannot thrust them from my mind. I've never wanted another woman as much as I want you."

Cerynise released a quivering sigh as his words flicked across her senses, awakening her own visions of her hard-muscled, bronze-skinned husband.

"Your breasts are so soft and fair," he breathed, yearning to cup a swelling mound in his hand, "they're like delicate pink rosebuds on a dewy morn, opening up to a rosy aurora of light. Their nectar is as sweet on my tongue as—"

The door across the hall opened without warning, startling them. Oaks looked from one to the other of them in sudden bemusement, sensing their unease. "Is anything wrong?"

"No!" they both denied simultaneously.

"There is nothing—" Cerynise began, hardly able to breathe. Even in the presence of the mate her breasts tingled as she recalled the warm bliss that her husband's mouth had evoked within her.

"We were just talking—" Beau began.

Looking very guilty, they glanced at each other. Oaks cleared his throat and stepped away from the cabin door. "I think you'll find everything you need, Mrs. Birmingham, but if there should be anything..."

"She'll manage," Beau informed him dryly. "You do have duties elsewhere, don't you? Or have I been lax in assigning them?"

"I do indeed have duties, sir," Stephen assured him hastily. "And I'll get about them this very moment." Giving Cerynise another smile, he hurried toward the companionway.

"I really do regret putting him out of his quarters," Cerynise murmured.

"He put himself out," Beau stated bluntly. "I'll send Billy down to help you get settled in your new accommodations."

Cerynise inclined her head stiffly. It seemed they were on opposite ends of the fray again. "That would be appreciated, Captain."

It gave her a measure of security to shut the cabin door quickly behind her. Only then would she be safe from his heady cajoling.

When Billy Todd knocked on Cerynise's door some time later, he bashfully delivered the announcement that her husband desired her presence at dinner later that evening. "He'll be entertainin' some English gentlemen tonight, mum, so's ye're ta dress special for the occasion since he'll be presentin' ye as his wife. An' ye're ta be there afore his guests arrive, 'bout six if'n ye're able."

The delicate chimes of the clock in the captain's cabin were just tolling the sixth hour when Cerynise rapped lightly on the portal. At a call from Beau, she swept inward and found him standing before his shaving stand trying to tie his cravat. He looked extremely handsome in a dark gray double-breasted tailcoat, large-lapeled silver-hued waistcoat, which truly ended at the waist, and slender, thinly striped pale gray trousers that were secured by straps beneath polished ankle-length boots. Her eyes warmly devoured his admirable form until he turned to her in some distress.

"Can you help me straighten this damn thing?" he growled, still struggling with the cravat. As his eyes lit on her, he forgot his exasperation with the neckpiece and slowly lowered his arms to his sides as his eyes skimmed the entire length of her. Her hair was dressed

214

high on her head in an intricately coiled and looped coiffure that staggered his imagination as to the length of time it might have taken her to coif such elegance. She wore a pale pink creation that shimmered like tiny diamonds in the candlelight. The bodice was cut straight across her breasts, displaying an enticing cleavage while molding the ripe fullness divinely. Around her slender neck she wore a stiff, dainty ruff of a translucent fabric sewn with the same beading that bejeweled her gown. No costly necklace could have added such a charming accent to her evening attire. Her wide, gossamer sleeves were gathered in narrow, beaded bands at her wrists, yet they seemed to flow around her like a thin veil. The skirt swayed in undulating waves about her long, shapely limbs, and Beau could only admire the effect. Indeed, he found his tongue far too weighty to express his full appreciation of her unparalleled beauty.

Subjecting herself to his heated gaze, Cerynise floated enticingly near and began to repair his cravat. Beau didn't know what to do with his hands, and although the temptation to spread them over her buttocks was nigh to overpowering, he shoved them into the pockets of his trousers instead, deeming it safer by far to keep them to himself rather than cause another war between them. To be sure, the desire to indulge in a little husbandly familiarity at that particular moment caused him to have definite doubts about his wisdom in ever mentioning the word *annulment*.

"Billy said you're having guests for dinner tonight," Cerynise murmured, rising on tip-toes to search out the front portion of the cravat and sweep it forward over the knot near his neck.

Beau stretched his chin upward, submitting himself completely into her care. "Aye, some of the young gentry of the city. We were hunting the other day, and we bagged some partridge, which Philippe has been keeping on ice for this occasion. I thought they might enjoy his exceptional flare with food. I actually invited them before I realized this would be our wedding night."

"You have acquaintances here in London?" she asked in amazement. "I thought that with the way you sail about the world and flit from port to port, friendships would be hard to foster."

"Aye, 'tis difficult," he admitted, "but I've managed to garner a few."

"I'm surprised that you've managed to socialize at all. You seem far too busy when you're in port to fraternize with the local inhabitants."

Beau cast a gaze down his lean nose at her and promptly became enthralled with the enticing gap which permitted him to see into her gown as she worked on his cravat. It was obvious that she wasn't wearing a corset, for her breasts had a more natural fullness to them that seemed to flow into the shallow top of her camisole. He was sure he had never sur-veyed anything quite so delectable in all of his

216

mature years. His palms itched to caress those creamy orbs, and it took an effort of will to keep his hands where they were. Not wishing to disturb his view, he casually lifted his shoulders before she decided to glance up at him. "What's the sense in working hard, my sweet, if you can't enjoy the benefits?"

Cerynise laughed, warmed by his blandishment and equally approving of his wisdom. "Oh, I agree, sir. Most heartily, in fact."

"My guests are unaware that this is my wedding night, and if you're at all in agreement, my dear, I'd rather let them assume that we've been married for a while, although as young as you are, I doubt they'd believe we've been wed longer than a year or two."

Cerynise lifted her eyes in wonder, sending his own chasing upward to meet her gaze. "And if they ask?"

His dark brows flicked upward in a tiny shrug. "No help for it. We'll have to confess."

"May I be allowed to know your reasoning, sir?"

Beau couldn't resist the urge any longer and slipped his arms carefully around her waist. He felt her stiffen momentarily, and then smiled when she yielded to his embrace without a quarrel. She even relaxed back against his arms. "Because I don't want them to get the impression that you'd marry a man without a lengthy courtship."

"Because I might seem a fickle sort?" she dared.

"*Because* I don't want them to get the idea they can steal you away from me," he corrected with a rankled sigh. "I've heard them boasting of some of their conquests, and I don't want them to think you're susceptible."

"Have you, in turn, boasted of your conquests in their company?" she asked carefully. "If you have, I doubt 'twould shed a good light on our marriage."

"My father taught me long ago 'tis unseemly for a gentleman to talk about such things in the presence of others. Those who do usually are seeking to puff up their own image. I've never felt inclined to do so."

Pleased with his answer, she twined her own arms around his neck and gave him a light peck upon the lips. Then she slipped quickly out of his grasp, leaving him groaning in frustration.

"I think you're an unsympathetic tease, madam, but you'd best be wary," he warned. "I cannot tolerate the torture of holding you one moment and letting you skip out of my grasp in the next. If you play with fire, 'twill eventually burn you."

Cerynise pouted prettily, daring a flirtatious flick of long, silky lashes as she cast him a coy glance. Just because he had said that he would have their marriage annulled once they reached Charleston didn't entirely prevent him from having a change of heart before then. Nor did she feel constrained to dutifully concur with their separation without putting into play some guileful temptations that would perhaps spur him into accepting her as his wife on a permanent basis. Since she had been in love with him for most of her life, she couldn't imagine herself ever desiring another man as her husband. "I don't mean to tease you, Beau, but I do enjoy the idea of being able to kiss you now and then. If that's too much for you to bear, then I'll limit my attentions to nothing more than a gentle pat on the hand."

"Bah!" His frustration came down to the simple matter of being damned if he did and damned if he didn't!

Cerynise squelched a grin as he glared at her playfully. They were on safe ground again, and she could play his wife to her heart's content while his guests were there. Then she would retreat to her lonely bed and spend a wakeful night yearning for his consuming kisses and stirring caresses.

The three gentlemen ranged in age from a score and three to six years more. Their eyes gleamed with delight when Cerynise came into view, but they maintained a respectful reserve after Beau presented her as his wife and, in gallant manner, briefly kissed her hand. Their titles were readily dismissed as they bade Cerynise to call them by their first names, and the group soon entered into a relaxed and amiable conversation.

The partridge was excellent served with a delicate sauce, and after tasting it, the guests begged an introduction to the chef. With unquenchable humor they offered the grinning Philippe outlandish fees if he would but come and cook for them. He waved away their pleas, assuring them that he had much to teach his captain about the French and that it would probably take years before he came to the end of his instructions, seeing as how his pupil was reluctant to learn. His teasing banter was met by hearty laughter, even from the one whom he playfully harassed.

Before the evening was out, all four of the men were chortling and vying for Cerynise's witty repartee on a variety of subjects. Upon making their departure, each of the three gallantly bestowed a kiss upon her fingertips again, albeit under the watchful eyes of her husband, and happily waved farewell, assuring the couple that it had been a delightful evening.

Soon after their departure, Beau became lost in thought, so much so that Cerynise dared to ask him, "Are you still angry with me?"

He heaved a sigh and leaned back in the chair behind his desk. "I expect Alistair will be coming back to the ship tomorrow, possibly with the magistrate."

Cerynise traced a finger around the cover of the pewter inkwell residing on the massive desk. "You said our marriage would supersede any claim Alistair might present as my legal guardian," she reminded her husband. "Have you changed your mind?"

"If our marriage was one in fact as well as deed, madam, then I'd have no qualms about the strength of it holding up in any court of law. Unfortunately, Alistair will be inclined to question its authenticity and encourage the magistrate to accept it as nothing more than a sham since our vows were spoken right after his visit. And frankly, madam, I don't think you're a very talented liar."

Cerynise became apprehensive. "You're not suggesting that we consummate our marriage just so we can convince that toad we're married?" Her tone became skeptical. "Come now, Beau...."

"I'm not," he snapped, and then repented of his caustic anger. Reaching across the desk, he took her hand and squeezed it reassuringly. "I'm sorry, I didn't mean to do that. The evening has been so pleasant, I've no desire to see us end it in sour discord."

"What do you think we should do?" she asked contritely, regretting her suspicions. "They can't very well have me subjected to an inquisition—" She gulped at the thought that intruded quickly on the heels of that idea, but she could not bring herself to say it.

Beau read the repugnance in her face and tried to put her at ease. "They wouldn't dare subject you to anything more than an interrogation, but if they have serious doubts about it, they might simply assume the marriage is a farce, have the vows annulled and give you over into Alistair's care."

"*Care* is hardly the word for it," Cerynise replied with a noticeable shiver. "If there was a dungeon in the depths of Lydia's house, I'd have cause to fear. I'm sure Alistair would outfit it with gruesome implements to wring whatever he wants from me. Truly, I cannot believe he has any desire to become my guardian. He wants...or *needs*...something from me that is beyond my ken to understand at present."

"If you can listen for a moment, Cerynise, without getting up in arms about what I may be wanting from you, perhaps we can work this out together and come to a proper solution."

Deciding she needed fortification for what he was going to suggest, Cerynise reached for the goblet of wine she had left on the desk some time earlier, for she seriously doubted that he'd offer anything she could calmly accept, considering he had warned her against jumping to conclusions.

Beau raised a brow as he watched her drain the contents. That simple act alone lent him great insight into her trepidation. The little girl who had adored him from years past had apparently come to fear him...or at least his proposals.

Cerynise promptly hiccuped and pressed her fingertips to her lips in wide-eyed surprise. "Excuse me."

"No more wine for you," Beau chided, moving around to the table and locking away the decanter. He didn't need half his wits to realize she wasn't used to imbibing.

"So you don't think I can lie and make them believe me," Cerynise harped, and flushed with embarrassment as she hiccuped again.

His mouth quirked at the merest thought.

"I think you blush more readily than most people breathe." He sighed heavily. "If your father had anything to do with establishing your values, young lady, I have no doubt that you've had little experience with duplicity. Therefore, you must make use of your strengths."

"And what are they?" She smothered another hiccup and immediately grew fearful that she would have to endure them for a while.

"Innocence, naiveté. Obviously you know little of the world, and perhaps, if the magistrate can recognize a lady when he sees one, he'll be reluctant to think you'd lie about our marriage." Sitting on the edge of his desk, he stretched his long legs out before him and folded his arms across his chest as he peered into her flushed face. "Try not to be too nervous when he starts asking you questions. If you can, let yourself imagine that we've made love together and that you're no longer a virgin."

Cerynise fanned herself, feeling decidedly heated by their discussion. Her hiccups didn't help her discomposure in the least.

"You do know what follows, don't you?" Beau probed, studying her keenly.

She refused to submit herself to his close scrutiny and, with a casual shrug of her shoulders, strolled across to the shaving stand. There she could see his face in the mirror without him being aware of it. "Lydia told me some things years ago."

Beau rolled his eyes in disbelief. "That must have been informative."

"I know that a man and woman must merge to make a child!" she declared, irritated that he thought her such an innocent. "I'm just not aware how it all comes about exactly."

"Would you like to know *exactly*?"

Even as inquisitive as she was about it all, Cerynise didn't think it proper that *he* should be the one to instruct her. " 'Tis unseemly for you—"

"Who else has a better right? I *am* your husband...."

"Not for long, you said...."

"For the time being, I am," Beau pointed out, and watched her closely as he added, "But perhaps Alistair can tutor you when you become his ward."

Cerynise made no effort to hide a convulsive shiver. The revulsion she had felt when Alistair's eyes had passed over her in a prurient leer came back with startling distaste. "What *exactly* do you think I should know?"

Beau enlightened her in great detail, making it as stimulating to her womanly senses as he was capable of doing. Explaining the act of mating to her was nearly as satisfying as kissing her breasts, he thought, but it would never be as thrilling as the real thing. Still, he'd take what he could get.

When Cerynise faced him in rapt attention, Beau knew he had evoked a comparable sensuality in her. He could feel a familiar tightening in his loins and made no effort to either hide or display that fact. It became obvious enough with his slimly tailored trousers, drawing flitting glances from his wife until she raised her eyes to his and saw his smile. Her cheeks flushed scarlet, and in quick response her gaze went chasing off to the far wall.

"I couldn't make love to you without that happening," he explained, for he knew she'd be inclined to think he was making a deliberate overture. "Despite the control I would like to have over my body at times, I cannot prevent my arousal when I think of being intimate with you."

"Don't think," Cerynise flung over her shoulder, mimicking his earlier dictate to Oaks. " 'Tis better for us both if you don't."

"You may see it as unfortunate, madam, but I've been bequeathed with these manly instincts by nature for the purpose of procreation. 'Tis sure there'd be fewer babies in the world if men weren't driven at times by their primitive inclinations."

"Have you informed me of all of this simply for your own pleasure, sir?" she inquired with a hint of sarcasm. "Or did you do so only because you wish me to be thoroughly aware of what the magistrate might ask me? 'Tis apparent that you think I'll be unable to answer the man unrehearsed."

Not wanting to arouse his wife's suspicions more than they were already, Beau carefully avoided her first question. "I just don't want you to blunder into revealing the fact that I wasn't able to consummate our marriage."

Feeling absurdly slighted, Cerynise wished

vainly for some witty retort that would impress him. When none came to mind, she argued her case. "I'm not a bumpkin actress who has to be instructed in her repertoire every hour on the hour so she can speak her lines even moderately well."

Beau eyed her closely. "Then tell me this, if you will, madam. If you have to swear tomorrow that we became man and wife in my bed tonight, can you do it credibly after what I've told you?"

She found it difficult to breathe suddenly, for her whole being felt as if it were aflame. "I...I..."

"Come now, Mrs. Birmingham...*if* that's who you are exactly. You must tell me whether or not you have shared a bed with your alleged husband, because if you cannot swear that your marriage is valid, I'll have no other recourse but to give you over into Mr. Winthrop's care." Beau leaned forward and stared intently into her astounded visage as he continued his authoritative inquiries in a softer tone. "Now answer me truthfully, Mrs. Birmingham, did you and your husband make love together and consummate your marriage?"

Cerynise was speechless for a moment until she finally blurted, "Surely they wouldn't be so forward!"

"For whatever purposes he has planned, Alistair is desperate to have you," Beau averred. "He'll stop at nothing to get his way. The magistrate, however, will hopefully be a bit more delicate. For his benefit, you must be able to say honestly that we spent tonight together." He gave an abortive laugh. "Looking the way you do, you shouldn't have to say anything more than that. The rest will naturally be assumed."

If Beau had thought she blushed a lot before, then he was quickly learning that it was nothing compared to what she had done within the last hour since their guests had left. "I know this isn't easy for you, the idea of sharing a bed with me for the night, but frankly, it's the best solution I can think of for alleviating the problem of you telling a lie. And though I'll be hard-pressed to withhold my attentions, I promise you I won't resort to rape."

Cerynise finally realized the hiccups had fled. No doubt being shocked out of her virginal innocence had squelched that small problem. "If that's the only thing you can suggest, I guess we should try it for a time...but you'll have to keep your trousers on."

Beau smiled. "If you insist."

His young wife heaved a wavering sigh. "In that case I'd better go and get into my night-clothes."

"Nothing too enticing, I hope," he teased.

"You needn't worry. I'm well aware of just how fast your trousers come off, sir."

A moment of silence passed between them as each of them entertained memories of what had happened earlier in the day.

"Feeling more relaxed?" Beau finally asked.

Deciding it wouldn't be wise of her to mention that her knees seemed to have melted,

Cerynise gave him a careful nod. "Yes, thank you."

Their polite conversation didn't make it any easier when the time came to go to bed, nor did Beau's deliberate tarrying at his desk to straighten out his log and all the receipts and documents that had been thrown chaotically about. Cerynise was still wide awake when he doffed everything but his pants and stretched out beside her in his bunk. For a long time they both stared at the ceiling of the cubicle, each unable to ignore the presence of the other. Finally Cerynise curled on her side away from him, but with his weight depressing the mattress on the outer side, it became a struggle to keep her distance. She was just beginning to relax when she felt his large body against her back. She tried to wiggle closer to the wall but found the tail of her nightgown imprisoned beneath him.

"I always thought this was a fair-sized bunk," Beau commented as he levered himself up slightly to give Cerynise a chance to reclaim the hem of her garment. She scooted over to the wall, but it did little good on an incline. She was soon back where she had started, and much to her chagrin, seemed ever destined to return.

"I could sleep on the floor," she volunteered.

"Absolutely not. If I have to do something chivalrous, I might as well do it up royally."

"Well, then, you could—"

"I said chivalrous, not saintly," Beau

retorted, having no doubt that he'd resort to rape before committing himself to the floor.

Cerynise tried to curb her giggles, but they soon raised Beau's brows to a curious level. "What's so funny?"

"Oh, nothing."

"Tell me," he urged.

He was too close, too compelling. Her stomach did a slow, leisurely roll as she realized just how very hard it was for her to thrust him out of her thoughts for longer than a moment. Lying back upon the bed, she cast a glance askance at the broad expanse of his chest, wishing fervently that she could touch him again in ways that would make him gasp. "Earlier today I was thinking of you as a knight in shining armor. It struck me as funny, that's all."

Beau looked appalled. "A knight in shining armor?"

"Only for a moment, but it was pure fantasy. I couldn't even get you to kiss my hand, and we both know you've done much more...."

"You couldn't *what*?"

"In my imagination," Cerynise explained hastily, and then waved a slender hand to hopefully dismiss the discussion. "It doesn't matter. The idea was absurd anyway. Why don't we try to get some sleep?" *As if that was remotely possible.*

"I'm not sure I like that."

"What?"

"Not kissing your hand."

He was right about her being an innocent.

It actually took her a moment to recognize where she had neatly led herself. Cerynise almost panicked, having already become aware of the fact that with his charmingly winsome cajolery, he could wheedle his way into a girl's pantaloons with very little effort. "Beau, don't...."

Too late!

Turning her palm upward, he kissed it in a slow caressing way that made her suck in her breath. By the time he raised his head again, the bunk had narrowed alarmingly.

"I don't think you should have done that," Cerynise whispered, already feeling the molten heat flowing into her loins.

Beau's expression was grim. "Neither do I." Without another word, he fled the bunk, grabbed a blanket from one of the lockers, and returned to the chair at his desk. Cerynise remained where she was. Long moments passed before she had to accept the fact that he did not intend to touch her again. She should have been relieved. Instead, there bloomed a hungry ache deep within her womanly being that yearned to be filled and assuaged.

CHAPTER 7

There was something very intriguing about waking up with a soft, womanly form curled in the curve of one's body, Beau mused sleepily as he became aware of the very first light of a new day casting its glow through the stern windows. The whole bunk was bathed with a strangely bright, reddish gold aura that gilded everything it touched, making the tawny tresses upon which he lay shine as if with a luster of their own. His wife's long hair had tumbled across his pillow, and its delicate scent lured him to rub his cheek against the soft curls. But that was not the only enticement he was aware of. His thighs were tucked beneath her trim buttocks, and had he been without his trousers, he might have more fully appreciated the fact that her nightgown had wandered up nigh to her hip, leaving him a view that was breathtaking. His quickening pulse warned him that if he didn't soon leave her side, he'd be remiss in his promise to her, because he was definitely thinking of waking her with soft, tantalizing caresses.

Carefully he eased away from her and crept across to his shaving stand, where he splashed cold water over his face. What he needed was a frigid plunge into the river to wrench his mind away from what he was leaving behind in his bunk. In fact, there would just be time enough to indulge himself in a more humane bath in the first mate's temporary quarters before his crew started stirring. He tossed a glance over his shoulder as he stepped toward the door, then promptly halted, feeling as if he had been hit in the gut. She was still lying in innocent repose upon her side, but the sight of her unclad backside was almost as compelling to his manly senses as a smiling invitation from her lips. He just couldn't leave her like that when the mate might walk in, unaware of her presence.

Returning quietly to his bunk, he reached across to the far side of the bunk and, lifting the sheet carefully, spread it over her. He stood staring down at her for a long moment, feeling his vitals twisting in knots in his belly as his eyes caressed her delicate features resting in profile against the pillow. For the life of him, he couldn't resist stroking the backs of his fingers over the wisps of hair curling softly at her temples. A fluttering sigh wafted from her lips, and still deep in slumber, she rolled upon her back, flinging an arm wide across his pillow. It seemed only a momentary lapse of time before her hand started searching for him, and then her eyes flew open and found him leaning over her. Instead of fear sweeping her visage, a smile as sweet as the breaking dawn curved her lips and illumined her eyes.

"Good morning," she murmured sleepily.

"Good morning, my sweet. I trust you slept well."

"Amazingly well...*after* you finally came to bed."

He cocked a brow in surprise. "Madam?"

Giggling, Cerynise shook her head, refusing to answer the question that was implied rather than spoken. Turning on her side away from him, she curled in a knot, muttering something like "Never mind" behind the hand with which she scratched her nose.

"You're not having second thoughts, are

you?" he inquired hopefully, bracing a hand on her hip as he leaned over her to peruse her profile again.

"Only if you are," she whispered, biting her bottom lip to keep it from curving upward in a grin. The fact that she was inviting him to accept the lengthy position of being her husband was subtle, but he was keenly astute and had no need of further explanations.

"Oh."

The single syllable sounded much like a note of dejection, Cerynise thought, abruptly losing her elation. She blinked away a start of tears and, to hide her disappointment, made much of rubbing her nose into her pillow as if it itched. Finally, after clearing her throat and trying to swallow the lump in it, she cast a glance askance to find that he hadn't moved.

"Would you mind turning your head long enough for me to get out of bed and put on my robe?"

The lilting buoyancy had gone out of her voice, causing Beau to suffer feelings of regret. Although he was intensely aware of just how much he wanted to make love to her, there was still that rational side of him that refused to be herded into a long enduring situation without allowing himself enough time to think everything through very carefully. He knew her from years back, but with their lengthy separation, he could not swear that he wanted to spend the rest of his life with her without first becoming acquainted with the woman she had become.

Stepping away from the bunk, he presented his back to her and waited. In the next instant he heard her bare feet padding swiftly toward the door and whirled to see her fleeing through the open portal. A brief moment later he heard the mate's door slam loudly in the silence.

Gnashing out a curse through gritted teeth, Beau flung his own door closed, ending the pleasantry of the morning.

Beau wasn't overly impressed with the magistrate who was ushered aboard by Alistair Winthrop and Howard Rudd. The judge was a stout, florid-faced individual who seemed pompously aware of his own importance, and it was evident from the amount of bowing and scraping the two unworthies did in his presence that they were vying for his favor. Indeed, they seemed confident of it as they bade Beau to call Cerynise up to the deck.

"You will see, Your Honor, that this Yankee has taken advantage of an innocent young woman and enticed her to forget her proper upbringing," Alistair assured the judge from as near as his elbow. "Having been ensconced on his ship for some days now, one must wonder what she has already given over to the rascal."

Mr. Oaks had been summoned to fetch the lady, and when she arrived, the deck grew hushed as the sailors halted their labor to watch what promised to be an exciting confrontation. Confident grins were worn by those wagering that their captain could handle the judge as well as the two pipsqueaks who were with him.

Cerynise moved with elegant grace across the deck and arrived at her husband's side before facing the three. The fact that Beau's steadying arm came around her helped to buttress her for the task ahead.

"You see!" Alistair declared, thrusting a finger toward the couple. "This blackguard even has the effrontery to handle the girl in your presence. I told you he was a lecherous scoundrel!"

"Yes, I see," the magistrate mused aloud, flicking his bushy brows upward. The girl was delectable enough to tempt the most staid gentleman, so it was understandable that she would arouse the attentions of a lusty, seafaring man. "Perhaps the lady and I should be introduced...."

Alistair stepped forward to do the honors. "Miss Cerynise Kend—"

"Excuse me," Beau interrupted curtly, "but I think I'd better make the introductions, since this is my ship."

The thin man sneered, unable to see what difference that made, but he bowed mockingly, permitting the captain to perform the services.

"Cerynise, this is the Right Honorable Judge Blakely," Beau said, and as she dipped into a polite curtsy, he swept his hand toward her, "Your Honor, this is my wife, Mrs. Birming—"

"What?" Alistair croaked in outrage.

A twitter of amusement ran through the crew, and elbows were prodded as the men waited to see what would follow.

"This is my wife, Mrs. Birmingham," Beau repeated for the benefit of the magistrate.

The cords in Alistair's neck became visibly distended as he stretched it far out of his collar and railed, "He's lying!"

The official looked perplexed. "But I thought she was—"

"This is too much!" Alistair flared, this time rising on tiptoes to shake a fist threateningly beneath the captain's nose. "Just who the hell are you trying to dupe?"

Beau calmly reached into his coat and removed a folded parchment which he handed over to Judge Blakely. "I'm sure you'll find everything in order, sir."

"This is a recent marriage," Blakely stated, studying the document and paying particular attention to the signatures. Then he peered up at his host with blatant suspicion. "Are there any witnesses?"

"Every man of my crew, sir."

"Can't have married her," Howard Rudd broke in. "The girl is underage! Without permission from her guardian, the marriage isn't legal!" Bobbing his head like a child who was wont to gloat, he smirked at Beau in triumph.

"Cerynise's guardian is deceased," Beau rejoined as if he had never heard the man, directing his attention instead to the magistrate. "Besides, the officiating clergyman was

236

fully aware that Cerynise is a few months short her eighteenth birthday. Under the circumstances, he saw no reason to object."

"Under what circumstances?" Blakely queried.

"I'm about to set sail for the Carolinas," Beau informed him. "Naturally, I meant for the young lady to accompany me."

"As your wife, you mean," the judge mused aloud, leveling a pointed stare upon the younger man.

"Exactly."

Alistair glanced between the two men, all of his senses alert to the fact that shortly after Cerynise's appearance, the judge had seemed to vacillate between the two entities that strove to possess her, as if the elder only wanted to do the right thing by her. That idea certainly didn't bode well for his claims. "None of this makes any difference," Alistair insisted, overly loud. "The marriage can't be valid unless it's sanctioned by her guardian! And since I've been given that authority, Cerynise must return home with me."

Blakely turned a perturbed stare upon the lanky man. "I can hear you better if you don't shout in my ear, sir."

The corners of Beau's lips quivered as he struggled to subdue his amusement. His sparkling eyes passed on to Rudd, who seemed suddenly petulant.

The magistrate bestowed a fatherly gaze upon the girl. "Miss...your pardon...I mean, Mrs. Birmingham. I hope you'll understand that my duty is to make certain that nothing untoward is happening here."

The gracious smile she bestowed upon him belied her desperation and did much to win his approval. "I understand, Your Honor. However, I must confess that I'm bemused because Mr. Winthrop has dared to pretend any interest in my welfare when I've seen no evidence of such...."

Alistair opened his mouth to argue, but Blakely held up a hand, forestalling him. "He claims to be your guardian."

Cerynise scoffed. "I would soon perish with such a guardian as he has proven to be. Indeed, he threw me out of Mrs. Winthrop's home without cloak or coin. I very nearly froze to death, and now he's back here claiming to want only my good. 'Tis a farce if I've ever come across one."

"He has presented a codicil to his aunt's will which places you in his care," Blakely informed her, eyeing her closely.

She met his probing gaze unwaveringly as she calmly inquired, "Is there much difference between a farce and a forgery, Your Honor?"

Alistair snarled and stepped forward as if to lay hand upon her, but Beau swept her safely to the far side of him and lifted a mocking brow as he met the thin man's seething glower. "Perhaps you'd like to discuss this at length after the judge leaves," he suggested. "I'm open to pistols or fists, if you're of such a mind."

"Now, now, we'll have none of that," Blakely barked.

"The girl is lying, Your Honor," Alistair insisted. "She is set on going with this rake, despite the fact that he will probably fling her aside once he reaches his home port."

"Your wife has laid serious charges against this man," the judge informed Beau.

"Are they any less serious than Mr. Winthrop's efforts to challenge the legality of our marriage? Now tell me, Your Honor, what would a father do for his daughter in this situation? If you have daughters, perhaps you can instruct us."

"I have three, Captain. In fact, my youngest is the same age as your wife."

"What would be your reaction to any notion that a young lady can be married by a properly ordained clergyman, in full view of a crew of men, and spend the night with her husband only to be told the next day that she is not, in fact, lawfully wed?"

Blakely flung up a hand even higher when Alistair tried once again to interrupt. Then he cleared his throat and blustered over his answer. "I'd be set to see that they're properly wed if they're not already."

He hesitated a moment, and then looked at Cerynise. "I beg your pardon, Mrs. Birmingham, but I do have to ask. Were you and Captain Birmingham together last night?"

A hush seemed to settle over the deck as everyone awaited her answer. She caught as many as three glances cast surreptitiously at her, but they were hastily averted. Despite the fact that Beau had warned her, she found the situation acutely embarrassing, but at least she could tell the man the truth, even if it was with a blush. "Yes, Your Honor, we were together last night." And then, because she was completely fed up with Alistair and his claims, she added for good measure, "In the same bed."

That seemed more than the judge needed to hear. His face was quite red when he faced Beau. "My apologies for having disturbed you, Captain Birmingham." He settled his top hat snugly upon his head. "Have a pleasant voyage home."

Alistair stared after the magistrate in burgeoning disbelief as that one made his way toward the gangplank. "You don't mean-...You can't...You mustn't let this blackguard get away with this!"

Judge Blakely paused near the plank and turned to peer over a shoulder at Alistair. "Captain and Mrs. Birmingham have given every evidence of being lawfully married, sir. You'll not find another judge in all of England who'll say otherwise. 'Twould be a disgrace if any did. I'm afraid you'll just have to accept that, Winthrop."

"Why, you arrogant heap of slime!" Alistair railed back at him. "You should be denied access to the bench!" Shaking off Rudd's restraining hand, he wheeled on Beau, his fury rising to heights that shocked everyone around him. "And as for you, you bastard! You may feel like a cock of the walk now, but I assure you I won't let you get away with this travesty...."

Beau's eyes squinted dangerously as he fixed a glare upon the thin man. "What did you call me?"

Unaware of the peril he was in, Alistair shook a fist at the captain and gratified himself by enlarging upon his earlier slur. "A stinking bastard! A filthy, lying Yankee bastard who—"

In three long strides Beau was beside the man, catching him by the back of his collar and the seat of his britches. Alistair railed in shocked protest and sought madly to reach the deck with his toes as Beau whisked him swiftly a-port. At the rail, the captain swept his burden upward and outward, launching it from his ship. His unworthy guest scrambled with wildly flailing limbs to find a haven in midair, but alas, there was none. Alistair's horrendous screech dwindled to a wavering wail that ended abruptly in a significant splash, causing the crew to erupt in loud guffaws and cheers. Beau was not entirely finished with his wife's adversary. Snatching hold of the ratlines, he swung himself up with a dazzling display of strength and alighted with equal grace atop the rail. He paced forward to an open space and, with arms braced akimbo, roared down at the man who, upon bobbing to the surface of the water, promptly started coughing and gasping for breath.

"You can insult me if you have the gall, Winthrop, but if you *even think* of maligning my mother again, I'll see you horsewhipped till your flesh comes off with the lash! I'll let

241

no sniveling lout like you cast aspersions on a woman to whom I happen to be very devoted!"

Beau swung down from his perch and dusted his hands off in the manner of one who had just rid himself of so much garbage.

"That'll teach the bloke ta keep his lip in line, Cap'n," chortled one of his crewmen.

Beau waved an arm in ready agreement. "Break out a cask, lads, and we'll celebrate that toad's departure."

Thundering footfalls of those who went to fetch it nearly made the judge cringe, but he smiled in approval as the captain strode toward him. "I'm quite fond of my mother, too, sir."

Beau grinned, repenting of his earlier impression of the man. "I thought you'd understand, Your Honor."

Beau directed his gaze upon Howard Rudd, who had been immobilized from the moment he had seen his companion snatched up by the raging captain. The solicitor's dewlap seemed to flap in the wind as he struggled to find his tongue and deny the possibility that he would *ever* dream of defaming so noble a creature as a mother. Giving up that feeble attempt, he whirled and, with coattails flying, sprinted toward the gangplank, nearly bowling the good judge over as he brushed past him. A moment later he could be seen launching a rope out to Alistair, who was trying desperately to learn how to swim.

Cerynise's giggles joined her husband's laughter as he took her in his arms, and for much more his own pleasure than for the benefit of his cheering crew, he kissed her long and thoroughly.

CHAPTER 8

Cerynise lifted her head off the pillow long enough to search for the pail that Billy Todd had solicitously left beside the bunk. Emitting a small, miserable moan, she closed her eyes and kept as still as possible in a hopeful quest to forestall her stomach erupting, but every pitch and roll of the vessel seemed to incite rebellion from that queasy area. She marveled that she had *ever* considered the mate's cabin a haven of any sort, for it had become a place of writhing torment from which she longed to escape. The fact that they had encountered rough seas soon after their departure from England gave her adequate cause to solemnly vow never to sail again as long as she lived...*if* she managed to survive this particular voyage.

It seemed strange, but in the last five years she had somehow managed to thrust the more repugnant details of her voyage from Charleston out of her mind. Granted, it had been overshadowed by her grieving anguish over her parents' deaths and the loss of the only home that she had ever known. Still, looking back upon it all, it seemed that she would've at least remembered her inability to cope with unreasonable motion. The realization that she was not a particularly good sailor could hardly have been ignored.

A faint smile curved Cerynise's cracked lips and abruptly drew a wince of pain as she felt a tiny split open the skin. *Not a good sailor?* she mentally jeered. *Horrendous* would be closer to the truth. If she *ever* reached land again, no power on earth could compel her to get back on another vessel heading out toward the open sea. Indeed, if she had her way, she'd stay well away from the ocean and never look at another wave again or subject herself to the agony of a ship rising upon long, slow, roiling swells and then plunging into the deep troughs that followed. It seemed an endless, diabolical cycle of waves rolling past the ship one after another after another....

Cerynise barely reached the bucket in time, and it seemed an agonizing interval before she was able to lift her head again. Soon after realizing she was about to be sick, she had tried to hide her symptoms from Billy, who was ever pressing her to eat, but one glance at the well-gorged tray he had brought to tempt her was all it took. Then her secret came out. To her amazement her retching didn't seem to bother the lad as much as it had her, for he had rushed to give her aid, supplying a bucket and a wet cloth with which she could bathe her face. Afterwards, she had sobbed and pleaded with him not to tell anyone, most especially her husband. Billy had been reluctant, deeming it unwise to withhold such information from his captain, but he had finally acquiesced.

Thereafter he had personally attended her few requirements, bringing fresh water and a bowl of light broth now and then, a supply of clean towels, and surreptitiously emptying the pail over the side along with buckets of scraps left over from the galley.

Beau had knocked on her door more than a few times and, with each passing day, had grown more insistent that she let him in. Burrowing beneath the bedcovers, she had sent him away with muted refusals to see or even talk with him. That he had assumed she was sulking had allowed her to avoid a visitation that would have caused her a most excruciating shame.

Her strength had continued to ebb, and her parched lips were now susceptible to bleeding whenever tiny splits occurred. She tried drinking water, but even that would come gushing up soon after it was downed. Sleep was her only refuge throughout the endless hours of torture, but waking was difficult, for it usually came with a need for her to heave up what little she had on her stomach. She couldn't even fathom getting dressed or garbing herself in anything more than a nightgown. Her hair was now hopelessly snarled beyond repair, but she cared not a whit about anything, much less the way she looked.

Three light raps on the door signaled Billy's return for the bowl of broth he had left an hour ago. It was still sitting untouched on the tray beside the bunk. At her weak call, he quietly entered the cabin and then halted in astonishment. He was certain he had never seen anyone looking so deathly ill before. He was sure she couldn't have looked any worse had she been near the grave. The shadows underneath her eyes were darkly pronounced, giving them a hollowed look. Her cheeks were sunken, and those previously soft, winsome lips were marred from dehydration. Indeed, the sight of her frightened him so much that he whirled about-face and ran to get the captain, having no doubt that he had just cause for going back on his promise to her.

A short moment later, Beau stood beside her bunk, hands on lean hips, short raven hair tousled from the evening wind that had raked across the deck, and an unholy light burning in his eyes. "Dammit, Cerynise, why didn't you tell someone you were ill? You look like death warmed over."

She hadn't seen him in days, and the fact that he loomed over her like some divinely perfect fabled god only made her more aware of her weak, sorry state. She had been immensely relieved that he had accepted her croaked commands to leave her alone without barging in, for she had known only too well that he possessed the all-too-manly temperament to do that and much more. Nevertheless he had been constantly in her thoughts, like a strain of music that kept running over and over through her head. Now here he was, glaring down at her as if her condition was somehow her fault.

"Go away," she moaned, turning her face

aside to hide a start of miserable tears. "I don't want you to see me like this."

"In sickness or in health, my dear," he rejoined with more sarcasm than she could bear.

"Just throw me overboard," she whimpered, clasping hold of the covers as he began pulling them away. "I don't want to continue on another day."

"Come on, sit up," he urged, ignoring her pleas as he slipped an arm beneath her shoulders.

She started to shake her head, but promptly decided that was not a good idea. "I can't! It only makes it worse. Just go away."

"And let you die in peace?" Beau laughed shortly. "Never!"

Cerynise's eyes widened in disbelief at his cruelty. "You're a callous brute."

"So I've been told." He drew her up to a sitting position on the edge of the bunk and swept her bare feet to the floor, then proceeded to slip her arms into her dressing robe.

"Oh, what are you doing to me?" she groaned listlessly. "I'm going to be sick."

"Take deep breaths," he urged, hunkering down on his haunches to slide her slippers on her feet. "You'll be fine...."

His words had scant calming effect on her stomach. In sudden panic Cerynise collapsed forward toward the pail and relented to the dry, convulsive heaving of her stomach. At last, her queasiness ebbed and she fell back weakly upon the bed. The cooling strokes of a wet cloth on her face, throat and into the opening of her gown brought her a measure of relief, but she hardly had time to catch her breath before Beau was hauling her up again and pressing a tin cup to her lips.

"Wash your mouth out," Beau urged, refusing to let her turn away from him.

Wrinkling her nose in distaste, Cerynise accomplished his directive and spat out the water into the pail. She sank back upon the bunk and lifted a doleful stare to her husband. It didn't help in the least that he looked so hale and hearty.

"Now drink the rest," Beau pressed, holding the cup to her lips again. "You're as dry as an unearthed skeleton."

"You hate me," she mumbled against the rim, but relented enough to take a sip.

"Not true, madam." He continued bathing her face and throat as she clasped the cup between trembling hands and drank tiny draughts. "But I *am* angry with you for allowing me to think you were pouting in here like a spoiled child when all the while you've been sick. If not for the fact that Billy thought he was being loyal to you, I'd have it out with him for not informing me of your plight immediately."

"I begged him not to tell you," Cerynise mumbled into the cup as he pressed it back insistently to her lips.

"Drink!"

"Oh, Beau...I can't! Not any more!"

"I said drink!"

" 'Twill only come up."

"Not this time. Trust me."

"Only a little," she groaned in petulant tones, but he refused to take away the cup until she had drained it down to the last drop.

Despite her attempt to fall back upon the bed again, he drew her to her feet, braced her upright with his own body as he wrapped a blanket around her, and then swept her up into his arms. Kicking the door aside, he strode from the cabin, bearing her toward the companionway.

Cerynise cast an apprehensive glance over her shoulder and saw the stairs looming before them. "Please, Beau," she whimpered, hating how frail and helpless she sounded. "I don't want to go up on deck where your men can see me."

"You need fresh air, madam. 'Twill help you feel better. Besides, after the way Billy came racing up to me in an anxious dither, my men will probably be expecting to see a funeral at sea."

"That will come," she assured him ruefully. "As soon as you finish me off with all that cold air you're insisting upon!"

Beau smiled down at her but never broke his stride. His long legs closed the distance to the companionway in short order as he murmured, "I'll keep you warm."

The short twilight of autumn had already deepened into a dark gloom, but the moon, shining overhead, poured a silver ribbon across the water. Chilled breezes wafted across the deck, making Cerynise catch her breath, but they did nothing to bring her relief from her anguish.

"If you don't put me down, you're going to regret it," she warned.

Beau complied only when he reached the nearest bulkhead and lowered her to it. Cerynise had little strength to hold herself upright and sank forward against him, leaning her brow against his neck and nestling her head against his shoulder. Had she been feeling better, she might have enjoyed his arms holding her close against him, but under the circumstances, she could only dread what might happen.

"Please, Beau," she breathed against his neck. "I feel as if I'm going to be sick again. I'd like to return to my cabin. At least there, I won't embarrass myself."

"Staying down there will only make it worse, Cerynise."

"But this isn't making it any better," she argued.

He turned her away from him, braced her slender form with his body and held her secure with an arm wrapped about her midriff as he pointed out to sea. "Look out over the top of the railing."

"Nooo," she moaned, and rolled her head in anguish. Was the man so merciless? Absolutely the last thing she needed to do was look at the water!

"Not at the waves," he whispered against her

hair. "Look at the horizon. There's enough moonlight for you to see it, so fix your gaze there."

Cerynise squinted in an effort to see the faint dark line between sea and sky. After focusing her gaze upon it, it took several moments before she became aware of its stability. "It isn't moving."

"Well, actually it is," Beau replied with a soft chuckle. "The earth is turning, but you needn't worry about that. As far as you're concerned, it isn't moving."

Glancing up at him, she sighed wistfully. "I wish I weren't moving."

He smiled down at her. "Don't look away from the horizon, Cerynise. Just keep your eyes fixed on the line, and keep breathing in the cool, clean air."

Cerynise obeyed, for the moment satisfied to lean back within his encompassing arms. Time slipped past, but she was hardly aware of anything beyond the sheltering comfort of his large body. By slow degrees she became cognizant of the fact that she was beginning to feel better. Drawing in a long, slow breath, she released it again in a pleasurable sigh. "I do believe I'm going to live."

Beau laughed and folded the blanket up close around her neck. "Warm enough?"

She nodded, snuggling back against him. "Quite comfortable now."

The seasickness that had plagued her since the *Audacious* sailed from the Thames into the

251

open sea was swiftly disappearing. But in its place was an exhaustion more profound than any she had ever known.

Her head found a niche between her husband's neck and shoulder and, with a sigh, she closed her eyes. By slow degrees her breathing slowed.

Beau didn't dare move. He was content to hold his young wife in his arms as the night deepened into a silky blackness studded with a myriad of stars. During her lengthy reclusion, he had been plagued by a nagging suspicion that something was not quite right in his life, a feeling that was, at the very least, unsettling. He had had to face the realization that he missed not being with the girl. Certainly those lively little wenches whom he had visited in the past had not been able to claim his mind longer than his departure from their doors. Yet day and night he had thought of Cerynise until he had been brought sharply to the awareness that he desired her company far more than the usual palette of women with whom he had been intimate.

The ship bucked at the contrary winds and, beneath the surface of the water, battled the Gulf Stream currents. Early in his sailing career, Beau had become cognizant of the fact that sailing westward was known as the uphill passage across the Atlantic. A downhill crossing could be accomplished in little over a month with prevailing winds blowing from west to east. But on the return leg, it could take as much as three months. Although that was hardly an appropriate length of time for a normal courtship, perhaps it would be enough for him to settle his mind on just what kind of commitments he wanted to make to this young beauty he held so closely within his arms.

When the watch changed, Beau carried Cerynise back to her cabin. She didn't rouse as he laid her in the bunk, and he could detect no evidence of continuing sickness. He pulled off her robe and briefly admired her loosely flowing nightgown with its rounded neck trimmed with a wide ruffle of handmade lace. He dared not linger beyond the simple task of tucking her beneath the covers. If the experience of their wedding day had taught him anything, he would do well to limit such ministrations to nothing more than a brotherly concern.

"Don't move," Cerynise bade, focusing intently on the lines that she was swiftly applying to the nearly completed sketch of Billy Todd. "I'll be finished in a moment."

Anxious to see what she had drawn, the lad squirmed in mounting suspense.

"Hold still now," she implored.

Curbing his curiosity, Billy managed to comply long enough for her to complete the drawing. But then, with such a view for him to look at, it was hardly any task at all. The lady had returned to her former health and beauty in a matter of days, and since then had been completely absorbed in something that had kindled the attention of nearly everyone

253

aboard the *Audacious*. To say that she was talented would have been putting it mildly by an extreme measure.

"Done," Cerynise declared in satisfaction, and finally turned the parchment around to let Billy see the results.

His eyes widened in growing amazement as he perused the results. "Would ye look at that, mum? That's me!"

"Or at least a reasonable likeness," Cerynise replied with an effervescent laugh. She studied the portrait with a fair amount of satisfaction, pleased that she had been able to catch the lad poised somewhere between childhood and maturity. There was still a telltale hint of softness in his cheeks and mouth, but the eyes were clear and steady. The chin was firm and hinted of strength to come.

"Do I really look like that?" he asked with a sheepish grin.

"Aye," Stephen Oaks confirmed, halting close behind the cabin boy's shoulder. "But it's not your winsome face she's caught, lad," he teased. "She's captured your nature right on the mark."

"Thank you, kind sir," Cerynise said, laughing as she dipped her head in an impromptu curtsy. "No artist could ask for higher praise."

"You wouldn't be in the mood to sketch another one, would you, ma'am?" Stephen inquired hopefully.

"I think I can be persuaded." Cerynise reached for a fresh piece of parchment and, with a graceful sweep of her hand, motioned for the mate to sit down in front of her. The site she chose for him afforded her a view not only of her subject but also of the horizon, toward which she continued to glance from time to time. Even after more than two weeks of fine health, she still refused to take anything for granted. Feeling well had certainly buoyed her spirits and changed her attitude toward sailing. She was fairly confident now that she could survive another voyage, but right now she was going home. *Home!* For so long now the Carolinas had been little more than a distant memory. Yet circumstances had changed, and with each passing moment she was drawing closer to all the things she had remembered and cherished over the last few years. Still, she couldn't help but wonder what awaited her there.

Since regaining her health and falling into a daily routine aboard ship, Cerynise had returned to her art and soon found herself sketching the seamen and their life aboard the *Audacious.* Most of her work she gave away, keeping only a few for herself, among them the ones she labored on in the privacy of the mate's cabin. She was beginning to suspect that she had the largest collection of drawings of Beau Birmingham in existence and, with each passing day, she was adding to it.

The afternoon watch came on deck before she finished Stephen Oaks's sketch and handed it to him with a smile. "A handsome man you are, Mr. Oaks."

255

"Well, I'm not sure about that, ma'am, but this drawing is a fine one," he assured her with a pleased grin. "Why, I bet the fancy folk of Charleston would pay a pretty sum for you to do this sort of thing for them."

Cerynise tossed her head upward with an amused chuckle. "I fear the contrary will be true, Mr. Oaks. People seem to look dimly upon a woman painting portraits, perhaps because all the great masters have been men. I'm sure the people in Charleston will be just as skeptical as those in England."

"Then 'twill be their loss, ma'am, not yours."

"Thank you," she replied cheerily, accompanying her words with another pert dip of her head.

Becoming aware of a presence looming over her, Cerynise marveled at the tingling rush of excitement that affirmed Beau's presence even before she glanced around to find him standing close behind her, studying the sketch of the mate. He had come upon them unawares, unnerving her with his penchant for appearing without a sound from almost out of nowhere. She doubted that it was a propensity he consciously strove to maintain, for there were times when she was able to catch some warning of his approach and could fortify herself against the trembling that would then beset her. Today she found herself decidedly disarmed and equally aghast at her own fluttering response. She was sure if he ever became mindful of her reaction, he'd be wont to think her unchanged from that little girl whose heart had always leapt with joy whenever she had espied him coming down the narrow lane toward their house and the nearby school. To think that he'd perhaps be wont to dismiss such weaknesses as something only a silly youngling might suffer made her cautious about revealing her strangely chaotic emotions. The inhibiting constraints she suffered in his presence only served to remind her that thus far he had made no promises to keep her as his wife upon their arrival in Charleston.

"I really don't understand how someone so large can move around so quietly," she scolded, as if he might have startled her.

Beau gave her a slow grin that did strange things to her pulse, for it started leaping like frogs cavorting on lily pads. "I'll endeavor to give you more warning, madam," he replied. "Will tripping clumsily over my own feet be enough?"

Gaining no answer, Beau stepped around to look at her drawings, which she had spread out alongside of her on the deck and had weighted down against the whipping of the wind. He was ever amazed by the realism of the likenesses she portrayed, for he readily recognized each face she had drawn.

When Cerynise glanced up, she was surprised to find him so close. Indeed, she could see the pulse beating steadily at the base of his throat where his shirt fell open. If only she could remain equally unaffected, she thought. She closed her eyes for a moment against the sudden whirling of her senses. When she opened them again, she nearly stumbled backward in surprise as she found Beau leaning over her, reaching for the cloak that had fallen from her shoulders. She felt his chest brush her sleeve and peered aslant into the opening as his shirt fell away from his chest. All too keenly she recalled his hand leading hers in a leisurely caress of that tautly muscled expanse and to what it had quickly led them.

Beau straightened and became momentarily engrossed in spreading the cloak around her shoulders and fastening the silken frogs beneath the hood. "You shouldn't be out here without your wrap, madam," he admonished softly. "I wouldn't want you to come down sick again."

"I won't," she whispered, lifting her eyes to the ones that slid slowly upward from her throat. When his gaze paused on her lips, she had the strangest sensation that he was going to kiss her, but she quickly dismissed that notion as some fantasy of her own and rebuked herself for having such faulty illusions. Still, when those blue orbs captured hers, she found the simple act of breathing normally had become an impossibility.

"I'd be honored, madam, if you would dine with me this evening," Beau murmured, smoothing the hood of her cloak around her shoulders.

Sudden visions of them lying naked in his bunk came unbidden to her mind, halting her breath with the ecstasy that always came with that apparition. She could only assume from the way she came undone whenever he was near, that such a simple invitation as dining with him might well lead her into nine months of seclusion without a name to give their offspring. Since the onset of the voyage, she hadn't dared a return to the captain's cabin for fear of that happening.

"Mr. Oaks will also be dining with us," Beau added, seeking to ease the qualms she was apparently suffering.

"Oh."

A raven brow lifted wonderingly as Beau perused his wife's face. He could almost swear that he had heard a note of disappointment in her voice. He pressed a hand to his chest, solemnly promising, "I shall seek to garb myself more appropriately for the occasion, madam."

Cerynise accepted his statement as an invitation for her to gown herself with equal care. Dipping into a winsome curtsy, she tossed him a coquettish smile. "I shall attempt to do the same, Captain."

A silver-blue taffeta seemed the best choice for the evening, Cerynise decided after careful consideration. The bouffant sleeves and ankle-length hem were well in fashion, certainly as much as the demure baring of her shoulders. She wore no adornment on her throat, for the garment needed none. A draped sash of more brilliant blue swept upward from the right side of her waist to her left sleeve, where it was gathered in a flamboyant bow. Her hair was pulled back smoothly from her face, and from behind each ear, narrow ribbons of the brighter blue dangled prettily, adorning the small clusters of springy curls that bobbed there. The remaining tresses she had intricately woven in a weighty mass above her nape. The fact that she had spent over an hour fashioning the coiffure attested to her desire to win her husband's approval.

Beau swung open his cabin door at the first light rap of her knuckles, and for a moment he stood before the opening, drinking in her beauty in silent appreciation. Cerynise accepted his slow, exacting scrutiny as an unspoken compliment, for the warmth of those sapphire eyes had intensified significantly by the time they arrived at the smooth crown of her head. He seemed to enjoy taking his own sweet time perusing her, for he gave her a slow grin that was no less than hypnotic.

No doubt her own expression revealed a deep appreciation of the sight that greeted her, for Cerynise was once more struck by his penchant for garbing himself in fashionable garb. Crisply tailored buff trousers defined her husband's narrow hips superbly, while a tan waistcoat and a dark green swallowtail coat complemented his wide shoulders and lean waist. The high folded collar of the coat was set off to perfection by a creamy silk cravat, which had been neatly addressed prior to her entry.

"Too bad Mr. Oaks is coming," Beau remarked with a wayward grin that had turned a bit roguish. Taking her hand, he drew her into his lair and swung the door closed behind her, leaning near to whisper, "You look sweet enough to have for dinner."

His suggestive talk brought a blush of pleasure to Cerynise's cheeks and hastened the chaotic beating of her heart. Breathlessly aware of his encroaching nearness, she stood rooted in suspenseful alertness as he seemed to mold his long form against her slender back. She could feel his warm breath caressing her ear and his eyes devouring her. His fingers lightly brushed a bare shoulder, quickening her pulse.

"Lest you be confused by my recent efforts to avoid your cabin, madam," he breathed, nuzzling her hair, "I haven't stopped wanting you. The distance between us merely forestalls the possibility of rape."

Cerynise briefly considered the probability of his excuse being nothing more than a wily ploy, for she deemed it totally out of character for the man to evade any meeting with her that might have ended in his desires being placated. Despite the overwhelming and equally titillating evidence of his unswerving dedication to seducing her, she banished her suspicions, but only because she wanted to enjoy the evening with him without a quarrel arising between them. The presence of their chaperon guaranteed that nothing inappropriate would happen between them.

Cerynise braced herself against the sizzling assault on her senses as Beau's hand ventured slowly upward from her slender waist, but she could not subdue a soft fluttering gasp when his palm settled warmly around a breast. Indeed, the fires he lit as his thumb slowly strummed across a pliant nipple came nigh to stripping away her will. Of a sudden, it seemed a pulsing flame licked across the pinnacle, igniting a burning hunger within her womanly loins and setting her whole body ablaze with ravenous yearnings. She told herself that she should turn tail and run to the safety of her quarters before his hand moved on to other conquests, but her legs felt leaden and refused to obey her feeble command.

"I can't look at you without becoming affected," he whispered, closing his eyes as he savored the essence of her hair. "If you only knew how much I wanted you, you'd take pity on me...."

A loud knock sounded on the door, allowing Cerynise's breath to escape in a fluttering sigh of relief. The intrusion saved her from the quandary of submitting not only to her husband's wandering hand but everything else he had in mind. It also left her suffering a recurring disappointment that she could not give herself to him in the safety of an enduring marriage.

"Too late," Beau whispered, pressing a soft kiss upon her shoulder, causing Cerynise to close her eyes as she luxuriated in the warm brush of his lips. It seemed a moment of dreamy ecstasy, but with a last caress of her breast, he stepped away, paused long enough to cool his ardor, and then swept the door open.

Mr. Oaks had also taken pains with his appearance. He looked particularly well turned out in a wine-colored frock coat, gray trousers and waistcoat, and freshly ironed shirt and stock. He was an amiable fellow and a gifted storyteller. He regaled Cerynise with tales of his seafaring adventures with the captain and frequently had her waiting with bated breath for the conclusion of his story. Just as often he elicited her laughter with his wit.

They enjoyed yet another superbly delectable repast created by the talented Monsieur Philippe, and by the time the port arrived, Cerynise had cause to wonder when she had last spent so much time laughing. Beau seemed content to let his mate do the entertaining while he, for the most part, sat back and watched her.

"Which only goes to show," Mr. Oaks concluded yet another tale, "that you can go partners with a Chinaman and a Moor, and everyone comes out ahead in the end."

"I still don't know why the sultan didn't just imprison all of you," Cerynise replied with a laugh and then warbled, "But I'm glad he didn't." She glanced at Beau, whose daring exploits had filled her with awe and yet a sense of dread for the risks he was inclined to take. She wanted to rebuke him for not being more cautious about safeguarding his life, but then, that urge was no different than what she had experienced as a child when she had seen him racing recklessly across the countryside on the back of Sawney.

At the moment, her husband leaned back in his chair, his long legs stretched out to the side, very much at his leisure. It occurred to her as she eyed him surreptitiously that he didn't necessarily appear older than his years, yet he seemed vastly more mature than other men of the same age. He bore the weight of authority and experience remarkably well, she thought, for he seemed to casually accept the responsibility of his command, as if he had been born to it. It was also something he deftly maintained without a display of tyrannical demands.

Lamplight burnished his features, emphasizing the crisp line of his jaw and the noble elegance of his face. His eyes were darkened by the shadow which the hanging lantern presently cast across his face, leaving the color impenetrable, but she could sense his gaze hawkishly devouring her.

"When you left Charleston, Captain, did you deliberately pursue such an adventurous life?" she queried quietly.

Beau twirled a glass of ruby port between his long fingers and shrugged. "Our experiences only seem daring in the retelling, madam."

"No such thing!" Mr. Oaks objected with a chuckle. "Every word was true and the captain knows it."

"You've sailed rather close to the wind a time or two," Cerynise persisted.

"More like a time or a hundred," Mr. Oaks boasted. "There was that month we spent holed up in Majorca when—"

"I think that will do, Mr. Oaks," Beau

murmured tolerantly with a grin, but even so soft a rebuke was capable of shushing his mate. Beau was just lifting the decanter to refill the other's glass when a disturbance in the companionway interrupted. He rose almost leisurely and swung open the door, revealing several crewmen who glanced at each other rather dubiously. One was pushed forward to serve as spokesman.

"Beggin' yer pardon, Cap'n, but there's a spot o' trouble below."

"What sort of trouble?" Beau asked quietly. Stephen Oaks was already on his feet, moving around to stand beside his captain.

"Wilson's drunk, sir," another man blurted out. "He's already knifed Grover an' now he's got himself an ax. Choppin' away at the walls below decks, he is, sir. Thinks it's funny, he does."

Chopping holes in the walls of a ship while at sea didn't seem particularly amusing to Cerynise. Neither did wielding an ax while raging drunk nor, for that matter, knifing a man. Yet Beau showed no visible sign of alarm as he turned back to her. "Please excuse us, madam."

"Of course." She stood up hastily. "I'll go to my cabin."

"No, you'd better stay here." At her look of surprise, Beau further instructed, "Lock the door from inside, and don't let anyone in here until I return. Understood?"

"Yes, Captain," Cerynise acknowledged with an uncertain nod.

It might have been all well and good to challenge Beau Birmingham about their marital status, but she had the good sense to know this was not the time to argue about staying in his cabin. If truth be told, she was relieved that he was so well experienced in handling adverse situations, as Oaks's discussions over dinner had confirmed.

With that in mind, she softly begged, "Please be careful."

He was about to step through the door, but paused to give her a quick glance over his shoulder. He smiled faintly and left the cabin with Mr. Oaks following hard on his heels.

Cerynise released a quavering sigh, realizing just how anxious she had become, not for herself but for her husband. Oaks hadn't really done her a favor by bragging on his captain's daring feats. One thing she had learned from the mate's stories, that when there was trouble to be reckoned with, Beau usually took charge, and her imagination conjured up a whole plethora of diabolical things that could happen to him while trying to take an ax or a knife from a drunk.

Cerynise pressed a trembling hand to her brow as she faced the gallery windows. Darkness loomed beyond the stern, but she would have seen nothing beyond the square panes even if dawn had been breaking. Her awareness that Beau was in danger reduced her to a quivering mass of womanly concern for a man whom she dearly cherished. At that realization, Cerynise sat down abruptly upon the cushions, barely an instant before her legs would have given way beneath her.

She was still frozen with anxiety when she heard footsteps in the companionway. Without giving a thought to Beau's command, she raced to the door, unlatched it with fumbling fingers, and yanked it open. Her husband had lifted a hand to knock, but when she appeared, breathless and fearful, a sudden scowl darkened his countenance.

"Didn't I tell you not to unlock the door until I told you to?"

He was right. Her behavior had been no less than foolish. Anyone could have been standing in the passageway. But she didn't care at the moment. In a heartbeat, she flung herself toward him and clasped her arms around him. "Oh, thank goodness you're all right! I was so worried...."

Beau's arms encircled her and steadily tightened until she was held snugly against him. He pressed a cheek against her hair, somewhat awed by her fear. It was much like the time Sawney had bucked him off and he had been knocked nearly senseless after his head scraped a nearby tree on the way down. He had awakened from his daze to find his head in Cerynise's lap and her frightened tears pelting his face.

"Of course, I'm all right," he soothed near her ear.

Released from the depths of her trepidation, Cerynise felt like soaring. Indeed, she was nearly giddy with relief and, in an instant, was pulling his head down and covering his face with laughing kisses, expressing her joy with girlish fervor. Her delight increased significantly as his mouth began to snare hers with quickening zeal. Brief though they were, his kisses were exotic little morsels that made her hungry for more. Rising on tiptoes, she locked her arms about his neck and clung to him unashamedly as she answered his questing tongue and lips with frenzied rapture. Even when his hand wandered beneath her buttock and pressed her up against him, she felt no desire to pull away from the burgeoning hardness that became evident even through the layers of her skirts and petticoat.

Fate would have it that the hapless Mr. Oaks chose that very moment to enter the passageway. Upon espying them locked in an embrace ill suited for the passageway, he gasped in surprise and then, abruptly realizing his mistake, made to reverse his direction. But it was too late. The couple broke apart, and Cerynise, upon spying Oaks, fled to her cabin with a vivid blush while Beau turned aside.

"I beg your pardon, Captain," the mate apologized, horribly flustered. "I was just..."

"Never mind," Beau bade curtly, and drew in a ragged breath. A battle of wills raged within him as he debated the choices between following his wife or returning to his own cabin. After the interruption, it was doubtful that Cerynise would want to see him, and certainly not with the same enthusiasm she had displayed only a moment before. A wise man would wait until her embarrassment had eased. A wise man would return to his own cabin and spend a hellish night tossing and turning in his lonely bunk while he cursed his mate's untimely intrusion.

His eyes glittering dangerously, Beau strode to the familiar portal and, a brief moment later, slammed it closed behind him. Stephen Oaks winced sharply and retreated like a timid little mouse to the small cubicle that served as his temporary quarters. The captain hadn't elaborated on the status of his relationship with his wife, but from all previous indications, the lady hadn't seemed at all inclined to fall into her husband's lap like Oaks had seen other women eagerly do in the past. The fact that she had apparently been responding with a fair amount of passion of her own only made his embarrassment more acute. He had certainly bungled it for his captain this time.

Exhausted and aching from a wearisome night of restless turning, Cerynise rose, bathed, and garbed herself in a demure, dark blue woolen gown. She gathered her hair in a somber knot at her nape and tried to pinch some color into her cheeks. Billy Todd arrived with her breakfast tray shortly after her toilette, but this was not the grinning, gregarious Billy whom she had come to know. This morning he was pale and silent, and apparently was struggling to maintain a semblance of composure that he wasn't necessarily feeling.

"Is something wrong, Billy?" Cerynise asked

269

in growing concern as he set the tray down.

Avoiding her gaze, he shook his head. "No, mum. Everything's fine."

She wasn't at all convinced. Fevers could spring up so easily and even a strong boy like Billy could fall prey. "Are you perhaps ill?"

"Oh no, mum."

Billy had left the door open when he entered the cabin, and though she strained to hear, the usual morning sounds from the deck to which she had become accustomed were not in evidence. In their stead was a somber silence.

An undefined sense of dread filled Cerynise. "Billy, are you sure...?"

The lad hastened toward the door, reluctant to answer any questions. "I'll come back later to collect the tray, mum." He hesitated briefly before adding, "Ye'd best stay put for the morn'n.'"

He flushed, nodded quickly and withdrew. Cerynise stared pensively at the tray of food. All she could hear in her mind was the silence that had been more deafening than the rattle of drums and fife. Her curiosity got the better of her, and she went to the door, opened it, and stood in waiting silence. The ominous hush drew out in ever-lengthening degrees.

There were almost a hundred men on board the *Audacious*. What could possibly have rendered them so deathly still? Having little knowledge of shipboard life other than what she had gleaned since their departure from London, Cerynise was at a loss to explain the hush that had settled over the frigate.

They were making good time, but at present there was none of the thumps and rattles of daily chores being performed, the calls from the morning watch, the snatches of song or the low murmuring voices that were usually discernible in her cabin in the mornings.

There was only silence.

Cerynise slipped cautiously through the passageway and then ascended several steps of the companionway until she was able to have a look about the deck. To her amazement, she found the entire crew assembled in stony silence on the main deck, drawn up in ranks facing away from her. They stood with legs braced apart, hands clasped behind their backs, looking toward the forecastle. Cerynise couldn't see beyond them and had to climb a few more steps to do so. This she did only to instantly regret it. A man, naked from the waist up, was lashed to the backstays of the foremast against the starboard rail. His wrists were stretched outward above his head and were secured with cords. Standing beside him was the burly bosun's mate whose arms were as thick as battering rams. From his huge hand dangled a cat-o'-nine-tails.

That lash was the most wicked thing Cerynise had ever seen, and with an effort, she dragged her eyes away and sought Beau. He was also there on the forecastle, tall, stoic, his powerful body stiffly erect, a figure of immense power and authority, yet cold and distant as though devoid of all humanity. As she watched, her heart crept into her throat.

Mr. Oaks stepped forward and, in a clear voice, announced, "Seaman Redmond Wilson, having been found guilty of dereliction of duty, possession and excessive use of alcoholic spirits aboard ship, and endangerment of the life of one Thomas Grover, as well as the welfare of the crew and the condition of the vessel, is thereby sentenced to receive twenty lashes, punishment to be carried out forthwith."

No one moved except for the bosun's mate, who turned his head slightly in Beau's direction. With a single nod, the captain of the *Audacious* signaled for the punishment to commence. The cat hissed forward through the air like a striking snake, making contact with human flesh and drawing a roar of pain from the man. Cerynise cringed, hardly aware that a sharp gasp had been wrenched from her own lips. In the grim silence that ensued, all heads turned toward her.

Her first instinct was to escape, but it was all too obvious what she had done. Pride refused to let her flee the consequences of her actions. Scarcely breathing, she climbed to the deck and mutely awaited her reckoning. Billy Todd stood nearby, staring at her in horror. The rest of the crew regarded her with expressions that ranged widely from disbelief to sympathy.

A path opened as Beau strode across the deck toward her. Not for a moment could she mistake his rage. He gripped her elbow and, without a word, escorted her down the stairs and through the passageway to her cabin.

"You shouldn't have come on deck," he rumbled as he threw open her door. "Didn't Billy warn you not to?"

"He told me to stay put," she admitted in a hushed tone.

"Usually there's a reason for instructions of that sort," he stated crisply. "In the future, madam, you'll be wise to heed them."

"I will," Cerynise whispered, very close to bursting into tears.

Detecting an unusual brightness in her eyes, Beau stepped forward but caught himself abruptly, aghast that he should even think of apologizing. Whirling about-face, he stalked from the cabin, leaving her to close the portal behind him.

The muted sounds of Redmond Wilson's screams drifted down to haunt her, and try as she might, Cerynise could not block them out. She knew the man had deserved his punishment, and because she was a passenger on a ship that usually carried none, she was the intruder, the one who had blundered into her husband's affairs and caused him acute embarrassment in front of his men.

The screams grew silent at last and in a surprisingly brief time the customary noises of shipboard life began anew, but no one came to her door. Cerynise remained isolated in her cabin, and this time she vowed to stay until she was given permission to leave or they dragged her moldering from her crypt.

By nightfall, her nerves had been stretched taut. Billy Todd hadn't appeared with the noon meal or even supper. That didn't trouble her overmuch since she had grave doubts that she could've eaten a morsel. As full darkness descended, her agitation steadily increased. Obviously she was being left entirely alone to consider her guilt in disobeying an order, however casually it had been given.

Footsteps approached her door, and she forced her trembling limbs to perform the act of standing. A scowl still darkened Beau's visage as he entered, but he paused and looked around in surprise. "Why didn't you light the lamps?"

"I didn't even think of it," she admitted lamely.

He swiftly took care of the matter himself, and soon the light stripped away the gloom of the interior. It seemed to warm her with its golden radiance while it bathed her husband's face with its soft, caressing glow. When she finally committed herself to meeting his gaze, Cerynise realized he was no longer frowning.

The small confines of the cabin had definitely shrunk with his presence, at least in her mind. Beau moved restlessly about, touching the back of a chair, the frame of the bunk, straightening the ewer of water on the small dresser, all the while seeming pensive and uncomfortable.

"I'll send Billy with a tray of food for you," he said at last.

"You needn't bother the boy."

Beau looked around in surprise. "But you haven't eaten since breakfast."

"I ate a good bit at supper last night."

"I'll send a tray anyway."

"I said you needn't bother," she insisted. "I'm not hungry."

"All right then! Forget it!"

"Why were you so angry with me for coming on deck?" she blurted, unable to stop herself. She glared at him through gathering tears. "What harm did I actually do by being there?"

"Do you have any idea what a man's back looks like after a flogging, madam?" he asked, his jaw clamped, the muscles twitching in his lean cheeks. "The skin is sometimes flayed off in bloody strips. Do you think a woman should witness that?"

Cerynise blanched and shuddered. "No, Beau, of course not. You were right to expect me to stay in my cabin, and I was wrong to ignore Billy. But what actual harm did I do?"

Beau lifted his head to stare at the ceiling briefly before he gave her an answer. "You interfered with something that was none of your affair, Cerynise. Sometimes it's necessary for a captain of a ship to dispense punishment and take actions that a woman might not understand. Without discipline, seamen would feel no obligation to extend respect for officers of any command. Order would be impossible—"

"You don't have to explain all of that," Cerynise interrupted, but halted suddenly as she grasped the full import of what he was saying. His distress, masked by an iron will, was evident just the same. "You didn't want me to see what you had ordered done."

"That has nothing to do with it," he protested.

Despite his objections, she was confident that her conclusion had merit, but rather than press him, she asked gently, "Who disarmed Wilson?"

"I did, of course. This is my ship. I'm responsible."

Exactly what she had thought the previous evening when she had trembled with fear that he would be injured. "Just as you were also responsible for punishing him. Both actions had to be taken to protect others."

He looked uncomfortable.

"Do you expect me to think you're an ogre for having the strength to carry out justice when it's needed? Oh no, sir, I do not. I have full confidence in your ability to be fair when it's deserving and equally harsh when circumstances compel you to be. You're the captain of this ship, and your responsibility includes everyone aboard this vessel."

He came near and slipped a knuckle beneath her chin, tilting her head upward until he could search her face. His sapphire eyes were gentler than she had ever seen them. "That makes me responsible for you, too."

Perhaps it was the little imp resting on her shoulder that prompted her to goad, "Only until we reach Charleston, Captain."

Beau wasn't sure he liked the reminder. His brow gathering, he drew away and moved to the door. Pausing there, he glanced back at her. "Don't forget to lock your door."

This time, Cerynise did precisely what she had been told.

CHAPTER 9

Sketches of the crew remained very much in demand in the following weeks, for the sailors were much in awe of Cerynise's talent. They seemed to enjoy her presence on deck, not only because her drawings drew their interest but also for her friendliness and lively wit. To their relief, they soon discovered that she was no stuffy aristocrat who'd be inclined to look down a condescending nose at them. She was just as ready to talk with them as they were to a woman, yet they were careful to show her the proper respect due a captain's wife, calling her Mrs. Birmingham or ma'am or mum, seeming almost fearful to step beyond their boundaries. It was Cerynise who put them at ease about their rough manners. She had caught on to their jargon very quickly and used it deftly to mimic their comments or their way of talking, drawing hoots of laughter when she deepened her voice, hooked a thumb in her belt, and strode about with a hitch in her gait or a roguish swagger. She began to know many of the sailors by name, and plied them with such questions as where they were born, did they have any family, how long had they been sailing, and what were their hopes for the future. She talked with many who had no home life other than the sea, preferring to live unfettered by kith or kin, but they didn't necessarily impress her as entirely happy men. They had just never known another way of life, having signed on at an early age or been impressed in some fashion or another. A few had grown up on farms and, when they were barely old enough, were forced to do service in the English navy. Some had families in the Carolinas or along the seaboard and were anxious to see them, having been away a goodly number of months.

During all of this, Beau remained at a tactful distance, allowing his men the benefit of his wife's company whenever they were free from duty. He had bade Billy to find a way to stabilize her easel on deck and outfit her with a portable stand for her paints. The results keenly claimed his own close attention, for she vividly captured a mariner's life on canvas, showing sailors in their rough garb clambering up into the rigging with the wind whipping their hair and, ever beyond them, the sea with its tumultuous waves. She even painted the younger helmsman standing steadfast at the wheel, with brisk breezes raking his tan locks and clothing. Beau never saw any paintings of himself, but now and then, when he would glance up unexpectedly, he'd find her closely studying him while sketching on parchment. But upon his approach, she usually busied herself with shuffling her drawings, and by the time he arrived, he found someone else's face and form on the paper beneath her hand.

On a cold but gloriously bright day, dolphins

were seen cavorting alongside the *Audacious*, where they remained for several hours. Cerynise was so intent upon getting a closer view and, at the same time, capturing them on paper that at one point her feet were completely off the planking as she balanced precariously over the railing. Spying her, Beau leapt swiftly across the deck and, swooping her off the wooden rampart, set her to her feet with an angry reprimand.

"Kindly refrain from tumbling in, madam," he barked, scowling at her. The thought of her being caught unawares by a gust of wind or the bucking of the ship had sent piercing shards of cold dread through his heart. " 'Tis a long way down, and your skirts would probably drag you under faster than I can swim."

Cerynise blushed, realizing how foolhardy she had been. "I'm sorry, Beau," she murmured, humbly contrite. "I didn't even think about falling in."

Placated by her soft apology, Beau lowered his tone to a cajoling request. "Please don't get on the rail again while we're at sea, Cerynise. It isn't safe."

"Yes, sir." The words were muted, childlike.

He smiled down at her as his hand came up to caress her cheek with what seemed a husbandly display of affection. "Good girl."

Suddenly Cerynise's heart lifted, and with a smile, she leaned toward him until she found his arm about her waist. At the moment, she didn't care one whit that Oaks and several others were watching them. He was her husband after all. "I didn't mean to anger you."

"Worry would better describe my feelings, my sweet," he corrected, amazed that she had openly invited his embrace. "I'd hate to lose you after all my schemes and efforts to bring you with me. Falling off my ship would hardly show your gratitude."

Although Cerynise suspected where his statement would lead them, she inquired in a guise of sweet innocence, "How would you prefer I show it, Beau?"

He held her curious gaze for a long moment, knowing only too well what she expected him to answer. Then a slow grin stretched across his handsome lips. "We'll leave that to your imagination, madam," he murmured. "But staying alive would be primary above all else."

"I shall endeavor to comply with your wishes, sir."

"Good." With that simple reply, he slid his hand away in a slow, provocative caress of her waist, leaving her feeling wonderfully light-headed as he stepped away. It was only later, in the privacy of her cabin, that she was led to wonder if he was wont to observe her as closely as she did him, for she had barely dragged herself onto the railing when he was suddenly there behind her, hauling her off.

In the ensuing days, Cerynise ventured into the galley and coaxed Monsieur Philippe to allow her to sketch him at work. By this time the chef had taken on legendary proportions in her mind, and she wanted something to remember him by. Philippe chortled and fussed a bit but seemed clearly flattered that she would care to draw him. She completed several scenes of him working his wizardry in a space that seemed cramped to her but which, he informed her, was at least twice the size of a normal ship's galley.

At no time did Cerynise catch even a hint of any ill feeling on the part of the crew for the punishment Wilson had been given. She could only assume that they had accepted it as his proper due and had thrust the matter from their minds. As for Wilson himself, he had been confined to the cable tier for a week and then was given rigorous duties befitting his crimes and the task of correcting the damage he had done below deck, all of which he labored at beneath close supervision. In redress of his wounding of Thomas Grover, he was also assigned that seaman's normal duties and given the chore of waiting on the man until Grover was on his feet again. Whenever the announcement was made that Wilson would be working on deck, Billy cautioned Cerynise to stay in her cabin and, this time, made it evident that it was his captain's orders. She complied completely.

Three weeks out, Cerynise woke to an unusually red dawn. So vibrant were the colors that she pleaded for Beau to let her come on deck at that early morning hour and set up her easel so she could capture the stirring display. When Stephen Oaks paused beside her later to admire her work, she could hardly contain her enthusiasm.

"Isn't the sky absolutely beautiful?" she warbled eagerly. "I can't remember ever seeing so vivid a sunrise."

Oaks grunted, none too thrilled. "Oh, it's vivid all right, but just the sort of dawn a sailor would rather not see come along."

Cerynise looked at him in surprise. "What do you mean?"

Oaks took a long look around. "There's an old adage sailors have long taken to heart, ma'am. Red sky at night, sailors' delight. Red sky in the morning, sailors take warning. I would venture to guess that we'll be in for a bit of rough weather ere long."

Although the sky was void of clouds, Cerynise allowed that the man had far more knowledge about such things than she did. No one seemed affected by this daybreaking harbinger, however. Indeed, the sailors climbed into the rigging with their usual vigor to spread more sail. Even Beau went up, which was a sight that Cerynise could have done without. He seemed well acquainted with making his way along the foot ropes beneath the yard. He even hoisted himself up on top of the spar itself and seemed to stroll leisurely along as he looked off toward the horizon and then, changing direction, inspected the sail that billowed beneath him. Cerynise watched him in trembling disquiet and felt her heart lurch when a sudden gust of wind snatched at him, causing him to thrust out his arms to balance himself. Her fear was too much for her to bear with any semblance of calm in the presence of others. Clasping a shaking hand over her brow to sharply restrict her view, she fled the deck and sought sanctuary in her cabin, where she paced anxiously about, awaiting the dreadful news of her husband's fall.

Billy Todd brought her breakfast a short time later, and Cerynise feigned a casualness she by no means felt as she asked, "Is the captain having his breakfast, too?"

"Aye, mum. He just came down."

With tears of relief spilling over her lashes, Cerynise breathed a silent prayer of thanksgiving and sank weakly into her chair. Oblivious to her distress, Billy poured her a cup of tea and took his leave.

Cerynise hadn't calmed to any measurable degree by the time she returned to the deck. Since the weather seemed unseasonably warm, she ventured forth with only a shawl draped over her shoulders. As soon as she moved away from the companionway, her eyes went searching until she espied Beau talking with the quartermaster, a grizzled man with corded muscles and a steely gaze. Both men were standing near the younger helmsman, who had the morning watch at the wheel. For the most part, the helmsman listened intently to his superiors, but he would give comment when spoken to directly. Cerynise couldn't accurately fathom what they were discussing, but she rather gathered it had something to do with the forecasts of gloom Oaks had predicted. There was, she guessed, always a chance that changing the ship's bearings a degree or two might enable the *Audacious* to escape the worst of a storm. Still, how could anyone foresee where the bad weather was centered?

Mr. Oaks was engaged in an activity that had aroused her curiosity ever since she had first become aware of it. Desiring to know more about the instrument that had so absorbed him, Cerynise meandered casually across the deck until she reached his side and then waited patiently until he lowered the device he was using.

"Is that a sextant?" Cerynise asked with a smile, indicating the metal contraption that looked like a triangle with a curved base and several interesting attachments.

"Why yes, it is," he answered, surprised by her knowledge. He held it out for her to see more clearly. "With this and a chronometer, a sailor could almost plot a course through heaven itself."

"How is it done, may I ask?"

Smiling at her interest, Mr. Oaks gallantly offered, "Allow me to show you, ma'am. You see, one simply looks through the telescope here"—he tapped that part of the instrument with his forefinger—"and focuses it on an object in the sky, in this case the moon that has obligingly remained in the morning sky." He stepped behind her, extending his arms beyond hers to make the necessary adjustments, and then leaned close over her shoulder to correct it back a degree.

"One then measures the angle between the object and the horizon. With that angle, a sailor can refer back to the appropriate books of tables and, in only a few moments, calculate our latitude."

Cerynise was thoroughly engaged in studying the moon, for even as pale as it now appeared, she could make out vague shadows across the surface. "This is amazing, Mr. Oaks. I never thought I'd be able to see so much."

"Aye, 'tis," Mr. Oaks agreed. "Before the sextant was invented, sailors had to rely on the astrolabe, but that was a bad business in its day, for the instrument had to be sighted on the sun. Navigators who served a goodly number of years regularly went blind."

Cerynise felt a measure of dismay as she lowered the sextant and stared at him. "You must feel extremely fortunate to have an instrument as fine as a sextant at your disposal."

"Indeed, madam. Now let me show you how to calculate an angle."

He was in the process of doing that when a sudden awareness swept over Cerynise. One moment she was thoroughly occupied with learning the operation of the sextant. The next she was oblivious to everything but her heart gathering speed and the certain, inexplicable realization that Beau was close at hand.

That perception was swiftly confirmed with a gruff question. "What are you doing, Mr. Oaks?"

The mate stiffened apprehensively and,

dropping his arms to his sides, stepped back away from Cerynise. Blameless he was, for there had been no slightest hint of impropriety, yet in spite of that fact he started stammering. "B-begging your pardon, Captain, but your wife...I mean, Mrs. Birmingham expressed an interest in the workings of a sextant."

"I see," Beau replied, his eyes raking them both. The wind ruffled his raven locks as he considered each of them, increasing their discomfiture no small degree.

Cerynise felt a keen regret for having involved the mate in this situation that, although innocent, had apparently nettled her husband's ire. "Perhaps I shouldn't have interrupted Mr. Oaks while he was busy, Captain. I shan't do it again."

Beau turned his attention upon his first officer. "And were you able to finish with your instructions, Mr. Oaks?"

Stephen Oaks shifted his stance uneasily, folding his arms around the sextant as he clasped it to his chest. "I was just showing Mrs. Birmingham how to calculate an angle, sir, but I wasn't able to finish."

"Then carry on, Mr. Oaks," Beau urged, returning a grin to their gaping stares. "I don't know of anyone who can tutor her any better."

"Th-thank you, sir," the mate stuttered in relief.

Cerynise curbed her amusement as she watched her husband strolling leisurely away. She had the sinking suspicion that Beau Birmingham had deliberately set about to frighten them nigh out of their wits for no other reason than his own puckish enjoyment. Perhaps the boy he had once been, who had relished teasing her long ago, had not entirely vanished after all.

Cerynise hurriedly begged leave of the mate. "Excuse me, Mr. Oaks, but I should like to have a word with my husband."

Leaving the man, she quickened her steps to catch up with Beau and casually fell in beside him. He glanced askance at her, displaying some surprise at her presence. The coy grin she gave him was quite charming. "I gather you're feeling rather smug by now, Captain."

He seemed perplexed by her statement. "Madam? What are you saying?"

"You know very well what I'm saying," she challenged. "I've been acquainted with you far too long not to recognize that devilish wit of yours. You intentionally harassed that poor man, making him think you were jealous...."

Beau squinted as he lifted his gaze into the shrouds above their heads. "I *am* jealous."

His simple acknowledgment baffled Cerynise so completely that she could not find further words with which to accuse him.

"I'm jealous of any man who claims even a moment of your time when that moment is not also spent with me. I could have shown you the sextant and explained the way it works, but since we've left London, you've been avoiding me as if I carried the plague. The only way you'll consent to come to my cabin now is if I have other guests. Indeed, madam, you protect your virtue more adroitly than any chastity belt ever could."

His accusations brought home to her the truth of what he said. She *had* been evading him. What could she do when every enticing moment she spent with him in private drew her ever closer to his bed? "You know why I can't chance being with you."

Beau sighed heavily, wearied by her arguments, and looked out to sea. "A storm is brewing."

His abrupt change of topics took Cerynise unawares, and yet she was grateful for it. It put them on safe ground again.

"How can you tell?"

Stepping near the rail, he beckoned for her to draw near and pointed toward the gray churning mass curling away from the hull. "Was the water this choppy yesterday?"

Cerynise stared at the deep ripple of foam-capped peaks and the murk beyond before she shook her head.

"What about the wind? Notice anything different since you came on deck?"

She thought about it a moment before realizing that the air was cooler. "The wind has changed direction."

He nodded, pleased by her observation. "And may again." Noticing her sudden concern, he gave her a lopsided smile. "No need to fear, my sweet. *Audacious* has weathered many storms and has come through no worse for the wear of them."

"I'll never be able to find the horizon in bad weather," she commented ruefully, casting a sidelong glance toward the one still in evidence.

Beau threw back his head and laughed in hearty amusement. Laying his arms about her shoulders, he drew her close and settled his chin on top of her head. "Then you'd best return to my cabin, madam, for I can promise, be it the foulest tempest to cross these waters, I can give you something to stare at and hold that will occupy your mind so completely, you'll never even be aware of a storm passing."

"Beau!" she chided breathlessly. She was becoming too aware of his bawdy humor to miss his insinuations. "For shame!"

He chuckled, gathering her closer to him. It had been far too long since he had been able to hold her thus. "Why? No one can hear us with this wind."

"Perhaps not, but it doesn't seem appropriate that you should talk to me the way you do when we might not be married in a few weeks."

"We'll worry about that when the time comes, madam. Until then, you're my wife, and if you won't allow me to enjoy you like any normal husband, then you'll have to bear my poor humor, for 'tis the only way I can take my revenge upon you."

Feigning a pout, Cerynise started to push away, but Beau clamped his arms more tightly about her and, dropping his chin near her temple, whispered, "Stay put, or I'll embarrass us both."

Burying her face against his neck, Cerynise settled back against him, allowing him the protection of her skirts. She was glad that he couldn't see her face, for the heat of it nearly stifled her. Yet she felt a strange, delicious contentment that her nearness could affect him even in the company of so many.

It was a very long moment before her husband loosened his arms about her, but even as she moved away, his hand followed the line of her inner arm until only the tips of their fingers touched. Then, with a grin, Cerynise glanced back at him and broke away, racing toward the companionway. Beau watched her go with eyes that glowed as he acknowledged to no one but himself his growing fondness for the girl whom he had once casually befriended with a brotherly affection.

The sea began to churn and soon became a dark, angry gray. Just looking at it made Cerynise want to retch. Low, roiling clouds gathered, stealing away the sunlight, and what warmth remained was blown away by the rising wind. Spitting rain stung the face and hands, and then the night-born gloom settled in like a dark, depressing shroud.

Cerynise retreated to her cabin, ate supper from her lonely tray, and slipped into her narrow bed. Everything about the mate's quarters had grown suddenly stale and boring, and she fought a strengthening desire to flee to the comfortable masculine quarters just down the passageway. She seriously doubted that Beau would be there; he had spent many hours on deck during the day and as yet she hadn't heard the familiar creak of the flooring outside her door that would have indicated his return to his cabin, but if she allowed herself, she could conjure all manner of reasons and excuses for awaiting his return and then yielding herself completely to that compelling, blue-eyed gaze and everything else that would follow, no doubt in short order.

Reluctantly Cerynise stayed in her virginal domain throughout the night, but with the coming of morning, it seemed her world had taken on a drastic change, for the ship had already run afoul of rough seas. A strange, yellow-tinged grayness loomed above them, which made it terribly difficult for her to even look up. She hated the dull winding-sheet that lay morosely over everything within sight. Indeed, she feared it was a bad omen for what was yet to come.

"We're gonna have a real blow, we are, mum," Billy announced in an excited tone when he brought her breakfast tray. "Cap'n says so."

A wavering sigh escaped her, and with a small vein of hope, she queried, "Has he ever been wrong before, Billy?"

The cabin boy looked astonished. "The cap'n?" He seemed to search his mind a moment for an answer. "Why no, mum, I can't say as how I've ever known him ta be mistaken. He knows the sea like the back—"

"Of his hand," Cerynise finished gloomily. She groaned, pushing aside the tray. She had no doubt that her fear of storms was centered primarily on her memories of the one which had taken the lives of her parents. She just hoped this one would be kinder. "I feel as if I'm going to be sick all over again."

"Now, mum, don't do that," Billy pleaded anxiously. "I'll have to tell the cap'n, an' he's awfully busy right now. Besides, he asked me ta bring ye up on deck if'n ye'd like, seein' as how ye won't be able ta come up much more before we hit the full strength of the storm."

Cerynise mutely agreed and, wrapping a cloak snugly about her, followed the lad up. The moment she stepped on deck, she felt the wind slicing through her garments and the icy impact of it on her face. Waves crashed in quickening repetition against the craft, sending thick sprays of foaming water over the railing. The *Audacious* continually dipped into the troughs between roiling gray mountains of water and then surged upward again as more swells passed beneath the bow. Cerynise put out a hand to steady herself as the deck seemed to drop from beneath her, making her eyes widen in mingling amazement and fear. Ropes had been strung across the deck to provide handholds, and although none of the men were using them as yet, Cerynise wasn't that confident of her ability to stand upright without aid. She firmly gripped a cord and held on for dear life as she considered the world she had come to know. It now seemed very small, no more than a tiny speck in comparison to the immensity of the sea.

Instinctively she searched for Beau and found him talking to the quartermaster again. Both of them were looking out to sea, and their manner was calm but highly focused. Beau was garbed in a thick seaman's sweater and wore a cap that sat rakishly upon his dark head, no doubt to keep the wind from whipping his dark mane into his eyes. There was a moment when he turned his face into a sudden gust and laughed as if he were enjoying himself immensely.

Shaking her head at the unfathomable ways in which men faced danger, Cerynise took a last look around and decided she had had enough. She now considered the relative calm of the mate's cabin quite inviting.

The storm continued throughout the night into the following morning. Whatever light came with daybreak, it was barely detectable; there was only a thick, watery grayness that completely obscured everything, even the topmasts. Nothing was tangible beyond their small realm, and what would be left in the wake of the howling tempest remained to be seen, for it had become a demon that sought to wreak a terrible vengeance upon the vessel that had dared intrude into its midst.

It was well into the wee hours of two mornings hence when a sudden thump in the passageway snatched Cerynise awake. It was promptly followed by a muttered curse that set her heart to leaping. Flying from the bunk, she snatched open the door and leaned out to see Beau stumbling down the lurching corridor toward his quarters. He was tugging off his oilskins, which apparently hadn't helped much, for the clothes he wore beneath them were thoroughly soaked enough to leave wet trails behind him. Even from behind, Cerynise could tell that he was shaking uncontrollably from the cold.

Flinging wide his cabin door, Beau forged inward without bothering to push it closed behind him. Immediately he tossed the slicker and his cap aside and then started stripping off his sweater and the long-sleeved, finely knit shirt he wore beneath. Cerynise followed in his wake and swept the portal shut, then hastened to a locker beyond his shaving stand. Beau glanced around long enough to realize he had company. His eyes flicked briefly over her nightgown, the same one he had seen her wearing when she had been sick. Although the soft billowing fabric clung to the ripe curves of her young body divinely, for once he had neither the strength nor the desire to become amorous.

"Y-you'd b-better get back to b-bed before you c-catch your d-death, madam," he stuttered shiveringly, working open the fastening of his trousers with fingers that did not readily respond. They were so cold that he dreaded the pain of them being warmed again. Indeed, he couldn't remember ever being so cold, even in Russia. "If you s-stay, you'll be s-seeing a lot m-more than y-your virginal s-senses may be able to bear."

"You took care of me once when I needed it," Cerynise countered matter-of-factly as she gathered a handful of towels and a blanket from the locker. "Would it be so hard for you to let me do the same for you?" She shrugged at the notion that she would be shocked. "Besides, I've seen everything about you that a wife is allowed to see."

"That's right," he acknowledged, peeling down the sodden trousers and the long underwear he wore beneath. He dropped to the bunk and bent forward to drag off his boots, but with an exhausted sigh, he decided differently and sprawled back upon the mattress, flinging his arms wide. Immediately Cerynise was there. Kneeling at his feet, she tugged off the footwear and then his trousers and underwear.

Beau had closed his eyes, but he promptly flung them open again as he felt his long frame being vigorously rubbed dry with linen cloths. He was mildly amazed at his young wife's boldness in toweling not only the whole length of his body, but his private parts as well. As much as he would have rallied with eager zeal to her ministrations under different circumstances, he was too spent to muster more than a muted plea for warm soup.

"I'll get Billy up and send him to the galley to heat you some as soon as I get you under the covers," Cerynise murmured, pulling the feather tick and top sheet from under him. In a moment she was tucking the bedclothes up over his shoulders as he huddled on his side.

She slipped into the same elegant gentleman's robe which she had found in the familiar locker and tied it about her. Then she left to find Billy and give him instructions.

In a few moments she was back and made haste to turn down the lanterns that had been lit in anticipation of the captain's return to his cabin. She was aware of Beau's bleary-eyed gaze following her movements about the room, but other than that, he was as still as death. When the soup was brought, she propped the pillows behind his head to brace him up. Greatly surprised that he would allow her, she began to feed him, but his fatigue was acute and his eyelids sagged closed repeatedly between spoonfuls.

Making the decision to stay in his cabin, Cerynise spread a blanket out beside his bunk, but at a muted grunt from Beau, she glanced up and saw him trying to drag the covers down behind him.

"Join me," he pleaded in a low murmur and, with a heavy sigh, slowly closed his eyes again.

The hard floor hadn't been very inviting anyway, Cerynise reasoned as she crawled over her husband and settled into the warm, narrow space between him and the wall. Facing his back, she tucked her knees beneath his and slipped an arm around him. Her hand found its way to his chest, and briefly her fingers stroked across the furred expanse and a male nipple before his hand came up to enfold hers within his grasp.

In the very next moment his slow, heavy breathing made Cerynise realize that he had fallen asleep. With a smile she brushed her nose against his stalwart back, and then, snuggling even closer, found a comfortable place for her cheek to rest.

Far too soon, Beau roused himself from the cozy haven of his bunk and the soft form sleeping within it and returned to the battle raging overhead. The crew worked in six-hour shifts, but he worked continually, driving himself far beyond the limits of endurance. He spent little time in his cabin, but when he did, Cerynise was immediately there, helping him strip away his wet clothes and nurturing him in a myriad of different ways that Beau hadn't even deemed possible. He felt a sharp sense of disappointment that he was too exhausted to even enjoy the awareness of her soft body pressing warmly against his for the few moments he was able to snatch some sleep.

At last, the storm spent its fury, and the *Audacious* glided into a calmer sea. A full complement of sails were unfurled to catch the now beneficent wind, and once again they began to make good time. The quiet relief of the men was evidenced by their frequent smiles and their energetic eagerness to get on with the business of sailing.

Cerynise found her own contentment sharply dimmed by the realization that Beau hadn't yet fully recovered the hardiness he had exhibited prior to the storm. At times, she was sure his face appeared flushed, at other moments pale and drawn. His movements appeared strained and listless, as if it took a concerted effort for him to walk from bunk to chair or to make an ascent to the deck. Cerynise was there when, from a distance, she saw him speak a few words to Mr. Oaks, who frowned with sudden concern. A moment later, Beau went below.

Usually by the middle of the afternoon the captain was present on the quarterdeck, but he made no appearance on this particular day, nor was he seen when the evening watch took over. Cerynise became increasingly concerned, and although she was reluctant to intrude upon his privacy now that the stress of the storm had passed, it seemed the least she could do was to make sure he was all right. If nothing else, it would ease her own worries.

His cabin door was closed, and no sound could be heard from within despite the passage of time she stood beside it in a nervous quandary. Cerynise could resist no longer and rapped her knuckles lightly against the wood. After a moment of continuing silence, she eased the portal open and found her husband sprawled naked on his back with an arm folded over his eyes.

"Beau...?" she murmured, moving quietly to the bed. His lack of response compelled her to reach out a hand and touch his cheek. He had not shaved since the previous morning, and that was most unusual for Beau, who had always been meticulous about doing so except during the height of the storm. But of far greater significance was the fact that he was burning up with fever.

Cerynise promptly set to work. After bidding Billy to fetch a bucket of water and a fresh bundle of towels, she shushed the boy's concerns and assured him that she would do all she could to care for his captain. She bade him tell Philippe that a light broth would be needed as well as some of the medicinal tea which he had once boasted about while she sketched him.

Beau was mumbling incoherently by the time she returned to the bunk. He looked at her strangely when she sat beside him and tried to press a cup of water to his lips. It seemed as if the demons of hell had just threatened him, for his arm thrashed out wildly, sending the container and its contents flying. Cerynise managed to duck just in time to escape being hurt, but she was immediately back, spreading a wet linen across his brow. Soaking another cloth, she began to bathe his throat and body in an effort to reduce the fever, all the while speaking soft, soothing words to calm him. He raved on in disjointed sentences that made no sense to her, and she was constantly aware that any moment he could rise up and send a fist crashing into her jaw.

Bathing his body didn't seem to have as much effect reducing his fever as she had hoped, and Cerynise fretfully changed tactics. After dribbling cool water over his chest, she spread a wet cloth over it and left it there. She did the same for his lower torso, providing him a modesty cloth of sorts, though in truth she was no more concerned about his nakedness than he was. She was too upset to think of such a trivial matter when she was far more intent upon getting him well again.

The cooling compresses were soon warmed by the heat of his body, and once again she addressed herself to sprinkling him down and laying on freshly dampened towels. She was leaning over him and reapplying a wet cloth to his brow when he drew his breath in sharply and opened glazed eyes to stare at her. Cerynise had no idea if he recognized her or not, but of a sudden she found both her arms seized in his unyielding grip. A smile slashed across his hard features as he drew her down upon his chest.

"I need you...."

"Yes, I know," she replied pleasantly as she tried to pry his steely fingers loose from her arm. She managed to lay the cloth over his brow, but in the next moment she found her breast encompassed by a large hand.

"Behave, my love. You're sick," she cooed, stroking the hair at his temples. "We can discuss this at a later time, when you're feeling better."

Her attempts to brush aside his hand seemed to amuse him. "Don't be frightened, my sweet," he rasped. "I won't be rough with you."

"You're ill," she stated, trying to penetrate

his fevered trance. "You must rest. Now lie back and behave yourself."

The tug of war that quickly ensued for possession of her breast ended in a rending of cloth which promptly separated her bodice to a depth well below her bosom. The ripe fullness spilled outward through the rent, masked by nothing more than a filmy chemise.

"Now look what you've done," she gently rebuked.

"You're beautiful," he crooned, reaching to seize the pale orbs.

Cerynise promptly decided she needed to put some distance between herself and her feverishly amorous husband, at least until he sank again into uncaring oblivion. Gathering her bodice together, she flitted back to the mate's quarters, garbed herself in a nightgown and robe and then returned to the captain's cabin.

Beau had turned his face aside to the wall, and the twitching of his arms and legs indicated that he was in the midst of a dream that apparently had him waging a different sort of a game, perhaps one with a more aggressive combatant than she had proven to be. He began to mutter something about Majorca...the ship being threatened...a fight...men he had to free from a prison....

The next three days were an agonizing torture for Cerynise. At times, Beau recognized her and was aware that they were in his cabin. He would eat and submit himself to her wifely baths with barely a complaint, but then his fever would start rising again, and he'd be drawn back into the demented world of delirium. Though Mr. Oaks and Billy both tried their utmost to persuade her to get some rest, offering to take turns watching over their captain, she firmly refused. The thought of leaving Beau even for so short a time was unbearable. Instead, she moved her clothes back into the cabin, ate the food that was brought to her without being even remotely aware of its taste, and kept her vigil as faithfully as a mother over her child. When she slept, it was beside her husband, for she knew if Beau took a turn for the worse during the night, she'd become immediately aware of the change while lying next to him.

Command of the ship had fallen to Stephen Oaks, who came down frequently to see if there was any change. Billy Todd hovered nearby, his young face the picture of misery. Although the ship was in competent hands and no thought of shirking was ever entertained, the atmosphere on board had seemed to change drastically. Philippe fretted that he was not doing enough, and the quartermaster was seen talking solemnly to Mr. Oaks in the companionway outside the mate's quarters. When Cerynise passed them looking for Billy, the older man made inquiries that readily convinced her of his loyalty and concern for his captain. He offered to do what he could if she had need of him, but she graciously refused, assuring him that he would better serve his captain at the helm, steering them homeward.

In an effort to strengthen her husband, Cerynise was forever trying to force some kind of liquid into his mouth and would often press a cup to his lips and urge him to sip the water or a warm brew. When he sought to turn aside, she gently scolded him for being obstinate and declared his own words back to him: "You're as dry as an unearthed skeleton, Captain Birmingham. Now drink!"

Whatever hesitation she might have once suffered at the idea of touching his private parts was completely vanquished by the familiarity of bathing him and tending his personal needs. Though she remained virginal in actuality, her naiveté was no longer something Cerynise accepted as fact, for it had been nigh sundered by the intimacy of handling her husband's body. In those brief moments in which he was aware of her service to him, she no longer blushed or felt any shame for having to touch him in areas that even in his illness evoked his reaction. It definitely brought a sharper flush of color to his face when she performed the more debasing duties. When he was too weak to stand, receptacles were brought for his use, and as efficient as a well-practiced nursemaid, she would assist him and then dispense with the contents in quiet dignity, whisking the container out the door, where Billy took charge.

"Why don't you let the boy see to my needs?" Beau asked weakly, abashed after another such occurrence.

Cerynise smiled down at him with glowing

eyes and murmured considerably more sweetly than he had once done, "In sickness or in health, my dearest."

"Are you set on tormenting me, woman?" he asked gruffly.

"Never that, my dear." Cerynise paused to wash her hands as she teased, "I'm only trying to get you well so I won't have to wear widow's weeds for months on end."

"I don't want you to see me like this," he complained, grating a hand across the stubble darkening his cheeks. It was definitely not as bad as it could've been, for she had also learned the knack of shaving him, along with giving him a bath. It was just that he was tired of being sick and embarrassed by her wifely ministrations when he had always been so stalwart.

Cerynise came back to the bunk and laid out fresh sheets to change his bed linens. "Turnabout is fair play, is it not, Captain?"

Beau scowled. "You're deliberately antagonizing me when I'm too weak to do anything about it."

Gazing down at him, Cerynise allowed her lips to curve coyly as her eyes glowed back at him. "What would you like to do about it if you were stronger, sir?"

If his chin hadn't already been wedged against his neck by the pillows stuffed behind his head, Beau was sure it would have descended forthwith. Even with his dazed senses, he could detect an invitation when it was presented. "Careful, madam. I'll not always be hampered by this confounded weakness."

"Strange, I didn't realize you've been hampered in the least." Cerynise looked straight into his eyes, daring to remind him that only a moment earlier when she had been in the process of bathing him, the manly flesh had thickened beneath her hand.

" 'Tis the other I speak of...the lack of strength that afflicts me," he muttered grumpily. "I could be nigh dead and the sight of you would awaken that part of me. But you undoubtedly think you're safe, woman, else you wouldn't tease me."

"I think no such thing, sir," she asserted, and then, just as quickly, flashed him a smile. "But that is neither here nor there, sir." She twirled her finger in a downward circle, motioning him to face away. "I need to get dressed for bed, and since I've given Mr. Oaks back his cabin for the time being, I can't very well ask him to vacate his quarters so I can change, now can I?"

"You've seen enough of me," Beau argued. "Why can't I see more of you?"

"Because, dear husband, looking at you isn't going to place *you* in danger of being raped."

"Is it rape when a husband makes love to his wife?"

"We'll leave that for the sages to answer in years to come, my dear," she answered with a coquettish smile. "As for now, I would like for you to turn your head...*please*."

Beau started to roll over but was once again reminded of just how weak he had become, leaving him no more strength than a baby. He averted his face instead.

By the next evening, Cerynise sensed that a crisis had come. Beau's fever escalated sharply, and his delirium became more intense. At one point, he lashed out and sent a basin of water crashing to the floor, thoroughly soaking Cerynise in the process. It had been in her mind to don a nightgown, but perhaps not as soon as she was required to do so.

Beau finally quieted, and Cerynise was torn between apprehension and relief. When she felt his skin, she was led to hope that it might be a slight degree cooler than before, but she couldn't be certain. Taking no chances, she cooled him down with wet towels until she was at least assured that the fever was no higher than it had been earlier that day. Then she doused the tiny flames of all but one lantern which hung near the bunk and crawled over Beau to take her usual place on the far side. Mentally and physically drained of strength by her fretful worrying throughout the days and nights, she nestled close against his back and found her favorite area to rest her hand, feeling pleasantly reassured by the strong, sturdy heartbeat beneath her palm. She closed her eyes and let herself be swept along into deep, blissful repose.

It was strange the pleasures one could find in the arms of Morpheus. A warm titillating wetness drew on her nipple while a feverish hand moved beneath her gown, searching out the secret softness of her. Following the urging pressure of her dream lover's hands, she relaxed back upon the pillows and welcomed him with opening limbs. His naked body covered hers and seemed to scald her with more than the fervor he exhibited. The blunt probing of a blazing hardness against her womanly flesh was only one more caress she willingly accepted. Then a burning pain stabbed through her, bringing her up off the pillow with a shocked gasp.

Cerynise passed a hand over her eyes as if to wipe the sleep from them, but this was no dream thrusting intently at her loins. This was Beau, feverish, dazed and thoroughly engorged with lust as his narrow hips caressed hers in long, leisurely strokes that soothed the shock of his penetration. Down in the depth of her, where the hard flint struck, she could feel sparks beginning to flare in a tinderbox overflowing with womanly ardor. His detailed explanations of weeks ago were now made vividly clear, and she responded in ways that he had described were pleasing to a man, rising up against him, taking him fully into her, and meeting his hard strokes with a passionate zeal and desire to gratify his cravings completely. For too long he had wanted this from her, and now she was giving him everything she had within her.

His harsh breathing rasped near her ear, sounding thunderously loud, while her own quickening gasps seemed to be torn from the inner marrow of her being. His loins thudded into hers with increasing intensity until she was nigh moaning for want of some strange release that she could not fathom. The intensifying hunger within her became almost insatiable, driving her to a kind of wildness that made her dig her nails into his back. Then she caught her breath in surprise as she felt the first pulsing waves of bliss begin to wash over her. She was greedy to savor it all and began to writhe beneath him until they were straining against each other, forcing every pleasurable sensation that could be wrenched free to gush forth in a torrent of sizzling, scintillating ecstasy. It was a dazzling display, a thoroughly unique experience of being lifted aloft while tiny, rapture-filled bubbles burst in and all around their cleaving bodies. Cerynise felt a feverish warmth filling her and welcomed it in the cavern of her being, clasping her husband's tautly flexing buttocks as she lifted herself up to him so the feeling wouldn't be lost or wasted. Gradually the hard thrusts slowed, and Beau relaxed against her.

"Cerynise, don't leave me..." he muttered against her throat.

Her arms slipped around him, and she smiled, tears of joy filling her eyes. "I won't, Beau."

She held him close to her, aware of the thudding of his heart and his harsh, labored breath tickling her face. She didn't know how long she lay there. Her eyelids were sagging closed when she felt him move away. Turning on his side away from her, he huddled beneath the bedcovers and immediately began shivering.

"Cold," he mumbled. "So cold."

Fear spiraled through Cerynise, but when she rose up behind him and laid a hand to his brow, it seemed definitely cooler. She sighed in relief and then glanced down at herself in some surprise. The ties of her nightgown had been pulled free, and the garment now hung off her shoulder, falling open to an elbow and leaving her ripe breasts fully exposed. Minute pinpoints of red speckled the pale orbs where they had been scraped by her husband's beard. The nipples were equally flushed and tender where he had suckled her.

For some strange reason Cerynise found this new experience strangely satisfying, as if these tiny wounds were evidence of her new wifely status. The day of their marriage, Beau had been incredibly gentle with the sensitive peaks, leaving no hint afterwards that he had ever taken them into his mouth. But in his fevered state he had been mindless of everything but the fulfillment he had sought and, perhaps unwittingly, gave her in return.

Cerynise crawled over him, taking care not to disturb him, but he reached out a hand to halt her from leaving. As she climbed free, it fell back upon the mattress. For a moment she stood beside the bunk, gazing down at her handsome husband, feeling closer to him than she ever had before. Much in awe of this stirring tenderness, she knelt beside him and lightly kissed his ear, his cheek and his mouth. As she did, she realized that not once during his lovemaking had he kissed her. It was almost as if he had avoided doing so, which seemed very odd, since he had previously sought her kisses with fervent zeal.

From beneath heavily weighted eyelids Beau stared at her in a daze, and with a smile Cerynise sat back upon her heels, making no effort to cover her breasts as his gaze ranged over them slowly. He lifted a hand toward her, but with a sigh, he closed his eyes and sank again into a heavy slumber.

After a moment Cerynise rose and was surprised to feel a sticky wetness between her thighs. On closer examination she realized that part of it was her own blood. Her eyes flew back to the far side of the bunk, where she saw reddened blotches marring the whiteness of the sheet. She searched further still and found that Beau had not been excluded from the ritual of virginal sacrifice. It seemed a late hour for such a task, but baths were definitely in order, and the sheets needed to be changed.

Freshly garbed in a nightgown, Cerynise set about to cleanse Beau and strip away the sheets. Her fingers brushed his forehead in a loving caress, and a sob of pure relief broke from her as she found his skin much cooler than it had been in days. The flush of fever was gone. Already he seemed to be resting easier and deeper. He stirred slightly, his lips moving. She bent closer, hardly daring to breathe. It seemed but a spiraling thread of sound that issued forth. "Cerynise, don't hold yourself from me forever...."

Gloom settled in, thrusting a sharp pain

through her heart. He didn't even remember what he had done. Nor did it appear likely that he would when he came fully to his senses. Would he even believe her if she tried to explain? Perhaps, if she made such an attempt, he'd even be inclined to think that she had taken advantage of him in his delirium. Or more rightly, perhaps, insist that she continue letting him have his way with her until their marriage was annulled.

Painful as it was for her to consider that he might want to proceed with the nullification of their marriage upon their arrival in Charleston, Cerynise reaffirmed her intent not to stop him from obtaining his freedom. Better to let him think the consummation never happened at all than to see him vexed by a union he had offered only on a temporary basis. As painful as it would be for her to bear, she thought she could let him go more easily if he remained unaware of what had happened in his bunk. If he felt honor bound to do the right thing by her but eventually came to resent her being his wife....

Cerynise choked on a sudden welling of tears and couldn't continue with the thought, for her heart grew cold even as the idea formed.

No! It was better to pretend that nothing had ever happened. Though her decision filled her with trembling disquiet, she grew more dedicated to it with each passing moment. With no other thought in her mind but to allow Beau the liberty to make the final decision whether to continue with their marriage or to dissolve it, she lovingly bathed the now quiescent male form, kissing his arms, face and chest amid a profusion of tears. Then she labored to turn him over as she stripped away the stained sheet and spread a fresh one over the mattress.

She had just finished remaking the bed when she recognized Billy's footsteps in the passageway. Frantically Cerynise glanced around for a place to conceal the dirty clothes and espied the second locker beyond the bunk, the one that normally held his rain gear, which was now dry and stored away again. Surely, she reasoned, they'd be favored by a calmer voyage from now on and the locker would remain unused. Rolling up the sheet and nightgown together, she stuffed them near the back of the compartment and barely clicked the door shut before Billy knocked softly and asked if she needed him for anything or if he should go to bed.

"The captain's fever has broken, Billy," she called through the door. "He's going to be just fine, so go and enjoy your sleep."

His ecstatic response left no doubt in her mind that the news of his captain's recovery pleased him.

CHAPTER 10

Beau resumed command of the *Audacious* with a zeal that allowed no uncertainty to remain in anyone's mind that he had fully recovered from his illness. Neither could Cerynise entertain even the smallest hope that he remembered their intimacy. Upon waking to restored health and finding her beside him in his bunk, he had promptly started making overtures commensurate to a groom coaxing his virgin bride to yield herself to the delights to be found in a marriage bed. Plying her with persuasive kisses, he had promised to be gentle with her and assured her that, in spite of the initial pain, she would come to enjoy their union. During this heady beguilement, Beau slipped the ties at the top of her nightgown free, making it abundantly clear to Cerynise that he was feeling much like his randy old self again and was just as eager to make love to her as he had been before. His husky blandishments quickened her own hunger for what she had once tasted. Yet the fact that he still thought her a virgin frustrated her so much that she swung a pillow into his face in a fine display of flaring temper.

Moments earlier, Beau had drifted upward through a cloud of haunting impressions and entered the realm of full awareness with a strange sense of well-being, perhaps unlike any he had hitherto known. Almost at once, he had realized he had been ill, evidently very ill, and that made the odd contentment all the more perplexing. He couldn't quite lay a finger to the cause. The past days, for the most part, were lost to him. Yet something had happened which he could neither define nor deny, and for some obscure reason it all

313

seemed connected to Cerynise. His befogged recollections seemed distantly detached from reality, yet he was inundated with glimpses of his wife tending him and an awareness of her nestling against his back, her soft breasts pressed tightly to him and her slender thighs snuggled beneath his. At least that much he guessed was true. Yet fragments of more sensual impressions flitted through his mind, seeming so real that he could almost have sworn they were true. Still, they were so equally farfetched that he could only accept them for what they were. *Illusions!* How could he even consider that he had actually seen his young wife sitting on her heels beside his bunk with her gown falling down around her arms and her soft, lustrous breasts gleaming with an unusual rosy hue beneath the hanging lantern? Or that he had felt her nails clawing at his back as he poured his love into her? Or heard her rapturous panting as she soared to the lofty pinnacle of ecstasy? He certainly discerned no change in her. If anything, she seemed even more adamant that he not touch her, for the very moment his fingers tugged loose the delicate ribbon of her nightgown and pulled the garment open to allow his gaze to feast upon her bosom was the precise instant he got a face full of feathers. It didn't help in the least that the pillow she hit him with burst open, sending fluffy down flying everywhere, mostly, it seemed, into their noses and mouths, and all she could say was "Oops!"

His good humor sharply declined from

there, dropping to a roiling point when she scrambled to her feet in the bunk, albeit hunched over, and lifted her gown in a quest to jump over him. Challenged by a desire to keep her prisoner, if only to solve the mystery befuddling his senses, he raised a leg to block her path to freedom. He soon found out just how tenacious his wife really was to leave his bed. Planting a dainty foot upon his chest, she fairly sailed across his bulk, permitting him an enticing view that nearly staggered his wits. Almost at once she began throwing her clothes and possessions into a satchel, obviously scurrying in her haste to get out of his reach. Had he warmed her backside with hot oil, Beau was certain she could not have moved any faster. It was understandable, then, that whatever ebullience he had briefly relished upon finding her snuggled close against his side swiftly darkened into a sour irascibility.

Growling, Beau batted away feathers as he stalked naked across the room, not giving a damn how nervous he made his wife as he crossed to the washstand. "Well, you've certainly made a fine mess of my cabin," he snarled disagreeably. "Billy will no doubt be highly entertained trying to stuff this mess back into the pillow."

Cerynise kept her face carefully averted, but that didn't keep Beau from seeing her primly elevated profile as she responded with strained dignity, "I didn't mean for the feathers to come out."

"No, but you meant to hit me, didn't you?" He grunted sharply in derision. "Was it too much for you to take pity on a man who has been laid low by illness? Did you have to abuse me?"

"You were being rude," she accused stiltedly.

Beau slapped again at the feathers floating in front of his face. "I was being husbandly, madam," he corrected tersely, "but I guess that was too much for your fine virginal purity to bear. Like I've told you before, I happen to enjoy looking at your breasts. I've seen none finer."

Cerynise wondered if he would have been at all curious had she let him see her bosom, for she still bore a rash from his bearding. It was to be assumed that he had locked those moments of passion deep within the coffer of his mind and had forgotten their union like a besotted man who, upon sobering, could recall nothing of the moments he had spent in lewd debauchery. To her, the fusion of their bodies had meant far more than physical appeasement, perhaps the most significant being the realization that she was now truly, lawfully his wife. Swallowing her emotions was difficult, and though she could chide herself endlessly for having carelessly ensconced herself in his bed, it didn't change the way she felt now that the deed had been done. What grieved her was the fact that she couldn't release all those warm, tender emotions and respond to him as a loving wife should.

Making a valiant attempt to appear glib, Cerynise queried, "Have you seen many breasts, Captain?"

Beau looked at her closely, but again he saw only her imperiously held profile. Had he imagined a thickness in her tone? "I've seen enough to know you have many women outdone by a fair margin. Not only are your breasts full enough to fill my hands, but they're about as perfect as any man could possibly envision."

"You must have viewed a sizable number, Captain," she surmised coolly, refusing to look around. "Should I express my gratitude for your ability to make such a comparison?"

"No, dammit!" Beau barked, with long strides reaching her side. He opened his mouth to speak but instantly began spitting as he tried to dislodge the feathers that he had sucked in.

A giggle was wrenched from Cerynise as she realized what had happened. Dancing away to a safe distance, she turned and, pointing at him, dissolved into laughter. "All you need now is to be tarred, Captain," she declared through her amusement as her gaze lightly skimmed downward. "You certainly have more than enough feathers needed to complete such a task."

Bracing his knuckles casually on a narrow hip, Beau glanced down at himself and made a point of picking a feather off a very manly part. "I wouldn't be at all surprised to find a little dust there, too."

Cerynise couldn't resist a quick retort and did so loftily. "I would."

317

Beau's brow cocked at an inquisitive angle as he looked at her narrowly. It was right on the tip of his tongue to ask her outright if he had indeed made love to her. Still, if he had only dreamed it, then he'd be giving her cause to wonder if he fantasized about her morning, noon, and all through the night. He probed indirectly. "Not unless you know more than I do, madam."

Cerynise bit her lip in an effort to keep from blurting the truth and, by dint of will, managed to respond with a blasé shrug. "I assume you had your full share of harlots in London. I saw you with several the night before we were married."

If she had hoped to startle him with her revelation, then Beau was most assuredly willing to disappoint her. "You saw me leaving them, too, a moment after they met my carriage."

The complacent smile her husband wore convinced Cerynise that he hadn't been at all surprised by her remark. She lifted her nose in a guise of priggish prudery as she faced the gallery windows. "You certainly seemed to enjoy that hussy fondling you. She *was* rather pretty, as I remember."

"Strange," Beau replied in a museful mien as he rasped a hand across his bearded chin, "whenever you've touched me there, you've always gotten immediate results. But as I recall, madam, nothing of that nature occurred that night...a fact to which you can attest after having witnessed her invitation."

Cerynise shot him a curious glance. "How do you know what I saw?"

Beau chuckled briefly and shook his head. "Nay, madam, 'tis my secret, and I will never tell."

Feeling an urge to sneeze, Cerynise waved a hand through the air to fan the feathers away from her nose. She really wished she hadn't hit him so hard after he had been sick. The pillow might not have even come open had she endeavored to make it a more playful swat.

She sighed, wondering how long it would take Billy and her to put everything aright again in the cabin. "You'd better get dressed so we can start cleaning up in here," she urged dejectedly. "This may take all day."

Beau crossed to the locker and, taking out his robe, shrugged into it. "I'm going to take a bath in the mate's quarters. Then I'm going to shave and get decently attired once again. I'd really like for you to join me, madam, but if I dare ask, I may get another pillow thrown into my face."

With that bit of sarcasm, he stalked out, closing the door loudly behind him. That was the morning of Beau's first day back on his feet.

The second was no better, for by that time Cerynise had taken up residence in the smallest cabin, having had Billy help her carry her trunks and possessions into the tiny space. She hadn't wanted to put Stephen Oaks out of his quarters any longer and had given the mate the very same options that he had once given her, flatly telling him that she wouldn't use his cabin under any circumstances and that it was entirely up to him whether or not he used it. The mate conceded, for he had no other place to go now that she had become ensconced in the tiny cabin.

In an effort to make her new accommodations less menacing, Cerynise questioned Beau about the possibility of hanging up some of her sketches and paintings on the walls. Grudging the fact that she was serious about living apart from him even to the extent that she would endure a windowless cabin that heightened her apprehensions, he scowled and snorted like an angry bull. Even so, he relented enough to give his consent.

Billy offered to help, and Cerynise hovered near, making sure he drove the tiny nails into the seams where the planks of wood had been buttressed together against the wall, for she didn't want her husband to regret the fact that he had acceded to her request. She arranged the artwork to lend the cabin a feeling of depth as well as the open atmosphere and freedom of the upper deck. Having painted the porpoises in full color and flying motion on a larger canvas, she hung that piece where she could espy it upon waking. Once the individual groupings on the four walls were arranged in a manner that suited her, Cerynise found herself pleasantly surprised by the warm, comfortable ambience now pervading the tiny room. The paintings gave her considerably more to look at than dull blank walls, but most of all she no longer felt like she was in a dark dungeon.

After the upheaval and turmoil of the storm, her anxiety over Beau during his illness, and her startling introduction to the more erotic rudiments of being a full-fledged wife, Cerynise felt physically and mentally drained. Recognizing her own sense of depression, she promptly determined that she needed to take care of herself for a change and forewarned Billy that she would be resting for a while and didn't wish to be disturbed. She slept for several hours and awoke feeling refreshed and wonderfully rejuvenated. Then, just as a woman is wont to do while in fine spirits, she directed her attention to her appearance, which she had been too worried to care about during Beau's feverish bout. Since Billy had gathered several barrels of rainwater for such purposes during the storm-driven deluge, she bade him heat enough water for a tub bath and selected scented bath salts appropriate to her mood, a sweet jasmine fragrance that reminded her of home.

Cerynise settled back into the steaming water with a deep sigh of appreciation. She hated basin baths, preferring to soak on a daily basis, but a sea voyage wasn't always conducive to such luxuries. The bath was probably the only benefit from the tempest. At the moment she thought it divine.

Memories of those moments spent in carnal union with Beau swam provocatively through

Cerynise's mind as she dallied in the bath. The impressions were so overpowering and vivid that they rekindled fires, which she had naively thought had been smothered by the blunt realization of her husband's incognizance. If she closed her eyes, she could almost feel his large body moving upon hers, his hardened chest teasing her breasts, and his harsh gasps filling her mind. A long, trembling sigh slipped from her lips as she luxuriated in the sensations that flooded through her. Her yearning to have Beau's arms around her right then and there was acute, making her realize just how deeply she had been affected by their union and the bliss she had found within it.

Heaving a fretful sigh, Cerynise shook her head at the folly of entertaining such stimulating recollections. It didn't strengthen her resolve in the least to be lusting after her husband when she knew that, for her own sake, she would have to hold him at arm's length until he committed himself completely to their marriage, which she really couldn't expect to happen.

She was still in the midst of soaking herself when she heard the floorboards in the passageway creaking slightly as someone walked past her door. The distant closing of the captain's door identified that one to be her husband. A moment hardly passed before the squeaking came back to her portal and, after a long pause, a light rap of knuckles came against the wood.

"Cerynise," Beau called in a gentler tone than

she had heard from him since he had left his bunk. "I'd like for you to have dinner with me tonight."

She lifted a large sponge and dribbled water over her pale breasts, wondering what ploy he would use this time to get her into his bed. As much as she wanted to be with him, she knew that when her desires could be stirred merely by her memories of their intimacy, it was definitely better if she avoided the temptation of being with him. "I'm sorry, Beau. I'm busy."

Beau wasn't willing to be denied, not tonight. He was intrigued with fleeting memories of her snuggling against his back, which made him loathe their present sleeping arrangement all the more. But more than anything, he wanted answers to all those other tantalizing impressions that haunted him relentlessly and that refused to slip into oblivion. In a slightly stronger tone, he reissued his invitation. "Cerynise, I'm asking you to have dinner with me. I have something I wish to discuss with you, but right now I'm hungry. I want to relax and enjoy the meal with you *if* you will allow me the pleasure of your company."

Cerynise suffered no uncertainty what he was hungry for. Indeed, with his propensities, she wondered how he had ever managed to endure lengthy voyages without a harlot on board to service his on-going needs. In an equally sweet voice, she warbled, "I'm busy."

"You're sulking again," he accused testily, becoming a little more irate.

"I am not!" she denied, offended by his conclusions. "Now go away before your men hear you pleading at my door."

"I don't give a damn who hears me," he growled, close against the wooden barrier. "I want you to open this door so I can talk with you."

"And I told you I am busy!" she flung toward the door.

If Cerynise had thought she was safe in the cabin with a latch securely fastened across the portal, then she soon realized she had been in error to suppose that Beau Birmingham could be halted simply by a locked door. With nothing more than a hard jolt of a shoulder, he sent the panel flying open and the now-broken lock rattling to the floor. Before the door hit the wall behind it, he was already striding across the threshold, displaying enough surprise to convey the fact that he really hadn't expected to find her in the tub.

Beau barely had time to cast an appreciative glance across his wife's wetly gleaming breasts before he again found his face full, this time with a sopping wet sponge. The shock sent him stumbling backward over the same area the sponge had liberally sprinkled with water the very instant it met the intruder. His retreating feet hit the moisture and abruptly slipped out from under him, throwing him backward against the far wall of the passageway.

Cerynise winced as she heard his head hit the wood panel, and the sudden silence that ensued made her fear that her husband had

324

been knocked unconscious. Anxiety propelled her to her feet and she was out of the tub in a flash, seizing a robe and running toward him as she struggled to don it. Then one eye popped open in Beau's now-grimacing face and fixed on her in a painful squint. Only the briefest of moments passed as he considered her delectable form and the sound of footsteps descending the companionway. His reluctance to have another man view what he was rapidly coming to consider solely his by marital rights was decidedly more pronounced than his desire to feast his gaze. *"Woman, get some clothes on before you have the whole ship up in arms!"*

"Humph!" Decidedly miffed at being bellowed at, Cerynise caught the edge of the door and swept it forward. It banged against the broken jamb and promptly came back. After a slight pause to yank away the splintered wood sticking out from the frame, she whipped the portal closed again with a finality that sealed the doom of any conversation her husband had hoped to have with her.

In the lengthy silence that followed, Cerynise stared at the door, wondering if he would make another assault upon it. Having dinner with her was something he had really seemed to have set his mind upon, she sensed, for after getting to his feet in the hallway, he muttered sourly near her door, "I hope you enjoy your damned privacy, madam, because I sure as hell won't. But then, perhaps it's your intent to torment me."

It was unlikely the officers and crew on deck had been oblivious to what had gone on between the newly wedded couple on the lower deck that night. It was certainly more than Cerynise could hope for when Mr. Oaks knocked on her door the next morning and offered to take her for a turn about the deck. If not for the fact that she was feeling in rare need of fresh air after isolating herself in her quarters for the duration of the evening and into a late hour of the morning, she would have forgone the opportunity. She sensed that Beau was too vexed with her determination to separate herself from him to even consider offering his arm for such an outing.

Stephen Oaks seemed rather sheepish about meeting her gaze, but as she fell in beside him, he was led to speak in behalf of his superior. "The captain is a bit more surly than usual, ma'am, what with being sick and all." He didn't care to explain in any great detail what he meant by "all," but as a man he could understand his captain's frustration with her continuing obstinance to withhold her favors, which Stephen strongly suspected might be the case. On the other hand, he could also sympathize with the girl. The marriage vows had been spoken in such haste that she probably hadn't had nearly enough time to consider the demands her new husband would be making of her. "I'm sure 'twill pass ere long."

"Aye," Cerynise sighed somberly, having no doubt that Beau's irritability was caused primarily

326

by her presence aboard his ship. "The end of the voyage should see a turn in it."

Stephen Oaks searched his mind for something more encouraging to say. He could have told her that her husband was well liked, and with only a few exceptions, who were themselves not worth their weight in salt, the seamen held their captain in high esteem. When the man had risked his own life to save members of his crew as he had done in Majorca, what else could anyone, who had been around longer than the last voyage or two, have felt toward the courageous man? The mate even considered expounding upon the wealth of opportunities the captain had given him when no one else had even cared to lend an ear to his aspirations of commanding a ship one day. And if she thought her husband's gift to Mr. Carmichael had been a singular occasion, then Stephen Oaks would have enjoyed enlightening her on the generosity of the man, perhaps to the degree that she might have even been led to think that he was only making it up to ease her exasperation with the captain. All of this Beau Birmingham would probably never have even pondered, much less have mentioned to another soul. The captain could be damnably closed-mouth at times, even to the point of letting others think the worst of him.

"Ma'am, I understand that you've known the captain for a goodly length of time. You must have seen his good side, else you wouldn't have agreed to marry him. All you need is a little patience. He's sure to come around fairly soon."

Cerynise smiled ruefully. Come around to what? Their marriage? Doubtful! Captain Beauregard Birmingham enjoyed his freedom too much to seriously consider taking to wife any woman on a permanent basis. When a man as good looking as her husband, who could've had any lady of his choosing, had limited himself (at least as much as she could determine) to appeasing himself with strumpets, it was clear that he had long been dedicated to the idea of maintaining his bachelor's status, to the degree that he had carefully avoided the pitfalls of compromising the virtue of young, winsome maids.

Beau was on the quarterdeck with the bosun when she arrived on the lower deck. Now that it was colder, her husband had once again garbed himself in a sweater, this one a dark blue, and narrow trousers of the same hue. He had lost weight during his illness, which made the handsomely proportioned bones and tendons in his face even more pronounced. As soon as he caught sight of her, the lean cheeks started flexing. A cold despair descended upon Cerynise when she noticed those snapping sinews, for she didn't doubt in the least that his vexation with her was the cause.

The deep cowl of the knit garment had been lifted to provide him some further warmth and protection from the winds, but it seemed to her that every now and then an involuntary shiver would shake his frame. After tending him through a lengthy ordeal in which she had feared for his life, Cerynise grew concerned that he was chancing a relapse. When Billy hurried past her on some mission, she bade him to fetch the captain a coat. The boy was soon back, handing her the garment and speeding on his way before Cerynise had a chance to tell him that she had also wanted him to take it up to the quarterdeck.

Folding the coat over her arm, Cerynise told herself that there was absolutely nothing to worry about, that Beau Birmingham, as much as he might have wanted to, wouldn't gobble her up and spit her out in so many pieces. At least, she hoped he wouldn't. But from the way the muscles in his jaw were twitching, she was not about to make any wagers.

Cerynise couldn't subdue the nervous shaking that had suddenly seized her as she climbed to the upper deck and approached the two men. Even after gaining the higher level, she couldn't bring herself to intrude. Indeed, Beau seemed to go out of his way to ignore her presence. It was Mr. McDurmett who brought her husband's attention to bear upon her. Under the circumstances, Beau had no choice but to face her with a querying brow raised sharply. Against her better judgment, Cerynise moved forward with her offering.

"I brought your coat, Captain," she murmured timidly, holding it out with outstretched arms. She detected a ruddiness in his cheeks that gave her cause to worry, and she could only hope that it was due to the wind and not a returning fever. "After you've been so sick, I'd feel greatly relieved if you'd wear it." She shook the garment out as she offered, "Here, I'll help you put it—"

The blue eyes flashed a warning as his fingers closed around the delicate bones of her wrist, forestalling her attempt to drape the coat around his shoulder. "I'm not some mewling babe, madam, as you may be wont to think I am," he muttered savagely. "I can take care of myself now, and I don't need you to follow me about like an overanxious mother afraid that her weanling may catch his death. Now take the coat out of my sight."

His words stung far more harshly than the steely grip he had fastened on her arm. Abruptly he released her and pivoted about, giving her no further notice as he returned to his conversation with the bosun, who seemed to blush in embarrassment as he flicked a worried glance toward her.

Cerynise backed away hastily, averting her eyes to hide her swimming tears. Somehow she managed to descend the steps to the main deck without stumbling and quietly, gracefully made her way to the companionway with all the dignity she could summon. She moved past men who kept their gazes focused diligently on anything or anyone but her. The knowledge of her public rejection only intensified her distress. Indeed, her chest ached as if her heart had been ripped free.

In her unhappiness and haste, Cerynise was unaware of the man who watched her with carefully hooded eyes from the quarterdeck. Beau had dropped any pretense of

330

ignoring his wife, yet only the jagged pulse that had leapt to life in his throat attested to his own disquiet as he stared after her with mingled feelings of regret and concern. If not for his damnable pride, he might have broken his guise of stoic reticence and gone after her, letting the crew think what they would. His annoyance with himself was paramount, and try as he might, he could not stop those strange, tantalizing dreams from flaring through his mind where, with heightening recurrences, they conspired to form a memory.

With a broken sob Cerynise swung the door of her cabin closed behind her and threw herself onto the bunk, where she poured out her anguish in the muffling softness of the pillow. It seemed suddenly too much for her to bear, all of her fear and her love for Beau culminating in that brief interlude of passion that was her secret and her torment. But now, his manner was as cold as the sea they were sailing, as if her efforts to withhold herself had wrecked every chance she had ever had of staying married to him.

Cerynise's tears ebbed only with the onslaught of a traumatized sleep, but it was a nightmarish elapse of time, a horrible illusion in which she became desperately afraid for her life. She was running through a dark house with Alistair Winthrop and Howard Rudd following hard upon her heels while flashes of light burst all around her, startling her and sending her reeling away in fright and trepidation. In spite of her frantic attempts to flee, the two men came ever closer and, with each new discovery of her hiding places, set her to flight again and again until there was no place left where she could seek shelter. They seemed to swoop down upon her like banshees from hell, and in their hands they carried large black sheets in which to bind her for her burial. Her back was to the wall as they pulled them across her face, and suddenly she couldn't breathe....

With a muffled cry Cerynise came upright off her pillow, flinging away the hand that lay alongside her cheek. In rising panic she began to struggle against the one who reached out to take her by the arms. "No, you can't!" she sobbed pitifully. "I'm not dead yet! You can't bury me...."

"Cerynise, wake up," a familiar voice soothed. "You've been dreaming."

She glanced around wildly, her fear undiminished. Had all of the events from the time of Lydia's death onward been a dream? Had she even met with Alistair Winthrop and Howard Rudd to discuss the will? Perhaps she wasn't even married....

Her eyes fell on Beau, who sat on his haunches beside the bunk, and the desire to fling herself into his arms and sob out her relief against his shoulder almost tore her from her narrow bed, but the memory of his harsh rejection on the quarterdeck came winging cruelly back, making her pull away with a moan. "Please don't touch me."

Beau swallowed the lump in his throat with

332

difficulty as he tried once more to soothe her. "Lie back upon the bunk, Cerynise, and rest a moment longer until your thoughts come clear. It frightened me to hear your screams from the deck."

Startled by the realization that she had cried out in her sleep, Cerynise stared up at him in confusion. In growing dismay, she turned her face aside as tears gathered. "I'm sorry if I embarrassed you...."

Beau sought to calm her fears, just as he had done when she was a child. "Shhh, my love. Don't even think that. You merely frightened me, that's all. Your screams sounded very much like those of that little girl who had been locked in the trunk years ago."

"I suppose your men heard them, too," she muttered dejectedly, refusing to look at him. "Just like they heard everything else that went on down here last night?"

"So what if they did?" Beau laughed softly, trying to make light of it all for her benefit. "They're probably wagering which of us will win out, but I have a feeling they're not placing too many bets on me coming out ahead." He reached across and gently tugged at her chin. "Turn around, my love, and let me see your pretty face."

Strange how memories from the past seemed to recur from time to time, Cerynise mused distantly. He had quieted her sobs with almost the same magical words after letting her out of the trunk, but this time she denied his plea. "Don't call me my love," she whispered, stubbornly refusing to let him draw her face around. "I'm not your love, so don't pretend that I am with all those pretty words you use on other women. We both know what you want, and that is to mount me like some lusty bull."

Beau winced at her unladylike statement, but it only brought home to him all the things he had said in her presence. Perhaps she had been around him too long for *her* good. "Philippe has made soup for lunch. Can I talk you into coming to my cabin and sharing it with me?"

"I'd rather not," she replied dully.

"Dam—" Beau caught himself instantly. Flying into a temper every time she rejected his invitations did nothing to ease their dispositions. He tried again, this time more gently. "I've come to enjoy our meals together, Cerynise. I wish you'd change your mind. Besides, I have some things I'd like to talk with you about."

Her aloofness was unswerving. "I'm really not hungry right now."

Footsteps approaching the open door brought Beau's attention to bear upon the one who came to stand beyond the threshold. Stephen Oaks looked past him worriedly, settling his gaze on Cerynise, but the man could discern nothing of her present state when she refused to look around. Meeting his captain's gaze, he asked hesitantly, "Is Mrs. Birmingham all right, sir?"

"Aye." Beau sighed and straightened himself to his full height. "She just had a bad dream, that's all."

Even if it meant angering his superior, the mate felt pressed to let him know just how much his wife had endeared herself to many of the sailors on board. Perhaps such knowledge would help the man realize what a prize his wife really was, in more ways than just beauty and grace. "Billy is wary of coming down, Captain, for fear that something horrible might have happened to her. I'm afraid the rest of the men are up in arms, too, for the very same reason."

Beau looked at his second-in-command and realized the depth of loyalty the man had obviously come to feel for the lady during their passage from England. The mate's words came close to laying the blame for the difficulty in their marriage at his feet, not Cerynise's. And why not? His contrariness and tenaciously stubborn will could set the orneriest tar on his ear. "Then please assure Billy and everyone else that Mrs. Birmingham is resting now after waking from a nightmare. She'll be as good as new in no time."

"Aye, Captain." Stephen Oaks started to turn away but paused and solemnly met his captain's lingering stare. " 'Twould really be nice to see her smiling face on the morrow, sir."

Beau nodded, aware that the man was gently urging him to treat his wife with more care. "I'll see what I can do, Mr. Oaks."

"I know you will, sir," the mate replied, and with a brief smile, returned to the deck.

Beau looked around at his wife and found

that she hadn't moved. He bent down to tuck the covers in around her and smooth the stray tendrils of hair back from her temple. "You should have something warmer than these blankets. I'll bring in the feather tick from my bed...."

"Please don't bother. I'm just fine as I am."

Beau turned with a frustrated sigh and crossed to the door. He had done it up royally this time. She wouldn't even look at him or accept his efforts to help or comfort her.

Cerynise heard the door close gently behind him and, in the silence that ensued, finally found the privacy to bury her face in the pillow and sob out her anguish anew.

It was at least a good hour later when Cerynise poured water into the basin and, wetting a cloth, bathed her eyes and face until the red blotches that had been brought forth by her weeping began to fade. Patting her skin dry, she leaned forward to stare into the tiny mirror above the washstand.

No more tears, she promised herself in a whisper, fervently hoping she had shed the last of that salty river for the likes of such sapphire-eyed devils as her husband and others more akin to Alistair Winthrop. If Beau didn't want to keep her as his wife, then she could ill afford to let her despondency over her lost love wreak havoc with her moods. Somewhere, someday, there would be a man who'd love her and could accept her as his bride without caring that she was no longer a virgin. Until then, she would have to make a new life for herself. There would be enough challenges to face in Charleston without letting her dashed dreams get the better of her. Until her paintings started selling, she'd have to be financially dependent on her uncle, but he had lived a bachelor's life so long, she didn't know if he could abide having a female under foot all the time or her paints and sketches cluttering some area of his house. But then, he had always had his nose in a book of one kind or another, so perhaps he wouldn't notice her presence overly much.

Strengthened somewhat by the new goal she had set for her life, Cerynise turned to her sketches and involved herself in her work, but she sat back abruptly in stunned amazement when a charcoal sketch of Beau gazed back at her from the parchment, and not just one Beau but dozens upon dozens, fluttering from her hands to drift across the cabin floor, so many mute reminders of her infatuation with the man. With a groan, she swept them up and was about to consign them to wadded parchments when her more sensible self asserted itself. She wouldn't let him drive her to the destruction of her own work. Instead, she would keep the drawings as a salutary lesson in the penalties of allowing her heart to rule her head, and henceforth she hoped she'd be the wiser for it.

The sketches had been stowed away well out of sight and she was standing before her easel, industriously detailing figures on a canvas for a new oil painting, when some instinct halted her in mid-stroke. She raised her head, listening intently. She heard nothing save the muted slap of canvas in the wind, the creak of planks, the distant voices of men, all the sounds that had become so familiar to her that she had to make a concerted effort to hear them at all. Yet she couldn't deny the feeling that was now sweeping through her. She remained tensely alert, her heart beating with almost painful swiftness and her fingers gripping the brush so tightly they came nigh to snapping it in two. An instant before the rap of knuckles came upon the wood she knew who stood outside her door, the only man so at home on the *Audacious* that he could walk across a swaying deck or descend a companionway without making a sound.

Cerynise moved on trembling limbs and, with a stern reminder to remain composed, opened the door. Beau stood in the passageway, looking greatly troubled.

"I was harsh with you earlier on the quarterdeck," he said without preamble. "You didn't deserve that, and I've come to say I'm sorry and to make amends to the best of my ability."

She waited, mainly from the sheer surprise of his unexpected apology, while he, in turn, studied her with an intensity that convinced her that she hadn't been as successful at hiding the evidence of her weeping as she had hoped.

"Apology accepted," she murmured quietly, and waited through a long, uncomfortable silence. It seemed an eternity. "If that's all you wanted, Beau, I should get back to my work. I'll need to sell some of my paintings as soon as I reach Charleston so I can repay you for what you gave Jasper."

"You needn't worry about that, Cerynise. Just consider it a gift."

"I'd rather not be beholden to you any more than I am already," she said in quiet dignity.

Beau wondered if some peculiar affliction had stripped him of the ability to openly discuss the matter which had plagued him since arising from his sickbed. He felt equally inadequate in his search for a way to repair the hurt he had inflicted. More than his first mate, he wanted to see his wife smile again.

Another lengthy hush ensued, and Cerynise, uncomfortable beneath his unrelenting stare, stepped forward to push the door closed. Her attempt seemed to awaken Beau, for he promptly moved inward, gently nudging the wooden barrier back with a shoulder. At her look of alarm, he sought ineptly to justify his lingering presence. "Mothering me in front of my men, madam, doesn't inspire a lot of confidence. They must have no doubt about my ability to command."

"It must be a poor world that you men make for yourselves when any show of caring concern is taken as weakness," Cerynise replied stiffly. "It makes me doubly glad that I was born a woman."

The corners of Beau's mouth threatened to

give way to amusement. "Don't expect me to argue that point with you. Somehow I can't imagine that you'd be very convincing as a man." His brows gathered with concern as he continued to study her, and with husky gentleness he inquired, "Cerynise...is all well with you?"

He *knew!* The thought froze her in place, like a doe caught in sudden wariness by the approach of man. Frantically she searched her mind, wondering what she had let slip. Yet she could think of nothing that she had either said or done that would have given away her secret. That left one other option...he was now recalling the event himself. But why wouldn't he simply question her about it? He was a direct and plainspoken man, definitely not the bashful sort to approach any subject hesitantly. So why would he not ask her outright about the matter?

Cerynise's gaze delved deeply into those darkly crystalline eyes, searching for some hint of what he might know. They were as beautiful as always, but they revealed nothing. She was reading too much into his question. That was all there was to it, she concluded. She was simply grabbing at straws.

"Perfectly well," she finally murmured. "Now, if you'll excuse me, Beau, I must get back to work."

Unconvinced, he continued to study her, making no effort to leave. Slowly his gaze swept over her, heating where it touched, making her look away lest he see too clearly the helpless stirring he caused within her. "I'd like for you to join me for supper, Cerynise, and I hope this time you will accept my invitation. I've come to hate dining alone, and Mr. Oaks is no comfort. He seems intent upon chiding me about my uncivilized manners."

Sit near him at a table for an hour or more? Without Mr. Oaks's cheerful, stabling presence? Cerynise knew exactly where she would end up, and the way Beau was pressing her, she was certain he had come to the determination that she had no will of her own. Despite an overwhelming desire to yield to his plea, she could not. For her own preservation she had to think of what she would risk and not be taken in by his cajoling.

"I think under the circumstances, Beau, it would be better if we weren't in each other's company so much." That statement had an all too familiar ring to it that made her wonder how often she had said those exact same words. Thus far, they had failed to serve her purposes, for she was even more involved now than she had been when she first issued that proposal. She tried again, hoping to convince him...as well as herself. "We both seem to have difficulty honoring our titular arrangement. I've certainly allowed you far more liberties than either of us initially discussed, so I must consider that it's best for me not to be in your company at all. Forthwith, it should be as if we had never married."

If she had ever spoken words that wrung her heart more deeply, Cerynise couldn't remember

341

them. These took all her strength and will to say.

Beau neither smiled nor frowned. In silence he inclined his head ever so slightly and withdrew. It seemed an end of an era he had immensely enjoyed, but more than that, he was sure his heart had ceased its motion.

Cerynise was trembling uncontrollably by the time she closed the door behind him. She returned to the small desk beside the cot, feeling in no mood to continue her work on the canvas. Instead, she sat with her hands folded listlessly in her lap, her eyes unfocused, with a burgeoning emptiness filling every niche and fiber of her being.

It was that same horrible sense of being hollowed out from inside that sucked much of the joy out of her life through the days and weeks that followed. She kept to herself as much as possible and no longer felt fully connected to life aboard ship. It was as if invisible walls had descended around her, shutting her off from the world outside her cabin. She didn't even feel alive; she was just existing from moment to moment until the voyage came to an end. Then, somehow, she would have to collect her shattered heart and put it back together again in some semblance of order.

Following Beau's visit to her cabin, Cerynise had gone up on deck at Stephen Oaks's gentle urgings, just long enough to avoid inquiries from any quarter about her health. Once there, she responded to the greetings of the men but never initiated any conversation of her own. The mate tried to draw her out, as did Billy Todd and Monsieur Philippe, who oftentimes came to fetch her tray himself and would stay long enough for a quick chat in French. They all felt driven by the same kind of concern that she had seen in the eyes of other crew members. Deflecting it all with a soft smile, she let the well of emptiness draw her further in.

Christmas still found them close to a month from their destination. Cerynise consented to share the evening with her husband in a quiet dinner attended by Stephen Oaks. She gifted Beau with a lavish painting of his ship, and to the mate she presented a portrait she had painted of him on canvas, as she had done earlier for Billy and Philippe. In return, Oaks presented her with a miniature replica of the *Audacious* that he had carved and outfitted with string rigging and handkerchief sails. He grinned widely as she praised his talents, which took no enormous feat by any means, for she was mightily impressed that he had constructed it all so closely to scale.

They enjoyed a delectable repast, compliments of Philippe's enthusiasm for the season, and as Mr. Oaks took his leave, Cerynise made to follow to her room, but Beau laid a hand upon her arm and begged her indulgence a moment more. Seeing the wariness in her eyes, he assured her that he hadn't yet presented her with a gift, which he had wanted to do in private. Her nod of acquiescence hardly portrayed the emotions she was struggling

343

with. Almost as soon as she had entered his quarters, she had become aware of a potent sense of longing growing within her. It was a desire so strong that she wanted to cry at the lack of progress she had made in her endeavor to detach her heart from Beau Birmingham. With everything that she was capable of feeling, she yearned to return to the familiar comfort of his cabin and his arms. Feeling precariously vulnerable with such renegade thoughts racing through her mind, she waited in uneasy silence as he went to fetch the gift from a cabinet beyond the washstand.

Beau brought out an intricately carved rosewood box and swept it open to reveal a pair of jade figurines with carved lotus flowers adorning the teakwood base. They were the most exquisite pieces Cerynise had ever seen, but she could well imagine the cost of such treasures, too much for her to take from a temporary husband.

"They're beautiful, Beau, but I don't really think I should accept them."

He lifted the male figure of the matched pair and examined it closely. "I was told that these two are supposed to be fabled lovers who were finally able to marry after surmounting great difficulty. I thought the gift appropriate, madam, considering our adversities, and I'll be quite put out with you if you don't accept them."

"Suppose you should marry another someday?" Cerynise murmured and swallowed against the emotional knot that rose in her throat. Expressing the thought exacted a harsh toll on her composure, for she wanted to burst into tears at the idea that Beau might repent of his bachelor's status and wed another. "Would you not prefer to give them to your wife?"

"I'm giving them to my wife," he stated, commanding her gaze, "and I'd be honored if you'd accept my gift."

The tenderness in his eyes was so compelling, Cerynise could feel her heart already plucking a chaotic rhythm. She fought an overpowering longing to press close to that stalwart male form and rest her head in relief against his chest. She knew he'd welcome her gladly, and just as surely, she knew that her will would crumble beneath the kisses that would follow. Unable to trust herself within reaching distance of him any longer, she thanked him breathlessly and hurriedly took her leave, escaping to her room, where she spent another wakeful night wishing she didn't have to hold herself from him.

A returning bout of seasickness caused Cerynise to sequester herself in the loneliness of her cabin, and although she managed to retain what little she ate, she was nevertheless stricken with an unfathomable exhaustion. She hardly felt like painting anymore and spent much of her time sleeping, sometimes taking long naps in the mornings as well as in the afternoons. After waking her on three different occasions, Billy reported his growing concern to his captain, and when Beau hurried down to make inquiries and feel her brow, Cerynise assured him that sleeping was just her way of coping with the boredom of a lengthy voyage and that she hadn't really been afflicted with some strange malady. She also expressed confidence that she would revive once they reached Charleston and that she didn't need a nursemaid watching over her. Reluctantly Beau accepted her excuses and left her to her privacy, which was what she seemed to want.

Thereinafter Beau observed her with close attention, but only from a distance. Their paths crossed often, and with emotions carefully masked, they spoke briefly or merely nodded politely to one another. One evening, when Billy came in with her dinner tray and left the door open behind him, Beau paused beside it, having been on his way to his own cabin. As usual his tall, hard body radiated strength and healthy vitality, but his dark blue eyes were cautious as they swept her.

"Are you feeling well this evening, Cerynise?" he asked courteously.

"In excellent health, Captain. Thank you. And you?" Cerynise replied with feigned gaiety, making every attempt to appear the epitome of what she had just boasted.

Beau chewed his cheek reflectively as he pondered her paleness. She had seemed far too solemn of late to please him, and her forced smiles did nothing to convince him that she was feeling all that chipper. Yet, as much as he was inclined to, he could hardly command her to tell him the truth about her health.

"You are well, are you not, Captain?" she prodded, counting the moments until the door could be closed and she could breathe again.

"Most assuredly, madam," he said at last. And then, after another lengthy pause, he queried, "You won't hesitate to inform me of any needs you may have, will you?"

"Billy and Philippe have been seeing to my requirements perfectly well, Captain." Cerynise shrugged and spread her hands with a brief laugh that even she would have admitted sounded false. "I cannot imagine why I should have to bother you with such trifling matters. You have a great deal to occupy you, far too much for me to take up any of your time."

Beau didn't appreciate her answer, but he refused to beg her to give him just a wee bit of her time. He had already done enough of that. He continued on to his room.

In the weeks that followed, Cerynise came to the deck more often, primarily to dispel any notions that Beau might have been fostering about her health. While there, she looked out to sea rather than any place where he was. Watching him would have led her along a path that she was striving desperately to avoid, and though she tried to blank her mind to his presence, it took firm precedence over everything else. If she'd been able to simply will it into being, she would have wished for her torture to end by the sighting of land. Toward evening on a crisp late winter day, just a few days short of three months from their departure from London, her wish was granted.

CHAPTER 11

The *Audacious* approached Charleston on the morning tide in late January. At first light Cerynise ventured to the deck and strained to catch even a small glimpse of the city through the misty haze drifting tantalizingly along the coast. Seabirds soared overhead like welcoming friends or rode the white-capped waves that splashed against the bow, but as she watched them cavorting, she could only mark the contrast between their carefree spirit and her own growing despair.

The winds turned brisk as the solar orb began to rise to a lofty height, and the haze was swept away. Cerynise snuggled deeper in her velvet cloak, refusing to allow the crisp breezes to send her fleeing to the warmth of her cabin. Instead of the euphoria she might have expected to feel at her homecoming, she experienced only a growing measure of relief that the journey was at an end. Nevertheless she welcomed the sights as her gaze swept the glistening white beaches that framed the main channel into Charleston Harbor. Drawing a deep breath, she savored the mingled essences of the vast, stately cypress and mangrove forests growing along the shore that wafted toward them on buffeting winds.

How desperately she had missed her homeland. She hadn't realized exactly to what degree until now, when her eyes could feast on the familiar land. The shock of losing her parents mingled with the gratitude that she had felt for Lydia had overshadowed recollections of her homeland from years past, locking them deep in her heart. Now the seals were broken, and the memories came flooding back, filling her with a strengthening serenity. It had been a long journey indeed, traversed not across the ocean but through the years of her own life. But it was finally over, and once she stepped to shore, a new journey would commence, one that would see her striving to make a place for herself here in this land where she had grown up.

A familiar awareness swept over Cerynise. It was unmistakable as always, and she turned with bated breath to find Beau eyeing her from very close range. He was wearing the cap that had become well-known to her in the latter part of the voyage. It was angled jauntily upon his fine head, but beneath it, the short black wisps at his temples were being whipped by the wind. He had condescended to wear a coat, perhaps for her benefit, and to Cerynise he looked every bit as admirable and princely as he always had and, no doubt, always would. Just gazing at him, she could feel her heart nearly thumping out of her chest, reacting to his presence just as it always had and, no doubt, always would.

"You seem rather pensive this morning, Cerynise." Beau voiced the conjecture as he stepped near and leaned his elbows on the railing beside her. "Are you not glad to be home?"

"Oh, certainly," Cerynise replied, managing a smile the likes of which he had not seen in some weeks. "But I can't help but feel a stranger here after being away so long." When her pulse refused to slow to a normal rhythm, she wrenched her gaze away from her handsome husband and fixed it with great resolve on the steadily emerging shoreline. "I wonder how much has changed since I left or if I'll be able to recognize it as the same city I used to visit."

"I don't think you'll have any trouble. It hasn't changed that much."

"I hope not." Being thought of as an outsider by the inhabitants of the area was a fear that plagued her, but she avoided mentioning that fact. Her uncle would welcome her, she was confident of that, but he had always been a rather solitary, self-sufficient man who had always been content to be alone with his books even when he wasn't teaching. As for her acquaintances from years past, she knew her childhood friends would all be grown and undoubtedly involved in various activities and the usual endeavors of young women. Some would even be married, perhaps with a child on the way....

Cerynise felt a faint shock at her own wifely state, and in sudden distraction smoothed a hand down the front of her gown, over the softly gathered fullness of her skirts. The inadvertent inspection halted abruptly when she realized that Beau was observing her with a curious frown.

"Will you have family meeting you in

Charleston?" she inquired nervously, facing into the wind as she sought to cool a blush.

Beau was sure he had seen a tiny kitten facing a pack of wild dogs with more aplomb than his wife presently displayed. He lifted his wide shoulders in a casual shrug. "Since most of them are probably at Harthaven, I doubt they'll be advised of my ship coming into port. I'll drive out later to see them once I get settled. I have some gifts for them, and of course, my mother wouldn't take kindly to me staying in the city and not informing them that I've come home."

"Mr. Oaks said your arrivals here are well-anticipated and that you're usually beset with throngs of people anxious to see what you've brought back. I'm sure if that is the case, it will be some time before you're able to leave." Cerynise made a concerted effort to appear insouciant as she added, "If that should be the case, Beau, I think we should discuss how you'll handle the annulment."

It had been in Beau's mind to suggest that they give themselves plenty of time to think over their relationship before actually proceeding with the division. During that period he intended to ask his wife's uncle if he could pay court to her like any normal swain considering marriage. In light of his previous tenacity to avoid marriage, he had amazed himself to a goodly degree by coming up with that particular plan, but he just couldn't imagine giving the girl up. Indeed, the very idea of her being wooed by some other suitor rankled him sorely. "We'll have enough

351

time to discuss all of that later, Cerynise. I'm in no rush."

Cerynise took a deep breath, willing herself to be calm. Being Beau Birmingham's temporary wife certainly had its drawbacks, but only because their marriage was destined to end. She knew that by delaying the task, her heart would be entangled that much more when it came time for her to sign the papers. Indeed, as tormented as she was now, she could imagine the emotional upheaval she'd suffer if she began to hope that their marriage might continue, only to see it dashed to smithereens at some later date. She couldn't continue indefinitely with the cool, stilted facade that she had, by dint of will, managed to maintain after begging him not to think of them as a married couple anymore. And then, of course, she was forever reminded of another reason which she tried not to dwell on while the subject of their annulment was being discussed. To do so would have seriously threatened her composure. Quietly she murmured, "Perhaps the sooner the better, Beau."

Was it her imagination or did he stiffen?

"I thought we should allow ourselves a couple of months—"

"No, it's better to get it over with," she pressed, nearly panicking.

"Are you in that much of a rush to dissolve it, madam?"

Perplexed at his acid tone, Cerynise lifted her gaze to the carefully hooded eyes that studied her closely in return. How could she explain to him that in two months' time no lawyer in his right mind would think of drawing up papers for such a division? And Beau would only hate her because he'd then feel trapped. With measured care Cerynise gave her well-recited excuses. "Once I set up my studio, I won't have much time to dally if I intend to sell enough paintings to repay you and have some funds left for myself. 'Twill be better if we proceed with all possible haste while I still have some free time available."

"Of course, your paintings take precedence," Beau replied snidely.

Cerynise was overwhelmed by his sarcasm. Didn't he know that he meant more to her than her ability to paint? Couldn't he understand that she was desperately, hopelessly in love with him? Or had he foolishly imagined that because she had withheld herself from him that she wanted no part of him? If he had, then he was both blind and witless!

Cerynise allowed her impatience with such a notion to be conveyed with her own practicality. "Sir, if I must make my own way in life, my art is of great importance to me. It means my livelihood."

Beau chafed in darkening humor. "What will you tell your uncle?"

"The truth," she answered simply. "I'm sure he'll understand and be grateful for everything you've done...as I am."

The hard glitter in his eyes warned her that she was treading unwarily over uncharted ground. "Just that? Grateful?"

353

Cerynise was growing more confused by the moment. "Should I not be?"

Though he searched her eyes, Beau saw no hint of what he was looking for. "About the annulment..."

Facing the shoreline, she replied with all the serenity she could muster, "I don't wish to inconvenience you in any way, Beau. At least, not any more than I've already done. Please proceed as you see fit."

"I see...."

She looked back at him, drawn irresistibly to the virile power and manly grace of his person. He was regarding her with the same care he'd lend an uncertain sea, to the extent that had she not known better, Cerynise might have imagined he was irritated with her because she was insisting that they progress with the annulment posthaste. But surely their separation was what he had both wanted and expected. And just as certainly, it was folly for her to yield to any weak-minded hope that he didn't want their marriage dissolved any more than she did.

Beau was frustrated by the shuttered look that forbade any insight into his wife's thoughts. It seemed to him that her feelings were no different now than they had been for the better part of their journey. She wanted nothing to do with him.

Regret surged upward within him and was so intense, he was nearly taken aback by surprise. When he had hatched his plan to whisk Cerynise out of Winthrop's clutches, he had never dreamed he'd come to care so deeply for her in three months' time. But it seemed his reluctance to have their marriage invalidated was all for naught, and he realized he had been foolhardy to nurture even a slender thread of optimism that she might wish their marriage to continue and could come to feel some wifely fondness for him. His thwarted aspirations were further sundered by a willful pride that set his jaw to snapping. "In that case, madam, my solicitor, Hiram Farraday, will be in touch with you."

Cerynise nodded rigidly, unable to force a verbal response through the choking misery welling up in her throat. It was a long moment before she realized she was gripping the rail with a white-knuckled tenseness that set her fingers to aching. Keeping her gaze fixed on the approaching shore, she eased her grasp by slow degrees and managed to feign indifference even when Beau left her side without further ado.

Wind and tide conspired to favor the *Audacious*, speeding her into the deep blue bay toward the spit of land dividing two great rivers. The white-washed city sparkled in the morning sun and claimed the eye with its bejeweled appearance. Beyond the tall masts of the vessels that crowded the harbor, church steeples could be seen rising into the belly of the sky, while along the point and beyond, graceful two-and three-storied edifices nestled. Memories proved but a poor reflection of reality, for Cerynise found herself as awed as any new arrival coming upon Charleston for the first time.

Beau called an order, interrupting her reverie, and men scrambled into the heights to obey. The sails were soon furled and the necessary preparations made to bring the ship against the quay. As the last mile flew by, Cerynise found her eyes sweeping over the crowds gathering along the wharf. From her past visits to the city, she recalled the various reports that had flowed like quicksilver throughout the streets and byways whenever a particular vessel was sited rounding the headlands. News of the *Audacious*'s return would already be spreading, but, of course, no word of her own. Her uncle wouldn't be anticipating her arrival, but with a little luck, she hoped to slip away unseen amid all the excitement of the sailors' homecoming and make her way unaided to his house.

Cerynise went below and hastily gathered the belongings she had planned to take with her. Her trunks and satchels had been packed well in advance. With the exception of the smallest valise, in which she had put basic essentials, the rest would have to remain behind until her uncle could come back to fetch them.

When she was ready, Cerynise stood in the middle of the cabin and took one last look around. The small room that had been her home during the last leg of the voyage was already losing its familiarity. She was sure she'd be hard-pressed to remember it with any great detail in a few weeks. Not so the cabin down the passageway. That one she would distinctly recall, perhaps to her dying day.

A brief series of bumps signaled journey's end. After thousands of miles, through the midst of nature's tempest and her own personal turmoil, Cerynise found such a conclusion striking because it seemed so ordinary. She sighed, unable to relieve the tightness in her throat, and made her way for one last time along the corridor and slowly ascended the companionway.

By the time Cerynise emerged, the *Audacious*'s moorings were secure against the dock and the gangplank laid in place. The quay swarmed with families shouting greetings to various members of the crew who were just as eager to catch a glimpse of loved ones. People were still streaming in from adjacent lanes and alleys and crowding into the area until it seemed that no space would be left for those still on their way. Several elegant carriages drew up, and after alighting, their passengers hurried with unswerving dedication to come aboard. A pair of young ladies were handed down from a landau by their black driver and, in laughing excitement, nearly flew up the gangplank. Upon spying Beau, they called out to him, waving ecstatically until they gained his attention.

"Suzanne! Brenna!" he cried happily. "What are you both doing here?" He quickly closed the distance between them and, sweeping first one and then the other up into his embrace, gave each a kiss on the cheek.

Cerynise could only imagine from the dark

hair and vividly hued eyes of the two ladies that they were part of the Birmingham clan, whom he hadn't been expecting. Not wishing to appear overly inquisitive, she turned aside slightly, permitting herself the advantage of observing them without being obvious about it. Even amid all the other noises around them, their voices were borne on the wind to the rail where she stood.

The taller and older of the two gaily explained the reason for their presence in the city. "We came to shop, Beau, but when we heard that your ship had been sighted, we had to hurry over, if only to catch a glimpse of our brother before he sailed off again."

"Now, Suzanne, it's not as bad as all that," Beau protested, chuckling. Then he stood back with arms akimbo and a grin that nigh split his face as he perused the smaller one. "Brenna, you're looking quite mature nowadays. And what? No pigtails?"

"Humph!" The young black-haired, blue-eyed beauty tossed her bonneted head with feigned exasperation at his teasing. "I've never had pigtails, Beauregard Birmingham, and you know it! And if you'd care to remember, dear brother, I'm now ten and six, definitely old enough to be mature."

"It seems the last time I saw you, you were stumbling over your own feet, but it certainly seems as if you've acquired more grace since then. Now tell me, are you still being chased by all the landed gentry in the area?"

"Oh, hush, you rascal!" Brenna chided

with a pretty pout, and then wildly exaggerated her predicament. "You know Papa pulls out a gun every time he sees a potential suitor approaching. I swear I'll *never ever* be able to get close enough to a man to even decide whether he's handsome or not with Papa always standing guard."

"Believe me, dear sister, he has every reason to protect you with such dedication," Beau assured her jovially. "As a man, I can vouch for that."

"Oh, you men are all alike," she fussed sweetly. "You defend each other with unswerving dedication, and saints preserve the woman who'll argue with you."

"When you're older and *wiser*, my dear, you'll be appreciative that Pa is so dedicated about protecting you. If not for him, the rakes will see you as a tempting morsel just waiting to be devoured."

Brenna took exception to his remark. "I'm not *unwise* now."

"Let's just say that you're not experienced enough to handle men who are more worldly."

"It takes one to know one, I suppose," she declared with a teasing twinkle in her eyes. "You and Pa are certainly chips off the same block."

"Perhaps," Beau acknowledged. "But then, I've heard him say that you're the very image of Mama when he first saw her."

"Yes, and she wasn't much older than I am right now when she married Papa, but left to him, I'll be an old maid of twenty ere he lets a gentleman come calling."

"I thought Mama was closer to eight and ten when she got married," Beau prodded with a grin.

"Well, I'm almost that," Brenna claimed, and quickly stuck her tongue out at him.

"What did Mama say about that?" Suzanne scolded her younger sister, and then sighed heavily, as if nearing wit's end. "You'll never be considered anything but a naughty little girl until you stop embarrassing us like that."

"Oh, you're always so staid, Suzanne," Brenna complained. "A body would think you're my mother."

"Girls, girls!" Beau gently rebuked, breaking into their tiff. "Stop your fussing. It isn't becoming." As his sisters scowled at each other, he lifted his gaze to search for the slender form of his wife. Perhaps by renewing acquaintances with his family, Cerynise wouldn't be inclined to think him an ogre or be so intent upon flying away like a singed bird. "Besides, I have someone to whom I'd like to reintroduce you." Taking each by the arm, he led his sisters across the deck to Cerynise. Even before he reached out to take his wife's elbow, she was already turning to face him.

"Cerynise, these are my sisters, Suzanne and Brenna." Sweeping a hand toward her, he turned to his younger siblings. "I'm sure you both remember the Kendalls. Well, this is Marcus Kendall's daughter, Cerynise...."

"Cerynise Kendall, of course!" Suzanne cried, briefly taking the younger woman's hand in her own. "You used to come to

Harthaven with your father, but my goodness, you've changed so much! I'd never have known it was you if Beau hadn't told us. But what are you doing here? The last we heard, you were sailing off to England to live with that lovely Mrs. Winthrop." Suzanne turned black-lashed green eyes to scan the deck in search of the tall, dignified elder whom she had always considered a figure of stately grace. "Did she come with you?"

"No, I regret to say that I've come alone," Cerynise answered quietly. "Mrs. Winthrop died shortly before my departure from England."

"Oh, Cerynise, how tragic for you! We're so sorry," Brenna said sympathetically, gathering Cerynise's fingers in her own. "But we're so delighted to see you again. You must come out and visit with us at Harthaven after you get settled."

Cerynise became aware of Beau stepping behind her. Perhaps it was some shared understanding that did truly link her mind as well as her heart to the man, for every instinct within her screamed a warning that he was just waiting for an opportunity to introduce her as his wife. She could foresee the confusion that would cause.

Brenna gave her brother no opportunity to break in as she continued her reminiscing. "I remember, Cerynise, how clever you were with a paintbrush when we were attending that girls' academy together for a time. The thing I recall most about your paintings was the fact that they always looked like their subjects. Even back then, I longed for you to paint my portrait, but I was a year or two younger than your circle of friends, so I never dared ask. Do you still paint?"

"Like Rembrandt," Beau volunteered with a grin.

"Oh, how exciting!" Brenna cried, her sapphire blue eyes flashing with enthusiasm. "I must tell Papa! Just recently I heard him say that he wanted to have Mama's portrait painted with her daughters, so now I can inform him that we've found an artist who can do it to his liking."

Cerynise smiled at the girl's ebullience, but she thought it prudent to handle the matter delicately, lest they all be caught in an embarrassing situation. "Perhaps you shouldn't press your father unduly until he can see what I'm capable of. He may not even like my work and would prefer to hire another artist for such a task." The greater distance she could put between the Birminghams and herself, the better off she'd be, Cerynise decided, for they would only remind her what she'd be missing after her marriage to Beau was dissolved. As a girl, she had been made to feel very much at home by the cordial hospitality of the Birminghams, and at times she had even dared to imagine herself their daughter by marriage. Since that was definitely not going to be the case, she preferred not to suffer the anguish of knowing they could have been, if only...

"If Beau says you paint as well as the masters, then we suffer no doubt that you're among the best," Suzanne assured her with a friendly chortle. "If you're not aware of it yet, our brother has quite an eye for excellent art. But we'll let you get settled before we start pestering you about painting us all. Will you be staying with your uncle?"

"Yes, but I'm afraid he isn't aware of that yet."

"Which reminds me," Brenna chimed in. "Beau doesn't yet know what's in the wind for our family."

"Doesn't know what?" Beau queried a bit suspiciously. At a very early age he had learned that there were always surprises in the Birmingham family.

"Suzanne is engaged to be married," Brenna announced happily. "Michael York finally bought that plantation a mile or two down the road, and as soon as everything was finalized, he came over, asked Papa for Suzanne's hand and then went down on his knees to propose to her. Oh, it was so exciting watching them from the doorway...."

Suzanne was clearly astonished. "Brenna, you didn't!"

"Oh, I did!" Brenna confessed proudly before she faced her chuckling brother again. "The middle of April we'll be having a ball to celebrate the occasion. You've come home just in time to set all the young ladies aflutter with similar dreams of engagement balls and such...."

"Well, actually I'm already..." Beau began, but he had no time to finish as Mr. Oaks stepped near and touched his arm to claim his attention.

"Forgive me for intruding, Captain, but there's a man over here who seems to be serious about buying all the furniture you've brought back."

"But how can that be?" Beau asked in amazement. "He hasn't even seen any of it yet."

"Aye, but he knows what you brought back last time, and he came too late to even get a pedestal from the last bunch. He's quite adamant about speaking with you about it now, Captain, before someone else starts buying it off."

Brenna laid a hand upon her brother's sleeve. "We won't keep you any longer, Beau, but we shall expect to see you later tonight. Mama will be thrilled to hear that you're back, and of course, you know that she'll be wanting to see you before the sun sets." Her lips curved with a teasing smile as she launched into other outrageous speculations. "You always were the apple of her eye, you know. Her little baby. Why, the way she prides herself in her firstborn, anyone would think your birth was something special."

"Now, don't be jealous," Beau reproved, chuckling softly as he settled a doting kiss upon her forehead. He bestowed the same on Suzanne before facing Cerynise. "I shouldn't be too long," he murmured before stepping away with Mr. Oaks.

Cerynise said her own farewells to the two sisters, who again encouraged her to come out fairly soon to see them. She nodded, but she knew that wouldn't be anything she could easily do. Visiting them would bring more pain than she could bear.

The deck was now crammed with people, and with Beau occupied elsewhere, Cerynise found it a favorable time to make good her escape. It was far better to make a clean break before her distress over leaving Beau encumbered her heart. She knew to say farewell to any of the seamen would likely see her undone emotionally, and as much as she wished to thank Mr. Oaks, Billy, and all of the others for their kindness to her, she'd have to write it out in a missive and send one to each, for she didn't want to embarrass herself by breaking down in front of everyone.

No fancy carriage awaited Cerynise, nor did she have the coin to hire one. Alone, she made her way through the jostling crowd until she reached a spot well back from the wharf where she could pause to calm the sudden queasiness that had come upon her in the crush of people. Looking back at the graceful vessel, she felt a piercing regret that she wasn't still there, patiently waiting for her husband to conclude his business so they could leave together. Such wayward thoughts made her eyes sting, but she blinked away the start of tears, refusing to indulge her melancholy. Yet, in spite of her efforts, a deepening forlornness intruded, and with a dispirited sigh she averted her gaze and, hefting her satchel, began to make her way along a familiar lane that led away from the docks.

Sterling Kendall's house was set just within the boundaries that had once been marked by the city's walls, and although those particular defenses were now gone, their influence had nevertheless remained amid the cobblestone lanes that had been laid out during the first tentative stirrings of the city. Her uncle's residence was on one such lane, set back from the busier streets and made even more secluded by the fact that only one nondescript side of the house faced the lane itself. The other three were enclosed within a walled garden that, apart from his beloved books, was his greatest pride. Cerynise had many fond memories of having visited the pleasantly modest house with her parents on innumerable occasions.

Cerynise paused on the opposite side of the lane from the same structure to await the passing of a lorry, then she slowly traversed its width. Now that her long-awaited homecoming lay before her, she found herself overtaken by uncertainty. What would her uncle's reaction be to her unexpected arrival? When it came to explaining the circumstances by which she had returned, would she find Sterling Kendall as tolerant and forbearing as she had hoped?

Her increasing anxiety over the kind of welcome she would receive slowed her approach, and with heavy heart, Cerynise swung open the wrought iron gate. A seashell path led her through an extended trellis that had, over the years, become almost lost beneath trailing vines of Carolina jasmine. The vine hardly looked its best now in winter, but she remembered the delectable scent that wafted from it in warmer months. She broke off a dead twig as she passed beneath, and then fixed her eyes on the portal. Her hand trembled as she reached out to lift the brass knocker, but she paused, searching for the courage to face her uncle unashamedly.

A clatter of hooves on the cobblestone lane behind her made her turn, and her eyes widened in surprise when she saw Beau pulling a snorting stallion to a halt near the gate. He swung down and, after looping the reins over the riding post, strode toward her. One quick look at his face convinced Cerynise that he was absolutely furious with her. Not only were his eyes glinting with icy shards, but the muscles in his cheeks were tensing and vibrating to a degree that she had never seen before.

"Just tell me one damn thing!" he growled upon reaching the step where she stood. "Was it too much for you to wait and let me serve as your escort? It was my intent, you know. Or have you become so impatient for the annulment that you couldn't wait to leave me?" Beau's frustration was supreme, and yet he couldn't entirely decipher where it was centered. The pact that they had mutually agreed upon three months ago called for the termination of their marriage soon after their arrival in Charleston. According to that bargain, she could go her separate way. The fact that she had, had cut through his heart like a knife, leaving him with a dark sense of having been betrayed, like a husband whose wife had just taken off with a secret lover. He knew he was being unreasonable, but he just couldn't seem to help himself. Even if their marriage had only been a travesty, he had gotten too comfortable with the idea of her being his wife. In spite of all his past qualms about being tied down to a wife and family, he was reluctant to let her go and see it all end without making some effort to hold her to him. "Is it really your design to provoke every contrary emotion I'm capable of feeling? Is that what you're doing?"

Agog with an unwilling fascination at the fury of her handsome husband, Cerynise blurted out an answer totally unrelated to his question. "I was just about to knock on the door."

She truly hadn't meant to sound flippant. Indeed, nothing had been further from her mind. But in the face of such flaring emotions emanating from this man who towered over her, all reason had fled.

The dubious scowl that Beau slanted down upon her suggested that he had serious doubts about her sanity. "You left the ship without even so much as a whisper to anyone," he accused. "You didn't even say good-bye. Nor did you even hint of your intentions to leave the ship without me."

"You were busy, and I didn't wish to disturb you," Cerynise replied in a soft, quavering

368

voice. "It seemed an appropriate time to leave."

"Appropriate, hell!" he snarled. "Inappropriate would be more like it. I left everything to come after you."

"I'm sorry if I angered you, Beau," she murmured contritely. "I really didn't think it would matter."

"Well, it did matter! A lot, in fact! One moment you were there, where I could see you, and the next, you had fled. I searched the ship for you, unable to believe that you'd leave without a word, and then one of my men told me that he had seen you slipping through the crowd. As difficult as it was to accept, I should have known. You've proven yourself quite adept at escaping at the most inconvenient times. In fact, if I didn't know better, madam, I'd be inclined to think you have a wide, yellow streak running down your back."

Taking offense, Cerynise raised her chin a notch at his insinuation. "I'm no coward, sir."

Beau snorted in disagreement. "Right now, madam, I'd say that isn't exactly the truth. But then, I'm the one from whom you fly away every chance you get and, in so doing, leave me so riled up inside I've oft considered the pleasure it might give me to commit mayhem on your very fetching backside."

Cerynise stepped back, unconsciously clasping a hand over her abdomen. "You wouldn't dare...."

Beau was incredulous that she should even suggest that he was serious. "Do you honestly believe I would?"

Her slender shoulders lifted in a lame shrug. "I've never seen you so angry with me before."

"That's understandable," he quipped sarcastically. "I've never *been* this angry with you before."

"I saw no need in delaying our separation," she explained mutedly.

"That was obvious," he retorted cuttingly. Her simple statement only heightened his irritation. "You might as well have slapped my face or spit in my eye, the way you sashayed off without a word to me."

"There was no insult intended, Beau," Cerynise whispered, looking up at him with pleading eyes. "I'm sorry if you took offense."

He was unable to resist her worried appeal. Taking a step closer, he murmured distantly, "I even begged a loan of a mount in my haste to find you."

"But you must have known where I'd go," she said, somewhat heartened by the fact that the muscles in his cheeks were no longer tensing beneath his bronzed skin.

"Aye! I did, and that's why I'm here." Beau moved even nearer until Cerynise could see nothing beyond his broad shoulders, but then, with her eyes riveted on his face, she wouldn't have seen anything else anyway. He advanced with measured care, and instinctively she stepped back, only to bump into the door. His long body was there to meet hers when she stumbled forward again, and as if by magic, his arm was suddenly around her, steadying her and pulling her near. She breathed in raggedly, inhaling all the scents that bestirred her womanly being and awakened her senses to his manly virility. Her head whirled, leaving her a little dizzy and faint. She lifted a hand to brace herself, only to encounter the hard, unyielding wall of his chest, that same muscular expanse she loved to caress. She seemed naturally inclined to do so, for her hand moved unbidden in a slow, circular motion around a male breast.

Trembling, she raised her eyes to his and saw in an instant that his anger was gone, transformed into a longing so intense, it left her amazed that after all their quarrels and strife, this proud, indomitable man desired her just as fiercely as he always had. *Annulment, be damned!* she could almost hear him saying. His dark head lowered, his opening mouth came near, and she waited with emotions winging out of control.

The clatter of a passing wagon intruded, reminding her of the fact that they were standing beside a public lane in the middle of Charleston. Anyone could see them if they chose to look through the arbor, and yet, everything within her cried out with yearning for this man in spite of all the conflicts that might follow. Her soft lips parted in a sigh of surrender....

"Beau—"

In an instant her whisper turned to a startled

gasp as the front door opened suddenly, jolting her forward against Beau. They both stumbled away from the wide step and stared in surprise at a gray-haired man with wire-rimmed spectacles who gazed back at them with the air of a startled owl.

"Oh, I do beg your pardon," he apologized. "I thought I heard something and came out to see—" He broke off, a tentative smile lighting his solemn visage. "Cerynise...is that you? Oh, but it can't be. She's—"

"It is!" Cerynise reassured him eagerly. This was hardly the reunion she had envisioned. Fully aware of her flustered state, she could perceive his curiosity being aroused by her bright blush. It was too much to hope that he'd lay the cause to her arrival. "I've come home to stay, Uncle Sterling."

The man seemed suddenly bemused. "But what about Mrs. Winthrop...."

Cerynise's voice thickened with emotion. "She passed away some three months ago."

"Oh, I'm sorry to hear that," Uncle Sterling said, losing some of his elation. "She was a fine woman." Looking at his niece again, he smiled, this time gently. "But you can't believe how relieved I am to have you back. I've missed you so. You're the only family I have now."

With those simple words, Cerynise felt the wall she had erected in fear crumbling away. He opened his arms to her, and with a catch in her breath, she flew into them. Sterling gathered her close, embracing her affectionately and blinking away a flood of tears. "Dear

372

child, you've been in my thoughts constantly. Your letters were a delight, to be sure, but I cannot tell you how your arrival has lifted my spirits. I had begun to despair that I'd never see you again."

"Now I'm back," she murmured, wondering how she could have ever thought him cold and distant. Perhaps she hadn't really even known him. Yet she had every hope that would soon change.

Beau had stepped back a respectful distance to allow them this moment together, and after a time, Sterling Kendall faced him with a smile. "I gather I have you to thank for my niece's safe return, Captain Birmingham."

"There are some things you should know, sir," Beau replied, startling Cerynise with his declaration. "And I think we should talk about them at length."

Uncle Sterling glanced curiously from one to the other and, after noting the sudden dismay in his niece's face, decided it was a matter of some urgency. "Of course, Captain. Let's go into the parlor, where we can have some tea while we talk."

They followed him through the lemon-scented hall to a room overlooking the garden, which now in winter was mostly dormant except for the camellias that were still blooming. In the summer months all manner of flowers and neatly clipped shrubs created a view that was immensely pleasing to the senses. Cerynise had always loved roaming through the mulched lanes, looking at the colorful array of blossoms and the charming gazebo where climbing roses and ivy trailed upward through the white lattice walls. It had once been her hope to create that same scene on canvas, but as yet she hadn't done so.

"Find yourselves a seat and get comfortable while I go and see where the housemaid is," Uncle Sterling urged them. "Cora is getting rather hard of hearing, and lately she hasn't been seeing too well either, but she declares that she's fit enough to carry on just as well as she always has."

Cerynise remembered Cora from her childhood and roughly guessed the woman was at least sixty-eight. From the neatness of the house, she could ascertain that in spite of her limitations Cora was still fully capable of cleaning and cooking for her uncle. The woman had done so for the last thirty years.

Cerynise crossed the room and settled on a settee facing a wide expanse of square-paned windows that showed off the garden. Less than a moment later Beau followed, ignoring more comfortable chairs to take a place beside her. Everywhere their eyes flitted, there were books nestled in little crannies, on shelves, and larger volumes carefully arranged on tabletops. Beau picked up one and began leafing through it until his interest heightened. Besides the historical text, there were also drawings representing ancient Greek and Roman statues, many of which were rather graphic in detail. A quick glance upward confirmed the fact that Cerynise's interest had also been stimulated, and he turned the pages much more slowly for her benefit.

"Nice drawings," he commented with a grin, finally turning his gaze upon her.

Cerynise had been leaning toward him ever so slightly, but at his words, she sat upright, her face flaming. She couldn't very well lie and deny that she had been gawking at the male statues on the page. The best she could do was respond with a casual shrug. "I suppose."

"Not as nice as the real thing though."

"Put the book up," she cautioned in a whisper. "My uncle's coming."

"Is that what you did when you were a little girl?" Beau queried, laying the book back upon the table in front of them.

"What do you mean?" she asked in wide-eyed bemusement.

"Devour all the pictures of naked men and women and then scurry to hide that fact when your elders approached," he explained with a soft chuckle.

Cerynise wished she could cool her cheeks with a wet cloth, but then, she seriously doubted even that would help, for her blush warmed her whole body. "I don't remember ever seeing that kind of book here before. Perhaps my uncle was more careful about leaving it out for children to find."

"A historian would never imagine that kind of book lewd," Beau argued, "so I doubt the good professor would hide it."

"Well, I never saw it before in my life!" she hissed hotly.

"All right!" He could not quell an amused grin, and then, because he loved to tease her, he leaned near to whisper, "Have you ever painted a man in the nude?"

"Certainly not!"

"Didn't know what they looked like before me, eh?"

"Be quiet! My uncle will hear you."

His broad shoulders lifted casually. "I don't mind."

"Well, I do!" she protested in a barely audible tone. "We're supposed to be considering an annulment. Or have you forgotten?"

"You won't let me," he prodded.

Startled by his answer, Cerynise looked up to search his eyes, but she had no time to question him, for her uncle opened the door and held it wide as Cora pushed the tea cart in.

Tea and crumpets were served, and Cerynise nervously partook of both. She had no idea what Beau meant to tell her uncle; she only knew that whatever it was, it would come as a shock to the elder.

After closing the door behind the housemaid, her uncle faced Beau over the tea cart. "What do you wish to tell me, Captain?"

"Simply that Cerynise and I are married...."

Cerynise cringed, awaiting her uncle's reaction. He would no doubt take offense because he hadn't been informed prior to the event.

Sterling sat back in his chair in stunned disbelief. "How did this come about?"

376

In an anxious rush to have it all behind her, Cerynise gave Beau no opportunity to say what was on his mind. "It was all rather sudden, Uncle Sterling, and most needed at the time. You see, Mrs. Winthrop's nephew tried to claim me as his legal ward upon her death, and when Alistair threatened to have the authorities halt the *Audacious*'s departure, Beau...I mean, Captain Birmingham offered marriage as a way to get both me and his ship out of England. We have plans to get our marriage annulled as soon as possible, but we thought you should know immediately...."

The clatter of a china cup being set upon a saucer with unusual force drew Cerynise's startled attention to her husband, who at the moment seemed genuinely perturbed with her.

"Did I not explain our situation precisely?" she queried uneasily.

"Very concisely, madam."

Sterling looked from one to the other and wondered what he was presently seeing in the younger man's face. It was not pleasure, by any means. He sought to soothe whatever irritation the captain might be feeling. " 'Twould appear that you both found a resourceful solution to a difficult predicament."

"Perhaps," Beau muttered. "At least your niece seems to view it that way." Then rather abruptly he put his cup and saucer back on the tea cart and came to his feet. "I must get back to my ship now. I left Mr. Oaks in charge without giving him adequate instructions how I wanted to handle certain matters. I'm sure he'll be at a loss until I get back."

"Certainly, Captain," Uncle Sterling said, opening the door. "I'll show you out."

As the elder entered the hall, Beau paused briefly to glance back at Cerynise, who could find nothing more to say than "I suppose you'll be sending the annulment papers around for me to sign."

His smile was stiff and terse, his mood dark. "If you insist, madam."

Then, whirling on a heel, he followed her uncle through the hallway.

The hard lump in Cerynise's throat threatened to dissolve into a burst of tears as she listened to the striding footfalls of her husband, who apparently was in no mood to walk softly. The men exchanged a few murmured words at the door, and then the portal was swept open. She sat frozen until it closed again with a firmness that had a definite ring of finality.

CHAPTER 12

More than a month after her return, Cerynise came down to breakfast much later than usual, wearing a painting smock and looking for all the world as if she had finally found the heart to return to her work. Uncle Sterling had already settled in the dining room, where bay windows overlooked the garden. He had been addressing his morning meal with enthusiasm, but at her entrance, he rose in gentlemanly manner.

"I was wondering where you were, my dear," he greeted jovially. "Please forgive me for starting without you. I have an early appointment this morning that I mustn't be late for."

Cerynise spared a quick glance at the shirred eggs, hominy cakes, sausage, and applesauce available on the sideboard and swallowed with difficulty. The housemaid waddled in with a warmed plate which she set before the girl, but Cerynise shook her head. "Thank you, Cora, but I think I'll just have tea this morning."

The older woman poured a cup and served it with an ample piece of her mind. "Miss Cerynise, you ought to eat more than you do. You don't eat enough to keep a cricket alive."

Cerynise started to lift the cup, but her stomach chose that moment to do a slow, dizzying flip-flop, making her feel just as she had aboard the *Audacious* in the earlier days of the voyage. She set the cup down hastily and quickly averted her gaze.

"Is something wrong?" Uncle Sterling asked, glancing up to find her eyes closed and her face pale.

"No." Cerynise looked up to find him in the process of spreading thick orange marmalade on a warm corn muffin. Cautiously dragging her gaze from him, she watched her tea do an odd little back-and-forth motion in her cup.

With trembling hands she reached out to steady the cup, but immediately discovered that it wasn't moving. It was only her stomach turning. Her hands began to shake noticeably, and she yanked them back quickly, clenching them together in her lap.

"Something *is* wrong," Uncle Sterling stated with conviction, dropping his muffin. He pushed his chair back and came around to her side of the table. "You're as pale as a ship's canvas this morning, my dear. What plagues you? Are you feverish?" He pressed his knuckles to her brow to judge for himself.

"No, I'm fine," Cerynise muttered in a weak, unconvincing tone. She felt perfectly well—...aside from her inability to keep food on her stomach...and the strange lassitude that had continued on unswervingly since her first bout on the *Audacious*. "I'm just a little tired, that's all."

"Well, no wonder," Uncle Sterling replied, resuming his seat. "The way you've been moping around here lately, you've undoubtedly become bored after the excitement of the voyage. A young girl like you should be out meeting new friends and going to balls and such. Perhaps a stroll would improve your frame of mind. 'Tis a lovely day, and my appointment shouldn't occupy me above an hour. When I return, I shall expect to have the pleasure of your company for a walk."

"If you insist," Cerynise acquiesced listlessly, finding no enthusiasm for such a task. In spite of her careful explanations to Beau

380

about her need to set up a studio and get back to her painting, she had progressed very little toward that end. Even when Uncle Sterling had suggested that they should get together with old family friends, she had politely put him off, not wishing to go anywhere or see anyone.

"Perhaps we could stroll along Broad Street and do a little shopping," he suggested. Women always enjoyed such things, and he was in a rare mood to be out and about with his niece on his arm. "I understand there are some excellent modistes there."

Cerynise didn't know whether to laugh or cry. All she needed was to be fitted and measured by a seamstress. That would definitely raise havoc. But her dear, sweet scholarly uncle was so concerned about her that he imagined a new gown would be effective in bringing her out of her doldrums. She knew he couldn't have recited more than one or two facts about feminine fashions, but he was offering to spend his own money and time escorting her to dressmakers with the hope that it would somehow make her feel better.

Cerynise smiled at him gently. "I'd love to go with you, Uncle Sterling, but perhaps we could visit some bookstores instead. I'm just not feeling in a mood to shop for material or fret over fashions right now."

Her uncle's relief was obvious enough to make her laugh in appreciation for the sacrifice he had been willing to make on her behalf. Soon he left for his appointment, but only after wringing a promise from her that she'd eat something. Barely had she sampled the smallest portion of a hominy cake than her stomach rebelled. She just managed to get to her room in time, but afterwards, she felt so weak she had to lie down. Finally her nausea faded, and she began to move about in a halfhearted quest to get ready.

When Uncle Sterling arrived a little more than an hour later, Cerynise was waiting for him in the entrance hall. She had garbed herself in a pale blue woolen gown trimmed with brown velvet cording and a wide band collar of the same hue. It was the only one among her day dresses loose enough to allow her to forgo wearing a corset. Since there was only a slight nip in the air, she had shunned the idea of wearing a cloak and, instead, had draped a large, enveloping cashmere shawl of pale blue and brown paisley around her shoulders. Over her neatly coiled coiffure, she had tied a pert blue bonnet handsomely arrayed with pheasant feathers. Although the converse was true, her smile suggested that she hadn't a care in the world.

"You're ready!" Uncle Sterling exclaimed, pleased that she was looking so winsome. Gallantly he offered his arm. "Shall we?"

The day fairly sparkled beneath a clear sky, while the air was imbued with just enough scent of the approaching spring to tantalize the senses. Everywhere Cerynise looked, she espied finely garbed men and women making their way in and out of shops. They were certainly eloquent testimony to the prosperity of Charleston. Some, she guessed, were from nearby plantations, others perhaps from the area near the mills nestled on the Ashley River or from places much farther afield. Her ears caught enunciations with a northern twang amid the leisured drawls of the Carolina inhabitants. There was also evidence of Europeans aplenty everywhere they went. After living in a city as immense as London, Cerynise could hardly think of Charleston as a great metropolis, yet it had a charm all of its own. Most of its citizens seemed to combine a love of adventure with shrewd business sense and genuine southern hospitality, which certainly made shopping an affable experience. Cerynise found herself involved in more than a few delightful little chitchats with store owners and clerks. Their discussions ranged anywhere from passing comments on their balmy March weather to lighthearted observations on the various plays presently being performed at the local theaters. After catching herself laughing in response to some witty remark, it dawned on her that merely being out and about had helped considerably to lift her spirits.

Or at least it had until she rounded a corner with her uncle in time to see an elegant carriage roll to a halt in front of a shop belonging to one of Charleston's most renowned couturiers, one Madame Feroux. A tall, broad-shouldered man alighted and held out a hand to assist his female companion in her descent. The young lady was of such doll-like beauty

Cerynise might have stared in admiration had she not recognized her own husband serving as the woman's escort. From then on, she was helplessly caught in the throes of acute despondency with a fair amount of jealousy blended in.

Beau's teeth flashed whitely in sharp contrast to his darkly burnished skin as he threw back his head and laughed at whatever the ravishing creature had said. He was exceptionally well garbed and looked every bit the Carolina aristocrat that he was. Indeed, no London dandy could have matched his debonair appearance. His fine, charcoal gray swallowtail coat was set off to perfection by thinly striped gray trousers and a shawl-collared vest made in a wider, complementary striped silk. A rich, waffled-silk cravat of pearl-gray was a stunning addition to his elegant garb. The fact that it was neatly in place beneath the stiff collar of his white shirt led Cerynise to wonder morosely if his little friend had had anything to do with its natty appearance. His dark gray top hat was angled jauntily upon his dark head, and if anything, his dashing good looks were even more striking than before. The petite brunette evidently thought so too, for she swayed against him, brushing her small bosom against his arm as she smiled up at him enchantingly and lightly touched a hand to his broad chest.

"Really, Beau," she warbled, "where are your manners? Surely, it isn't too much for me to expect that you—" She broke off abruptly when she realized she no longer had his attention. In sudden confusion, she followed his gaze to the source of his distraction, and for the briefest of moments her dark eyes chilled in arrogant displeasure as she appraised the tawny-haired beauty at whom he stared.

Beau stepped aside, deftly detaching himself from the brunette, which by no means was an easy task since she had actually taken hold of his lapel. Smiling, he tipped his hat gallantly to his wife. "A pleasure to see you again, Cerynise."

Beau doubted that he had ever uttered a more truthful greeting in all of his life. He hadn't seen her since the day he had stalked out of her uncle's house, but it couldn't be said that he hadn't thought of her, for he definitely had. Constantly, in fact. The time during which they had been apart had been an agony of memories running over and over in his mind. When he had helped Sterling Kendall load her belongings in a carriage, every instinct within him had goaded him to ask news of her, but his stubborn pride hadn't allowed him to do so. She had seemed so adamant about getting the annulment that he had hoped to assuage his anger by totally ignoring her, even to the point of refusing to visit his lawyer, which would have awakened his ire all over again. What he had deemed as suitable punishment for her had resulted in a living hell for himself. Thus, it came as no surprise to him to realize just how much her appearance delighted him. Indeed, his eyes feasted on her with ravenous hunger, and it was almost a full moment before he remembered that she, too, had an escort.

"Professor Kendall, how nice it is to see you again."

"And you," Sterling responded, cheerfully unaware of the emotional currents running between his niece and the captain. Not so the pocket Venus. When a man perused another woman in her presence the way Beau Birmingham was doing at this precise moment, her hackles were inclined to rise like those of an enraged feline. She had never been confronted with a situation in which she had to share a man's attention with another female, for she was quite popular and had many admirers, to the extent that she could pick and choose her escorts. The fact that Beau Birmingham, the most reticent toward her, was probably the richest and, to be sure, the most handsome among Charleston's male populace only solidified her objective of wooing him into matrimony. This tawny-haired Aphrodite whom he zealously perused was unmistakably a rival she'd definitely have to dispense with in one fashion or another.

The brunette tugged on Beau's sleeve in an effort to break his unwavering stare. He seemed startled as he glanced around, and for barely a moment he looked at her as if he hadn't the slightest idea who she was. Abruptly recalling his manners, he hastened to make the introductions. "Cerynise, this is Miss Germaine Hollingsworth. Germaine, I'm sure you remember Cerynise Kendall from your—"

Germaine managed a small frown and blinked her long lashes in a close resemblance of confusion as she looked up at him. "No, Beau, I'm afraid I don't."

He was taken aback by surprise. "I'm sorry. I just assumed your paths had crossed at some point in time."

It was a reasonable conjecture, considering that Germaine was only a year or two older than his wife, and as much as the brunette denied it, his premise was correct. Cerynise recalled her only too well. The pampered Miss Hollingsworth had attended the same academy to which most of the wealthy families and parents with more of a professional scholarly bent sent their daughters to be instructed in a manner suitable for young ladies. Germaine had been one of those who had enjoyed tormenting a somewhat gawky twelve-year-old who had failed to believe the world revolved around bonnets and beaus. More than once in the presence of Germaine and her friends, Cerynise had been made the target of tongues that could have flailed the hide off an alligator. Yet, at the approach of an attractive male, those same young ladies had had the ability to mask their shrewish dispositions with chameleon-like swiftness and drip sweet honey with every syllable they uttered.

"Beau, dear, we really mustn't linger," Germaine coyly pressed. "You did promise..."

"To give you a ride to Madame Feroux's." He swept his hand to indicate the shop behind them. "And you have arrived."

387

"Silly me." Germaine laughed and tossed her elegantly coifed head as if embarrassed by such a foolish mistake. "Why, I hardly noticed where we were." With a flutter of dark lashes, she looked up at Beau with a pleading expression that, in Cerynise's mind, wouldn't have been misplaced on a hungry wolf. "I always have such difficulty deciding what looks best on my tiny frame, and everyone says that you have the most divine taste, Beau, so I was wondering if you could assist—"

"I'm afraid not." He didn't even look at Germaine as he answered, for his gaze was fastened on Cerynise, who found herself unwillingly fascinated by the other woman's charming endeavors.

Germaine's pretty mouth tightened, but she was not about to relent. "Why, Beauregard Birmingham, how can you be so nasty to little ol' me? I've heard rumors about you being a tough sea captain, but you're also supposed to be a gentleman, and a gentleman would never deny a lady's—"

"Am I?" he queried in distraction.

"Are you what?" Germaine asked petulantly.

"A gentleman?" Although the question seemed primarily addressed to Germaine, he never looked away from his wife. "Would you say that to be true, Cerynise?"

Cerynise was distantly aware of Uncle Sterling eyeing them both fairly closely now, no doubt bewildered by her high blush and the sudden trembling that had beset her. She was averse to praising her husband in front of the little coquette and answered him as diplomatically as she could. "Were you not one, sir, you'd certainly be unwilling for me to announce that fact," she rejoined, her voice sounding faint in her own ears. "And yet, if I were to laud your character for your companion's benefit, I wonder where that would lead." *To bed?* Cerynise dolefully wondered.

Sensing her tension, Uncle Sterling cleared his throat. "Are you planning to remain in Charleston very long, Captain Birmingham?"

"Perhaps a bit longer than usual, Professor Kendall. I have important matters that need my close attention." The fact that his gaze shifted from the man to Cerynise seemed to indicate that she was at the forefront of those important matters. "I should still be here well into mid-summer, if not longer."

Sterling was growing more bemused by the moment. "Has your fascination with the sea waned, then?"

The wide shoulders lifted in a brief shrug. "I wouldn't say that exactly, but I have other interests that have plagued me much of late, and I'd like them settled one way or the other before I'll even think of leaving."

Cerynise was certain that he was referring to their annulment, but he could hardly blame her for the delay. For more than a month now she had been expecting papers to arrive and had recently begun to suspect that they wouldn't. Beau could hardly have forgotten about their marital division, but then, when he was so dedicated to remaining a bachelor, he probably thought he had all the time in the world. He'd have been shocked to learn differently.

Germaine was ecstatic over the idea of his lengthy stay. "Oh, Beau, it would be so nice to have you around Charleston for a change. I really think you'd love attending the Spring Ball this year, and since I'm still available...well, we can talk about that later. Still, I've always thought that sailing off to all those other countries must be terribly dangerous. Every time you leave, I wonder if you'll be coming back. Now I won't have to worry, at least for a while."

"I doubt that we'd be standing where we are today if our forefathers had been afraid of danger," Beau replied distantly, again without the slightest flicker in the woman's direction.

"I do hope your business here proceeds smoothly, Captain," Cerynise murmured, and couldn't resist a gentle prodding to remind him that their annulment was something that he was supposed to arrange. "Perhaps you've been so busy lately that you've forgotten about Mr. Farraday."

"Mr. Farraday?" Germaine began, her brows gathering in perplexity. "Does she mean the solicitor?"

The woman received no answer, for none of the others was paying her any heed. Uncle Sterling was far too absorbed eyeing his niece and the captain. Cerynise could only stare in helpless fascination as Beau's lean jaw tightened dangerously. At present, he was looking at her so coldly that, had he been a dastardly pirate, she might have found herself run through. She could hardly ignore the fact that she had vexed him again, but she wasn't at all sure how she had done so. He *had* been talking about the annulment, hadn't he?

"Henceforth, I'll be certain to assure Mr. Farraday's speed in all matters, *Miss Kendall,*" Beau answered coolly. "Now good day to you both." With a curt nod to her uncle, he slipped a hand beneath Germaine's arm and escorted the delightfully surprised creature into the shop.

Uncle Sterling hesitated a moment before offering his own arm to Cerynise. When she continued to stare blankly in the direction in which the pair had gone well after they had disappeared into the shop, he took her hand and slipped it gently within the crook of his elbow. She walked stiltedly, rather like a lifeless doll, as he drew her along with him. "I've been meaning to ask you about those papers, my dear. Are you sure the annulment is what you want?"

Cerynise was still very much in a daze and didn't hear a word he said. She could only rebuke herself harshly for driving Beau not only away from her but straight into the clutches of Germaine Hollingsworth. Where he was concerned, it seemed she could only act the part of a complete simpleton. When she foolishly, systematically destroyed every chance that she had of keeping what she truly, desperately wanted in life, it was obvious to her that she was hell-bent on her own destruction and misery.

As if to emphasize her distress, her stomach began to roil very strangely. Completely shocked by what she was feeling, Cerynise gasped softly and swayed on her feet, coming very near to buckling to her knees. Sterling caught her arm and looked at her in sudden concern. Her pale, drawn face was enough to convince him. He raised a hand to summon a hired livery and quickly handed her in.

"If this continues, my dear," he said as the carriage rattled along the cobbled street, "I shall insist that you see my physician."

Cerynise shook her head and turned her face toward the window to hide her tears. "I'm fine. Really. I just got too warm, I guess."

Her uncle murmured something about it not being very warm at all outside, but he didn't pursue the topic any further. He was beginning to have his suspicions, and he was not above laying the blame on Captain Birmingham.

When they reached the house, Cerynise excused herself and went up to her room to rest. She doffed her gown and shoes before stretching out upon her bed. With a feeling of awe, she moved her hands slowly over her abdomen, where a definite curve was beginning to form. How long since that single night of love? Four months, give or take a week? At least long enough for the movements of the baby to become strong and sure. All of her efforts to withhold herself from Beau after that one brief episode had been for naught. His seed had already found fertile ground, and in her womb she was carrying part of him, possibly the only part she would ever be allowed to keep. It wouldn't be long now before people began to notice her ever-growing belly and begin to whisper snide comments. Yet she couldn't bring herself to beg Beau to give up his freedom for the sake of their child. It was a choice he'd have to make on his own.

It was a long, sleepless night. Cerynise spent most of it wondering how best to proceed with motherhood. She finally decided that it would probably be better for herself and her baby if she moved away to another southern city where she wouldn't be known and where she could make a pretense of being a young widow. She *had* gotten with child while married, except that it was the death of that union that would leave her greatly bereaved. Once she was settled, she could start painting again and hopefully sell her work surreptitiously as she had done before. If things went well, it wouldn't take her long to establish a life for herself and be fairly situated before her baby was born the middle of August.

It was late the next morning when she finally went downstairs with a smock covering her gown, which had become a necessity. Since her uncle was engrossed in writing a book about the ancient Greeks, she fully expected him to be secluded in his study, where he usually worked. The study doors were closed, and with a wavering sigh of thankfulness, she went into the small morning room just off the kitchen. Her stomach was no calmer now than it had been in recent days, and she wondered if her lingering nausea was due in part to her wrought-up emotions. She had heard of women suffering from queasiness even into the later stages of their pregnancy, but she sincerely hoped it wouldn't be true in her case. Knowing that she had to force herself to eat for the sake of her child, she took a small serving of eggs and biscuit onto her plate and had made only minute progress when Cora entered.

"Your pardon, Miss Cerynise, but this package arrived for you earlier this morning."

Even after she had been left alone again, Cerynise made no effort to examine the contents of the large envelope of stiff vellum. It was carefully folded and sealed with blood-red wax, just the sort of package a lawyer might send. Listlessly she went to the window, looked out upon the garden for a time and then returned to her place where she forced herself to eat. Gradually, she armed herself with the mettle required to open the packet.

Inside was a sheaf of legal documents written out in meticulous copperplate. The last page also bore an impressive-looking seal and room for several signatures. One was already in place.

The dark, heavy ink emphatically implied that Beau had signed without hesitation. After flipping back to the first page, she began to read the content. There was a great deal of legal terminology, but it all meant the same thing. They had never lived together as man and wife. Therefore no true marriage had existed or would ever exist in the future. They both agreed to surrender any legal rights and obligations to one another in perpetuity.

It was very quiet in the morning room. Cerynise could hear a few distant sounds of carriages and horses passing on the lane, but they did little to pierce the dark cloud that hung over her life. She knew what she was about to do was at the very least illegal and quite probably immoral, for she was about to swear to what was untrue. However briefly, she and Beau *had* lived together as man and wife. The fact that her pregnancy had occurred with no awareness on his part changed nothing.

She had no doubt now that what she had dreaded for nigh to three months was true, yet she was about to condemn her unborn child to bastardy, all in service to a private sense of honor she could hardly explain even to herself. The enormity of the chasm looming before her unnerved Cerynise, yet she refused to draw back now. She would never entrap Beau against his will, not when he had made it abundantly clear that he wasn't ready to commit himself to a wife and family. Nor would she sacrifice her own sense of what was fair and right, even if the whole world thought her mad.

Despite the nausea that had returned with a vengeance, Cerynise reached for the quill and ink on the serving board, sparing a pensive smile for the habits of a scholar who never knew when he might want to jot down a thought. Though her hand was shaking violently, she took a firm grip on herself and painstakingly signed her name:

Cerynise Edlyn Kendall

Beside Beau's bold declaration, her own seemed pale and insignificant, but it would have to do. She sanded it quickly, closed the document, and returned it to the envelope. Before she could allow herself even a moment's hesitation, she rang for Cora. When the woman appeared, Cerynise gave her the envelope with the request that it be sent posthaste to Captain Birmingham.

Early that same afternoon, Cora came into the room which Uncle Sterling had given Cerynise to use as her studio. The younger woman's paints, easel and paintings and sketches from the sea voyage cluttered the room. Most of the latter were on the floor, leaning against the wall as the girl strove to organize her work area.

"Miss Cerynise, there's a lady at the front door who says she'd like to talk to you about a portrait she wants you to paint."

"Did she give her name?"

"No, ma'am. She just said you'd know her."

Cerynise frowned, thinking it odd of the visitor, and then questioned, "What does she look like?"

"Oh, real pretty, miss," the maid assured her. "Small with black hair."

"Oh, that must be Brenna." The interest Beau's sister had shown in her work assured Cerynise that it could be no other. In spite of everything, she was delighted to be visited by the girl, and with a smile, she cleared a place for her guest to sit. "Please show her back here to my studio, Cora, and prepare us some tea."

Cerynise was so busy arranging a place for them to sit and chat over tea that she didn't even think of donning the smock that she had taken off only a few moments earlier when she had gotten too warm in the room. Cora didn't see well enough to notice much detail beyond a handbreadth from her nose, and Cerynise had felt no qualms about doffing the covering. She was just finishing her task and still had her back to the study door when a soft rustle of taffeta brought her to the awareness that her beautiful caller had arrived.

"I never imagined that you'd come so soon, Brenna," she said, turning to face her visitor. Her smile of greeting froze in an instant as she saw Germaine Hollingsworth smirking back at her from the doorway.

"I'm sorry to disappoint you, Cerynise," the

brunette said, arching a dark brow sardonically. "I can understand how much you may have wanted Beau's sister here, but I'm afraid you'll have to contend with me instead."

"So you *do* remember me after all," Cerynise goaded, trying to appear casual as she moved toward the stool where she had left the loose cotton smock. Without a shawl or some other protective covering, she was too far along in her pregnancy to hope that people wouldn't notice her thickening waist or rounding shape. All they would have to do was take a close look at her and they'd know instantly that she was with child.

Germaine laughed caustically. "Oh, yes, I remember you. You were that prim little artist who wanted to be left alone with her work and her own circle of friends. What was it we used to call you? Stilts? Or was it Sticks?" She laughed snidely. "Both were appropriate names at the time, but I must admit, Cerynise, you've acquired a more pleasing appearance since last we met."

"Then I take it you didn't come to inquire about a portrait."

The woman released a pompous sigh as she strolled about the room to look at the paintings. "I really don't know what my parents would do with another one," she rejoined. "Last time they hired the best, you know, and I rather doubt that you'd be capable of meeting their expectations, as much as Beau was wont to laud your talent when I asked him about you. But if I've learned anything about men over the years, I'm willing to guess from the hungry way he looked at you yesterday, he has designs on your person, *not* on your paintings."

Cerynise turned aside as Germaine blocked her access to the smock. "Then why did you come?"

"I wanted to warn you away from Beau," Germaine replied with blunt frankness, "just in case he may come calling. You see, I intend to marry the man as soon as I can bring him around to the notion, and in the meantime, I wouldn't want him to dally with another woman who might see some advantage in entrapping him in marriage." She reached down to tilt a painting of a seaman outward from the wall in a quest to see a slightly larger one hidden behind it and gasped in surprise as she recognized the very person she had purposed to marry. Though she wouldn't have admitted it, the portrait was a stirring likeness of one Beau Birmingham, garbed in a sweater and a cap with sails billowing behind him.

Germaine whirled to face Cerynise, only to find the other's back turned toward her. Angrily she demanded, "When did you paint this?"

Cerynise glanced around at the piece that Germaine was now holding up. Those blue eyes staring at her even from the lifeless canvas made her heart lurch in misery. "On the *Audacious*."

"When were you *ever* on the *Audacious?*" Germaine questioned in a sneering tone. "Beau never mentioned anything about you visiting his ship."

"I was a passenger aboard her," Cerynise explained simply.

"That's a lie! Beau never takes passengers! If he did, I'd have bought passage myself to wherever he was going."

Cerynise lifted her shoulders briefly. "I was the exception."

"I think you're still lying, and if you are, I'll find out! You're not going to steal Beau away from me, do you hear?"

"Is he yours to claim?" The fear that something of a passionate nature had already occurred wrenched Cerynise's heart. "Or are you just being hopeful?"

"Look at me!"

Cerynise folded her arms across her midsection and reluctantly faced the woman. "I'm looking."

"Don't *even think* of trying to win him for yourself. I've been after him too long to let a little nobody slip of a bitch like you get in my way! And believe me, if you think 'Sticks' or 'Stilts' was bad, that will be mild compared to the rumors I'll initiate in your behalf."

"Really, Germaine, you could have spared yourself a visit. I doubt that I'll ever be seeing the man again," Cerynise said forlornly. As if protesting her statement, the baby moved abruptly within her womb. The sudden sharp roll caught her completely by surprise, and she gasped, pressing a hand to her abdomen for

400

barely an instant before she remembered herself and hurriedly faced away.

Germaine's eyes widened in amazement. She had seen enough to solidify one thought. The fullness detectable beneath the other's softly gathered skirt was definitely not the natural curve of a chaste maid, of that she was sure. And she was just as certain that Beau Birmingham didn't know a thing about the pregnant state of the little slut whom he had ogled only the day before.

"Well, now that we've settled that matter, I guess I should be going. I have some more shopping to do if I'm going to attend Suzanne Birmingham's engagement ball with Beau next month. Ta-ta."

Looking decidedly more cheerful than when she had entered the room, Germaine fairly sailed down the hall toward the front entrance. She wouldn't have missed this visit for all the world, for she now had enough fuel to cinder Cerynise's reputation and turn to ashes any infatuation that Beau Birmingham might have felt for the girl. Although the day before he had casually mentioned the fact that he'd be away from his house today, she had provided herself with the perfect excuse to visit him on the morrow.

The day was just breaking, but Beau was already up and dressed, *not* because he had risen early, but because he hadn't even gone to bed. Having given up any attempt to sleep with the turmoil roiling within him, he had spent

401

the night pacing his study, steadily drinking his way through a goodly amount of brandy. He had finally slumped into the chair behind his desk, where he now glared at a sheaf of papers he had left on top in full view. The documents were those that Cerynise had signed and returned to him. Once he forwarded them on to Farraday, the barrister, in his usual efficient way, would successfully conclude the matter of their marriage once and for all.

For perhaps the thousandth time, Beau inspected the delicate but unfaltering signature, as the dark cavity consuming his heart deepened progressively.

Damn her! he mentally growled. Had she even wasted a moment's breath of notice before finishing him off? Had she, even for an instant, considered the alternative? No, of course she hadn't, at least not since he had angered her aboard the *Audacious*. And he was a damned fool for regretting it all. Women definitely had their uses, but with rare exceptions a man would be well advised to consider them just another appetite in need of satisfying. He'd been lax about leaving himself open, falling for her, wanting their marriage to continue, and now he was paying for it. But no more! He was now in a mood to set Charleston on its ear. He'd drown himself in females, wallow in them, sate every urge he'd ever felt and then some. He wouldn't stop until he was damned well numb!

Resolved on what seemed a likely course to take to rout Cerynise out of his thoughts,

Beau left his desk and went to stand at the front windows, from whence he could glimpse the bay. He'd launch into preparations for another voyage as soon as Mr. Oaks returned from plying the seaboard for new cargo. Sailing to far-off ports would help ease the remorse that still throbbed within him. After all, there was no more reason for him to stay in Charleston. In a few days Cerynise would no longer be his.

With a heavy sigh, he left his study and made his way upstairs with lagging steps. He thought he could finally rest now, but only because he was too exhausted to stay awake. He passed through his spacious bedchamber and entered the dressing room, where he took a good hard look at himself in the mirror above his shaving stand. He definitely needed to rid himself of the overnight growth that darkened his cheeks, brush the taste of foul brandy out of his mouth, and wash and comb his hair in some semblance of order. He spied the bath that had been left untouched since it had been prepared for him the night before. It was now cold, but the shock would probably do him good. Perhaps it would even bring him to his bloody senses.

In a moment he was lying chest-deep in the chilly water with his head resting on the rim of the huge tub, but even there, he was continually inundated by visions of Cerynise. He had no particularly favorite memory, for they were all titillating to his senses. Yet, if he had to make a choice above the rest, it would be the one wherein he had plied her with kisses after their marriage vows. Teaching her how to kiss in a way that was sensual and arousing had been a very gratifying experience for him. Then, too, there was that moment when he had caressed her womanly softness and found the thin virginal flesh preventing easy passage. It had warmed his heart to realize that no other man had been there before him. And, of course, there was that dream of her rising up beneath him in answering passion, her soft gasps filling his mind, and her nails scratching his back....

Beau swore suddenly, realizing that he was doing it again. For the life of him, he just couldn't stop thinking about her! Indeed! Every memory of her seemed as dear to him as his own lifeblood.

A half hour later he whipped the bedcovers down and sprawled naked onto his bed. Sleep came upon him very quickly, but even as he finally began to relax he saw in his mind's eye the vision he had created from his imagination and had nurtured ever since, that of Cerynise sitting on her heels beside his bed with her round breasts gleaming with a luster of their own beneath the softly glowing light of the hanging lantern.

Sterling Kendall rose at his accustomed hour and dressed absently while following a train of thought that had nothing whatsoever to do with Greeks. When he left his

404

chamber and went down the corridor to the bedroom that his niece occupied, he was still debating how to go about questioning her. Pausing outside her closed door, he recalled the first time he had seen Cerynise, when she was but a scant two days old. Childless himself and already suspecting he was destined to remain so, he had taken one look at the lovely, squalling little creature and fallen hopelessly in love.

Over the years, he had watched her grow into an unusually thoughtful, intelligent child and had taken enormous delight in her achievements. When tragedy had struck, taking his dear brother and sister-in-law well before their time, he had despaired at his lack of fatherly experience. Other than taking her into his home, he hadn't known what to do for the precious girl whom they had left behind. Kind Lydia had proven a godsend, and yet he couldn't count all of the times in the past five years that he had regretted giving in to her pleas to let Cerynise live with her in England. Even coming as it had on the heels of yet more grief, his niece's return had filled him with joy. Yet, for all of that, he could no longer ignore the fact that something was very, very wrong.

He was a simple man, content with his books and his garden, yet it would have been a mistake for anyone to think him unworldly. What he hadn't experienced himself, which he admitted was a great deal, others had.

Moreover, they had been thoughtful enough to write about it. Through his studies, he had absorbed considerable knowledge about human nature. He certainly hadn't missed the tension between Cerynise and Beau Birmingham on the two occasions he had seen them together after their return to Charleston. Nor had he been entirely ignorant of what they had been doing at the very moment when he had opened his front door to find Cerynise on his front stoop, all of this despite a union his niece had continued to assure him was no marriage at all. He could only believe that this was something the captain had insisted upon, for no young woman in her right mind would willingly face what the future held in store for his niece without a husband.

As profoundly as Sterling was wont to hope that his fears were misplaced, he couldn't postpone confronting Cerynise another moment. Drawing a resolute breath, he raised a hand to knock on the door. He promptly halted, a startled expression sweeping over his face as he heard a strange sound coming from the room. A moment later, it was repeated. He was about to thrust open the door when it came to him what was actually happening. Cerynise was suffering repercussions caused by nausea.

It was possibly a testament to Sterling's character that he made no attempt to convince himself that his niece had merely eaten something disagreeable. His shoulders straightened as his hand came down to clench into a fist at his side.

He wouldn't disturb her; there was no point now. His business was with Beau Birmingham.

It was almost mid-morning when Monsieur Philippe answered the summons from the front door and explained to the beautiful visitor, "Your pardon, mademoiselle. *Le capitaine* was not expecting anyone. I think he's still upstairs."

"Are you the butler?"

Philippe laughed at the very idea. "Oh, no, mademoiselle. I am *le capitaine's* chef, Monsieur Philippe Monét. Zhere is no butler at present, only a housemaid, and she is busy scrubbing zee floor in my kitchen."

Germaine Hollingsworth was greatly puzzled. As rich as Beau undoubtedly was, she had difficulty imagining his house being equipped with anything less than a full complement of servants. She would certainly demand a full assortment when she became mistress. Curious, she probed for an explanation. "Isn't it rather strange to have such an exquisite home without enough help to maintain it?"

"Oh, zhere are servants coming fairly soon to replace zee last ones who were let go, mademoiselle," Philippe explained. "But zhey have not yet arrived." He shrugged as he added, "Zee others were too lax while *le capitaine* was away. He came home unexpected and found only zee housemaid working." Philippe made a gesture across his throat that highly suggested that their heads had been removed from their shoulders. "Zhey were quickly finished here."

"Captain Birmingham doesn't have any slaves, then?"

"Oh, *non,* mademoiselle. Not *le capitaine.*"

She smiled sweetly. *That too will change,* she determined. Graciously she requested, "Would you kindly inform the captain that Miss Germaine Hollingsworth is here and would like to have a word with him if he could possibly spare a moment."

"Oui, mademoiselle." Philippe swept his hand inward. "Won't you come into zee parlor to wait?"

"I'd be delighted." Germaine followed him into the front room and, at his invitation, took a seat on the settee.

Several moments later Beau came downstairs garbed in trousers, shirt, and black ankle-length boots. Not being in the best of moods, he was frowning sharply, for he hadn't been able to get more than an hour's worth of sleep before Philippe tapped on his bedroom door. At times, he had found Germaine amusing even though she seemed to chatter on incessantly until his mind wandered. He guessed in that respect he also found her a bit boring. In fact, come to think of it, he hated all that inane prattle she was inclined to coyly spew for his benefit.

"Oh, Beau, I do hope I didn't disturb you," Germaine cooed worriedly with a sweetly contrite expression as she rose and crossed the room to him. "I left my shawl in your carriage the other day, and I do miss not having it. Would you mind terribly asking your driver to fetch it for me?"

"Certainly," he replied, wondering why she hadn't thought of asking Philippe to do the same. He found the chef waiting outside the kitchen and sent him on the errand, then returned to the front sitting room, where his guest was now contemplating the painting of the *Audacious* hanging above the mantel.

"CK?" Germaine looked back at him inquiringly. "Does that stand for Cerynise Kendall?"

"Yes, it's one of her paintings," he answered, averting his gaze from the oil. As much as he liked the painting, he knew that henceforth it would always remind him of the young woman who had managed to firmly ensnare his heart.

"You certainly must admire her work a great deal to hang the oil in such a prominent place," Germaine gently nudged, hoping to gain more information.

"I happen to think it's an excellent likeness of my ship."

"I understand that she sailed with you on your last voyage from England."

Beau glanced around, wondering where Germaine had gotten her information. He was not above asking outright. "How do you know that?"

"Oh, Cerynise told me when I visited her at her uncle's house yesterday. You see, I was mistaken about not knowing her, and when the realization finally dawned on me that we had gone to the same academy for a time, I wanted to apologize to her personally."

"That was nice of you," Beau commented, with only a slight trace of sarcasm. He was no witless fool when it came to detecting the wiles of certain women. He could sense that Germaine had something more to say and that she was just waiting for the appropriate moment to launch her cannonball, for he was sure whatever she was working around to would be delivered with devastating precision. "How did you find Cerynise? Was she well?"

Germaine shrugged prettily. "Oh, I suppose so, but you know how it is with women in their early stages of...well, you know...her condition."

Beau looked at her inquisitively, wondering if she had lost her mind. "No, I don't know."

Germaine managed a blush. "You know that *word* ladies are not supposed to use..." She lowered her voice to a whisper. "*Pregnancy...*"

He scoffed in disbelief. "That's absurd!"

"Oh no, it isn't," Germaine argued, and leaned near to further confide in a low voice. "I saw her myself. She's rounding quite nicely. If I were to guess, I'd say she's at least three or four months along if she's a day. I'm sure you'll be hearing about it through the grapevine fairly soon. A young, unmarried woman like that can hardly hide her condition much beyond the first months, and Cerynise is so slender, every bulge shows."

Beau was speechless with shock. Four

months ago he had been seriously ill and out of his head. And that was precisely the time that those haunting memories of making love to her had begun. Distracted by his thoughts, he turned away and went to the large cabinet against the far wall. There he poured himself a drink from a crystal decanter, tossed it down with a flick of his wrist, and then shuddered as he realized it wasn't something he particularly liked.

"Beau, are you all right?" Germaine queried worriedly. Even her father, who was wont to drink overmuch in private, waited until after lunch to have his first tipple of the day.

Beau wanted to laugh at the very idea that anything was wrong. He knew now that Germaine had come in a quest to destroy Cerynise's reputation, but she had just told the wrong person. "Aye, but it will take me a while to get used to the idea."

His guest was still trying to decipher that statement when he faced her. When she finally gave up her futile attempt, she inquired, "Get used to what?"

"Why, to the idea of being a father."

Germaine's jaw dropped substantially before she managed to gasp, "Whatever do you mean, Beau?"

"Well, it comes as something of a shock, but I guess from what you say I'm going to be a father."

"You...and Cerynise Kendall?" Her jaw sagged even more, pulling open her mouth until it gapped as much as a widemouthed bass's.

She stared at him, horrified. "You mean you're the father of her bastar—"

Beau was suddenly delighted to be able to make the statement, "I mean that my wife is pregnant with our first child."

Germaine's reply was barely a whisper. "I didn't know you were married...."

He shrugged his wide shoulders. "Few people in Charleston did. My crew knew it, of course. Cerynise and I were trying to keep it a secret for reasons you wouldn't understand, but now I suppose there's no help for it. 'Twill have to be told."

"But when were you married...?" For once in her life Germaine was feeling very close to a genuine faint.

"Several days before we set sail from England," Beau informed her. Lest the woman be mistaken about the length of time it took for the crossing, he added, "In late October, about five months or so ago."

"I find that hard to believe." Germaine would have used a stronger statement, except that she didn't think Beau Birmingham would tolerate being called a liar quite as well as Cerynise had. "It makes no sense. Why would you keep your marriage to her a secret?" Germaine's skepticism strengthened the longer she thought about it. "You're just being gallant, trying to save her from a scandal."

"You think too highly of me, Germaine, but if you're suffering any doubts, wait here a moment." Beau stepped across the hall to his study and, from a drawer in his desk, withdrew the marriage document that Mr. Carmichael had given him. When he came back, he handed it to the woman. It was only for Cerynise's benefit that he took the time to show such evidence. Otherwise, he'd have let the woman wonder till her dying day. "You see, it's all been duly signed and documented, and if you'd care to notice the date, you'll see it's just as I said."

Germaine was greatly tempted to shred the parchment in tiny pieces. Seeing his name along with Cerynise's scrawled at the bottom made her want to scream in rage. Slowly she lowered the parchment and quirked a brow as she stared up at him. "This is most curious, Beau."

"Aye," he agreed, plucking the document out of her hands. He smiled for the first time in at least two days. "But I'm rather relieved that it's out now. There will, of course, be some changes made...."

"What kind of changes?" she asked, hoping against hope that they would be to her liking.

"I'll have to discuss them with my wife." Beau stepped to the parlor door and called down the hall. "Philippe, could you run out and ask Thomas to ready my carriage?"

"*Oui, Capitaine.*"

Beau returned to the parlor and, taking Germaine's arm, escorted her to the front portal. "Now, I hate to be rude, but I really must be getting along before too much time has elapsed. I hope you'll excuse me."

Before she knew it, Germaine was standing

outside the front door which had been closed without preamble behind her. She had never been so swiftly evicted from a home in all her life, and probably never would be again.

On the elegant cobblestone street that contained the residences of Charleston's most prosperous sea captains and merchants, Sterling Kendall paused to consider the darkening clouds overhead. Other than that, he didn't hesitate as he walked away from the same address that Germaine had left a half-hour earlier. The captain had just left, he had been told by a Frenchman, but even before departing his own home that morning, Sterling had already decided what his next course of action would be. Now his plan seemed to unfold of its own volition.

A wave of his hand secured a passing carriage. Sterling spoke the name of a well-known plantation to the driver before he settled back within the interior. The ride would take less than an hour, and he was not at all certain what his reception would be at its end, but he had no doubt what he was now required to do.

CHAPTER 13

The painting of Beau had been lifted to a place of distinction on the easel, and it was where Cerynise's gaze was focused as she sipped tea in the loneliness of her studio. No one knew how much she yearned to have the real man sitting across from her, but that would never be now. He was probably destined to become Germaine's husband, and they'd no doubt have beautiful, dark-haired children who would have rightful claim to their father's name.

Cerynise blinked away a start of tears and, taking a deep breath, determined that she wouldn't cry again, at least not for another moment...or hopefully, even two. Cora was outside, taking in the clothes. With the wind that had sprung up, tiny twigs and dead branches were constantly being flung against the windows or falling onto the roof. The noise had ceased to startle Cerynise, for she was far more apprehensive about the storm that was sweeping toward them. Her dread deepened apace with her gloom as dark clouds continued to roil overhead and lightning sizzled in jagged streaks across the sky. The rumble of distant thunder grew steadily louder as it followed the flashes of light making their way toward the city. With the flying debris bombarding the house, she was surrounded by a wild cacophony of different noises, so much so that she wasn't even motivated to investigate a distant rapping. A moment earlier she had responded to a similar noise and had gone to the front door to see if a visitor was there, only to find a broken branch rattling down the steep roof.

Yet in the midst of all of this chaos, unbelievably, a keen awareness swept over her, causing Cerynise to lower her teacup shakily to its saucer. She wanted to turn and search the hallway behind her for the familiar figure, but she knew the foolishness of that farfetched idea. No one would be there. Beau Birmingham had gone out of her life like the dousing of a candle. Indeed, if she went to live in another city, they would probably never see each other again.

Tears blurred her vision, and as much as she tried to halt them, they quickly erupted into harsh sobs that shook her whole frame. With an agonized whine, she shoved the teacup and saucer aside and, folding her arms upon the table, buried her face within them. She wept bitterly, her shoulders shaking with the violence of her sorrow.

A soft thump on the table beside her startled Cerynise, and she sat back with a sharp gasp, her tears for the moment forgotten. She wasn't at all certain what had happened, but when she could blink away some of the moisture from her eyes, she saw a small stack of torn papers that she could only guess were remnants of what used to be a sheaf of documents. She picked up one curiously and saw her own signature on one section and then Beau's on another. Then she saw the word *annulment*. Could it be? But how...?

Catching hold of the back of her chair, Cerynise turned upon the seat and saw a tall, broad-shouldered form advancing toward her from the doorway. She blinked, wiping desperately at her tears, and somehow managed to push herself to her feet despite the trembling limbs that threatened to give way beneath her. Then she saw Beau's smiling face and his arms extended toward her, and all of heaven opened up to her. In an instant she was flying into his embrace and being lifted off her feet. She wrapped her arms tightly about his neck. Laughing and crying crazily, she covered his face with ecstatic kisses. Then his searching mouth snared hers, and it became a wild, ravenous meeting of lips and tongues, a hungry consuming search that left Cerynise fairly faint with joy as he held her closely against him and slowly turned in a circle in the middle of the room. Finally she drew away for a breath.

"Oh, I've missed you so much!" she whispered, brushing her lips across his brow, down his lean nose and pressing them once again to his mouth.

"Why did you sign the papers?" Beau asked huskily between her teary, salt-tinged kisses.

Cerynise leaned back in his arms to look at him. "I thought you wanted me to."

"Never!"

"Never?" She frowned in confusion. "But why...why did you sign them?"

"Because it seemed that you were demanding them."

"But that was only because I knew you wouldn't be able to get an annulment if we waited much longer." She gulped, hoping she wouldn't destroy their happiness by what she was about to tell him. "I know you don't remember making love to me during your illness, but we made a baby together, Beau, and my condition is getting very noticeable."

Beau stood her to her feet and turned her about until her front side was silhouetted against the storm-darkened light streaming through the windows. His hand followed the gentle curve of her belly, and as she awaited his reaction in suspenseful trepidation, he began to grin and then to chuckle. "Many times I wanted to ask you if I had dreamed it all or if I had actually made love to you. I remembered bits and parts, but I was half-afraid I was fantasizing, and I could only imagine that my inquiries would convince you that I was a lecher."

" 'Twould seem our marriage has often been foiled by our own reticence." Cerynise tilted her head aslant as she peered up at him. "In fact, the way Germaine left here after she took a close look at me, I thought she'd search you out posthaste to tell you the news."

Beau laid his arms around his wife's slender shoulders and pulled her close again. "Aye, she did, but she only gave me the proof I needed to hold you in our marriage. Had I known sooner you were carrying my child, I'd never have consented to an annulment."

"Even though it meant losing your freedom?" she queried timidly.

"Freedom be damned," Beau rejoined, and then stated emphatically, "I lost all interest in my freedom as a bachelor soon after we were married. I began to want you as my wife on a permanent basis, and that's the way it will be from now on."

"Oh, how happy that makes me!" Cerynise exclaimed joyfully, slipping her arms around his waist and snuggling close.

"Is your uncle here?" he asked, pressing his cheek against her hair.

"No, he's been gone for several hours now, and I really don't have any idea when he'll be back."

"Then we'll leave him a note if he's not here by the time we've finished packing your belongings."

Cerynise pulled back again to search his sun-bronzed face. "Where are you taking me?"

"Home! Our home, where you belong."

"And my paints..."

"We're taking everything. I've got my carriage outside waiting for us, and I'd like to leave before it starts raining." Even as reluctant as he was to turn her loose, he was even more anxious to get her home with him. "Where are your trunks?"

"Upstairs in my room."

Beau took her hand. "Show me."

Cerynise was soon escorting him upstairs, a climb that was just long enough to permit a little marital familiarity. Laying a slender hand over the much larger one that inspected the tautness of her breast, she smiled up at him. "Still rutting, I see."

"Aye," he acknowledged huskily, meeting her gaze. He raised a dark brow inquiringly. "Do you have any arguments against me indulging my husbandly rights?"

"None in the least, sir," she murmured with a smile as she swept her own hand down

419

the front of him, making him catch his breath at the sudden pleasure she evoked. "As long as I can indulge a few wifely ones as well."

Greatly relieved, Beau nuzzled her neck. "By all means, madam, but let us not tarry here lest we shock your Uncle Sterling out of his scholarly wits."

Once in her bedroom they began packing her clothes, and soon Beau was toting her trunks down the stairs. Returning to her bedroom once more, he found her trying to lift one of the heavier satchels. He quickly relieved her of it.

"Madam, believe it or not, I'm quite capable of carrying everything you've packed if you'd but give me the chance," he gently scolded. "You'll have to think of our child from now on and refrain from exerting yourself. Now, while I'm getting the rest of your paintings and supplies, you'd better write a note to your uncle and tell him the annulment is off and that you'll be living with me from now on as my lawfully wedded wife."

Cerynise made no attempt to subdue her grin. "Aye aye, Captain!"

Beau gave her a wink above his own wide grin. "Good girl."

In less than an hour they were in the carriage and on their way at a brisk pace. Upon their arrival at his residence, Beau lifted his wife down and then hefted a trunk on his shoulder as Cerynise paused to look at the house. At present, several large trees around the structure were being buffeted by the wind, but she gave little heed to the gusts with her husband near.

It was a large Georgian-style mansion surrounded by a pleasant garden behind a wrought
iron fence, situated well back from the street
to assure both privacy and serenity. The
weatherboards were painted white, the shutters on either side of the windows a deep
forest green, and the front door a matching hue
trimmed in white beneath a fanlight of cut
crystal depicting a vessel under full sail. In all,
the residence reminded her of a countryside
estate though it was located only a short stroll
from Charleston's busy wharves.

Cerynise smiled up at her husband. "Oh,
Beau, I feel like a princess being brought
home to a castle."

"Well, in that case, madam, you should be
shown in royally," he replied, setting the
trunk on end and motioning Thomas to fetch
the others. When Beau turned back, he swept
his wife up into his arms and bore her swiftly
to the door as the rain began in earnest.

In the entrance, he set her to her feet. "Why
don't you look around a bit while Thomas and
I carry in your things? If it's all right, I'll put
your paintings and oils in my study. You can
work in there if you find the amount of light
acceptable."

"But won't I be disturbing you if I do?"

"You may, but only because I'll be indulging
my second favorite pastime...watching you."

Cerynise giggled. "I need not ask what your
first is."

"That will come shortly," he promised her
warmly.

She ran to open the door for Thomas, who was struggling with her largest trunk. Then, as Beau and the driver returned to the carriage for the rest of her baggage, she looked around at the rich, tasteful appointments. Cerynise couldn't have imagined herself *not* liking the interior, for Beau, in his own right, was an artist of exceptional abilities. He had a keen eye for elegant furnishings and decor and applied that talent well. An entrance hall with a beautiful floor of variegated marble in tones of white, gray and magenta opened onto a more spacious, airy central hall where a curving staircase, replete with polished mahogany steps and handrail that sat atop gracefully turned spindles of white, twined gracefully upward to a second-story landing. The interior woodwork was painted white, and abundant greenery complemented it. Everywhere she looked, Aubusson carpets were plentiful, and furnishings of Chippendale, Queen Anne and similar pieces were fully in evidence throughout.

Once again Cerynise returned to the front portal and held it open for the men. They carried in the last of her trunks, satchels and paintings just in time, for the rain, driven by the wind, had begun to pelt the windows. Thomas ran out to bring the carriage around to the back, leaving Cerynise to close the door behind him. With a vivacious smile, she turned to face her husband. "You leave nothing for a wife to do but stare in awe," she said with pride. "The interior is even more lovely than the exterior."

"Want to see the bedroom?" Beau invited with a teasing leer.

Her eyes shone as she scanned the length of him. "Only if you're willing to show it to me."

"I'm eager to show you a lot more than that," he assured her with a chuckle. "But Philippe is in the kitchen, and he'll want to see you ere I whisk you upstairs. The way I've been yearning for you, it may be another week before I allow you to leave my bedroom. I'm definitely not going to tolerate any interruptions until I've sated my every craving." Beau stepped near, and his wife lifted her face expectantly. He lowered a soft, warm kiss upon her lips before he urged huskily, "Now hurry, my love. Go see Philippe while I get your baggage upstairs. Then we can be alone together."

The kiss was so nice Cerynise wanted more and rose on tiptoes to steal another. Her husband readily accommodated her, this time making it far more sensual as his tongue slipped inward to play chase with hers. When he drew back, it seemed she had no strength of her own, for she leaned heavily against him.

"More," she pleaded wistfully.

"I dare not, madam, lest you'd have me wear your skirts."

"Beast," she fussed with a pretty pout as she rubbed herself against him.

"Wench," he whispered back, smiling as he brush his lips against her temples. "Ere long,

423

you'll have my heart in your hot, greedy hands if you don't desist, my winsome wench. I'm not two seconds away from taking you upstairs and pleasuring myself with you. Philippe and your trunks be damned."

Cerynise heaved a sigh, exaggerating her disappointment. "I suppose I must leave you since you put duty before pleasure."

Beau's eyes glowed as he watched her wander dreamily toward the kitchen. He could only marvel at the significant change that had taken place since he had let himself into her uncle's house. His knock on the front door had gone unanswered for several moments, and when he had finally ventured in and traversed the hall in search of his wife, he had found her seated at a table in a back room, staring dejectedly at his painting. She had reminded him of a small child who had been severely rebuked, for with shoulders hunched, her slender frame had clearly conveyed an attitude of defeat. He had expected her to turn at any moment after she had straightened, for he could have sworn that she had sensed his presence, but what had followed had nearly torn his heart. He couldn't remember ever having heard a woman sob with such deep, harrowing anguish.

Her cheery voice now came from the hallway leading to the kitchen. "Philippe? Where are you?"

"Madame Birmingham?" the chef cried in surprise. He ran into the corridor and, upon seeing her, took both her hands in his and liberally pressed happy kisses to them. "Oh, it is so excellent to see you, madame." Immediately cautious of what he was about to say with her husband in the house, he slipped into his native French and began to confide how the captain had nearly sunk into the depths of despair without her warm glow lighting his life. "He would not eat, madame, and drank far more than he ever did." Then with a knowing smile and an upward flick of eyebrows, Philippe sighed. "Ahh, *l'amour*."

"Cerynise?" Beau called from upstairs some moments later.

"Coming," she answered happily, and blew a kiss to the chef as she pushed through the swinging door. The storm was now upon them, but she hardly noticed as she hurried into the hallway. Beau was waiting for her at the landing above the stairs, and when she came into view, he held out a hand to hasten her flight. The windows behind him displayed roiling black clouds, and now and then, streaks of lightning tore across the sky, ending in great, bellowing peals of thunder. The wind was equally as fierce, but even with her fear of such turbulence, Cerynise could think of nothing but being in her husband's arms.

She was breathless by the time she arrived, but the radiance in her eyes evidenced the precise cause. Taking her by the hand, Beau whisked her into the master bedroom of his home and then nudged the door closed behind him. He reached around to lock it and, leaning back against the sturdy plank, pulled her within his embrace and kissed her with all the passion he had been saving up for her alone. His fingers freed her hair, and then he was lifting her up in his arms and carrying her to his bed. He stood her to her feet beside it, and immediately they were seized by a frenzied haste to undress one another. Soon they faced each other in all their naked glory. Cerynise's hands moved down the hard length of her husband's body in admiration while he stroked her soft breasts and covered her with greedy kisses. In the next moment they were wrapped in each other's arms and tumbling to the mattress. This time, there was no lengthy, tantalizing prelude, for Beau had endured an agonizing abstinence and wanted nothing to hinder their union. His wife was soft and willing, and he was hard and ready. There was enough kissing, tasting and handling to elicit sharp gasps of pleasure from each as they boldly searched out familiar territory. Then Beau was loving her in a most physical way and snatching her breath with his fierce ardor. In the midst of their intimacy everything came flooding back to him in a newly awakening reality, her panting breath in his ear, her nails digging into his back, her silken limbs entwining his hips...it was just as he had thought he had dreamed it.

Though the storm continued to rage outside, they lay in each other's arms, kissing, touching and whispering. Beau finally questioned her about what he now suspected to be true, and Cerynise confirmed that they were no illusions he had had, for she had actually sat beside his bed that night luxuriating in her new wifely state. He also told her of the many times he had tried to question her about it, but she had refused to accept his invitations. Cerynise was rather appalled at her countless blunders. If not for her mistakes, they could have been enjoying the intimacy of marriage months ago.

She snuggled against her husband's side and idly caressed his chest. "Do you hate me for what I almost did to us?"

"Hate you?" Beau was incredulous. "Good heavens, woman, can't you understand by now how much I love you?"

Bracing up on his chest, Cerynise searched his handsome face. "It's not just your rutting instincts?"

His hand caressed her naked back. "If it were, my dear, I would have been able to find appeasement with any woman, but I wanted no one but you....You've held my mind ensnared from that moment I put you into my bed and brought you close to my heart."

"The day we were married, you mean."

"No, the night I carried you aboard my ship."

"So long ago?"

"Aye."

Cerynise traced a finger along the hard ridges of his muscular chest. "You must know I've been in love with you ever since I was a child."

His dark eyebrows lifted in a small shrug.

"I had always thought that, but you led me to believe otherwise when you wouldn't have anything to do with me."

"I was afraid you'd hate me if I got with child. You'd have felt obligated to do the gentlemanly thing...."

"So you were willing to let our child be born a bastard rather than tell me that you had gotten pregnant? Madam, you must think me a cad to have gone to such lengths to hide that fact from me."

"How could I possibly think you a cad when I'm sure the sun rises and sets just for you?"

Without another word, Beau turned with her, pressing her flat upon the bed as he rose up on an elbow beside her. He gently caressed her breasts, noticing again how much firmer they had become since her pregnancy. His hand moved downward to examine the gentle roundness of her small belly, affirming once more that it was true, that she was going to bear him a child. He needed no further proof, but the sudden hard knot that formed beneath his palm made them both laugh. He slipped farther down into the bed and pressed the side of his face close against her stomach to listen.

"He's kicking me." Cerynise giggled and moved her husband's hand over the spot. "Do you feel him?"

"Aye, I do," he replied, and chuckled as he pressed his lips to the place. "Papa's first kiss."

One kiss led to another and soon his tongue

and mouth were tracing upward over his wife's body until they blended with hers in an erotic exchange that left them both heady with desire. Quickening fires were lit beneath provocative caresses and titillating kisses until Beau rolled, pulling her on top of him. Cerynise caught her breath at the sensations aroused within her as he settled her over the hardened shaft and directed her hips in a long, languid caress of his loins. His mouth greedily claimed a soft peak, and the fires of passion leapt higher still, sweeping away her restraints. Slipping her forearms beneath her heavy tresses, she lifted the tawny length above her head, capturing his gaze. Her lips curved in a sensual smile as she looked into his lusting eyes and moved her hips in a slow, undulating motion, much like a dancer before an Arabian prince. The hotly pulsing flame within her quickened her blood until her movements became more concentrated and increasingly forceful, igniting their fervor. His hands seized her breasts as he rose up beneath her, and soon their passions were soaring out of control, driving them onward until their harsh gasps were finally muted and became soft, blissful sighs of contentment.

Beau was certain he had never experienced the like of such fulfillment. He also knew he wouldn't have traded all the freedom in the world for what he now held within his arms, his wife, his mate for life. She had been delightfully creative in her innocence, and he could only imagine, with a little more instruction, that she'd entangle his mind so thoroughly that he'd be willing to yield her anything for a few moments in her embrace.

"How would you like to accompany me on another voyage after our baby is born?"

Cerynise didn't even have to think about his question. "Oh, yes! That would be absolutely heavenly…that is, as long as I don't get seasick again."

His finger sketched a pale pink nipple. "I had thought you were pretty much over that until your last bout."

Cerynise smiled up at him. "I don't think that particular sickness was caused by the motion of the sea, my love. By that time, I had already begun to suspect that I was with child after missing my monthly."

"Did you always come at a regular time?"

Cerynise was somewhat amazed that he was so knowledgeable about women. "Yes, but how…"

Beau chuckled at her naiveté. "You'd be amazed what boys talk about while they're growing up, my love. But then, I also had a sister a couple or so years younger. As much as it appalled our mother, Suzanne would fly into a rage whenever I'd tease her about hiding out in her room. She let me know in no uncertain terms that she was suffering a woman's curse and threatened to pray it down on me, too. I never dreamed her threats would have much effect, but I suppose a husband must endure monthly self-restraints when his wife isn't pregnant." He feigned a thoughtful frown as he measured her small belly. "We'll have to become a little more creative when you grow too round to mount, madam."

Happy laughter spilled from her lips. "With your propensities, my lecherous husband, I don't think I'll have too much time between the birth of one and the conceiving of another."

"Definitely a possibility, madam, but then, I can afford as many as our love may bear."

"I'll likely be having more than a fair share of them while you're away sailing the seas."

"One more voyage, madam, and then Mr. Oaks will captain the *Audacious*," he promised. "I have found something I love far more than sailing to distant climes. I want to be wherever you are."

Lifting her gaze again to his, she searched his face. "But what will you do if you give up sailing?"

Beau chuckled. "Stay at home and make love to you."

Cerynise caressed the hard, muscular ridges of his chest once again. "And when you're not doing that?"

"My uncle would like me to help him out at his shipping company. His two sons haven't shown much interest in doing so as yet. The oldest one definitely prefers managing their plantation. Uncle Jeff said he'd give me a full partnership if I wanted it. But then, of course, my own father would like me to help him run the plantation."

"You won't miss the sea?"

"Not with you beside me."

She nestled close against his long body and murmured drowsily, "Then I will endeavor to make your existence on land as interesting as possible, sir."

"And I will attempt to do the same for you, madam," he murmured, pressing a kiss to her brow.

It wasn't long before Beau heard the soft, steady breathing of his young wife and realized she had fallen asleep in his arms. With great care, he drew the sheet up over them and closed his eyes, allowing himself to drift off in sweet, relaxing slumber, the best he had had in some time.

A soft rap of knuckles against the door tore Beau from dreams that were very much like those he had savored only a pair of hours ago. Sliding ever so cautiously from his wife's side, he snatched on his trousers, padded barefoot across the rug to the door, and opened it a crack. Philippe was standing at the threshold looking very apologetic.

"*Excusez-moi, Capitaine*, but your father is here. I asked him to wait for you in your study."

Beau nodded sleepily. "Tell him I'll be right down. Can you make us some coffee?"

"*Oui, Capitaine.*"

Closing the portal, Beau stumbled into the dressing room, splashed cold water onto his face and then brushed his teeth. Garbed just as he was, he went downstairs.

432

If not for a definite graying at his temples which contrasted handsomely with his black hair, Brandon Birmingham could have passed for a man twenty years his junior. His sun-bronzed face seemed amazingly free of wrinkles, with only a slight deepening of crow's-feet at the corners of his black-lashed, green eyes. His tall, broad-shouldered frame was still taut and muscular, evidence of an active, hardworking man.

Brandon had been staring out of the window at the churning sky, mulling over what he needed to say to his son. After Professor Kendall's visit, he had done a lot of thinking back on his own life, especially that moment when he had been threatened with harsh consequences if he refused to do the right thing by the pregnant girl whose virginity he had taken while under the mistaken belief that she was a harlot. The intimidation had served to arouse his ire and spite, which he had later taken out on Heather soon after they were married. He recognized the fact that his son had inherited not only his looks and his larger frame but his temperament as well. Because of that, he knew that force was not a judicious way to handle a delicate situation with his offspring.

"Afternoon, Pa," Beau mumbled, smothering a yawn as he passed through the open door of his study.

Brandon's eyebrows lifted in sharp surprise as he faced his son and saw that he was only half dressed. " 'Tis a poor late hour in the day for you to be rising from bed, son. Are you ill?"

"No." Beau shook his head. "Just trying to catch up on a little sleep. I didn't go to bed till dawn."

Though he wasn't necessarily proud of the fact, Brandon also knew his son had followed too closely in his footsteps to imagine that he was a teetotaler in regard to spirits and women. It seemed practical to assume that his first-born had been too busy indulging those propensities during the past evening to get any sleep.

Philippe entered with a silver tray bearing the coffee service and, after pouring each man a cup, took his leave.

Brandon downed his in a hurry, and then cleared his throat, not knowing exactly where to begin. He settled on a more direct approach. "Professor Kendall came to see me today."

"Oh?" Beau's brows gathered in some bemusement. "What did he want with you?"

"To talk, mainly about you. When you came out to deliver Cerynise's painting, you never mentioned the fact that you had married the girl. Why?"

Beau swallowed another sip of the hot brew before he shrugged his naked shoulders. "I didn't want Mama to get her hopes up when an annulment was in the offing."

Brandon had had the task of explaining to his wife instead, at least as much as he had been told from Sterling's point of view. So far as Heather was concerned, there was only one

434

problem with Beau: He spent too much time away from Charleston. Otherwise, he couldn't possibly do any wrong, at least not in her eyes. She had been certain that he would do the right thing by Cerynise without interference, but Sterling had all but insisted that Brandon talk to his son, since no gentleman would even dare consider an annulment after taking a wife to bed. "Your mother always thought well of Cerynise. In fact, she'd like it very much if you kept the girl as your wife."

"You mean you discussed everything with her?" Beau queried in some amazement. He knew well enough what conclusions his mother probably came to after the good professor went and babbled about the intended separation.

Despite the tenseness he felt over the situation, Brandon managed a chuckle. "I'm sorry if that distresses you, Beau, but you should know by now that there is very little your mother and I don't discuss together."

Beau had long known his parents were very close. Throughout the years they had shared a love so profound that he had come to believe that he would never discover such devotion for himself, but since Cerynise had reentered his life, he was of a different mind entirely. He was also aware that his parents were in a habit of conferring on matters pertaining to their family, but in this situation, it just seemed that his father should have consulted him before causing his mother to fret.

Brandon eyed his son before stating carefully, "I think you and your sisters are well aware that your mother and I are very devoted to each other, but that hasn't always been the case."

It was a full moment before his father's words registered on Beau and alerted him with a faint prickling of his senses. While living at home, he had overheard bits and parts of vague allusions to something that had happened very early in his parents' marriage or, perhaps, even before. Uncle Jeff had seemed wont to tease his brother about whatever had occurred back then, but no one had ever cared to enlighten the offspring of that union, and whenever Beau had asked what they were talking about, he had always been told that his father would tell him one day. He had a feeling this was the day.

"What was the case exactly?" Beau inquired cautiously, not at all certain at this point that he wanted to know. He set his coffee cup aside, lending his sire his undivided attention.

Brandon went back to stand near the window and looked out once again as the slashing rain pelted the window. With a sigh he finally faced his son. "There was a time when I was forced to do the honorable thing by your mother, and as a result, my own stubborn pride caused a great conflict between us. Heather was clearly afraid of me, and my resentment and anger incited much of that fear."

Beau stared at his father, unable to believe what he was hearing. "You mean Mama was pregnant with me before the both of you were married?"

Even after so long a time, Brandon still

suffered the blushing heat of deep chagrin over what he had done to the young girl who had been brought aboard his ship. "Aye."

In all of his years, Beau had never experienced a moment of greater shock. He knew his parents were human beings. Even now, they were susceptible to being surprised during an intimate caress or a passionate kiss, but they seemed so honorable and respectable that he was stunned to learn that there had been a time when they had seriously transgressed the accepted boundaries of morality.

Very carefully Beau questioned his parent. "Are you telling me that Mama was your mistress before she became your wife?"

"Absolutely not!" Brandon shook his head emphatically. "It was what I wanted from her after I took her into my bed, but she would have none of it. She ran away from me instead. No, it was entirely different from that...." He fell silent as he realized he was probably confusing the issue. What he needed to do was to start from the beginning. Taking a deep breath, he plunged into the mire of the story. "I had just docked in London and was feeling in need of some feminine companionship. Unbeknownst to me, Heather had been brought to the city under false pretenses and threatened with assault by her aunt's brother. In defending herself she became convinced that she had killed the man and fled in fear. She was found wandering on the docks by two of my men who mistook her for what she most definitely was not."

"But when you realized their mistake, surely you—"

"I didn't realize she was an innocent until too late. Even then, I believed she had been led to sell her virginity...." His skin darkened perceptibly. "It must be obvious what I thought. At any rate, I played the rutting stag and acted reprehensibly, even to the point of trying to force her to stay with me. She escaped me, and when next she was hauled before me, it was not only her aunt and uncle demanding satisfaction, but a prominent lord who had the ability to hinder my departure from England. I could do nothing else but placate their wishes. I took my resentment out on Heather, making her dread the very sight of me. I told her that I would own up to the fact that she was bearing my child, but in all other areas she would be no wife to me at all. I kept my distance, vowing no woman would get the better of me." He laughed harshly. "Except the more I was around her, the more I wanted her, and it became a torturous rack that I had made for myself. She was everything I had dreamed of as a woman, and yet it wasn't until after you were born that I finally submitted to what my heart was urging me to do. During that time I never once touched another woman, nor have I since...."

Beau couldn't help himself. His amusement was too much to bear in silence, and his laughter came spilling out, causing his father to cringe in growing discomfiture. For all that Brandon Birmingham was his father,

Beau realized he was a man like himself, possessed of a fiery nature and a keen appreciation of the joys a woman could provide. The idea that he had kept his distance from his beautiful wife for nigh to a year was absolutely on the far side of astounding.

"The reason I tell you this," Brandon continued with a rueful smile, "is to warn you against the folly of making the same kind of mistake with Cerynise as I once made with your mother. Sterling Kendall has assured us that his niece is an honorable young woman who is in love with you. But he strongly suspects that she is carrying your child and, for some mysterious reason of her own, will not tell you that fact even though it may mean the babe will be born a bastard after the annulment. If you truly believe she is pregnant with your child, then search your heart well before you abandon your offspring and its mother to the consequences those two will surely reap."

"Some changes have occurred which I think you should know about, Pa—"

Beau's words were rudely interrupted by a loud, insistent tapping of the front door knocker, which was quickly followed by Philippe's frantic assurances that he was coming. As the portal was swung open, a voice barked irately from the entrance hall.

"Where is he?"

"*Excusez-moi, monsieur.* Do you mean *le capitaine*?" Philippe inquired, sounding a trifle haughty, as if he had been deeply offended by the other man's harsh demand.

"*Capitaine,* ha! I have better names for that despicable scoundrel!"

"I will see if *le capitaine* is at home," the chef replied stiltedly. "If you would identify yourself—"

"Kendall! Professor Kendall!"

Upon hearing the name, Beau hastened from the study, followed by his father, and gestured for Philippe to let the visitor in. The gray-haired professor seemed clearly distraught as he stalked through the foyer. Upon espying Beau, the elder approached him with glaring eyes. Since an angry confrontation seemed imminent, Philippe took himself briskly back to the kitchen, having no doubt that his captain could handle the situation without any help or listening ears.

"My niece has left for parts unknown! She has packed up her belongings and taken off like a scalded pup." By this time Sterling Kendall was close enough to jab a forefinger repeatedly into Beau's naked chest as he asked angrily, "It is *your* child she's carrying, isn't it?"

"Yes, but—"

"I'm sure Cerynise has fled to another town," Sterling raged on, giving the younger man no chance to explain. "I can't much blame her for not wanting to face the trauma of bearing *your* child without a name to give it. The very idea that you would even consider an annulment under the circumstances makes me ashamed that I once mistook you for an honorable gentleman."

"Beau?" a muted feminine voice called

440

worriedly from upstairs. "Where are you?"

Beau could imagine that his wife was frightened by the storm after being left alone, and he raised his head to allow his voice to carry to the upper rooms. "I'm down here."

Abruptly Sterling came to his own conclusions and, facing Brandon, jeered in distaste, "No wonder your son didn't want to tie himself down to my niece. He's too busy entertaining all the other women."

Brandon was just as surprised as the professor and glanced at his son with a curious brow raised.

Beau held out a hand toward the interior door that he and his father had just stepped through a moment ago. "Professor Sterling, perhaps you'd care to come into my study, where we can discuss this matter rationally...."

"Aren't you anxious to get back to your little doxy?" Sterling queried sarcastically.

"She's not going anywhere," Beau casually assured the man. "Now, please, come in here where we can talk."

Brandon wasn't at all certain that he shouldn't join Philippe, considering the present predicament his son had gotten himself into, but when Beau motioned for him to follow, he reluctantly complied. He was the last one through the door and made no effort to close it as he paced forward uneasily.

"You didn't find a note from Cerynise?" Beau questioned, facing the professor.

"There was none that I know of," Sterling rejoined tersely.

"In your study..."

"A blasted mess with that limb breaking a window and all my papers scattered about the house. I was too worried about Cerynise to do anything more than board up the window. If my niece left any kind of note there, then it will probably be weeks before I find it."

Beau glanced toward his father, who seemed to be having some difficulty settling down. Perhaps Sterling's accusations were coming too close to home for his sire to feel at ease with what the man was saying.

"Beau?" the feminine voice came again in a hushed, wavering tone, this time from the area of the parlor.

"In the study," he called in response, realizing that Cerynise was searching the house for him.

Sterling rose to his feet, muttering sourly, "I'd better go so you can get back to your little wench."

Beau waved the man back in his chair. "I think you should meet this little wench."

He stepped outside the door and beckoned to his wife. "Come in here, my love. I have someone to whom I want to introduce you."

"Oh, but, Beau, I'm not dressed," Cerynise whispered in protest, clutching the collar of his robe up close around her neck. Her feet were bare, and her long hair was a tousled, swirling mess that fairly bedazzled the eye. "I can't meet anyone looking like this."

"I insist," he announced, holding out his arm invitingly. As she came near, he slid his hand

442

to the small of her back, where it rested comfortably as he propelled her into his study.

"Cerynise!" her uncle gasped upon seeing her. Immediately he pushed himself to his feet as his eyes swept her in amazement. Then he glanced toward Beau to consider the younger man's inadequate attire. It was all too obvious what the two had been doing in the middle of the afternoon. He blustered, his face burning. " 'Twould seem you've been disturbed."

"Cerynise, I'd like for you to meet my father," Beau said, turning her to face his sire.

"Pa, this is my wife, Cerynise."

Self-consciously she clasped the edges of the voluminous robe together and dipped into a nervous curtsy. "Nice to see you again, Mr. Birmingham."

"Well, I'll be dam—"

Beau cleared his throat and grinned pointedly at his father, who usually tried to restrain himself around young ladies. Brandon was visibly apologetic, evidenced by his wry smile and the sharp quirk in his eyebrow.

"It must run in the family," Cerynise quipped with a teasing gleam in her eye.

"You're looking at the one from whom I learned it," Beau assured her.

"Your pardon, Cerynise," Brandon begged, bending forward in a shallow bow. "My son seems to delight in astounding me out of my senses."

She chuckled in sympathy. "I've had the same experience, sir."

"Your wife, you say," Sterling challenged, drawing their attention. "Does that mean the annulment is off?"

"Aye," Beau affirmed with a grin. "And we're extremely sorry that you didn't get our note. I went to fetch Cerynise this afternoon and helped to pack up her possessions. She made a point of leaving the missive in your study, but no telling where it is now." He paused briefly at his wife's perplexed frown and explained what had happened. Then he directed his attention once more to her uncle. "I think you should know that neither Cerynise nor I wanted to be separated from one another, but we were both confused by what the other wanted. We beg your apology for worrying you; we worried ourselves no less."

"You'll have to tell your mother all of this yourself," Brandon broke in. "Tomorrow night at dinner will hardly be soon enough. If you have other plans, you'd better cancel them. Your mother is not going to take it kindly if she doesn't get to meet her new daughter-in-law very, very soon."

Beau chuckled. "We'll be out, Pa."

Brandon stepped forward and, taking Cerynise's hand, gallantly bestowed a kiss upon it. "You do us up proud, my dear."

"Thank you, Mr. Birmingham."

"Pa will do," he assured her. "Beau's the only one who calls me that, so I give you leave to do the same." His handsome lips twitched with amusement as he winked at her and added drolly, "That boy likes to make me feel old at times just to test my temper, but he knows that's a damned lot of nonsense."

Cerynise clapped a hand over her mouth to subdue her laughter, but it did little good as Beau threw back his head and gave way to his own mirth. They were soon in each other's arms, relenting to their gaiety as Sterling Kendall joined in.

CHAPTER 14

The Birminghams, one and all, gathered at Harthaven to officially welcome Cerynise into the family. Sterling Kendall had been invited as well. Having led a singular life for a goodly number of years, he found himself a bit flabbergasted by all the effervescent chattering of the women and the sharp, witty humor of the men. Besides Beau's immediate family, there was Suzanne's fiancé, Michael York, and Brandon's brother, Jeff, and his sister-in-law, Raelynn, and the couple's four offspring, the oldest of whom was Barclay, a young man of twenty who preferred to be called Clay. Stephanie, an auburn-haired woman of eighteen, was engaged to be married the following year to Cleveland McGeorge, a prosperous art dealer. Although Cleve was originally from New York, in recent years he had moved to Charleston, where he presently owned a shop and lived in a townhouse. Jeff's second son, Matthew or Matt, had just turned fifteen, and his youngest child, Tamarah, was nine.

Of all of them, she looked the most like her father with her black hair and green eyes. After meeting and conversing for a time with each of the family members, it didn't take Sterling long to come to the conclusion that they were all an integral part of a vivacious collection of interesting, intelligent and extraordinarily fine people who were wont to make even strangers feel completely at home and at ease in their close-knit unity.

Cerynise was just as overwhelmed with their eager acceptance of her, and in no time at all she found herself exchanging confidences with Brenna, whom she could readily envision becoming a steadfast friend. Although she guessed Beau's mother was less than two score and five years old, Heather Birmingham looked no older than a woman of thirty. She was small and petite, like Brenna, with no hint of gray in her black hair. Upon meeting her new daughter-in-law, Heather had smiled and gathered Cerynise's hands in her own as she assured her how delighted she was to have her in the family. Then the mistress of Harthaven had ushered her through the introductions while Beau did the same for Sterling. Heather had also shown Cerynise around the house and led her on a tour of the bedrooms upstairs, starting with the one Beau had grown up in, which she assured Cerynise was now hers as well. Heather then made her acquainted with the help and did so lauding the praises of each and, most especially, a large, gray-haired black woman named Hatti. The fact that the old woman had helped to bring Brandon and, thereafter, all of the other Birminghams into the world solidified her as a respected pillar in the family.

It was not until everyone had taken seats around the long dining table that Cerynise glanced across the room and realized that the painting she had once warned Beau against buying was hanging in a prominent place on the wall above the sideboard between two large porcelain sconces. Lighted tapers cast a warm glow upon it, setting it off to perfection. Cerynise's surprise was so complete, she gasped and looked around at Beau, who was just helping her into her chair.

"What can I say, madam?" He grinned as he shrugged. "I liked it well enough to buy it for my parents."

"I think it's absolutely beautiful," Heather said proudly from her place of honor at the end of the table. "And it pleases me so much more to know that my daughter-in-law painted it. Stephanie's fiancé thinks it's the best thing he has ever seen and would be very interested in looking at more of your paintings with the idea of selling them for you. The fact that the artist is a woman didn't seem to faze him in the least. Cleve assured us that what really counted was the quality of art, not the gender of the person who painted it."

"More of her work should be arriving fairly soon," Beau announced, "but I get first dibs... as her husband."

" 'Twould seem you rather enjoy that distinction," Heather rejoined fondly.

"Aye, Mama," Beau admitted, tossing her a grin as he settled into his own seat and gathered his wife's slender fingers in his. And to remind his mother of all the times she had cautioned him not to waste his time with either this winsome maid or that one, he added, "This one is definitely worth keeping."

"I can see that for myself, dear," Heather sweetly averred. "Which, of course, reminds me. I must invite some of the ladies out from Charleston and the surrounding area to meet Cerynise." Her gaze shifted to her new daughter by marriage. "Would that be amenable to you, my dear?"

"Yes, of course, Mrs. Birmingham."

"You're in the family now, Cerynise," Heather replied, waving off the formality with a soft chuckle. "None of that Mrs. Birmingham stuff now, or there'll be a lot of confusion. Call me Heather or Mama or some such thing."

"Hey, Tory," Jeff called from near the opposite end of the table and winked aside at Brandon as he did so. "I hear you're going to be a grandmother. Are you sure you're old enough?"

"Hush up, you rascal," Heather rebuked with another graceful wave of her hand as she grinned back at him. "Just because you and your brother took your own sweet time finding the right woman to marry doesn't mean that my Beau should have followed your examples. He's done as well in nearly half the time."

"Ouch!" Jeff chortled. "You do get wicked when you're riled, Tory."

Heather delivered a smiling riposte. "It only took you a score and five years to catch on to that fact. If I didn't know better, I'd be inclined to think you're a little backward."

The exaggerated expression of distress that Jeff assumed evoked as much amusement as their bantering. Sitting beside him, Raelynn stifled a giggle behind a napkin and exchanged an amused glance with her sister-in-law before she dipped her head in approval.

"You'd best be warned, brother," Brandon cautioned with a chortle. "Heather is feeling her oats with a new daughter under her wing."

"She's getting feistier by the day," Jeff quipped. "I think I'm already bruised."

Raelynn patted his hand consolingly. "No one deserves it more than you, darling."

"Egads!" Jeff looked appalled. "What shrews we've married!"

"Oh, Uncle Jeff, you're such a tease," Suzanne accused, laughing along with her beau. "You know you love every one of the Birmingham women and wouldn't trade any of them for all the gold in China."

"Are there any other women in existence?" Jeff queried, feigning confusion as he glanced around.

When the hilarity died down, Suzanne looked across the table at Beau and Cerynise and eagerly asked, "You are coming to my engagement ball, are you not?"

"Of course, Princess," Beau replied fondly. "We wouldn't miss it for the world."

"I hope I can find something to wear that's

suitably large," Cerynise interjected wryly. "Otherwise I may have to wear a barrel."

"Madame Feroux may be able to help you," Brenna suggested. "I'm sure all the other ladies have had their gowns made for some time now." She tossed her brother a mischievous look. "Madame Feroux is especially fond of Beau, and I'm sure if he asks her, she'll work night and day to outfit you with a marvelous gown just to please him."

"Hush, minx," Beau cautioned. The teasing grin he wore belied the baleful gleam in his eyes. "You're only trying to stir up trouble."

Brenna's blue eyes sparkled impishly as she turned her attention to the far end of the table. "Mama, you wouldn't believe what I heard from Madame Feroux the other day. Can you believe that Germaine Hollingsworth had the nerve to tell the couturier that she thought it wouldn't be long before Beau asked her to marry him? The dressmaker was all aflutter, thinking it was true."

"No doubt," Heather murmured, extremely grateful for the way things had turned out.

Though Brenna's fine brows puckered in feigned confusion, a teasing glimmer could still be seen in her dancing eyes as she looked toward her brother. "What are you going to do with two wives, Beau?"

Acutely aware that Cerynise was awaiting his answer, Jeff chafed uneasily. "I merely gave Germaine a ride in my carriage the other day after we happened to find ourselves sitting beside each other at a wedding of a mutual friend."

"Just happened?" Brenna rolled her eyes in disbelief. She had gotten wind of a whole plethora of rumors that Germaine had deliberately started, no doubt with the idea of keeping other eligible maidens a respectful distance from Beau. Brenna had no doubt that Cerynise would eventually hear the same stale rubbish from some unwitting soul if she frequented the shops in Charleston in months to come. Perhaps more than any member in the family, Brenna had been confident of her brother's indifference toward Germaine as a possible wife. She wanted Cerynise to be aware of that fact, as well. To bring Beau's reluctance clearly into the open, she offered several conjectures. "I suppose you were sitting in the pew first, and Germaine *just happened* to sit beside you, and I *also suppose* that she asked you for a ride when her carriage was probably just around the corner. When are you ever going to learn, dear brother, that you've always been viewed as the large fish in a very small pond? Your admirers have been casting nets in hopes of scooping you up for some time now, which might explain Germaine's overconfidence. She *was* the most dedicated."

Heather exchanged a glance with Brandon, who sat at the head of the table. Only he had known the true depth of her concern when they had noticed Germaine's zealous campaign to win their son for herself. In past years, there had been a lot of vague scuttlebutt about the beautiful young woman, but as yet, none of it had been established as true. They

451

had been acutely aware of the hazard of their son relenting to Germaine's appeal and taking her into his bed. Pregnant or not, she'd have gone to her highly volatile father and complained that she had been trifled with. Mr. Hollingsworth was certainly not above forcing appropriate responses in a wedding ceremony by surreptitiously holding a gun directed toward the groom's head.

Brenna persisted with a sisterly penchant for needling her brother. "Madame Feroux said you came into the shop with Germaine the other day, Beau, and it was right after that that Germaine predicted her marriage to you. If you're not going to marry Germaine, why would you go to the dressmaker's with her?"

Beau sighed in exasperation. "Have you ever noticed that Madame Feroux has an amazing ability to spill everything she knows except what's pertinent to the situation? What she probably failed to mention was the fact that I stayed no longer than ten minutes at the most, and then I was on my way out again...without Germaine."

"My goodness, Beau, you really don't need to get so upset," Brenna chided sweetly, amused by the ruddy hue that had swept into her brother's face. She was rather pleased with herself, for she had goaded him into revealing his hasty departure, which she had known about through Madame Feroux. "I'm sure Cerynise hasn't a jealous bone in her body."

"On the contrary," the tawny-haired beauty

corrected with a smile. "I most certainly do where Beau is concerned. And since Germaine warned me away from him, I still suffer qualms whenever her name is mentioned."

"You mean Germaine actually warned you away from Beau?" Heather gasped in astonishment. "How could she even dare?"

"Would this family allow me to change the subject for a moment?" Brandon begged in an effort to help his son out.

"All right, Pa," Beau readily agreed, immensely relieved for the intrusion, for the topic of conversation had begun to nettle his good humor. "If you think you can get a word in edgewise in this family, go right ahead and try."

"You're just the one I wanted to talk to," his father replied, cocking a brow at his son. "So just answer me one thing."

Beau spread his hands to convey his willingness to comply. "I'm listening, Pa."

"Now, I don't have any argument against Monsieur Philippe. He's quite an exceptional cook, but don't you think that you're taking advantage of the man by expecting him to serve as your butler and houseboy, too?"

His son shrugged casually. "When I returned from my voyage and walked into my house, only the housemaid was working while the others were lounging around on their backsides watching her doing their chores. Except for her and Thomas, the rest have been let go. In fact, I couldn't get rid of them fast enough."

"That may well be, son," his father responded

dryly, "but I find it damned unnerving to have a front door opened and find myself confronting a man with a meat cleaver. My hackles may never go down again."

The whole table erupted into guffaws and giggles at the vision of their tall, broad-shouldered host standing in wide-eyed alarm before the much smaller chef, who, if anything, had probably been oblivious to the reaction he had caused with his cleaver.

Cerynise was launched into a laughing fit that left her holding her arms across her midsection in misery. "Oh, this family is absolutely the most wonderful group of people I've ever met in all my life," she declared, wiping away tears of mirth. "But now, I shouldn't laugh anymore. It hurts too much."

Brandon raised his glass of wine in salute and grinned at her. "Welcome to the family, my dear."

An enthusiastic chorus of ayes followed, affirming the fact that the greeting was unanimous. Undisputedly Cerynise was now in the family.

A fortnight later Harthaven overflowed with women who had been invited out to meet Beau's bride. All morning, carriages had been arriving at Harthaven, disgorging guests who were eager to take a close look at the new Mrs. Birmingham, who by all reports was already with child.

Certain things were known about Cerynise Birmingham. She was originally from the area, which some ladies accepted with relief, considering the obvious preferences the elder Birmingham brothers had displayed for foreign women. She had lived in England for a time and had finished her education there, which seemed a further point in her favor since the fading from memory of the unpleasantness surrounding the struggle for independence had presently made all things English fashionable. Her guardian, the late Lydia Winthrop, had indulged the girl's love of painting to the extent that she had been instructed by the very best teachers and, as a result, was quite talented with a brush. Heather and her two daughters were now sitting for a portrait, which Cerynise was in the process of painting, and the three usually went into Charleston for this, visiting the residence of Beau Birmingham at least twice a week. At times, they were even accompanied by the elder Birmingham, and on occasion, the whole family could be seen dining out or attending the theater, accompanied by Suzanne's fiancé, Michael York.

It was also rumored that Cerynise was from a good family, albeit one that had always been a bit outside the social mainstream. The Kendalls were of a scholarly background, and Cerynise, it was said, was no exception, a notion that frankly astounded those who had known Beau for some time. In their opinion, it wasn't the female mind he valued as much as other things, which made them all wonder privately if she pleased him in bed.

In the last week or so, Madame Feroux had eagerly yielded a few more details about Cerynise to every lady who came into her shop. *Mr. Beau's gifts of jewelry to his young bride are exquisite! Miss Cerynise brought the pearl necklace with her just to see how it would look with the gown I'm making for her, and my dear, I must say the beauty of the piece is beyond anything I've ever seen. Why, it's simply extravagant. Which reminds me, did you happen to see her wedding band? It's entirely crusted with diamonds! And the gown she intends to wear at Miss Suzanne's engagement ball is probably the costliest I've ever made. Mr. Beau personally requested it after he accompanied his wife to my shop. Oh, and you should have seen the way they touched! Why, it was divine! Never have I seen a gentleman display so much affection for his bride with only a casual grazing of his hand. And Miss Cerynise is as elegant as a swan, even if she is in a motherly way....She's at least four months along, you know, but I have it on good authority that they were married in England. Can you imagine meeting there by coincidence after knowing each other here for so long a time?* And so on and so forth.

All of this talk served to whet the ladies' curiosity even more than it had already been, and of course, they decided that they'd have to view Cerynise Birmingham for themselves just to see what sort of wife Beau had chosen for himself. Thus, a veritable avalanche of women descended upon Harthaven.

"Your mother said that no one declined

her invitation," Brandon remarked over his shoulder as he stood before the French doors in his study, where he and his son had adjourned in search of a peaceful haven amid a houseful of prating women. Another carriage rolled to a stop in the circular drive, and this time a white-haired ancient was handed down by her driver and assisted in her ascent of the front steps. "Good heavens, there must be a hundred or more already here, and now it looks like even the great-grannies are toddling in."

Beau joined his father at the doors and peered out across the porch. "Why, that's Mrs. Clark, isn't it?"

"Aye, Abegail Clark."

"I haven't seen her in years. In fact, I thought she was dead."

"That old woman is too feisty to lie down and die."

Beau glanced at the grandfather clock in the room and then, stepping near the interior door, opened it and peered out like a small, wary mouse from a peephole. He was vividly aware of his own dismay when he realized that even the entry hall was filled wall to wall with guests. "I think you're right, Pa. There must be a hundred or more in the house. How long is this damned thing going to last anyway?"

"Not long enough for what you're planning," Brandon responded with a wayward grin.

Beau turned with a question. "What am I planning?"

"The way you keep looking at the clock, I'd

guess you're wanting to escape here with Cerynise fairly soon. I think your expectations are much too high to be believable."

Beau's eyebrows shrugged upward briefly. "Well, I had hoped to. I've been expecting a shipment of goods from England to be arriving at the dock any day now, and I wanted Cerynise to go with me."

"What is it this time?"

"Well, her paintings for one thing."

Brandon couldn't curb a grin. "I thought you were just wanting to get her back to your bed."

Beau shot his father a look of surprise. "Why should you think that?"

"Well, boy, you've been drooling over her ever since she moved into your house, and from your obvious good humor, I must assume she pleases you very much. I can only commend your wisdom in not waiting a whole year before you settled her into your bed. Some men aren't that smart."

Beau laughed at his father's dry wit. "Don't be too hard on yourself, Pa. You have a better relationship with Mama than most men have with their mistresses."

"Aye, but she's better than any mistress."

Beau's lips twitched as he sought to restrain his amusement. Teasing his father was much more fun now that he was married, too. "Tell me, Pa, when a man gets as old as you, are you still able to...function...well, you know...in bed?"

Brandon looked appalled at his son's

suggestion that he couldn't perform his husbandly duties. "Egads, boy! What do you take me for? A damned eunuch? It may well surprise you to be told that your mother still wonders on a monthly basis if she's pregnant."

"I'm sorry!" Beau spread his hands and backed away, as if afraid that he was going to be thrashed. Of course, the merry gleam in his eyes contradicted that idea. Puckishly he rubbed more salt into his father's tender hide. "One never knows with older couples...if they have the strength to...ah...finish...what they start."

Brandon snorted. "I have half a mind to get your mother pregnant just to show you, boy. Why, you're not even dry behind the ears yet, and you're wondering if I'm too old. Ha!"

"Mighty touchy about your age, aren't you, Pa?" Beau needled, having difficulty keeping a straight face. "Seeing as how Mama is so young, maybe you're worrying that in a few years you won't be able to satisfy her."

"You've got a mouth on you that I'd like to wash out," Brandon retorted.

Beau dared to get close enough to settle a hand consolingly on his father's shoulder. The fact that it was just as hard as his own was clear testimony that no weakness of any kind troubled his sire. "That's all right, Pa. I'm sure Mama will understand when that time comes."

"I swear, this damned house just isn't big enough for the two of us...and it's not your mother I'm talking about."

Grinning, Beau casually shrugged his shoulders. "I know that, Pa. That's why I have a house in Charleston."

"Good thing." Brandon relented enough to chuckle. "Although with the baby coming, your mother is definitely wishing you lived closer."

"I gather she's as pleased as a cat with cream over my marriage to Cerynise."

"Oh, indeed. She couldn't be more delighted, especially since it seemed for a time that you were headed in a more...ah...worldly direction."

Beau had to decipher that statement a long moment before he asked in surprise, "You don't actually mean Germaine Hollingsworth, do you?"

"I never thought you'd go that way," Brandon assured him. " 'Twas your mother who worried."

Beau laughed at the very idea. "Mama would have gotten her dander up for sure if I had brought Germaine home as my wife."

"Now how can you say that?" Brandon queried with a chuckle. "We both know your mother is the sweetest, gentlest woman imaginable."

"Never mind that Irish temper of hers or that pure steel backbone?"

Brandon grinned. "Well, I've never minded any of that. She never gave me cause to. Germaine might have, though."

At that very moment, Germaine was indeed feeling some antagonism toward the mistress of Harthaven. Scarcely a room away from where Beau and his father were chatting, she sat with a false smile pasted on an equally stiff face, but inwardly she was seething. She couldn't abide the fuss presently being made over the girl whom she and her friends had delighted in mocking years ago. From every direction she was hearing extravagant praises heaped upon the one whom she had once derided as 'Sticks.' Cerynise certainly didn't seem so tall now after filling out. Germaine accepted that fact almost as a personal affront and mentally jeered, *How dare the twit return so lovely, serene and self-possessed? Like some otherworldly creature.*

Heather Birmingham evidently doted on her new daughter-in-law and was making every effort to protect her, at times even displaying the ferocity of a mother cat. For years now people had been generously inclined to describe Heather as such a nice person, so kind and compassionate, so gentle and lovely, and so on. Well, the fact of the matter was that those sapphire eyes could freeze a person with a positively frightening chill that even now sent shivers up Germaine's spine. It didn't matter that the icy glare was being bestowed upon the culprit who zinged Cerynise with a sharp barb. It was still the deadliest glower Germaine had ever been the recipient of.

Perhaps that was how Heather had thus far managed to keep a firm grasp on her husband, Germaine mused sullenly as she picked up her cup and sipped the tea. Being the wife of a strong-willed man like Brandon Birmingham all these many years couldn't have been easy. Yet, by all reports, Heather had handled him amazingly well, and at times, even strangers had remarked that the sensual richness of their marriage could almost be felt when the couple came together in a room.

If Germaine had ever suffered any qualms about her goal to marry Beau Birmingham, those trepidations had primarily been caused by the worry that he was too much like his father and couldn't be easily maneuvered. Then, too, she had been half-afraid that he wouldn't indulge her in a manner to which she had become accustomed. Her parents had always seen her every wish fulfilled, and she had often wondered if Beau would prove more stubborn, but that possibility hadn't been borne out in Cerynise's case, considering the fact that the tawny-haired twit was now wearing a sapphire ring and a diamond wedding band that almost made Germaine choke with envy.

Germaine set her cup down on her saucer and, seizing an opportunity presented by a lull in the conversation, remarked sweetly, "You know, Cerynise, I don't believe we've heard how you and Beau actually met. Was it terribly romantic?"

Despite the fact that she had grown leery of the woman and her snide questions, Cerynise laughed gaily. "Oh, I've been in love with Beau Birmingham ever since he was a student in my father's school."

Germaine managed a tight smile as she corrected her rival. "That's not really what I meant. We all know that he was your father's student. I was wondering how you met up with him in London. Surely your guardian forbade you to fraternize with seamen."

Cerynise had learned how to respond to catty girls and women during the five years she had been away. Dealing with them calmly, efficiently and as truthfully as possible was always the best way to blunt their thorny pricks. "It seemed reasonable for me to return to Charleston after Mrs. Winthrop's death. When I started making inquiries about the ships bound for the Carolinas, I was told that Beau had a ship in port. One thing led to another, and we decided to get married before we sailed."

Heather smiled with delight at the gracious way in which Cerynise had answered her would-be tormentor. Heather knew there was much more to the story than either her son had cared to elaborate on or her daughter-in-law was now revealing, and that she hadn't personally been informed of all the details. Nor did she think she needed to be. Contrary to what everyone in the family imagined, she knew her son was no saint. He was too much like his father for her to have nurtured such a farfetched notion. And she really didn't care whether it was by hook or rook or by the book, she was immensely relieved that Beau had managed to marry a woman of whom she could be proud and who all but idolized her son.

"I really don't understand," Germaine

463

responded, frowning prettily as if greatly perplexed. "Was Beau in London long enough for a formal courtship? Or should I dare imagine that your marriage happened through a whirlwind romance?" She tilted her head aside and laid a fingertip to her chin reflectively. "It seems terribly odd that when we met that day outside of Madame Feroux's shop, it was almost as if the two of you barely knew each other."

The little conversations that had been going on among some of the other ladies died away. Soon every ear was attentive and every eye was fastened on the guest of honor.

"Beau and I were trying to keep our marriage a secret," Cerynise answered smoothly. "I believe that has been explained to you. I was naturally shocked when I saw him with you, but he later told me that you had asked for a ride after he went to a wedding of a friend with whom you both were acquainted. Beau also told me that once inside of Madame Feroux's, he was there ten minutes at the most."

Germaine felt as if she had just surprised a porcupine at very close range. She had hoped to embarrass the girl by letting everyone know that Beau had actually escorted another woman to the dressmaker's, but when Cerynise explained precisely how everything had taken place, as if she had been lovingly reassured by her husband, it was she, Germaine, who was now abashed because it was now obvious to every lady present that the man had been in a hurry to leave her.

"You were staying with your uncle, Professor

Kendall, when you returned, were you not?" Irma Parrish inquired. She was a woman past her prime, yet she clung to youth with raiment far more suitable for someone half her age. She was also a notorious busybody and Germaine's cousin, which made her a natural ally. "Was there some reason for that?"

"I hadn't seen my uncle in five years," Cerynise replied. "And since Beau and I didn't want anyone to know we were married, staying with Uncle Sterling seemed the appropriate thing to do."

"But why were you trying to keep your marriage a secret?" Irma persisted.

"We *did* get married on very short notice, and with people wont to make much of our haste...Well, you can probably understand that it would have seemed far more proper for us to have a long courtship and a lengthy engagement before the nuptials. Do you not agree?"

Irma's mouth opened and closed several times, similar to that of a fish drowning on land. Finally she answered lamely, "I suppose I do, but I really don't see why you stayed with your uncle...."

Either the woman was harping on the subject or she was a half-wit, Cerynise decided, but she deigned to answer as patiently as possible. "With whom should I have stayed? Uncle Sterling wanted me to, and of course Beau was kind enough to allow it, considering our efforts to appear no more than casual friends."

465

"Beau being kind again," Germaine remarked thoughtfully. "How terribly noble of him. Did he marry you out of kindness?"

The statement was slipped in with a smile so adroitly that Cerynise was momentarily taken aback. She had forgotten how malicious Germaine could be, but by quickening degrees Cerynise was growing more experienced in her dealings with the woman. As a child she had just wanted the raven-haired beauty to leave her alone, but her ire now rose and her back stiffened at the implication of her words. The time seemed ripe for Germaine Hollingsworth to rue the day that she had ever tried to make a public spectacle of Sticks.

"Do you actually imagine that Beau would have married any woman out of kindness, Germaine? If so, you're greatly mistaken about what he wants from a wife. Beau is no simple, mild-mannered, benevolent gentleman who waits upon the whimsical moods of his wife. He is much more demanding than that. But I suppose only a wife would be cognizant of that." The smile with which she concluded her remarks was enigmatic, hinting at what more she could have said about her husband to enlighten Germaine and the rest of her attentive audience. She had said enough to imply that as a modest young woman, she was being, at best, discreet.

Heather grinned in glee. "More tea, anyone?" she inquired cheerily and, with a slight movement of her hand, summoned a servant to put out more sandwiches and cakes for the ladies.

466

Abegail Clark shifted her meager weight in a chair with the help of her cane. "All this interrogation reminds me of what Heather went through when Brandon first brought her back from England. I didn't like it any better then than I do now."

The deciding factor came when Martha Devonshire, who was linked by birth and marriage with every family of significance in the Carolinas, gazed through her lorgnette at the Birmingham bride. "I was never of the opinion that travel benefited a woman of quality. Yet I must admit that I may have been mistaken. Never have I met a young lady with such poise and graciousness."

That judgment rendered, the formidable matron sat back to observe the obedient nods of the assembled females, the vast majority of whom would never have dreamed of gainsaying her.

An hour later, the assembly ended and the guests reluctantly left. More than a few were inclined to linger, having discovered that Cerynise was a genuinely interesting person to talk with. Having been the recipient of a meaningful frown from her son, Heather graciously eased them on their ways with cheerful reminders that they would be seeing Cerynise at Suzanne's engagement ball. Even so, by the time the last guest departed, it was nigh the middle of the afternoon.

Beau strode in from outside, where he had gone to walk off his frustration and, upon his reentry, hurriedly collected his wife's cloak and bonnet. "Pardon my haste, Mama, but I've got to get back to Charleston. This *tea* took much longer than I expected."

He brushed a kiss on his mother's cheek as they bade farewell, and Brandon came out on the porch to stand beside his wife and to wave them off. When the carriage had rolled away, he slipped an arm about Heather's narrow waist and leaned over her ear to whisper, "How would you like to have another son, madam?"

Heather's head snapped up in surprise. "For mercy sake, what brought that on?"

"Beau doesn't think we're still capable of copulating."

She chortled in amusement as she slipped her arms around her husband's lean waist. "He doesn't know you very well, does he? But he'll find out differently when he's your age. Until then, I think we should consider a sea voyage on the *Audacious* instead of another child. Beau is planning on taking Cerynise with him after their baby is born, and you know you've never forgotten your love of sailing."

" 'Tis your grandchild that lures you, madam," Brandon accused with a grin.

Heather rubbed his hardened chest admiringly as she lifted blue eyes coyly to meet his. "We could spend a lot of time in our cabin making love. And who knows what will come of it?"

"When did you say Beau was leaving?"

Beau reached for the knob to open the front portal for his wife, but before he could turn it, the dark green, white-trimmed door was pulled inward by a man outfitted as a butler.

"Jasper?" Cerynise gaped in astonishment. "My goodness, what are you doing here?"

The butler's eyes swept down her briefly before he smiled. "Your husband invited me to come and work for him, madam. He even paid our fare."

"*Our* fare?"

"Yes, madam," Jasper replied with a nod and another smile. "Bridget and the others are here, too. In fact, the lot of us were able to personally escort your paintings to Charleston. They arrived undamaged, and I took the liberty of putting them in the study with your other ones."

Bridget had heard the muted voices from the back of the house and approached rather hesitantly as she made her way down the hallway leading from the kitchen. Cerynise took one look at her and, sweeping inward, hurried to greet the maid. They embraced and wept a little, but only with joy.

"Ye're lookin' grand, mum...I mean...Mrs. Birmingham. Never have I seen ye lookin' so fine." Her twinkling eyes dropped to the slight curve of Cerynise's belly, which had now become evident even beneath a shawl. "And ye're going to have a wee one. Oh, I'm so happy for you, mum."

"Thank you, Bridget," Cerynise replied, patting the woman's hand affectionately. "But tell me, have you met my husband?"

"I only saw Captain Birmingham on the

ship that day we brought yer clothes, mum. But had ye asked me at the time, I'd have told ye somethin' would come o' the two o' ye bein' together. I just never dreamt ye'd be married afore ye left London. At least, that's what Monsieur Monét told us. Ye must've been fairly dazzled by it all, what with it happenin' so fast an' all."

"I've known my husband ever since I was a child, Bridget, and have been in love with him for just about as long, so it wasn't all that sudden for me." She giggled as she added, "For him, perhaps."

Beau joined them, and after his wife made the formal introductions, he asked the maid, "Did Philippe show you where you're going to be housed?"

"Oh yes, sir. Past the garden in the servants' quarters, an' may I say, sir, I've seen no finer accommodations for servants."

"I hope you'll be comfortable there."

"I'm sure we will be, sir, an' thank ye most kindly for helpin' us out with our passage an' all. We couldna've made it here without ye givin' us so generous a purse. Jasper kept a careful accountin' sir, so's ye'd know what exactly was spent."

"Good servants are hard to find, so I performed a better service for myself by paying your way here," Beau assured her.

"Just the same, sir, we all appreciate what ye've done for us."

Cerynise cocked her head musefully at her husband as a sudden realization dawned.

"Are they the reason why you were so anxious to get home?"

Beau moved his shoulders briefly upward and grinned. "I thought they'd be arriving any day now, but since there were so many factors that could hinder their arrival, I could only guess at the approximate date. I've been checking the ships arriving from England on a daily basis, but I didn't have time this morning."

"You seem to enjoy keeping secrets from me, sir," Cerynise accused with a soft chuckle.

His smiling eyes dipped to her small, protruding belly before they met hers again. "Aye, madam, but no more than you."

The night of Suzanne's engagement ball arrived, and Cerynise took special pains with her appearance, knowing that she'd not only be confronting Germaine again but others who might have once set their hopeful sights on Beau as a possible husband. Madame Feroux and her assistants had worked tirelessly on an ice-blue creation to have it ready in time. At Beau's request, the gown had been made similarly to the pink one his wife had worn the night he had entertained his hunting companions on board his ship in England. The design had been changed slightly in that it had a longer bodice to conceal the curve of her stomach as much as possible. The weighty skirt of beaded silk was gently gathered beneath it. The sleeves were long and flowing, much like in the days of knights and ladies fair, but the neckline had definitely been made on the order of the pink gown and was cut squarely across her breasts. Beau had found it the most intriguing asset about the earlier version and had insisted that it remain exactly the same.

Cerynise's hair had been dressed high on her head to display the pearl-and-diamond earrings that dangled prettily from her dainty ears. For a belated wedding gift, Beau had given her an eight-strand pearl choker bedecked with a beautiful pink-and-white cameo encircled by diamonds. Cerynise had expressed her gratitude with gushing pleasure, for she had never *seen* anything as exquisite, much less owned it. Yet, even as costly and fine as the necklace was, the method by which it was given failed to compare with the ceremony of devotion with which her husband had presented her a new wedding band. He had gone down on one knee before her and, after removing the gold filigreed band from her finger, had ardently pledged his troth to be a faithful, loving husband. He had slipped the diamond ring on her third finger, kissed it, and then rose to seal his pact with a more thorough caress of her lips. What had followed was an evening that neither of them would likely forget, starting with a private dinner in their bedroom, a shared bath in Beau's huge tub wherein they had lain side by side, and ending in a night of love such as one would expect of a newly wedded couple.

When Beau requested help in folding his cravat in the late afternoon preceding his sister's engagement ball, it was no longer such a rare occasion that Cerynise had cause to be dubious about his motives. She only began to sense that something was different when he bent his head near hers and warmly whispered, "Delectable view."

Cerynise glanced down to find her breasts generously displayed by a gaping neckline and the shallow bodice of the lace chemise she wore beneath. Lifting her head, she smiled into his shining eyes. "I was sure you had seen it all before."

"Aye, but this time I don't need to keep my hands in my pockets. I can handle the sights to my heart's content, anytime or anywhere we can find a bit of privacy, madam," he breathed, brushing a kiss against her temple as his fingers plucked open the back placket of her gown. The heavily bejeweled bodice slid from her shoulders like weighted silk and plummeted to her waist, leaving the gossamer batiste and lace chemise molding the fullness of her breasts.

Cerynise stood before him like one bewitched by a strange enchantment, her eyes glowing with sultry warmth as he tugged the straps down and hastened the descent of the undergarment with his hands until that, too, lay bunched around her waist. The pale, pink-crested orbs thrust forward proudly, seeming to invite him to taste and touch. His mouth took possession, moving over the tempting fullness in a leisured caress, savoring the sweet nectar from the soft peaks and drawing blissful sighs from his wife, who stood in assenting, quiescent rapture as his lips and tongue stroked across her

473

naked skin. Her nipples tingled for more, and she arched her back to make them more accessible to him. Her breath was snatched inward in small gasps as he availed himself of the opportunity. He devoured them completely, leaving them glistening with moisture from his warmly licking strokes. A long moment later he traced his lips upward along her graceful neck and captured her mouth in the same greedy quest.

When at last he drew back, Cerynise had no strength left in her limbs. She swayed against him, begging breathlessly, "More."

"After we return home," Beau murmured huskily. Searching her soft, liquid eyes, he pulled the garments up over her bosom and shoulders and refastened the placket. "That will be my promise for later, madam."

"But you took away all my desire to leave," she whispered tremblingly. "I'll be yearning for you all night."

" 'Twas my intent, madam." His warm breath caressed her skin as he chuckled near her cheek. "Every waltz we dance, every glance and touch we exchange will be fired by this interlude and the thought of what will await us once we return home."

Cerynise moaned, exaggerating her disappointment. "Do you suppose it's possible for a wife to rape her husband?"

"You have more power over my body than I do myself, madam, but how can it be rape when I'd be a willing participant?"

She smiled shrewdly as her fingers plucked

open his trousers and repaid him in kind, giving him a full measure of his own heady potion. Pleased with the results, she drew back for an admiring gaze.

"Now I'll be ready for you all night," Beau groaned, drawing her hand back to him and closing his fingers hard over hers.

"Just desserts," she breathed, licking his mouth with the tip of her tongue. She could feel the pulsing warmth of him, imploring her to continue, but with a last enveloping stroke she pulled away. "If I must suffer, sir, so must you."

Beau was sure that it would be at least an hour before his blood cooled. "Did I ever tell you what a vixen you are?"

Cerynise smiled contentedly. "Only in bed, sir. Only in bed."

Many of the guests had already arrived by the time Beau's carriage pulled to a halt before the door. He handed Cerynise down and paused to kiss away the small, fretful frown she now wore. During the long ride out to Harthaven, her mood had become entangled by worry over what the evening would bear. She was especially anxious about being bombarded by catty questions from at least a handful of rejected maidens.

"If you only knew how beautiful you are, my love," her husband crooned near her ear, "you wouldn't let anything bother you, especially Germaine."

"I'm sure she has spread it abroad that I lured

475

you into marriage by devious methods,"
Cerynise muttered. "And everyone else will
be wondering how far along I am...or giving
me chiding looks and saying that I shouldn't
be here at all under the circumstances."

"You're a Birmingham now," Beau reassured
her. "You belong here more than all of the
others put together. As for your condition, we
have no reason to be ashamed, my love. We
were quite properly wed when you got with
child."

Cerynise heaved a forlorn sigh. "That may
be well and good, Beau, but tongues are still
bound to wag."

"They'll stop...when we're about eighty
years old," he teased, placing a doting kiss upon
her brow.

She smoothed his black lapel admiringly.
Except for his white shirt, cravat and a burnished silver brocade waistcoat handsomely
adorned with a high, crisply folded collar,
he was dressed entirely in black and looked every
bit as debonair as that day when she had seen
him with Germaine. "You'll stay with me,
won't you, Beau?"

"You'll probably find me so close at hand,
madam, that you'll want to shoo me away."

"Never."

Beau pulled her arm through his and,
climbing to the porch, whisked her through
the front door. The butler took her royal blue
velvet cloak, and then, as Beau escorted her
toward the guests, who had turned to stare,
Heather slipped through the crowded ballroom

to greet her son and daughter-in-law. After giving each a doting kiss, she turned a brilliant smile to the roomful of people and shushed their conversations with a graceful wave of her hands. She was promptly reinforced by her husband, who settled a hand upon her shoulder.

"Ladies and gentlemen," Heather called as her sparkling blue eyes swept over the faces of friends and acquaintances, "for those who haven't met her yet, I'd like to present our new daughter-in-law, Cerynise Birmingham, only offspring of the late Professor Marcus Kendall, whom many of you probably remember. Beau and Cerynise were married in England in late October before they set sail for the Carolinas. They wanted to keep their marriage a secret, and as yet they haven't confided in me as to the reasons why. I'd like to think it was to allow us the honor of seeing them wed in a church. Yet, as things have a way of developing in real life, Brandon and I are going to be grandparents in August."

Hearty applause, blended with laughter and congratulations, soon followed. A sigh of relief slipped from Cerynise's lips as she felt her tension easing, having been becalmed by the affable way Heather had handled the situation. Her mother-in-law had cut cleanly through to the heart of the matter, skillfully dispatching innuendoes and conjectures with a graciousness that was irresistible.

Beau was close at hand to introduce his wife to the guests who came forward eagerly to wish them well. Many of Beau's male companions from years back had been students of her father, and they briefly related amusing tales from their association with their dedicated schoolmaster. Names soon became a confusing tangle that fairly boggled Cerynise's mind, for it seemed a whole avalanche of amiable guests wanted to extend their congratulations on the couple's marriage and welcome them back from England. Her softly pleading eyes made her husband chuckle, and he begged for time out to dance with his wife.

"Feeling better?" he asked as he whirled her about in a waltz.

Cerynise laughed, evidencing not only her relief but her pleasure at being able to dance for the first time with her husband. She found him every bit as smooth on his feet as the dance instructors whom Lydia Winthrop had hired for her had been. Indeed, he was like some fairy tale prince, who swept her around the ballroom, continually turning in ever-widening circuits until the faces of those who watched became an indistinct blur beyond his broad shoulders. But then, her eyes strayed rarely from his face.

"Your mother certainly simplified the situation," Cerynise remarked, reveling in the fact that nearly everyone had been informed of their marriage. "Right now, I feel as if I'm floating on a cloud. Definitely a great weight has been lifted off me."

A devilish grin stretched across Beau's lips. "Is that the way you feel after I make love to you?"

She looked perplexed for barely a moment and finally understood his risqué remark. "Your weight is immensely more enjoyable to bear, my love, but I think you know by now how much I crave your body. I've not seen any finer."

Beau's eyes glowed as he challenged her. "As if you've seen more than mine, madam." He shook his head. "Nay, when you blushed to the roots of your hair the first time you saw my chest, I became convinced that you had never seen a naked man before we were married, but that's exactly the way I preferred it. I want you all to myself."

"And you can have me, sir, anytime you want me."

"My old bedroom is upstairs," he suggested with a warm leer.

Cerynise gave him a coy smile. "Of course, you know we'll be missed."

Beau sighed, sorely regretting that fact. "Aye, and we'd never get your hair up quite as nicely as it is now. As much as I desire to take my ease of you now, madam, I guess we must wait until we get home."

"You're a terrible tease, sir," she fussed flirtatiously. "Of that I'm now thoroughly convinced. You know very well I would be leading the way if you'd invite me to dally upstairs with you for a while."

Beau tossed his head back and laughed in hearty amusement. "I might yet, madam...but only when I can be sure that no one will come searching us out."

The couple's graceful flight around the ballroom aroused a seething black rage within the heart of at least one who watched with close attention from the sidelines. For the moment, Germaine Hollingsworth stood alone in the crowded room, feeling quite envious of her rival. If not for Cerynise, Germaine had no doubt that she would have been dancing in Beau's arms this very moment. He was the very essence of masculinity, tall and powerful, darkly sensual in his good looks, supple in his movements, yet hard as an oak, a fact which had both excited and delighted her whenever she had casually touched his broad chest. She could envision herself running her hands over his naked body, marveling at its firm structure, and bestirring him to a passion that would have made him her willing captive. But it was obvious now that he was Cerynise's slave. Indeed, if he had *ever* looked at her the way he had visually devoured Cerynise that day outside of Madame Feroux's shop, Germaine would have had cause to nurture some hope for herself in the weeks and months to come. Diligently applied temptations could tear apart the noblest intentions if the heart was at all willing. But as long as Cerynise remained the coveted jewel in his eye, Germaine couldn't foresee that happening. Frankly, she wished that Sticks would drop dead, preferably now, but dying in childbirth would definitely suffice.

Beau was completely entranced with the soft pools of adoring hazel that he beheld before him. They glowed with a shining luster that radiated her love for him. Feeling immensely blessed to have found such devotion, he swept his beautiful wife around the ballroom floor. Her pliant body moved with his, as if their minds were joined in sweet accord. He had no doubt they were, for he could read the desire flaming in those darkly translucent depths and knew that his own shone with equal fervor.

For Cerynise, nothing existed beyond her husband's encircling arms and the endless glitter of blue eyes that held hers captive. Their words were muted, an intimate sharing of comments, affirmations of love, and secrets solely their own. There was a warm, underlying excitement within her that he had kindled with his earlier promise, and the slightest brush of his thigh or the gentlest squeeze of his hand on her waist made her breasts tingle in anticipation of that moment when she would be alone with him again. Though her fingers lightly brushed the fabric of his coat and casually caressed him in ways that were totally acceptable even in the midst of so many people, each glance they exchanged was charged with erotic meaning, each smile a reminder of what awaited them upon their arrival home, for it was only there that they could be assured of adequate privacy. It was nothing less than a slow, rhythmic dance of building desires, a sensual ritual in foreplay that excited them, yet no one else could discern.

The music continued to fill the ballroom, and Beau reluctantly yielded his wife to the other Birmingham men who came to claim a dance for themselves. He, in turn, performed his duty by his mother, sisters, and cousins. Tamarah was included in that list, and though she pleaded with her parents to be allowed to stay up for the whole affair, she was sent off to bed in Brenna's room at an hour appropriate for a girl her age. As for the other young women in the room, for Beau it was as if they didn't exist. His heart and his gaze were firmly fixed upon his wife who, even while being escorted around the dance floor by his relatives, seemed to have eyes only for him.

Beau had been drawn aside by several of his hunting companions and as he laughed and chatted with them, Cerynise and Brenna accepted glasses of punch from a servant. The two women were engrossed with watching the dancing couples, but it wasn't long before both of them became aware of Germaine urging Michael York out onto the floor. The man didn't seem to know how to respond to her invitation except to accede to her plea, yet apparently it wasn't where he wanted to be. He seemed terribly discomfited by the depth of her bodice, for the woman was all but spilling out of a dark violet confection which appeared more of a marvel of engineering than a generous endowment. Making a concerted effort to appear casual, Michael looked everywhere but at her, and as soon as the tune ended, he quickly excused himself and beat a hasty retreat to his fiancée, who listened with smiling attention to what had all the appearances of being an anxious explanation. After a moment he kissed Suzanne's hand as if relieved and drew her out onto the ballroom floor, where he danced divinely, at ease.

It didn't take much imagination for Cerynise to come to the determination that it would only be a matter of time before Germaine also cornered Beau. The thought was barely formed when she saw the woman moving toward him with an inviting smile.

Brenna leaned near Cerynise to whisper, "Do you see where that woman is heading now?"

"Toward *my* husband," Cerynise answered in a muted tone.

Brenna ground her teeth in vexation. "Wouldn't you like to pull that hussy's hair out?"

"By the roots," Cerynise affirmed, remembering the jealousy that had once been aroused when she had seen Beau handing Germaine down from his carriage that day in Charleston.

Brenna patted her sister's-in-law hand consolingly. "Trust Beau to do what is right."

A pensive sigh slipped from Cerynise. "He must be cordial to her, of course."

Germaine's popularity among the men might have heightened her confidence to the degree that she fully expected any member of the opposite gender to drop whatever he was doing at her approach. But Beau was so busy conversing with his friends, that he looked right past her, never even realizing she was near. It caused the woman an undue amount of shock and frustration, for he seemed genuinely unaware of her presence. The tiny brunette set her arms akimbo and stamped her foot to demand his attention, but upon realizing she was there in front of him, Beau promptly introduced her to a young gallant who was far more eager to lead her onto the dance floor.

"Superb!" Brenna exclaimed cheerfully in a whisper and turned to meet Cerynise's radiant smile. "Isn't he marvelous?"

"Oh, indeed!" Cerynise agreed happily.

"Now look," Brenna urged. "He's coming back to you."

Beau cast a questioning grin toward his sister as he took Cerynise's arm. "Do you have any objections if I dance with my wife, Little One?"

Brenna willingly accepted the cup from her sister-in-law. "None at all, Tall Man."

As the couple moved away, Brenna turned to find a place to set the two cups and was somewhat startled to find a russet-haired young man a few years her senior approaching her. She recognized him immediately as Clay's closest friend.

"Your pardon, Brenna, but I was wondering if you'd care to dance. Clay said that you might be acceptable to the idea."

"I'm very acceptable to the idea, Todd," she replied, bestowing a dazzling smile upon him.

Gleaming white teeth were readily displayed in a jubilant grin as Todd hurriedly took the cups from her and passed them on to a servant. Gallantly he swept her a bow and then drew her small, slender hand within the bend of his arm, causing her father's eyebrow to jut sharply upward, even from across the length of the room.

With a coy smile Heather sought to smooth her husband's ruffled feathers as she rubbed a hand down his lapel. "Todd is only asking our daughter to dance, my dear, and I'd be very appreciative if you'd do me a similar favor."

He clicked his heels in a debonair bow. "May I have this dance, madam?"

"I'd like nothing better, my love."

Brandon laid a hand possessively on the small of her back and led her toward an open space on the ballroom floor. Still, he couldn't resist a complaint as they began to dance. "I overheard Clay talking to his brother about Todd Phelps's growing infatuation with our daughter, madam."

"Well, he's definitely a nice young man, from an upstanding family, but Brenna is only sixteen...."

"My sentiments exactly, madam."

Heather smiled as her husband strove to keep their youngest daughter in sight. Brenna was *his* baby girl, and from all indications, he was going to be extremely reluctant to give her up to just any young swain. A man would have to prove himself an exceptional individual before he'd find favor with her father.

Some time later Beau and Cerynise stepped out onto the front porch for a bit of fresh

485

air. They meandered arm in arm to the far end of the veranda, where a huge live oak allowed only mottled moonlight to pass through its rustling leaves, which left the area swathed in deep shadows. The chill of the evening soon elicited a shiver from Cerynise, motivating Beau to open his coat invitingly. Bracing his legs apart, he pulled her close against him as he leaned back against the white facade and folded his arms around her shoulders.

Cerynise sighed dreamily. "Little did I imagine when I was a girl hopelessly smitten with you that I would actually be standing on this very porch someday, married to you and with your child growing within me. Though I nurtured the fantasy of being your wife for many years, my love, it finally seemed so outlandish that I forced myself not to think of it anymore. Being so far away, I had serious doubts that I would ever see you again. Alistair will probably never know how great a favor he did me by throwing me out of the Winthrop house when he did."

Beau chuckled softly. "I'd almost be of a mind to show my gratitude with a kiss instead of a fist in the face."

"Kiss me instead," Cerynise whispered warmly, lifting her face expectantly.

He indulged her request well beyond a simple husbandly peck, and soon she was straining up close against him with her arms locked about his neck, returning the favor. It was a thoroughly passionate kiss, one that stroked across their senses and awakened familiar fires. His left arm was tightly clasped about her waist, allowing his right hand to move over her back with the freedom he was wont to enjoy, caressing her hip through the soft layering of her gown and underwear, dipping into the tempting crevice and following its path downward until his hand was firmly clasped between her buttocks.

A feminine clearing of a throat ended their kiss abruptly. Cerynise would have stepped away in acute embarrassment, but Beau had the presence of mind to keep her close against him. It was certainly no time for his wife to desert him.

Trying to identify the woman who approached, they peered into the shadows enveloping the porch. Finally the specks of light converged sufficiently to illuminate the smirk on Germaine's face.

"Well, it's certainly evident you two can't leave each other alone." Though her words belied the fact, she had been titillated by the display, for it only affirmed in her mind that Beau's appetites were nigh as vast as her own.

"That's the benefit of being married. We don't have to," Beau returned casually.

"Really, Beau, you should consider how you might embarrass other people," Germaine chided. "Such wanton displays should be reserved for bedrooms, not open verandas where anyone may pass."

"Strange, I can usually hear when someone is coming toward me, especially on a wood floor, but I didn't notice even the lightest sound of shoes scraping against the porch." Beau's gaze descended curiously to her hem, which swept the floor. The open study door indicated the area from whence she had emerged, and the way she was holding her arms behind her back led him to believe that she was keeping something carefully out of sight. "Which leaves me, of course, to believe that you're not wearing any shoes at the moment."

Germaine laughed, clasping both shoes in one hand, and casually swept her free hand before her to make light of his conjecture. "I don't go around spying on people, Beau, and even if I did, that wouldn't excuse your lewdness. I'll have to complain to your mother about your actions. It's certainly not safe for an innocent young girl to meander around Harthaven. Why, she'd be shocked out of her senses by such coarseness."

Beau was now able to face the woman and did so, leaving an arm wrapped around his wife's waist, for he was reluctant to have her flee and leave him alone with the woman. "I'm sorry if we offended your tender sensibilities, Germaine, but I find it hard to believe that you're shocked. In fact, if there's an innocent among us, I'm inclined to think that it's my wife."

Germaine's dark eyes glittered dangerously in the dappled light. "What do you mean by that?"

Beau cocked his head thoughtfully aslant. "Do you really want me to tell you?"

"If you're going to insult me, I'd like you to explain why you think you have the right," she insisted unwisely, "because I've never done anything that I would be ashamed of."

"Not even skinny-dipping with Jessie Ferguson last summer...?"

Germaine's jaw dropped in astonishment. There was only one way he could have known about that! That clod Jessie! He just didn't know when to keep his mouth shut! "That's an outrageous lie, Beau Birmingham! I would never—"

"Oh, then it must be another Germaine Hollingsworth who likes to cavort naked with her escorts. You see, Jessie isn't the first one who has boasted of his conquest. Let's see, his ride happened beneath a sycamore tree. And then there was Frank Lester. She rode him in his father's stable. In fact, from what I hear, there have been quite a number of men in her life, and it seems that this other Germaine Hollingsworth usually initiates the seductions and will do absolutely *anything* when she gets heated up. Word has gotten around that the difference between her and the ones who do it for a living is that she does it for free and enjoys it more."

Germaine sneered caustically. "From what I hear you've visited those bawdy women often enough."

"Well, at least I've never pretended to be a Goody-Two-Faced."

Germaine's chin lifted in haughty arrogance. "Obviously some other woman has been going around using my name for devious purposes, but she'd best be warned because

489

I'm a fair shot with my father's rifle, and anybody spreading such gibberish about me is in danger of being mistaken for a rat. In fact, Beau Birmingham, you may be taking your life in your hands if you try to tarnish my reputation with all that nonsense you've just babbled."

Beau smiled blandly. "You'd be surprised at the reputation you have, Germaine. All the studs in the area know where you live. That's why you're so popular with the men. I'm just surprised that you haven't gotten caught yet."

"You mean like your simpleton wife?" Germaine sneered in disdain and fixed a cold glower upon Cerynise. "I'm sure the other Germaine can tell you a name of a woman who'll take care of you in an afternoon's time, and no one will be the wiser."

"My wife probably doesn't even know what you're talking about, Germaine, but we're not interested in your offer. In fact, we're thrilled that we're going to have a child. Thank you for nothing."

Germaine's lips curled in contempt as she stepped to the outer edge of the porch and leaned against a column to slip on her shoes. Then, smoothing her skirts down, she assumed an air of ladylike grace and strolled back to the French doors through which she had slipped some moments earlier.

Cerynise finally let her breath out in a relieved sigh. "I have a feeling Germaine doesn't like you much anymore."

Beau's eyebrows flicked upward briefly. "I

doubt that she liked me all that well before. It was probably the lure of being able to call herself a Birmingham and the idea of spending my money that interested her far more. After being spoiled by her parents, it must be difficult for her to imagine herself marrying a man of meager means."

"Not even if that man were you?" Cerynise came back into his arms. "Poor Germaine. How foolish for a woman to set her heart on riches when a man like you is far more valuable. But then, I'm sure there is no duplicate for Beauregard Birmingham."

Beau leaned down to savor the fragrance of her hair. "You're prejudiced, madam."

"Aye, terribly," she agreed, snuggling against him. "Now kiss me again before we have to go in."

CHAPTER 15

Only a few of the azalea bushes were still in bloom as the end of May approached, but after being arrayed in their vivid fuchsia, snowy white, and deep magenta hues, the city and countryside lost much of its splendor when the blossoms finally wilted. The same held true with the gardens around Beau's house. On a morning near the middle of the month, Sterling Kendall arrived at the Birmingham residence bearing boxes upon boxes of seedlings he had started as well as shrubs and several flowering trees with their roots carefully bound. With the younger man's full approval, the professor spent several days transforming what had been a pleasant enough area into a garden that promised to be spectacular. After mulching around the tender plants, Sterling instructed his niece on their care, advising that such work was not only nourishment for the spirit but also provided, he was wont to suspect, useful lessons in nurturing a child.

Although Cerynise approached the task as an apprehensive novice, she soon realized the joy to be found in horticulture. It was an unexpected thrill to see a profusion of flowers bursting forth after weeks of careful tending. The garden soon became one of her favorite places in which to work and relax. When she wasn't painting in the study, she could often be found outside, tilling the beds, trimming away spent blooms, or trying to capture the beauty of the flowers on canvas before their color faded. It gave her an equal sense of satisfaction to create extravagant bouquets for the house, and soon the rooms that the couple were most wont to use bore the rewards of her work. Even Beau began to take an interest and, when he had time, would join her in her endeavors in the garden. New wrought iron furniture was purchased and placed in cozy settings beneath trees, in the gazebo where they frequently took breakfast and lunch, and here and there alongside the brick paths. At times, the two laughed and cavorted like puckish children, throwing dirt or sprinkling each other with watering cans until one or the other gave chase. But with Cerynise's growing girth, it was usually Beau who caught her and swooped her up in his arms amid her gleeful squeals.

As dirty and muddy as they sometimes got in their frolicking, it was not long before a small, white, brick-based shed was built in the garden area. It had a separate compartment for washing and another for dressing. Latticework extended vertically above the flat roof, masking from normal view a large, lidded, rectangular copper box which, after being fully exposed to the sun for several hours, heated the water it contained. The bottom portion of the box was perforated, but to control the flow of water, another sheet of copper could be raised or lowered by a lever attached to a pull chain. Once it was completely down, more water could be added and saved for another day. The contraption provided the couple with a warm rain shower of sorts, allowing them to freshen up after doffing their dirty work clothes. Clean clothes, soap and towels were always on hand, and though they delighted in showering off together, Beau was inclined to slip outside in the morning and indulge himself in a morning cleansing before he dressed for work. Though it was much easier than filling the tub in the dressing room upstairs, the water was not always warm at that early hour. Nevertheless he found it refreshing.

Beau was now managing the shipping company and warehouses which his uncle owned.

In that capacity, he also directed the unloading of company ships. He excelled at his work, but as yet he had refused to accept a full partnership, avoiding the commitments that would tie him down to land when he had every intention of making another voyage.

Stephen Oaks had returned from his northerly venture along the coast, having made a considerable profit on the cargo he had taken with him. From his trip, he had gleaned much needed machinery for the area of Charleston, proving himself a shrewd merchant as well as a competent sea captain. More recently he had been prone to visit his captain's residence on a regular basis, not so much to talk about business with Beau but to pay court to Bridget who, from Cerynise's viewpoint, was falling head over heels in love with the man. In her free time the maid could often be seen strolling arm in arm along the street with the future captain of the *Audacious*.

Cleveland McGeorge had set about to prove that he could sell Cerynise's paintings even with her name on them. It had taken him a while, but he had been successful on three different occasions, selling two to New York gentlemen and the last and best of the three to Martha Devonshire. Thereafter he had had inquiries from almost every wealthy family in the Charleston area. It gave him great satisfaction to create a demand for them and stir up competition among the interested parties by telling them that they would have to wait their turn, for in truth, Cerynise couldn't paint fast enough to appease everyone now seeking to buy one of her paintings.

The portrait of Heather and her daughters was coming along very nicely. Soon the faces would be done, which was always the most challenging part. Filling in the gowns and hair would be fairly easy, and Cerynise had all hopes of finishing the painting well in time for Heather's birthday in July.

Cerynise had come to the realization that she had never been happier in her life. She was married to the man whom she had always adored, and with each passing day it seemed their love for each other deepened. They were looking forward to the arrival of their first child with great enthusiasm, and they began to make lists of acceptable names for both genders. The room beyond their bathing chamber was soon designated as the new nursery, and although it was mostly furnished with new pieces, Beau's own cradle was brought to them from the attic at Harthaven, where it had been stored for at least a score of years.

Any moment in which Cerynise and Beau found themselves alone together was greatly enhanced by their growing love for one another. They enjoyed being secluded and were wont to make much of those interludes in the privacy of their home. Their courtship equaled or even surpassed what fabled lovers from Shaksperean, Chaucerian, and a whole host of other bygone tales had supposedly luxuriated in and was as close to an adventure in paradise as anyone could imagine. Still, they were inundated with invitations from nearly the whole social block of Charlestonians. Cerynise left Beau with the task of choosing which engagements they should accept and those they'd have to graciously refuse. An elegantly penned note from Martha Devonshire was among those they responded to with a visit. Beau hadn't been at all sure how the evening would turn out, for he hadn't been around the woman that much to speak of, but after no more than a few moments in the elder's presence, Cerynise had taken to Martha as quickly as she had Lydia Winthrop years ago. To their delight, they found the normally reserved lady had a marvelously dry wit that even had Beau holding his sides with laughter.

On Saturdays and weekdays, Beau usually came home to have lunch with Cerynise a little before noon, but if an appointment had been scheduled near the time he was supposed to return, he'd arrive as much as a half hour early just so he could spend the same amount of time with her and not be late for his meeting. Whether they dined in the garden or at the long, imposing table in the dining room, they sat close together, laughing and talking about numerous things. Cerynise was always anxious to hear what he had been doing at the shipping company or what interesting character he might have met. Beau willingly appeased her curiosity, sparing her the more boring details, and at times would even discuss some small annoyance that he had

had to deal with, for his wife had a way of easing his irritation with gentle, judicious reasoning when nobody else could. After the meal, they would either wander in the garden together or retire to the privacy of the study until he had to return to work.

One morning near the end of June, shortly before noon, Cerynise was cutting flowers for the house when the creaking of the garden gate drew her attention. Curious to see who was arriving by way of the street, she faced the portal just as a harsh male voice rasped "Kill!" In the next instant a huge black dog came bounding through the entrance. Immediately the gate slammed shut behind him.

Never in her life had Cerynise seen the likes of such a dog. Not only was the beast tall enough to reach almost to her waist, but it was solidly built with a chest as broad as a large oaken bucket. He had a massive, square head and eyes that gleamed like yellow fire. For a moment, Cerynise stood frozen with prickling horror, staring into that fierce gaze. Then the animal's hackles rose on end, and his fangs were slowly bared in a low, growling snarl as a whitish drool dribbled from his muzzle.

Cerynise's heart leapt into her throat as the beast began moving forward menacingly, watching her every movement as she backed cautiously away. The word *Kill!* had shattered any illusion about his reason for being there. The dog intended to dispense with her in a most brutal fashion. Unless this was some kind of prank it was an imminent possibility. Indeed, she was afraid that she was looking death fully in the face, but this one was black with brown markings.

Cerynise searched behind her for the closest haven and caught sight of the bathhouse. As she neared it, her throat constricted with fear, for the dog seemed to be advancing upon her faster than she was progressing. Even if she managed to reach the shed in time, she wasn't at all sure the structure could withstand an assault from such an enormous brute.

Her mind flew in a frantic search for a swifter and surer escape. The servants were upstairs cleaning the front bedrooms. If she screamed, she had serious doubts that they would be able to hear her. Philippe had gone to the market to buy fruit for lunch, and though he had said he'd be back shortly, he hadn't had nearly enough time to return. Cerynise didn't know the exact time, but she guessed it was too soon to hope that Beau would come strolling in, yet she prayed fervently that this was one of those days when he'd arrive home early.

Cerynise calculated her chances for gaining the safety of the house. Even if she started running, she couldn't hope to reach it in time, for the dog would surely quicken his pace. With his long legs it wouldn't take any time at all before he attacked her. Indeed, the chances of her effectively bringing about her own deliverance seemed beyond her capability.

"Nice dog," she cajoled fearfully, willing to try anything.

Much to her alarm, the sound of her voice seemed to incite the animal. He started barking furiously. Frantically she peered through the open slats of the board fence, hoping to spy its owner and demand his help or at least a reason for this attack, *if* by some strange fluke the order to kill had been meant for someone else. If, on the other hand, this was some kind of prank, she wasn't feeling the least bit amused. To be exact, she was frightened nigh out of her wits. Yet her sweeping search found no one; the culprit was either hiding and awaiting her death or had already left.

Suddenly the barking ceased, to be replaced by a throaty growling, which Cerynise found infinitely more intimidating. His fangs showing in an evil grin and his yellow eyes feeding almost hungrily upon her movements, the dog crouched lower to the ground, preparing to launch himself upon her. In a panic she whirled and fled toward the bathhouse. Even so, she was hampered by her bulk. Hearing his huge paws thumping against the brick path behind her and coming ever closer, she screamed in dread of the animal sinking his teeth into her flesh. She careened around a tree and threw a quick glance over her shoulder just in time to see the animal plow headlong into the same sturdy trunk she had just rounded.

The dog was momentarily upended and dazed, giving her time to lengthen the distance between them, but he quickly twisted around and got his legs beneath him. Her feet flew, propelled by fear, but as fast as she raced, she could hear the hound loping behind her once again, swiftly closing the space between them. She shrieked in terror, knowing that any moment she'd be taken down and possibly killed. Then, to her overwhelming relief, she espied Beau charging out of the house with a poker in his hand. He raced past her, and the vicious snarling was swiftly turned to surprised yelps punctuated by a repetitive thudding of the iron bar. Cerynise winced at the gruesome sounds, for it seemed she could actually hear the grating of metal scraping against bone. The yelps and pitiful whines rapidly dwindled until Cerynise could hear nothing behind her but the movements of her husband as he dragged the animal out of sight. A moment later she heard Beau striding hurriedly back to her by way of the brick walk. Trembling to the marrow of her being, she faced him and saw that he still clasped the now-bloody poker in his hand. His shirt and arms were bespeckled with red, but to her he looked as resplendent as a knight in shining armor.

"Are you all right?" Beau questioned worriedly as he halted before her, not daring to touch her with all the gore on his hands.

"Ye—" Her voice faltered before she could get so simple an answer out, and she responded with a dazed nod before she collapsed against him in relief, not caring how bloodstained he was.

Beau tossed aside the poker and, holding his hands carefully away from her, clasped her close

500

within his arms. For a long moment Cerynise could do nothing more than sob and cling to him until the worst of her terror began to subside. Drawing a handkerchief from his pocket, she began to dab at her eyes and took a long, deep breath that seemed inclined to catch in her throat.

"How did that beast get in here, anyway?" Beau asked when she had recovered enough to talk.

"Someone...let him in...through the gate," she explained haltingly. "I couldn't see who it was...but I heard the man give the dog a command to kill."

Beau jerked back enough to search her face. "Kill you? Are you sure?"

She nodded. "I remember that part distinctly. Whoever the man was, he held the gate open just long enough to let the dog in. He wasn't taking any chances on being seen. If not for you, that beast would have killed me."

"Stay here, my pet," Beau bade, gently easing her back into a wrought iron chair behind her. "I'm going to have a look at the gate. I won't be long."

He strode across the lawn to the portal and, stepping through it, looked up and down the street. As he might have suspected, there was no sign of the scoundrel. Beau searched closer around the garden entrance, finding nothing of any great significance except a large shoe print left in a small worn patch of rain-softened dirt where the grass had been killed back by constant passage through the gate. Only that morning they had had a light sprinkling, which left Beau no other choice but to believe that the footprint was fresh. He had seen that same kind of impression many times before, for it was exactly like those made by the canvas shoes of common sailors. The idea that a seaman was to blame led Beau to wonder if the attack on Cerynise had been intended as a way to take revenge on him for some unknown offense, for he couldn't imagine any deed that would have devastated him more than the murder of his wife.

Beau closed the wooden barrier to test the degree of ease with which the lock could be unlatched from outside. The gate was primarily used by servants, who, on their days off, came and went through this particular portal rather than traipsing through the house. The portal was tall enough for him to rest his chin squarely on its top. Thus, in order for someone to unlatch it from the street side and still keep his head down so as to remain hidden, it would have required a man of his height to be able to unfasten the lock on the inside without aid, for the latch was too far down for a shorter man to reach it without stepping onto the wooden block which was available nearby. To reach it himself, Beau had to step into that same bald area of dirt where the footprint had been left.

A tall sailor, Beau mentally concluded, and one who was now lacking a dog. Moon was in the Charleston area, and Beau knew the old tar was acquainted with many of the seamen in the area. He had certainly been around longer than anyone in his profession. Perhaps the ancient cabin boy would be able to supply him with names of sailors who fit that particular description. If Moon could come up with such a list, selecting the ones who held a grudge against him would be fairly easy, Beau concluded, for he didn't think he had that many enemies.

Beau returned to Cerynise and, after lifting her in his arms, carried her upstairs to their dressing room. As she doffed her bloodstained gown, he stripped his outer clothes, washed and donned fresh apparel. Then he led her to the bed with an exhortation to rest while he went and had a talk with the servants. Upon meeting Cooper in the hallway, he sent the young houseman out to bury the dog beyond the servants' privy and to put a padlock on the gate. Then Beau searched out Jasper and found him in an upper-story bedroom where he was industriously cleaning the ceiling.

"It seems that someone may be trying to kill Mrs. Birmingham," Beau surmised, drawing a shocked gasp from the man as he stepped away from the ladder.

"The madam, sir?" The servant looked appalled. "Why, it's hard for me to imagine such a dastardly thing, sir. Who would want to harm the madam?"

"I don't know, Jasper, but someone let a dog into the backyard after giving the animal instructions to kill. Mrs. Birmingham is quite sure about what she heard, and she was the only one in the garden at the time. It distresses me to think what I might have found had I come home at my regular time. If this was truly an attempt on her life, and I certainly have no reason to believe otherwise with the evidence I've seen, I must set up safeguards to insure that Mrs. Birmingham is protected at all times. From now on, during my absence, your first duty must be to watch over your mistress. If you see any strangers loitering around the house, in the road or anyplace else nearby, I wish to be informed posthaste, even if you have to send Cooper or someone else to fetch me home from the warehouse. I rather suspect that the blackguard is about my height, a seaman or at least garbed as one. From the impression he left in the mud near the gate, I would be inclined to say that his feet are larger than mine, which may indicate that he's taller, but not necessarily. I want you to keep an eye out for anyone looking even remotely suspicious. We can't take any chances."

"You can count on me, sir."

"You can also warn the other servants what to look for, but they must be discreet," Beau continued. "I don't want them prattling about this to anyone outside the house and possibly alerting the brigand."

"I will guarantee their discretion, sir. You needn't worry."

"Thank you, Jasper," Beau replied, and heaved a laborious sigh. "I doubt that mere words could adequately express what I'd suffer if something happened to my wife...."

A faint smile softened the butler's normally stiff visage. "Perhaps not, sir, but your love for the madam has been made significantly more evident to us by your tender care of her. In my mind, that is proof of far greater value than mere words. I shan't disappoint you, sir. I once shamed myself by allowing Mr. Winthrop to throw the madam out into the cold rain. I couldn't live with myself if I allowed a similar occurrence to happen, much less something of a more serious nature."

Beau nodded, unable to find further words to speak, and returned to the bedroom. Upon espying the empty bed, he crossed to the dressing room, where he found his wife sitting before her dressing table smoothing her hair. She had garbed herself in a fresh gown and was looking beautifully unaffected by what she had just experienced. He stated the obvious. "You're not resting."

"I'm going down to have lunch with you," Cerynise informed him in a way that brooked no argument. "After you leave, I'll come back and rest."

Beau approved of her plan well enough to offer his arm. "Philippe should be back by now, madam. When I came home, I passed him on his way to the market. He told me that he was going to get you some fruit." He grinned down at her. "It seems you've been craving more of it lately."

"Philippe pampers me too much. And so do you, sir."

Affectionately Beau caressed her distended

505

stomach. "We both relish doing so, my pet, so let us have our pleasure."

"Yes, sir," she murmured with a loving smile, and yielded her brow to the doting kiss he placed upon it.

Several days later Beau walked home after work with a short, bald-headed companion. He ushered the man into the study, where Cerynise was filling in the background for the portrait of his mother and sisters, painting highlights and shadows to depict folds in a silken drapery, the soft sheen of which nearly amazed him with its realism. As she turned with a smile to welcome him, she caught sight of the wiry sailor and clapped her hands together in glee.

"Moon! My goodness, what are you doing here?"

The old tar had politely doffed his cap and now used it to punctuate his statements, first by indicating Beau. "Well, missy...yer husband... that is, Cap'n Birmingham here, wants me ta watch around this here house for a while just ta see if'n I can spy the toad what tried ta do ye hurt. I've been around a long time an' met a goodly number o' seamen, but I knows nary a one what's got a dog as mean as that there beasty the cap'n described. If'n I'm right, though, that brute might've been the one what was stolen only a few days ago from a couple o' English gents. They matched him for blood sport with other dogs. The animal kilt e'er one he fought, an' when he weren't fightin', his owners kept a muzzle on him ta make sure he didn't take a bite out o' none o' them. I knows for a fact they'd set off his temper by lettin' him go a day or two without food, which in me mind should've made him weaker. Not Hannibal. Whene'er they'd throw meat ta the other dog an' turn Hannibal loose, it became a savage fight ta the death."

"How gruesome." Cerynise shuddered. If it was truly the same one, then the poor animal had been sorely abused.

"Moon will be staying in the servants' quarters for a while," Beau informed her. "I've told him to watch over you in the garden while you're out there so Jasper can keep an eye out from the house."

Cerynise didn't really like the idea of the men having to watch over her. "I can't imagine the brigand trying anything like that again, Beau. He'd be a fool to. He'll surely get caught the next time."

"The sod may try to do something far worse, my pet, and I want to be ready for him when he does," Beau stated. "So oblige me by letting Moon look after you."

Cerynise moaned in petulant tones. "I hope the scoundrel is found ere the baby decides to come. Otherwise, Moon might get in the way."

Hurriedly setting her teacup aside, Heather left her chair and ran to pull the study door back for Cerynise, who was struggling to carry in a framed canvas which, only a moment ago, she had gone to fetch. The painting seemed far too immense for a woman to maneuver, especially one due to give birth in a month's time. "My goodness, dear, you're going to hurt yourself. Let me take that."

"Just help me get it through the door," Cerynise urged, huffing a bit from the exertion of her feat. "And don't look! I want this to be a surprise."

Together they wrestled the massive piece through the opening, and then with a sigh of relief, Cerynise braced the bottom of the frame against the Oriental rug that carpeted the room. "Now, Mama Heather, I'd like for you to take a chair beside Beau's desk. The light from the window will display the painting better from that angle." As she waited for her mother-in-law to take the indicated seat, she explained, "Beau selected the frames for both your portrait and this painting, and as I'm sure you'll agree, his choices are superb."

Heather's brows lifted in surprise. "But I thought this *was* the portrait...."

"Oh, no, this is a different one entirely. I'll bring your portrait in after you see this one. I just thought you might enjoy looking at your birthday gift first."

Heather waited eagerly as the framed piece was slowly turned, and then she caught her breath, overwhelmed by the girl's generosity. It was a portrait of Beau, lovingly painted and quite true to character. "Oh, Cerynise! It's magnificent! But how could you dare part with it?"

Cerynise smiled, pleased to bring such

delight to the woman who had proven to be as good a friend as any she had ever known. "I have the real Beau with me daily and can paint another one for myself."

"Bless you, child," Heather said fondly, struggling with a wealth of tears as she came forward to embrace the girl. "I don't know when I've ever been more pleased with a gift. Of course, you and Beau must come out now and help us decide where to hang the portraits. And then, I want to commission you to paint one of Brandon...*if* he will sit still long enough to let you."

Cerynise cast a dubious glance down at her protruding belly. "I'm afraid that project will have to wait until after the baby is born, Mama Heather. As round as I am now, I have a hard time reaching the canvas, and with another month to go, I know 'twill be nigh impossible."

A glow of amusement replaced the tears in Heather's eyes. "Oh, it will be such fun having a grandchild. I can assure you that everyone at Harthaven is thoroughly excited at the prospect of having a baby in the family again. Hatti is nearly beside herself at the prospect of another generation of Birminghams being born in the family."

Cerynise looked at her mother-in-law hesitantly. "Beau has been wondering if Hatti will be wanting to assist me during the birth. I'm afraid he's worried that she's getting too old. I've been seeing a doctor who lives down the road a piece, and I guess if it won't offend Hatti too much, I'd like for him to help in the delivery. He seems quite knowledgeable, and from what I've heard from some of the women who drop in for tea, he tends most of Charleston's elite...." She lifted her shoulders in a tiny shrug as she added, "Though I'm not sure that fact verifies his abilities very much."

"By all means, Cerynise, you do what you're most comfortable with," Heather urged with gentle understanding. "That's important to your well-being. Besides, Hatti realizes that she's not getting around very well anymore and can't take charge like she used to, but I'm sure she'd like nothing better than to be on hand when our grandchild is born, if only as a witness. And as for that, I think Brandon and I would like to be here, too...if that's all right with you."

"Oh, of course! You must! Beau will expect it." Cerynise laughed gaily. "We shall plan on having houseguests that last week...."

"And let us all hope there'll be no delays," Heather interjected with a chuckle.

"Now," Cerynise said, pressing her hands together, "the moment you've been waiting for has arrived. The portrait of you and your daughters is finished, and this time, I think I'll have Jasper bring it in for me. Would you like more tea in the meantime?"

Heather waved away the idea. "I may have another cup after the painting is fetched, but definitely not now, dear. You haven't allowed us to see the portrait at all, remember, and my curiosity is nearly eating me up."

510

After another moment of suspenseful waiting, Heather was presented with a second portrait, and all she could do was stare at it in awe, feeling much honored by the beautiful likeness of herself sitting between her two daughters. Cautiously she asked, "Do I really look like that? Or are you trying to be kind, dear child?"

Cerynise smiled, totally charmed by her mother-in-law's lack of vanity when, in truth, the woman had every right to be proud of her looks. "It's the way I see you...and the way Beau sees you. It's also the way Papa Brandon sees you. He said as much when he gave final approval to the painting. In all, I think it's a fair likeness of you and your daughters. They're just as beautiful, you know."

During all of her visits to acquaintances' residences in Charleston and the surrounding area, Heather couldn't remember ever having seen a more exquisite likeness of individuals than this portrait that Cerynise had painted. "I have no doubt that you'll be in high demand once visitors to our home view this painting and the one of Beau. Truly, Cerynise, there's no question that your talent far exceeds other artists in the area."

"I'm thrilled that you think so, but frankly, Mama Heather, I don't know that I'll have much time...or even the desire to paint that much after the baby comes." Cerynise smiled as she picked up the teapot and stepped near her guest to pour her another cupful. "I'm sure I'll be quite enchanted with having a little one to care for."

Heather laid a hand over the cup, fore-stalling Cerynise's effort to fill it. "I've changed my mind about the tea, my dear. How would you like to accompany me to Madame Feroux's? I'm having some new gowns made for fall, and I would greatly enjoy your company while I'm there. Sometimes that woman's incessant chatter wears on me. I'm sure you can understand since you've been there yourself. It would help tremendously if I'm fortified by a calmer companion."

Cerynise looked suddenly distressed. "I fear Moon would have to accompany us, Mama Heather." Then she pressed her hands alongside her belly worriedly. "And what will Madame Feroux think of me coming into her shop so late in my pregnancy?"

"You're looking absolutely beautiful, my dear," Heather rejoined with fervor, "and since you're Beau's wife, Madame Feroux will be eager to hear all of the details so she'll have something more to talk about. But tell me, dear, why must Moon accompany us?"

Cerynise lifted her shoulders briefly. "Beau is afraid something will happen to me and has given both Jasper and Moon the task of guarding me."

Heather raised an eyebrow wonderingly. She suffered no uncertainty that Beau and Cerynise were blissfully happy, but she hadn't realized her son was so possessive of his wife that he would set guards to spying on her. She didn't want to pry...well, perhaps not much.

"How long has Beau had these other men observing you?"

"Since the incident in the garden last month."

"What incident?"

Cerynise didn't want to worry the woman, but she had to talk to someone, and she thought Heather would understand. "I was cutting flowers in the garden when a man opened the back gate. He let in a monstrous dog and gave it a command to kill. The next thing I knew, the animal was snarling viciously and coming after me. Beau arrived home just in time to save me from being attacked. He killed the dog, and ever since then he refuses to let me out of his sight unless Jasper or Moon is watching after me. I know Beau is genuinely concerned, and heaven knows, the incident left me shaking for a whole week. But can you imagine having Moon and Jasper constantly underfoot?"

"I hadn't heard about the dog," Heather said, clearly worried. "Did the man get away?"

"Yes, that's why Beau is so anxious about my safety." Cerynise heaved a forlorn sigh. "Frankly, I'm beginning to feel like a prisoner in my own home, and although I keep telling myself that's not really the case, I always have someone standing guard, especially when I venture out to the garden. Why, I can't even go to the privy without Moon or Jasper being close by. It's terribly embarrassing, considering how often I have to go now."

"Would you like to come and stay at Harthaven until the man is caught?"

Cerynise shook her head and smiled. "Thank you for the invitation, Mama Heather, but I think I'd miss Beau too much if I did."

It was an unusually fine day, sunny but not too warm for July. The gentle breezes wafting in through the interior shutters that shaded the windows were heavily scented with the delectable fragrance of the tiny blossoms covering the sweet olive tree growing just outside. The drone of bees hovering over the profusion of flowers could be heard amid the soft, gentle cooing of doves. It was a day for strolling hand in hand with a beau or a husband, and if a walk took a couple in the direction of a secluded bower, then it was to be expected. It was definitely not a day for moping about.

"If you're willing to go with me, my dear, then Moon can sit beside my driver and escort us to the door of the shop. Would that suffice?"

"That should be enough." Cerynise smiled with more enthusiasm. "I think I'd enjoy an outing immensely."

" 'Twill do you good, my dear." Heather rose from her chair. "And you look delightful as you are, so if you'd like, we can leave now."

"Let me fetch Moon. No doubt Philippe will be relieved to have the man out of his kitchen. His temper has been sorely tested by the old sailor, who swears his French cuisine will be the death of him. Poor man, I think his stomach has been soured by all those sea victuals and hardtack he has been eating for most of his life."

Heather laughed. "Perhaps Moon needs an outing for Philippe's sake."

Beau had concluded his day's work at the warehouse and was just leaving when, from an upper-story window, he espied a familiar carriage pulling into the shipping yard. He recognized Moon sitting atop the conveyance and quickly concluded that his wife had been out and about with his mother. He hastened to lock up the safe and fetch his coat and top hat before taking his leave by way of the back stairs. By the time he descended, Cerynise was already out of the carriage and making her way across the yard toward him. She paused to await the passage of two six-in-hands that Beau determined were returning unusually late after unloading their cargo at another dock. The wagons were now empty and the teamsters, having finished their labor for the day, were no doubt anxious to tend the needs of the draft horses and leave for home. Beau waved to the men and then glanced down the street for some sign of the third one which had left the warehouse at the same time as the other two.

"Where's Charlie?" he called to the second teamster.

"He'll be comin' any moment now, Cap'n," the driver yelled back above the noisy rattling of his large dray. "He lost a wheel on the dock, an' we had ta stop an' help him. That's why we're so late."

Cerynise moved around the last wagon and, with a bright smile, hurried to meet her husband. "We thought we'd give you a ride home if you're acceptable to the idea."

"How can I resist such a winsome invitation?" Beau countered, his eyes glowing above a grin. He gallantly offered an arm and was in the process of escorting her back to the carriage when he remembered that he had left some important papers lying atop his desk.

Cerynise looked up at him as he stopped abruptly. "What's the matter?"

"I've got to go back to my office for a moment to get something, my pet."

"I'll wait for you," she eagerly volunteered.

He winked at her affectionately. "I won't be long."

As he left her, Cerynise tilted her bonneted head away from the late afternoon sun that now hovered above the rooftops of the tall warehouses across the street and readjusted her lace shawl around her shoulders, self-consciously trying as much as possible to conceal her rounded shape. The rumble of wheels and thudding hooves drew a brief glance from her, and she moved nearer the warehouse to give the third driver plenty of room to maneuver his six-in-hand and wagon toward the stables.

Barely an instant later, the energetic footfalls on the back stairs of the warehouse drew Cerynise's attention, and she turned to find her husband descending the last few steps. Beau tossed her a grin before opening his coat and sliding the papers inside an inner pocket, freeing his hands for the joyful honor of esquiring his wife back to his parents' coach.

When Beau lifted his head again, he noticed an elongated shadow of a man stretching across a portion of the cobblestone drive that separated him from Cerynise. He looked around, hoping to find a friend, but his hackles rose in sudden apprehension. Though a large floppy-brimmed hat shaded the fellow's face, his hulking form seemed distressingly familiar. Beau quickened his step, hoping to cut the man off before he reached Cerynise, but his haste seemed to provoke a similar response from the stranger, who sprinted toward her suddenly. As Beau raced forward, he cried out a warning to his wife, but in the next instant the man slammed his bulk into Cerynise, sending her reeling with a scream into the path of the oncoming team.

A startled shout erupted from Moon, who immediately began scrambling down from his perch. Treading on the heels of his cry, a higher-pitched scream was wrenched from Heather who clasped a quivering hand to her throat and watched in horror as her son hurled himself toward his falling wife. It seemed an impossible feat, and yet he swooped his arms around Cerynise in midair, enfolding her burdened form as he twisted. He lit on his back on the cobblestones, willingly accepting the brunt of their combined weights. Without pause, he rolled up on his knees and elbows and continued turning over and over, his large body protectively encompassing hers with limbs extended in a kneeling position as he exerted every measure of strength he was capable of mustering to protect Cerynise and their baby from harm.

Though the driver had slammed a booted foot against the wooden brake and sawed frantically on the reins to bring the steeds to a halt, the massive hooves thudded down upon the stones a hairsbreadth from Beau's still-turning form. When the couple finally rolled to safety, a fair amount of pandemonium erupted. With a curse Moon launched himself into action and struck out after the now-fleeing stranger at an amazing fleet-footed run. The two drivers raced from the stables while the third finally brought his draft horses to a standstill. He leapt down from his lofty seat just as Heather stumbled from the doorway of the carriage and ran on trembling legs toward her family.

"Are you hurt?" she demanded in a tone that approached panic. She was shaking uncontrollably, and though she tried to see what injuries they might have sustained, worried tears blurred her vision. "Oh, please, tell me you're both all right!"

"I think we are," Beau replied a bit uncertainly as he searched his wife's face for any visible signs of pain. Cerynise was too anxious about him to be concerned about herself. Even as he lifted himself off her and sat back upon his heels, she followed to examine his hands, arms and legs. It seemed only his clothing was beyond repair. His trousers were torn at the knees, which were now bloody, and his coat was badly frayed across the back and at the elbows.

"Yer pardon, Cap'n," the driver apologized in a shaky tone. "I just couldn't get me horses halted in time." He handed Beau his smashed top hat and the lace shawl that Cerynise had lost in their tumbling roll. The latter was now torn and blackened by hoof and wheel marks. "I was sure I had kilt ye both."

"It wasn't your fault, Charlie," Beau assured the skinner.

"I saw that awful man push her!" Heather exclaimed in outrage.

"Aye, we all saw it," the first driver declared. "He'd have kilt her if'n it hadn't been for the cap'n."

Even after her initial examination, the fierce set of Beau's features made Cerynise fear that he was still in pain. She pressed an unsteady hand to his breast and searched his face worriedly, seeing the muscles snapping rigidly in his lean cheeks. Only then did she realize that she was seeing a depth of rage that she had never known existed. The fierceness of it unmistakably diminished anything she had previously seen.

"Let's go home," she pleaded shakily, her eyes delving into those dark blue depths.

The seething rage in Beau's face ebbed until a tense smile tugged at his lips. "Aye, my love. Let's go home...where you'll be safe."

Several hours later, Beau sat in his study, turning over the events of the day in his mind as he stared fixedly at the top of his desk. His mother, who had been clearly distraught by the attempt on Cerynise's life, had been taken home by her driver. Cerynise was in their bedroom upstairs, sleeping beneath Bridget's watchful eye. From all outward appearances, his wife had managed to come through the incident like a trooper, yet her sudden lethargy convinced Beau that inwardly she was frightened. He had called the servants together and, after explaining what had happened, had informed them that effective immediately there would be someone on watch in the house at all times. Moon was the first to volunteer, declaring himself too vexed to sleep anyway.

Though for a few moments Beau had considered taking his wife to Harthaven, he had promptly decided that the plantation was not the safest place for her. In addition to all of the outbuildings, it was surrounded by literally miles of land that offered innumerable hiding places for the rapscallion to sequester himself. The main house itself had no fewer than a dozen entrances and far too many places for easy concealment. No, their house in Charleston could be defended much more easily until he could find the gutter-licking scum responsible and put an end to his miserable life. Nothing short of that solution would assuage his doubts that Cerynise was entirely safe from the knave.

Too bad he had let the man off so lightly on the *Audacious*.

When Moon had returned to the house bruised and bloody after trying unsuccessfully to stop the man from escaping, the old tar had reported that he had gotten a good look at the culprit during their brief scuffle. It was none other than Redmond Wilson, the same man who had taken an ax to the *Audacious* until Beau had disarmed him. In addition to the precautions Beau had set in force in the house itself, he also sent Stephen Oaks out with several crew members to prowl the streets for Wilson. If the renegade went into a tavern, visited a brothel, or so much as found a place to lay his head, Beau was confident that he would soon know about it.

Absently Beau rubbed his shoulder, feeling a painful twinge in the muscles there. At the time, he had hardly noticed the deep bruise he had inflicted upon himself when he dove across the cobblestones to save his wife from being trampled beneath the six-in-hand. But then, any harm to himself was insignificant when he compared it to the pain he would have suffered if Cerynise and their child had been harmed or killed. Such a loss would be similar to having his own heart ripped from his chest.

Thinking of what had almost been taken from him filled Beau with a sudden, insatiable need to hold his wife within his arms and feel the steady rhythm of her heart against his own. Purposefully he strode from the study and ascended the stairs. Bridget rose as soon as he entered the darkened bedroom. It was Cerynise's wont to leave the draperies open on moonlit nights, and by the dim glow shining through the windows, he readily discerned the maid's distress. The worry in her eyes readily conveyed the fact that she was desperately afraid for her mistress. Nothing was said. There was no need, for they shared a common fear.

Bridget left with a muted "Good night," and Beau quietly closed the door behind her. He crossed to the four-poster and, for a long moment, stood gazing down upon the delicate features of his wife. A shaft of silver light streaming across the bed illumined her face. She seemed untroubled by dreams and, to him, as innocent as an angel. How could any man in his right mind want to harm her? he wondered morosely. The idea was ludicrous and yet, all too true.

Doffing his clothes, Beau left them hanging on the silent butler in the dressing room. When he slipped underneath the top-sheet, he snuggled close to Cerynise and laid a hand upon the rounded mound of her stomach. In a moment he was rewarded by a movement of his child, and with a heart swelling with relief, he pressed his lips into his wife's fragrant hair. A soft, contented sigh slipped from her lips as she nestled her head beneath his chin and stroked a hand over his hardened chest.

"I love you," she murmured drowsily.

His voice was fraught with emotion as he answered her in kind. "And I love you, madam...truly, deeply, and forever."

CHAPTER 16

"No trace of the brigand has been found, you say," Brandon mused aloud. "Is it possible that he has fled the area?"

July had flown and August was advancing to a ripe old age, yet there was still no sign of Wilson. More than a week ago, Beau had come to the conclusion that the sailor had likely escaped to other climes after Moon had recognized him, causing Beau to give serious consideration to extending the search throughout the Carolinas and, if necessary, the entire South. Should it come to that, he knew by offering a generous bounty in every port in the world, the man would eventually be apprehended. There was no place where the beast could hide that a goodly sum of money couldn't find him. It would only be a matter of time.

Until then, it was impossible for Beau to rest entirely at ease either day or night. He was always on the watch for the rogue and acutely leery of taking Cerynise outside their home. If Wilson was still in the area, the man could easily resort to using a pistol and, from behind any tree, wait for them to appear. Yet, in spite of his own vexation, Beau had tried to spare his wife, making a brave show while keeping her entertained with stories of his seafaring adventures, revealing more than he would have ever done otherwise. Fortunately, his parents had joined him in his endeavors to keep her distracted. His mother had ventured to their house almost daily and had even brought Hatti in to stay throughout the next weeks just in case the baby decided to come in the middle of the night or while the doctor was away delivering another baby. His father was forever buying Cerynise books on art, babies, or any subject he thought she might be interested in reading. Finally Beau had decided that he needed his parents' company as much as his wife did and had asked if they'd be willing to come in and stay with them until after the birth of the child. The fact that they had arrived with baggage a mere trio of hours after he had sent the summons assured Beau that they had been anxious to come but reluctant to intrude unless bidden.

Despite the worry and rage that never strayed far from Beau, the days passed pleasantly enough even though Cerynise tired more easily in these, the final stages of her pregnancy. As a result, the household retired fairly soon after an early supper, allowing Beau to ease his wife's discomfort in the privacy of their bedroom. In recent days, he had noticed her massaging her back and getting around much more slowly as her burden lowered in her belly. She was usually more comfortable in bed after he rubbed her back or when she could prop her legs across his. Snuggling beside him with their heads on the same pillow was always relaxing to her. Sometimes they would talk for a time while he held her close within his arms, but more often than not she would fall asleep listening to the low murmur of his voice. Not so Beau. He remained alert for long hours afterwards, keenly attuned to the sounds of the house, his mind constantly roaming in search of a plan that could be set into play to fully guarantee his wife's safety.

It was the third week in August, into the wee hours of the morning, when Beau was snatched abruptly from a sound sleep, his mind instantly alert to danger. After bounding from the bed, he ran to the window where he searched the night-shrouded shadows cloaking the yard. Behind him, Cerynise murmured restlessly, no longer comforted by his presence. Beau cast his gaze over a shoulder and watched as she drew up in a small knot upon the mattress, as if distressed or disturbed by some discomfort. Whatever it was, caused her brows to gather in a harsh frown, but in the passing of a moment, the scowl eased. Without waking, she rolled to his side of the bed and snuggled her face against his pillow, breathing in deeply and then releasing a long, blissful sigh as if savoring the scent of it even in her sleep. Beau, however, was fully conscious, and the odor he was smelling didn't sit well with him at all.

It was smoke!

Peering intently through the windows, he searched the garden and surrounding area along the north side of the house for any sign of a fire. Everything seemed normal enough, but that didn't necessarily mean that it was. The acrid scent was growing stronger by the moment, wafting in with the soft breezes that swept into the room. He lifted his gaze to the tops of the trees and saw their boughs gently swaying to and fro, their leaves flickering beneath the light of the moon. There was some hope, of course, that the wind was carrying the smoke from a more distant place. He could only pray that was all it was, but he rather suspected the breezes were coming from a more southerly direction, for even at this early morning hour, they seemed much warmer than they had been in some days.

Beau snatched up a pair of trousers and, thrusting his feet through the leggings, stood up to hitch the garment up over his naked loins. He lit the wick of a hurricane lamp, adjusted it, and resettled the glass globe. Then he rechecked the pistol that he had been recently keeping in his bedside table and slipped it into his belt before taking up the lamp and making his way from the room. He passed the landing above the stairs and strode down the hall toward the bedroom where his parents were ensconced. He was about to rap his knuckles lightly against the door when it was yanked inward, revealing his father, who had donned his trousers with similar haste. He was also carrying a lamp.

"Where's it coming from?" Brandon whispered and glanced up and down the hallway as he stepped out. Reaching back, he closed the door behind him, taking care not to awaken his wife.

"I'm not sure, Pa. It may only be a fire farther away on the docks. If the wind is blowing in the right direction, we usually get some of the smoke here. Something happened like this last year."

"Let's look around downstairs to make sure," Brandon suggested. "But first, we'd better light some sconces here in the hallway just in case we have to race back and get the women up."

In a few moments, they made a cautious descent to the lower floor and prowled through each room, searching for some indication of a fire before moving on to the next. The house was wreathed in silence, but nothing seemed amiss despite their growing awareness of smoke. Going off in a different direction than his son, Brandon wandered down the corridor toward the kitchen. Upon entering the room, he found the back door standing open and a manly form crumpled across the threshold.

"Beau," he called quietly. "Come take a look at this."

Turning the unconscious man over, Brandon muttered a curse as he noted the bloody gash across the young houseman's brow. He glanced around as Beau joined him. "Whoever did this certainly meant for this poor fellow to be out for a while."

Beau raised his gaze and squinted against the light of his lantern as he peered past the covered terrace buttressing the house and probed the shadows of the garden. Noticing a flickering glow being cast into the area from the south side, he stepped over Cooper's prostrate form and crept to the end of the porch, keeping a watchful eye out for anyone lurking in the gloom. When he reached the end of the terrace, he finally discovered where the smoke was coming from. The fence along the street side had been set ablaze some time earlier. What remained of the barrier wouldn't have been enough to warm their backsides even for a few moments on a cold winter's night.

"Cooper was on watch tonight, Pa," Beau stated in sudden alarm as he ran back to his father, who was wrapping a cold, wet compress around the servant's head. "The culprit probably set the fence on fire to lure Cooper out and hit him as soon as he stepped out. Someone may already be in the house."

"You'd better check upstairs to make sure the women are all right and get them up," Brandon urged, lifting the houseman and draping him over a broad shoulder. "I'll take Cooper to his quarters and wake the rest of the servants."

As his father left, Beau ran down the corridor toward the central hall. He was about to leap up the stairs when he noticed the north garden area flickering with light. Snatching the pistol from his belt, he raced to the window, threw it open, and leaned out in time to see a large, darkly garbed man sprinting around the front corner of the house. Flames were already leaping up from a burning mound of dry kindling that had been piled up beneath the edge of the house. A torch had been dropped alongside, no doubt after the arsonist had heard the window open.

Beau dashed back to the kitchen door and yelled out to his father, "Pa! Wilson's trying to burn us out! He has already started another fire on the north side of the house. Tell the servants to hurry and put it out! If you see Wilson coming around the back of the house, yell! I'm going out the front now to see if I can catch him."

"Kill the bastard!"

"I plan to," Beau muttered, whirling back into the house. He set aside the lamp and ran to the front door, but to his horror he found the portal standing open. Barely an instant later a sudden scream from upstairs sent shards of ice-cold dread shooting through him. Pivoting sharply about, he raced across the hall and leapt up the stairs three at a time. He was less than midway in his ascent when he saw Cerynise and his mother above the landing, but they were not alone. A masked man in black garb, lean and of more than average height, had seized Cerynise from behind and had an arm clamped tightly around her, effectively keeping hers pinned to her sides. In his right hand the brigand held a pistol directed toward Beau.

Heather displayed a fair amount of outraged zeal as she pummeled the intruder with her fists and kicked him sharply with a satin mule. She proved too much of a distraction for the rogue, for the man turned on her with a snarl, lifting the hand that held the pistol. He tapped the butt of it against her chin and promptly sent her slithering unconscious to the floor.

Beau's ire soared to unparalleled heights as he bounded up the stairs, but the brigand whirled to face him once again, this time pressing the bore of his weapon against Cerynise's temple. Beau froze in sudden alarm, causing the man to chortle gleefully. Emboldened by the control he held over the seafaring captain, he motioned Beau to retreat, briefly flicking the hand that held Cerynise. Beau had no choice but to slowly, obediently retrace his steps down the stairs. The black-swathed villain cautiously followed, using Cerynise as his living shield.

Beau was nearing the middle curve in the stairs when the assailant paused above him. The eyeholes in the mask gleamed with reflected light as he swept his gaze about, taking close account of his surroundings. Though only a fourth of the way down, he could see part of the front door that was standing open.

In a deep, gravelly voice that seemed oddly exaggerated, the assailant mocked Beau. "I could kill your wife now, you know, and save myself the trouble of coming back later, but of course, if I do that, I'd lose a chance to escape, for I cannot hope to kill you both. As much as it displeases me to leave here without completing my errand, I guess I'll just have to wait until a more opportune time to finish the bitch off."

Without further warning, he yanked his arm from Cerynise and thrust her forward, snatching a scream from her as he sent her hurtling down the stairs toward her husband. Beau threw himself forward to catch her, but the impact of their collision knocked him backward, causing him to lose his balance. Even as he sought to hold Cerynise on top of him and cushion her fall with his own body, Beau saw their foe leap over the balustrade to the floor below and rush off toward the front portal. The slamming of the door attested to the brigand's success in fleeing the scene of his crime.

"Damnation!" Brandon roared as he came charging into the hallway and espied the tangled forms of his son and daughter-in-law thumping down the last few steps. They came to rest on the marble floor, prompting him to ask in concern, "Are you two all right?"

"I'm not sure," Cerynise answered, trying to subdue a wince as she pushed herself upright.

Having descended headfirst and on his back down the stairs, Beau was sure he had bruises he wasn't even aware of yet, but there was no time to think of himself. Twisting around to look up at his father, he urged, "Pa, you'd better see about Mama. That bilge scum hit her with a pistol hard enough to knock her out."

Rage tore through Brandon as he flew up the stairs, but when he caught sight of his wife lying unconscious on the landing, his fury soared. At that moment he was certain he could have committed outright murder on her attacker. Gently he picked her up and carried her into their bedroom, where he laid her on the bed. After wetting a cloth, he pressed it to the darkly swelling bruise on her jaw. To his relief, Heather's eyes soon fluttered open. Becoming cognizant of his concern, she tried to reassure him with a smile but caught herself and groaned as she gingerly tested her jaw. "Oooh, it hurts."

"Aye, madam, and so it should," her husband whispered, stroking his fingers affectionately through the tumbled curls snuggled against her cheek. "You have a very dark bruise on your chin where that toad hit you."

Everything came flooding back to Heather in an instant, and she had to be physically restrained from leaving the bed. "Cerynise!" she cried anxiously. "That man was trying to kill her!"

"Rest easy, madam. He wasn't successful," Brandon informed her. "Right now, your daughter-in-law is downstairs with Beau."

"Unharmed?"

"She appeared to be when I left them, but she was trying to untangle herself from your son at the bottom of the stairs, and they gave me no explanation how that came about."

"I'd better go see about her," Heather said, making another attempt to leave the bed, but the room promptly dipped and began to whirl around her, drawing a disconcerted groan from her. "Perhaps I won't after all."

At that precise moment, the object of Heather's concern was sitting beside Beau on the marble floor. Cerynise was clearly distressed but not for any reason her mother-in-law might have suspected after such a fright. Gingerly she smiled back at her husband before confiding in some embarrassment, "Beau, I hate to worry you any more than you are right now, but it seems that I'm all wet. I think the fall might have broken my water."

Startled, he looked down at the pool of liquid she sat in and the small spots of bloody discoloration of her robe. "That's not all, madam. You're bleeding."

She spread a hand over her belly and felt its tautness. Even before she had become cognizant of the heated reprimand that Heather had been diligently laying upon the intruder, Cerynise had awakened to a growing discomfort in her back and a sticky seepage between her legs. There was, of course, only one conclusion which could be rationally drawn. "I think our baby was making plans on being born today even before that horrible man came into our house."

"Great stars in heaven, madam!" Beau swore, scrambling to his feet. "I'd better fetch Hatti and send someone for the doctor."

Cerynise looked up at him pleadingly. "Do you suppose you could help me to our bed first? This marble is terribly uncomfortable."

"Should've thought of that first," Beau mumbled in some chagrin as he scooped her up in his arms. "Not very gallant of me to leave a lady in distress."

She giggled and looped her arms around his neck. "That's all right. I forgive you. After all, you're my knight in shining armor. But I must say, if you take too many more tumbles with me, you're going to be crippled before your time."

"As long as I grow old with you, madam," he replied softly, "then I'll be satisfied."

Once in their bedroom Cerynise bade him to stand her to her feet beside their bed and help strip away her soiled robe and nightgown. "I know I'm not very nice to look at without my clothes now," she said sheepishly, clutching her arms before her naked body as he brought back a clean gown from her chest-on-chest. "But hopefully it won't be too long before I get my shape back and we can make love together again."

"I think you're beautiful now, madam," Beau whispered, touching a kiss to her brow. He recognized the glow of love in her eyes and felt immensely blessed by his good fortune. Shaking out her nightgown, he lifted it above her head as she raised her arms. "After all, you're carrying our child, and that makes you more than lovely to me."

"Does it matter to you what we have?" she questioned through the garment as she slipped her hands through the sleeves.

"As long as the babe is healthy and well

formed, I'll be delighted no matter what gender it is."

Cerynise's head came free, and she grinned up at him as he pulled her long hair out of the gown, allowing it to fall in tumbling waves down her back. "Have I yet told you this morning that I love you?"

Beau glanced toward the windows. "Considering it's still dark outside, I guess you haven't."

Wrapping her arms around his lean waist, she pressed a kiss upon his naked chest. "Then I'm telling you now, sir. Your wife loves you immensely."

Beau laid his arms around her shoulders. "Well, madam, your husband *adores* you, so there."

Suddenly Cerynise turned aside and doubled over in pain. She clutched his fingers in a desperate grip as he supported her with an arm wrapped around her back. After a moment she gasped, "I think you'd better spread the linens that Hatti prepared on the bed."

"Wouldn't you like to lie down first?" he asked worriedly

"Not until the linens are laid out. I don't want to soil the mattress."

It was simpler to placate her than to argue, Beau decided, and made haste to perform her wishes. In another moment she was lying back upon the pillows.

"I'd better go fetch Hatti now," he told her and hurried out. He paused briefly at his parents' door to announce that Cerynise had gone into labor before making his descent.

"Hatti, where are you?" he called after reaching her quarters and finding them empty.

"Right here, Mistah Beau," the black woman answered from the yard. Stepping to a place where he could see her, she looked at him curiously. "What yo' be wantin' me for?"

"The baby's coming!" he declared.

Hatti nodded knowingly. "I 'spected 'twas time, the way Miss Cerynise's burden done lowered in her belly these past few days."

"She's upstairs in our bedroom."

"I'll be along directly, Mistah Beau," the woman reassured him, waving away his concern. "As soon as I get washed an' dressed, then I'll be up. There ain't nothin' gonna happen in betwixt time."

"I'd better send someone to fetch the doctor."

"If'n I was yo', Mistah Beau, I'd wait a spell for that, seein's as how this be Miz Cerynise's first chile. It may be hours before the babe comes...."

"Hours?" Beau felt the color drain from his own face, and suddenly his knees seemed far too weak to support him. "That long?"

"I'll know directly," she replied, taking pity on him.

Beau unwillingly turned his attention to other matters. The servants were extinguishing what remained of the fire on the side of the house. The damage was insignificant and could be easily repaired. For that, he was thankful, but the charred fence along the street would have to be torn down completely and rebuilt immediately to keep the backyard reasonably safe for Cerynise.

The wind had died away, and morning had softened the sky to a cloudy, sultry gray when Beau resettled himself in a chair in the master bedroom and raised his head in an effort to stretch the kinks out of his neck. Cerynise was still in labor, and at present, Heather was sitting beside her on the bed, holding her hand. His mother had refused to listen to any more of his pleas that she should go to her room and rest. Beau had finally, reluctantly, acquiesced to the fact that she would stay. Brandon had recognized his wife's unswerving determination from the very beginning and had known better than to argue. If he had learned anything in their lengthy marriage together, it was that Heather Birmingham could be quite willful at times. Obviously this was one of those occurrences.

"I think *you* should get some sleep," Heather murmured sympathetically, turning that same kind of consideration upon her son, who was trying desperately to cope with his growing anxiety. Several moments passed before her words finally penetrated, but Beau shook his head, not trusting himself to speak.

Cerynise's eyes settled lovingly upon her husband, and he returned her gaze in frank adoration. After a glance between them, Heather decided the couple needed some time to be alone together. Bestowing a smile upon her daughter-in-law, she patted her hand and moved away from the bed with an excuse. "I'm going down to see how that nice young man, Cooper, is doing, and then I'm going to have Philippe cook us up some breakfast. Until then, I think the two of you could stand some privacy."

Hatti agreed wholeheartedly and, with a chuckle, waddled toward the door. "Yell or somethin' if'n ya'll needs us."

Beau waited until the door had closed behind the two women before he crossed the room and stretched out on the bed beside his wife. Pressing close, he rested his head near hers on the same pillow. "Does it hurt much?"

Cerynise threaded her fingers through the long, lean ones that reached out to her and brought them to her lips for a kiss. "The pain comes and goes," she murmured, lifting soft, liquid eyes to his. "Otherwise, I'm doing fine, according to Hatti."

"Are you afraid?" he asked, gently sweeping his hand over the mound of her stomach.

"Not with you beside me."

His hand paused. "And when I have to leave?"

"I don't want you to." Her fingers lightly caressed the back of his hand. "I can stand anything as long as you're with me."

It was some time later when Beau heard Hatti's footsteps approaching the bedroom door. Immediately he pressed a kiss upon his wife's brow and swung his long legs over the side of the bed. As he collected clean clothes from his armoire, he tossed Cerynise a grin before he promised, "I'll be back as soon as I get washed and dressed. Then I'll stay with you through it all."

Her eyes filling with tears of relief, Cerynise nodded. She hardly took a breath before a long, slow tightening across her belly alerted her once again. Even so, she braved a smile, sending her husband on his way.

In the ensuing hours the pressure intensified, and by noon the contractions had reached a degree that Cerynise could no longer conceal her discomfort from her husband. Though no cry slipped past her clenched teeth, it was impossible for Beau to ignore the marked tensing of her body and the sharp grimaces that accompanied the contractions. While Bridget stood nearby fanning her mistress, he stayed beside the bed, his face taut with concern as his wife squeezed his fingers in a tenacious grip. Seeking to give her relief in the only way he could, he bathed her face gently with a wet cloth and brushed sweat-dampened tendrils from her brow and cheeks as he offered words of encouragement.

The heat of August could not be easily subdued. Not a breath of air stirred, and as the afternoon progressed, the second-story bedroom became stifling. Yet, for the sake of modesty, Cerynise tried to keep herself covered with a sheet. It was Beau who kept dragging the linen away to wash her arms, legs and feet with cool water. With the wafting breezes Bridget created with the fan, Cerynise had to admit that, when her arms and legs were lightly dampened, it brought her greater relief from the sweltering warmth.

Dr. Wilhelm was fetched about two in the afternoon, and upon his arrival, it became evident that he was used to taking charge and imposing his mandates in similar situations. Quite blatantly he told Beau that he was dismissed henceforth from the bedroom. The look of panic that swept over his wife's face wrenched Beau's heart, and he began to argue for a right to stay.

"I'll brook no refusal from you, young man!" the physician firmly declared. "I don't want to see you in this room until after your child is born. Now find yourself something else to do beyond the confines of this bedroom, because you're not staying."

Heather and Hatti exchanged worried glances, for both of them could see that Beau was preparing to wage war. To forestall such an event, Heather went to her son and sweetly urged, "Go downstairs with your father, Beau. We'll watch over Cerynise."

"I should stay here...."

Emerging from yet another pain-shrouded seizure, Cerynise eyed the doctor with a great degree of apprehension, wondering if she could abide his officious attitude. As if his confrontation with Beau wasn't enough, the doctor began complaining that there were too many people in the room to suit him and started banishing piecemeal those whom he considered unnecessary, beginning with

540

Bridget. The maid was uncertain whose orders to follow. Having been summoned for the purpose of cooling Cerynise as much as possible, she could see an ongoing need for her presence. She glanced from her mistress to Beau in plaintive appeal, hoping one of them would advise her.

"What should I do?" she whispered, searching Beau's tensed features.

"Your mistress needs you...." he began, but he was rudely interrupted by the strong-willed physician.

"Get out of here, girl! And you'd better be quick about it!" Dr. Wilhelm barked irately. Having seized dictatorial authority, he thrust a stubby finger toward the door, sending the maid fleeing in tears.

Abruptly he turned on Hatti, who calmly set her arms akimbo and stood like an invincible bastion, daring him to try the same tactic with her. From the stubborn set of her jaw, Dr. Wilhelm apparently decided that she was a hopeless cause and directed his attention once more to Beau, who hadn't budged. Cerynise could believe by the darkening glower on her husband's face that he was just as outraged with the doctor as she was. She thought it prudent to intervene. "Go sit with your father, Beau. I'll be all right."

The doctor took that as all the permission he needed to lay a firm hand on Beau's arm in a quest to hasten him toward the door. "We don't need fathers assisting in the delivery of their offspring," he announced impertinently.

"Your wife will be much better off without you fretting over her."

"Get your hands off me," Beau snarled, his eyes slicing through the man's pinch-faced frown. "If I leave, 'twill be without your damned escort."

Dr. Wilhelm blustered in the face of such rage and took offense. "I beg your pardon, sir!"

Hatti interceded before any harm could befall the unwise physician. Taking Beau's arm, she hauled him toward the door. "Go sit with yo' pappy, Mistah Beau. Leave de doctor alone so's he can help Miz Cerynise."

Beau was thrust into the hall and the door slammed shut in his face before he could argue with the woman. With fists clenched, he stepped back to the portal, but he quickly realized he wouldn't be helping Cerynise by getting into a row with the doctor. Heaving a frustrated sigh, he complied with Hatti's wishes...at least for the moment.

Brandon met his son at the bottom of the stairs and, laying a comforting arm around his shoulders, led him into the study. Once in the room, he pressed a brandy snifter into Beau's hand and attempted to take the younger man's mind momentarily off his problems. "Did I ever tell you about the night you were born?"

Beau gulped down half the fiery liquid without even tasting it. "No, Pa...I don't believe you did."

"Your mother insisted that she had to have a blue nightgown, something about boys not wearing pink. She drove me mad. I was

542

thoroughly convinced that you were going to be dropped on your head right there in the middle of the room." As he spoke, he refilled Beau's glass and pushed him gently into a chair. "Hatti finally kicked me out. I was in such a state, I didn't even know what I was drinking that night."

After having sampled for himself the stress associated with having a wife in labor, Beau could appreciate how distraught his father must have been. As for himself, he didn't know if he could bear the likes of such trauma more than once in a lifetime. "What about when Suzanne and Brenna were born?"

"Much easier," Brandon assured him. "Of course, they were also smaller, which helped."

Beau tossed down the contents of the glass and held it out for another refill as his eyes met his father's. "Hatti said earlier that she thinks this baby will be fairly good sized. I just hope not *too* large."

Neither said anything more after that, for there was nothing else to be said. Beau had expressed the depth of his fears in that one statement.

Two more hours passed, and there was still no word from above. Beau found it impossible to sit still and began pacing back and forth across the room. Brandon managed to get him into a game of chess, but when his offspring lost to carelessness three times in a row, he took pity on him. Philippe, who was himself anxiously fretting, came into the study to announce that he had finally managed to prepare some food if either man wanted nourishment. The chef could have saved himself the bother. Neither son nor father had any interest in eating.

Philippe had barely stepped out of the study when a muted cry from above brought Beau out of his chair. Even if it hadn't sounded like his name, Beau's reaction would have been the same. Sprinting across the hall, he vaulted up the stairs as the chef stared after him, much agog at the swiftness of his flight. In the years he had worked for the captain, he couldn't remember a time when the man had moved so briskly, impossible though it might have seemed ere this moment, considering the fact that the captain had proven time and again that he was just as nimble of foot as he was quick of wit.

Not bothering to knock, Beau flung the bedroom door open and strode in. Dr. Wilhelm whirled from the bed, totally aghast at this interference. Immediately he tried to shoo the younger man out. "I told you before that you weren't needed in here! Now kindly remove yourself forthwith!"

Heather laid a gentle hand upon the physician's arm and quietly murmured, "Cerynise needs her husband here, and he wants to be with her. I would advise you, sir, not to protest any more."

"This is absurd!" he ranted, ignoring her counsel. "I've never yet allowed a father to be present at the birth of a child. Why, it's unheard of!"

544

"Then perhaps it's time you revise your thinking," Heather suggested. "Who has a better right to be a witness than the father of the child?"

"I won't stand for this!" he rumbled.

"You may leave," Cerynise gasped from the bed. Her husband had fallen to his knees beside the bed and was gripping her hand in a way that was far more comforting than the presence of the doctor. "I think Hatti will be able to assist me from now on."

"Yas'um!" The black woman grinned broadly as the doctor turned a glare upon her. Angrily he whipped down the sleeves of his shirt and began buttoning the cuffs. Glaring about him, he swept up his coat, snapped his satchel closed, and stalked out of the room without another word. Hatti followed as far as the door and, from there, yelled down for Bridget to get herself upstairs and "Fan this poor, suffering chile in this beastly hot furnace."

Hatti won another glower from the doctor which he tossed at her from the stairs, but she cackled in glee and sashayed her broad self back into the bedroom.

The black woman had barely closed the door when Cerynise cried in alarm, "Oh, Hatti, I think the baby is coming! Truly I do!"

The soothing strokes of the wet cloth that Heather plied across her daughter-in-law's cheeks and brow did nothing to diminish the flush of color that flooded into Cerynise's face as she strained to thrust the child from her loins. The impulse was too great to be subdued. Clenching her teeth, she raised her head off the pillow and bore down, all the while squeezing her husband's hand in a grip that nearly astounded him.

"Yas'um! It's a-comin'!" Hatti affirmed after pushing aside the sheet, a covering which the doctor had insisted upon. She promptly swept the girl's nightgown out of the way and prepared the necessary items.

Bridget came running into the room but Cerynise no longer had her mind on preserving propriety. She was straining for all she was worth. Beau had risen and was staring fixedly at the bloody black head emerging from her body. It thrust free in a sudden surge, and immediately the wrinkled creature gave a muted squall, evoking laughter from everyone in the room, including Cerynise.

"Jes' rest yo'self a moment, Miz Cerynise," Hatti advised, " 'cause yo' gonna be pushin' again real hard any time now." She had hardly spoken when the pain began anew and the urge to bear down seized hold of Cerynise once again. A chortle came from Hatti as she observed the results. "Here comes the shoulders, an' they's as wide as I've ever seen. It's gotta be a boy with shoulders like that."

"He certainly has a fine pair of lungs," Beau commented, rather awed by the lusty wails and the relentless miracle of birth.

Bridget busily fanned her mistress while taking everything in. She had never seen a baby born before, but after Stephen Oaks's recent proposal of marriage, they were already dreaming of having a large family.

The newest Birmingham gave another outraged squall as he was thrust completely into the world and into the waiting hands of Hatti. He flailed his tiny fists and turned beet red as he was laid upon his mother's stomach. At that precise moment and forever afterwards, Beau would firmly attest to the belief that his son looked straight at him and stopped crying.

"Isn't he beautiful!" Cerynise cooed, still holding her husband's hand.

Heather proudly agreed. "He'll look like his father with all that curling black hair."

Bridget was just as enthralled. "Oh, he's darlin'."

"When can I hold him?" Beau asked eagerly.

"Aftah I ties an' cuts the cord an' cleans him up a bit, Mistah Beau," Hatti replied. "Jes' be patient."

It was several moments before the baby was delivered into his father's arms. Beau stared down at the puckered little face with a feeling of wonder. The child's eyes were wide open, and he looked back at his father with what Beau proudly surmised as keenly intelligent interest. With a laugh of sheer exaltation, he carried their son to Cerynise and gently placed him within the crook of her arm. Together they examined the wonder they had wrought, spreading the tiny fingers and smoothing the silken wisps of black hair.

Heather went downstairs to give Brandon the news of their grandson while Hatti finished

547

up what needed to be done. It was the grand-father's loud whoop of pure joy that brought Philippe running into the study.

"It's a boy, Philippe!" Heather announced happily. "A strong, healthy, black-haired boy!"

"And Madame Birmingham?" he queried hesitantly. "She is all right?"

Heather nodded enthusiastically. "She couldn't be happier."

"Excellent!" he cried jubilantly.

Upstairs in the master bedroom, Hatti leaned over for a better peek at the new Birmingham and grinned broadly. "Well now, li'l mistah, yo'd better thank yo' mammy for all she's done 'cause yo's the finest babe I've seen since Mistah Jeff's Tamarah was born. Yassah, an' dat's the gospel!"

Cerynise could hardly believe she was holding her own child in her arms, one sired by Beau Birmingham. The baby was not only fair-sized, he was also vigorous and alert despite the trauma she had gone through after being shoved into the way of the six-in-hand and, more recently, down the stairs. Already, he was rooting around with clear intent, and when he didn't get what he sought, he wailed again in indignation.

"Just listen ta that chile!" Hatti cackled. "He's gonna have a temper jes' like all de rest o' de Birmingham men!"

Cerynise raised glowing eyes to Beau. "Did we ever settle on a name?"

He stroked his fingers across hers. "What

about Marcus for your father, Bradford for your mother's last name...and Birmingham for me?"

Tears of joy filled her eyes. They had never once discussed his present proposal. She tested the sound of the names altogether. "Marcus Bradford Birmingham. Quite a name for such a tiny little boy."

"He'll grow into it," Beau averred with a chuckle. "Do you like it?"

"Yes, my dearest love. Absolutely, and thank you for remembering my parents."

"I owe them a debt of gratitude for having such a beautiful daughter. We certainly made a fine son together, didn't we, my sweet?"

Cerynise proudly surveyed their accomplishment and thought she glimpsed a sapphire glint in her son's eyes. Even the wee one's expression somehow reflected the more thoughtful facial cast of his sire. "As far as I can determine from looking at our baby, my love," she murmured with a warm, tender smile, "I did all the work, but you'll be getting all the glory."

"How so, my sweet?" Beau asked, perplexed.

"Like father, like son. I have a feeling he's going to look as much like you as you resemble your father."

"Do you really think so?"

His eager question drew an amused chuckle from his wife. "Don't preen your fine feathers too soon, my fancy peacock. I may find a little of me in him yet."

"Without you, my pet," her husband softly whispered above her lips, "our baby wouldn't even be here."

Master Marcus Bradford Birmingham grew at a rate that astounded his parents, thrilled his grandparents, and impressed even his Great-uncle Sterling, who, though admitting himself no expert on babies, pronounced the youngster as "very fine indeed." Beau was clearly besotted with the youngster whose very existence filled him with wonder and joy. He was eager to share in Marcus's care. He thought nothing of fetching the boy when he woke in the middle of the night and bringing him to Cerynise for her to nurse him. He held him, rocked him and talked to him as if the babe could understand every word he said. And truly, Marcus seemed attentive enough to watch the elder and purse his lips as if he were but waiting for his chance to speak. Beau even went so far as to scandalize Hatti by changing the small one's diapers. Already the sight of Beau and his son happily absorbed in one another was becoming commonplace in the household.

Cerynise found a joy in motherhood that vastly exceeded anything she had anticipated. Whether she sat with her son at her breast, bathed, rocked or merely sang a lullaby to him, she felt wonderfully complete as a woman. It was as if she had become connected to some emotion that was infinitely precious, loving and maternally fulfilling. When she was thusly involved, she was certain that all the ordinary concerns of the outside world had dwindled to nonexistence.

By the time the first month's anniversary of his birth had rolled past, Marcus had become quite enamored with the idea of being nurtured with sustenance from his mother's breast. He raised such a row when he wasn't punctually placated that almost everyone in the house was made aware that it was time for him to be fed. The moment he was either taken up in his mother's arms or laid in them, he immediately recognized the fact that she was the right person to satisfy his growing appetite and would start rooting at her breast. If anything hindered that connection, he let his mother know he was extremely upset. His appetite proved voracious, but to Cerynise's great relief, she had no difficulty meeting it.

"He's starting off rather young, isn't he?" Cerynise asked her husband, her lovely lips drawn up in a teasing smile. At the moment the baby was kneading her breast with his tiny fists as he sucked ravenously at her nipple.

Beau looked on with doting pride. "In what way, my dear?"

"He's not the only one in the family who likes to be nurtured at my breast."

Her husband gave her a meaningful look above a slow grin. "I'm anxiously awaiting my turn, madam. I quite clearly remember Hatti saying that you should have about six weeks to properly heal. So another week or so should see us back on intimate terms again."

"If I don't get waylaid in the meantime," she needled sweetly.

"A little fondle here and there keeps the spirits alive, madam," he argued, trying to curb the telltale twitching of his lips as he defended his entrapment of his wife in their dressing room earlier that morning. She had barely donned her chemise when he decided he wanted to take a longer look and do a little exploring. "You've gotten back your beautiful figure, and I just like to admire it, that's all."

"Oh, I don't mind," Cerynise smilingly asserted. Indeed, she had been very much a willing participant in all the fondling and kissing that had ensued. "But I must confess I didn't quite know how to explain my torn chemise when Bridget found it stuffed in my armoire. All the buttons gone and the lace on the strap ripped. I could hardly place the blame for your eagerness on Marcus."

"Bridget will be getting married soon," Beau rejoined with a chuckle. "She'll learn soon enough that those things happen when a man gets in a heat for a woman." He cocked his head aslant as he gave her a meaningful perusal. "Or you could tell Bridget that she might be able to save some of her shifts by not getting dressed at all in the morning until her husband has had his breakfast."

"Breakfast being...?"

His eyes glowed as they swept her again. "Are you playing coy with me, madam, or would you really like a demonstration?"

"Hatti said...''

"It doesn't matter what Hatti said. It all depends on how you're feeling."

Cerynise smiled coquettishly. "A bit tender perhaps."

"We could work into it *gradually*."

"You're tempting me again," she accused with a flirtatious pout.

Beau threw his head back and laughed in hearty amusement. Then, upon sobering, he stepped close and leaned down to kiss his wife. "Two more weeks at the most, madam," he whispered above her lips. "That's all I will allow. As for now, I have to get back to work or Uncle Jeff will dismiss me."

"Hardly!" Cerynise scoffed in amusement. "You're the best thing that has happened to the shipping company. Uncle Jeff said as much when he and his family came to see Marcus."

Beau shoved his hands in his trouser pockets as he straightened. "Uncle Jeff is only saying that because he'd like for me to stay on without making another voyage."

"Aye, I heard him, but he also said you were good for business and that if you'd stay, he'd give you whatever you wanted."

Growing wary of her motives for such talk, Beau searched his wife's face. "Are you trying to tell me that you'd like it if we didn't take another voyage together?"

"Absolutely not!" Cerynise denied, catching his hand and drawing him down to her again. "I will go to the ends of the earth to be with you. I'm just saying that you're blandly dismissing how important you've become to the company. Uncle Jeff can manage it for another year or so without you, allowing us to take the voyage, but I think he'd be absolutely delighted if you'd commit yourself fairly soon to taking over the business after your return."

"What about Harthaven? My father has mentioned that one day he'd like for me to take over."

She smiled and, gathering his fingers in her hand, lovingly pressed his knuckles against her cheek. "Do you honestly think your father would know what to do with himself if he gave over the management of Harthaven to you? I believe that running the plantation is an elixir of youth for him, as much as your mother is. Perhaps it will be for you someday, but I don't think you need worry that your father will be offended if you go into partnership with Uncle Jeff. Of the two men, your uncle needs your help more. Clay is clearly not interested in managing the company for his father, and since you've been there, Jeff has had more time to enjoy himself."

"It has been rather nice living so close to my work," Beau confessed. "And certainly living at Harthaven would be a problem with Pa and I so much alike. To be truthful, I guess I've enjoyed what I've been doing well enough to want to continue after the conclusion of the voyage. I'll talk with Uncle Jeff more about it in the next few weeks. As for now, I'll be late if I don't leave fairly soon."

After savoring a kiss from her lips, he fondly

caressed the small black head nestled near her breast before giving her an affectionate wink and bidding them adieu with, "I love you both."

CHAPTER 17

October swept in, and as Marcus advanced to a marvelous age of six weeks, he surprised his mother by settling down for longer stretches at a time, sometimes even sleeping through the whole night. Of course, Cerynise had to be prepared to devote herself entirely to fulfilling his needs once he woke, for he'd be outraged if he had to wait. She gladly yielded him that favor, for she rather enjoyed not being awakened to his demands in the middle of the night.

It was late afternoon on a decidedly nippy day. Beau hadn't yet returned home from work. The baby had been recently fed and, at present, was sleeping in the nursery. Hatti's granddaughter, Vera, a young woman of eighteen, had been ensconced as the boy's nursemaid and was now watching over him in his room. It had been established from the first that after the final feeding at night or upon the parents' retirement to their bedroom upstairs, the girl would return to her own room in the servants' quarters, allowing the couple the joy of tending their child in the privacy of their chambers, if such a need arose.

Surveying herself in the long, standing mirror in the dressing room, Cerynise was of a mind to think that except for a fuller bosom, no other evidence remained of her having given birth only a few weeks ago. The delicate clinging cloth of her chemise displayed a waist that was once more slender, and hips and thighs that were sleek and trim. Bridget had learned to create elegant coiffures for her, but for a more casual evening at home, Cerynise's hair had been coiled sedately on top of her head and softened by a few wispy tendrils falling against her neck. The maid had helped her into a soft creation of olive green and burgundy paisley, the rounded neckline, cuffs and hem of which were trimmed in the darker reddish hue. It was just the sort of thing that suited Cerynise's mood on this cozy autumn afternoon.

Accepting a burgundy shawl from Bridget, Cerynise adjusted it around her shoulders to properly hide her bosom. The fact that her breasts were much fuller now definitely made the garment more than a little risqué, for she was nearly overflowing the scooped décolletage.

"The cap'n is bound ta admire ye, mum. He won't be able ta help it," the maid said with an approving smile.

Cerynise felt her own senses racing. "I feel as giddy as a schoolgirl receiving her first beau," she admitted with an effervescent smile. "Are you sure I look all right?"

"Like the beauty ye are, mum," Bridget assured, laughing softly. She could sense her mistress's excitement over the coming evening and was wont to imagine that she'd be just as thrilled once Stephen Oaks became her husband and they could share the marital bliss that Cerynise and Beau Birmingham seemed to enjoy.

Cerynise fretted a little longer, wanting to look her best for her husband. "You wouldn't tell me that if there was something wrong, would you, Bridget?"

"Mum, take my honest word for it," the maid warbled cheerily, "ye're as close ta perfection as the master will be able to bear."

Cerynise drew a deep breath and released it slowly. "I'm just a little nervous, I guess."

Bridget patted her hand. "Ye needn't be, mum, for 'tis no lie that ye'd be fetchin' even in an ol' sack." The maid stepped to the door and paused there to gaze back at her young mistress. "Ye're a vision, ta be sure, mum."

Bridget took her leave, and as the sounds of her hurrying footfalls drifted back through the silence of the house, Cerynise continued to ponder her reflection, trying to imagine how she might look from Beau's perspective. No slightest evidence remained of that mere slip of a girl whom Germaine had once ridiculed as Sticks. Indeed, with her round breasts nearly overflowing the cloth boundary, she looked rather voluptuous for a woman approaching ten and nine years of age. She smiled as she remembered Beau pausing at the dressing room door that morning to take in the view as she stepped into the bathtub. The fact that he had been physically affected by the sight brought a smile to her lips even now. Time hadn't allowed him to assuage his lusts, which made his homecoming this evening even more anticipated. Still, Cerynise was wont to savor the memory of her handsome husband standing there completely dressed and fully aroused. The remembrance of the moment heightened her own excitement, and with a sly smile, she paused to dab a delicate fragrance in the cleavage between her breasts.

Making her own way through the bedroom, Cerynise glanced toward the huge tester bed where Beau had held her so tenderly and with dutiful restraint since Marcus's birth. It was not to say that they hadn't given themselves over to a fair amount of passionate kissing and erotic caressing during the past weeks. Indeed, if it had been left up to her, they'd have resumed their relations much sooner, but Beau had been afraid of hurting her. Now it was their night. Thus, it was with a light step that she went downstairs to await his return in the study which, except for their bedroom, had become their favorite sanctuary.

A breeze had sprung up from a northerly direction the night before, and a small fire had been lit in the fireplace to banish the chill that had invaded the study. Securing the cozy mood of the room, Cerynise flipped down the slats of the plantation shutters covering the windows and turned down the lamp that had been left burning on a table. A chaise lounge, residing in front of the fireplace, invited her to the comfort of its soft Moroccan

558

leather and the tapestry pillows that cushioned its sloping end. It was where she most often reclined with Marcus in her arms while Beau worked at his desk only a short distance away.

Smothering a yawn, Cerynise relaxed back upon the chaise and readjusted the pillows behind her back to a more comfortable position. With the warmth radiating from the fireplace she had no need of the shawl and allowed it to fall away from her shoulders. Then she leaned her head back to await the sound of her husband's return. In swiftly advancing degrees, she yielded to the increasing weightiness of her eyelids.

It seemed no more than a moment before a familiar awareness began to penetrate her befogged slumber. Struggling upward from her nap, she lifted drooping eyelids for a brief peek and then, closing them again, smiled sleepily. Her husband was sitting on the chaise beside her, having doffed his coat and waistcoat, stripped away his cravat, and loosened his shirt to the waist. The amused smile he wore assured her that he had been watching her.

"Good afternoon, my pet," he murmured when she finally managed to lift her eyelids and keep them open.

"I must have dozed off," she mumbled drowsily, trying to sit up. "And here I had intended to greet you at the door."

Beau leaned over her, preventing her escape as he pressed his lips to the fullness swelling above the shallow top of the bodice, very near a pliant peak hidden beneath. "I didn't mind, my sweet. I was enjoying the view."

She giggled. "Brief though it was."

He glanced up at the clock on the mantel. "I came home thirty minutes ago."

Her brows gathered in confusion. "That long? But why didn't you wake me?"

"As I said, I was enjoying the view."

Cerynise reached up and, slipping a hand in the opening of his shirt, caressed the muscular firmness. "I'm glad you're home."

"So am I," he breathed, bending near again, this time to caress her lips with his own. Her mouth parted eagerly beneath his, and he enjoyed a slow, languid search of the honeyed depth.

Cerynise sighed in contentment as he sat back. "You convey me away to ecstasy with your kisses."

A black eyebrow raised to a skeptical angle. "I thought I only did that when we made love together."

"Oh no, sir. Your kisses are very fine indeed."

He came near again, this time tracing his tongue with tantalizing slowness over her breasts, venturing across a swelling mound, dipping into the fragrant trough, and then rising again to the peak, much like a ship crossing a rolling sea. Tugging her gown down from her shoulder, he bared a pale pink crest and halted her breath as he leisurely stroked a warm, wet brand across it, causing Cerynise to shiver as a delicious excitement rippled through her.

"Do you like that?" he queried, lifting his mouth to tease hers.

"You know I do." Cerynise sighed, looping an arm behind his neck as he drew her up with him. Their mouths played in sweet union as his fingers progressed to the back of her gown and unfastened it. With a shrug of her shoulders, she swept it forward and pulled free of the bodice as he held the cuffs. Beau clasped an arm behind her and, lifting her until her hips were off the chaise, quickly banished the gown to the floor. He continued to ply her lips with kisses as his fingers plucked open the buttons of her chemise. The undergarment fell open, spilling the lustrous orbs into his eager grasp. His mouth took possession, setting off a flaring ecstasy in her loins.

"Have you locked the door?" she whispered, threading her fingers through his thick hair as his hungry mouth devoured the swelling softness.

"I couldn't resist with so beautiful a captive close at hand." The brush of his breath warmed a pliant nipple as he rasped out an answer. "I've been thinking of this all day, my sweet."

"So have I."

His hand slid underneath her petticoat and advanced over the top of a stocking. Then he pulled back in surprise and stared at her in amazement. "You're not wearing any pantalettes, madam!"

Cerynise smiled coyly as she drew an imaginary *C* upon his chest. "Are you scandalized?"

"Absolutely," he replied with a chuckle, belying his answer with a provocative search upward.

Cerynise moved to welcome him and gasped as small jolts of sizzling excitement began to surge upward from her womanly softness, setting her on fire for him. She writhed beneath his touch, wondering how long she could bear such rapture without being completely swept away. "Don't rush me, Beau," she begged breathlessly. "I want to wait for you."

He yielded to her plea and, standing back, began to unfasten his placket. She kicked off her slippers and, rising to her knees before him, tugged the tail of his shirt out of his trousers and pushed the garment over his shoulders. Her hands returned to stroke the hard, muscular ribs and followed his falling pants to caress his manly loins. Beau might as well have been frozen, so enraptured was he by her artful fondling, except that flames began licking upward through his being, threatening to consume him in one quick rush. He closed his hand over hers, for the moment forestalling her bold handling of his person.

"My plea is the same as yours, madam," he murmured huskily. "Give me a moment to cool down, and then we'll get on with the business at hand."

He kicked free of his boots and shed the rest of his clothes. Then he came back to her in all of his naked glory. Pressing close against him, Cerynise moved her breasts temptingly against his chest, teasing him until he moaned softly and clasped them greedily in his hands for another taste of the delectable fare. Soon their mouths and tongues blended in a rapacious search, and with eyes dark with desire, Cerynise drew him back with her upon the chaise. He came willingly, slipping an arm behind her and pulling her astride him as he took the place she had left. He freed the fastening at the waist of her petticoat and rose up to draw it over her head, leaving her clothed in nothing more substantial than a camisole and a pair of silk stockings fastened with frilly garters. The petticoat was thrown to the floor, forgotten in his haste. Lifting her slightly, he resettled her over the fiery shaft and pressed fully home. Cerynise gasped as his warmth filled her, making her tremble with the pure, shimmering ecstasy of it.

Beau enfolded her within his arms for a moment, enjoying the feel of her bosom against his chest and her womanly softness sheathing him as he kissed her eyes, her cheek and her softly yielding mouth. His lips slid down the graceful column of her throat as he breathed, "It seems like forever since I held you this way."

"Oh, yes," she agreed, arching her back to allow him free access. A soft gasp was snatched from her as his mouth enveloped the pinnacle of her breast. It seemed to pulse in eagerness beneath the wet, fiery torch, and she almost mewled in disappointment when he lay back upon the chaise. Yet when his fingertips moved to where they were joined and began to work their magic, she became a fascinated prisoner and, in quiescent repose, drank in each delicious stroke.

Her sultry eyes delved into his, conveying her deepening arousal as she began to move against him, deliberately drawing out their pleasure in long, leisured strides. Beau's own breathing grew harsh and ragged as she made love to him with an inventiveness that matched the studied art of a sultry temptress in her shuttered den. She touched him provocatively, brushing her fingers over his male nipples, his hardened ribs and between his steely thighs as her tongue passed languidly over her upper lip. Holding his gaze captive, she moved her hands over herself, inviting his hands to follow wherever she led, and they did, making her catch her breath as he answered with his own creativity. She sucked her breath in through her teeth at the scintillating sensations flooding through her and then leaned forward, bracing her hands on the uppermost part of the rolled end of the chaise to offer the swelling mounds to the warmth of his mouth. They hung temptingly above him, like golden ripe fruit bejeweled with pink crests. His hands eagerly clasped their fullness, and he nigh devoured them as her rhythm became more intense. He seized her buttocks, urging her onward until both of them were driven by the rapture that burst upon them, sweeping them to dizzying, soaring heights. Caught in the midst of this lofty flight, Beau strained upward against her, feeling totally regenerated by the pulsing heat of her. He had never experienced such a thing before, and yet it was utterly thrilling to go on and on and on....

When reason finally drifted back to them and he pulled his wife down upon his chest, Beau was still struck by the wonder of it all. He pressed another kiss upon her lips as her fingers lightly stroked his arm.

"That was extremely nice." Cerynise sighed contentedly.

"The best I've ever experienced," he admitted. "I'm so relaxed now, I can hardly lift my arms."

"Please don't," she whispered. "I like them around me."

He clasped her close, moving his chest beneath her in a slow, undulating caress of her breasts, and was amazed to feel himself tightening within her.

"Oooh," she crooned, "that's even nicer."

"You do strange things to me, woman," he murmured huskily.

"I'm glad. It assures me that you won't go searching beneath other skirts."

"Nay, never that. I'm quite content getting under your skirts."

"I'm hungry."

"For what?"

A giggle escaped her as she raised her head to search his smiling face. "Real food."

"Then I suppose we'd better get dressed again."

"Still, I hate to leave such delights," she replied, moving her hips against him.

"Make up your mind, woman," he urged with a chuckle, clasping her buttock. "Me or real food."

"I'll have you later." Laughing at his feigned growl of disappointment, she pushed herself upright until she sat astride him once again. "As for now, a nursing mother must be nourished."

He stroked a forefinger beneath a white droplet trembling on the tip of her nipple and brought it to his mouth to taste. "No wonder Marcus likes you so well," he commented, making a show of licking his finger. "You taste nice."

Cerynise wiped away a tiny pool that had collected on his chest. "I'm not very tidy."

The blue eyes glowed back at her. "Marcus and I don't mind."

"Come, husband," she urged, dismounting him. "I'm really, really hungry."

She turned away to pick up her garments, drawing him off the chaise in a bounding leap. He lightly slapped her buttocks, making her straighten and look at him with a querying smile.

With a casual shrug he gave her a jaunty grin. "When you offer such temptations to me, my dear, you can expect some kind of response. And since I've had you for the moment, I'll have to restrict myself to an affectionate pat. Now get your clothes on, woman, so we can eat, or by my word, I'll make you serve my pleasure again."

Laughing at his antics, Cerynise complied.

After they had donned their clothes again, they hurried upstairs for a quick check on their son and a more tidy cleansing before returning to the dining room.

The long dining room table had been set for two at one end of the table. Glasses of wine had already been poured and were awaiting them beside their place settings. Beeswax candles cast a warm glow over the array of crystal, china and silver as Beau gallantly pulled out a chair for his wife. Slipping it forward beneath her, he bent over her as she settled into the seat, motivating her to lean back for the slow caress of his lips against her throat.

"I enjoy looking at your breasts from this angle," he whispered, "but I think I hear Jasper coming, and I don't like the idea of sharing such sights with another man."

Gathering the shawl together, Cerynise assumed a gracious image of a proper young mistress well before the butler arrived with their soup. Beau couldn't help but smile at the contrast between her present sublime poise and that lusty vixen who, moments earlier, had driven him on with wild, passionate frenzy. He was as susceptible to her as any puppet. All she had to do was maneuver his strings, and he'd dance to whatever tune she played.

As the servant departed, Beau raised his goblet in toast to her. "To you, my love. May you never grow tired of stirring my pleasure and filling my heart with joy."

Smilingly she dipped her head in gracious

acknowledgment of his salute, and then, after taking a tiny sip, she raised her glass in like response to him. "To you, my darling knight. May you never grow wearied of slaying dragons and saving this damsel from distress and boredom."

"The pleasure is all mine, madam," he rejoined with a warm, meaningful twinkle in his eyes before quaffing his wine.

The lobster bisque was superb, as was to be expected with Philippe as chef. So were the winter vegetables and the roast fillet of beef with cornichon tarragon sauce. Cerynise relished it all like an eager child, drawing a chuckle from her husband.

"I don't know how you manage to stay so trim, my love. With what you eat, you should be rolling down the halls."

Teasingly she licked her fingers for his benefit, evoking his laughter. "Between you and Marcus, I'm sure you'll both help me use it up."

"The way that little pig grunts when he's nursing, he'll undoubtedly consume it all for himself."

"Now don't be jealous," Cerynise cajoled sweetly. "You'll have as many chances to gain my attention as you could possibly want."

Beau braced an elbow on the corner of the table and leaned toward her with a leer. "Promise?"

Her eyes glowed back at him, conveying such a vow to be duly sworn to.

After dinner they returned to the study,

but only to talk, hold hands and kiss. Soon, Hatti's granddaughter, Vera, rapped on the open door to draw their attention.

"Mastah Marcus is awake now, Miz Cerynise, an' he's a-squallin' up a storm."

"Duty calls," Cerynise drolly sighed to her husband and, leaving him with another kiss, went upstairs to feed their son. After finishing off the last of the wine in his goblet, her husband followed to the nursery. Vera had wisely dismissed herself, allowing them to enjoy their child in the privacy of their chambers.

After nursing Marcus, his mother readied his nightly bath, and the doting parents joined in this endeavor, laughing together at the many faces their son made in reaction to being bathed in warm water and then dried in a soft towel. After placing an indulgent kiss upon the tiny head, Beau departed the nursery, leaving his wife to rock and sing their baby to sleep while he soaked in a bath of his own.

Some time later Cerynise left her slumbering son in his bed and slipped into the dressing room to find a scented bath awaiting her. Hearing a faint tinkle in the bedroom, she stepped to the door of the adjoining chamber and found her husband withdrawing his hand from a wine goblet that he had just placed on his bedside table. He was sitting in bed with the covers drawn up around his waist, looking for all the world like he was ready for a long night of sensual delights. His eyes swept her in a slow caress as he asked, "Planning on standing there all night?"

"Absolutely not," Cerynise eagerly replied. "Give me a moment to get a bath...."

"You needn't bother with a nightgown," he warned her as she returned to the dressing room. "It may get ripped."

"Yes, sir," she called back. "Anything you say, sir."

"And hurry!" he urged. "I've been waiting for a whole quarter of an hour and am nigh besotted thinking about you."

Cerynise hurriedly stripped away her clothes, bathed and brushed out her hair before slipping into a negligee that Beau had bought for her earlier in the week. It could hardly be called a garment, for it was made of the filmiest, silkiest white cloth she had ever seen. It was long and flowing with sleeves that did the same. After touching perfume to her throat and down her arms, she paused and then, with a smile, dabbed several droplets between her breasts again. She slipped her feet into white satin mules and doused the light. The gossamer fabric billowed out behind her until it seemed as if she floated into the bedroom on airy wings.

The sapphire eyes took in the sights with a lusting greed that left her breasts fairly tingling. Beau held out a hand, inviting her to hurry, and then swept down the covers beside him. Pausing beside the bed, she lifted the negligee off her shoulders and let it fall unheeded to the floor.

When she slipped into bed, Beau was immediately there, gathering her close. This time it was he who made love to her, startling her with the passion he exhibited. Although infinitely gentle with her, he was more adventurous with her now that she was no longer pregnant. He remained heedless of her breathless pleas, delighting in his ability to bring her to frenzied heights of eagerness. Panting and writhing as if she were caught up in an insatiable quest that would never be fulfilled, she became a bit impetuous herself and made bold to copy his manner until a deep, guttural moan broke from him. As his manly hardness surged into her warmth, Cerynise rose up to meet him and, with quickening ardor, answered his deep thrusts. Once again they soared on shimmering wings of ecstasy, letting their hungering ardor sweep them ever upward.

When finally they floated down to earth again, they snuggled together in their bed, and with a blissful sigh, Cerynise laid her head upon Beau's shoulder as her fingers idly caressed his chest. The world outside their home had ceased to exist for her, for it was all here in her husband's encompassing arms.

The back door slammed early the next morning, and Beau and Cerynise both glanced around as Moon came charging into the dining room in an anxious dither. Beau had just finished his breakfast when the old tar halted near his chair.

"The blighter's dead, Cap'n! They found him on the docks this morn'n' with his belly sliced open from stem to stern."

"Who in the world are you talking about, Moon?" Beau queried, pushing away his plate.

"Wilson, Cap'n. He was as stiff as a frozen cod. Must've been gutted late last night."

Beau glanced at his wife and saw that the color had drained from her cheeks. He could imagine that Moon's morbid explanations were a bit too lurid for her. Laying a hand upon hers, he excused himself and then motioned for the tar to follow him into the study. Closing the door behind them, he asked the man, "Do the authorities have any idea who might have killed him?"

"Nay, Cap'n. He's been hidin' out in an ol' run-down inn from what I heared from someone this morn'n'. No one I talked ta had seen a trace o' him since ye sent yer men ta search for him. Then, all o' a sudden, there he was, curled up with a knife in his belly. It don't seem likely that Wilson would've let a stranger get close enough ta stick him, so's I'm a-thinkin' he knew the fella what did it an' maybe trusted him more'n a mite."

"That might definitely be the case, Moon. Since there were so many men looking for him, Wilson would probably have been wary of anyone approaching him. But we may never know the answer to that riddle now."

"This means yer li'l girlie is safe now, don't it, Cap'n?"

"I hope so, Moon. I truly hope so."

Several days later, Jasper answered the summons of the front door knocker with his

572

usual dignified poise, but his stiff jaw slowly descended when he recognized the two who were standing before the portal. The last time he had seen them was the night before he and the rest of the servants had risen at the crack of dawn and absconded with the paintings that belonged to his present mistress. From their startled expressions, it was fairly easy to ascertain that Alistair Winthrop and Howard Rudd were just as surprised to see him.

"I was wondering where you had vanished to," Alistair jeered. "Now I know. I just never figured you for a turncoat."

"Had that been the case, sir, I would have stayed with you," the butler answered him loftily. For the life of him, Jasper couldn't manage a lie for the sake of graciousness and tell them that it was a pleasure to see them again. "Whom do you wish to see, sir?"

"My ward, of course," Alistair informed him caustically. "Please tell her that I've come to call."

"Mrs. Birmingham, you mean," Jasper pointedly corrected. "If you'll wait there, sir, I'll tell my mistress that you're here seeking her favor."

Feeling no compunction to extend the usual hospitality of the house to them, the servant closed the door in their faces, leaving Alistair nearly bouncing up and down in outrage.

"Seeking the bitch's favor," he squealed in an outraged whisper. "Why, I'll tear that bastard's heart out with a crowbar for leaving us in such a blooming mess."

573

"You couldn't have paid him anyway," Howard Rudd reasoned, and then sought to counsel his companion. "Now you saw how fast Sybil skedaddled when you lost your temper and told her that you didn't have enough funds to hire more and that she'd have to do all of our cooking and cleaning. So I must urge you to keep tight rein on your temper while we're here. Flying into a blooming snit won't suit our purposes in the least if we have any hopes of luring the girl away with promises of her paintings being returned to her."

"I wish we could've brought one with us just to entice her."

Howard Rudd heaved a sigh of lament. "Most unfortunate that we weren't able to get our hands on any of them."

"I still say that dealer in the gallery knew where they were in spite of the fact that he was so incensed by our accusations and claimed we were daft."

"Didn't help that you bruised him up a bit," Rudd chided.

"I may yet finish him off if I find out that he was lying to us."

"Now don't be so forceful with the girl. As we've seen in the past, Captain Birmingham isn't at all the gentle sort. Bruise his wife, and he'll search every ship leaving the docks just to get his hands on us. Throwing us into the bay will hardly placate him as suitable recompense."

"Are you sure you saw him at the shipping company?"

Rudd's lips flapped in a heavy emission of his breath, attesting to his exasperation. "How could I mistake him after our last visit with him? I assure you, the sight of that man has been forever branded upon my memory." With a trembling hand the barrister took out a handkerchief and wiped his glistening brow. "Still think it's damn foolish of you to try this when he's only a few blocks away."

"You said he won't be home for another couple of hours. We'll be long gone before he arrives."

"Jasper poses a problem. Have to bribe him or something or he'll be telling the captain we came. We'll be lucky to sail away from here with our carcasses intact...."

"I'll leave that matter to you. If the girl won't come peaceably, then I'll have no other choice but to take her. We'll meet up at that old abandoned farm outside of town." Alistair glanced aside at his accomplice and arched a brow as he noticed how much the man was shaking. "Are you sure you can cover my rear if our lure fails?"

The lawyer gulped and nervously patted the bulk beneath his coat. "I wish there was some other way to handle this. I hate firearms."

"We don't have much time left," Alistair snapped. "Our funds are running out."

"Should have sold more of your aunt's possessions before we left. Had we done so, we'd have had the time and resources to see this thing done properly."

"Don't fret so much. You know it sours your stomach."

Cerynise had gone to the kitchen to show Marcus off to Philippe while the baby was wide awake and sweetly attentive to the faces that came close enough for him to peruse. The chef was jovially giving the child his first lessons in French, declaring that Marcus would be highly appreciative of the language once he started sailing to foreign shores like his father. The child was responding to him with happy gurgles, drawing chuckles of delight from both chef and parent, but when Jasper came rushing in, Marcus quickly shifted his consideration to the highly agitated butler and puckered his brows in a curious frown.

"Madam! Prepare yourself," Jasper urged excitedly. "In fact, you'd better give the baby over to Monsieur Philippe before I tell you who is at the front door requesting to see you."

Cerynise clasped her baby more securely in her own arms, clearly bemused by the butler's anxiety, and inclined her head to assure him that she had the situation well in hand. "Who is it, Jasper?"

"Mr. Winthrop and Mr. Rudd, madam...."

Cerynise swayed in a stunned daze and quickly passed the baby over into the arms of the chef, who grew alarmed at her sudden pallor. "Madame! Are you all right?"

She nodded stiffly and begged him, "Please take the baby out to Vera...."

Without another word she turned and left the kitchen ahead of Jasper, who paused to give Philippe instructions of his own. In the dining room, Cerynise waited for the butler to join her and then bade, "I'll receive the visitors in the parlor, Jasper."

"Madam, are you sure?" he questioned worriedly.

"They wouldn't dare harm me here in my own home."

"Even so, madam, I cannot bring myself to trust the men. They're scoundrels through and through."

"That may well be true, Jasper, but I'm curious to know what they're doing here and what they want of me."

"No good, I fear."

"I'll hear them out. That's all."

Cerynise went into the front room on the north side of the house while Jasper reluctantly complied with her wishes. He opened the front door to admit the two, and then announced, "Mrs. Birmingham will see you in the parlor."

Stepping past the servant, Alistair strode into the front foyer and then, sweeping off his hat and tossing it back to the man, approached the study, on the opposite side of the house.

"The other way, sir," Jasper corrected, his ire rising as he took note of his former employer's interest in the room, where an older painting of Cerynise's was hanging above the mantel. It was one that her husband had especially reserved for himself, an English country scene of a thatched-roof cottage nestled beside a stream in the midst of a wooded glade. Personally Jasper had always considered it one of her best landscapes.

577

"Haven't I seen that painting before?" Alistair asked, turning a calculating frown upon the butler.

Jasper's nose lifted imperiously. "I wouldn't know, sir." Once again he extended his hand in the direction of the parlor. "Mrs. Birmingham is awaiting you in *here*, sir."

Howard Rudd passed his own headgear to the servant and smoothed down the lapels of his wrinkled frock coat before he followed Alistair into the parlor.

Jasper set the hats aside on the entrance table and stepped to the door, gaining his mistress's attention. "Do you wish tea or refreshments, madam?"

Howard Rudd eyed the large cabinet standing against the wall and licked a coated tongue over his parched lips as he took note of the crystal decanters residing on a silver platter there. "Glass of brandy if the captain wouldn't mind."

"*Nothing* at all," Alistair stated with emphasis, his eyes narrowing warningly as they shifted to the barrister, who was growing noticeably disconcerted by the ordeal of entering the domain of that seafaring worthy who had once set them on their ears. "We won't be staying that long."

"I'll have a cup of tea, Jasper," Cerynise replied, letting them both know that she was the one to whom the butler had spoken and the only one in the room with the authority to make such decisions.

Despite the moments that she had been allowed to compose herself, Cerynise realized she hadn't been expecting the sudden surge of abhorrence that had swept through her when she had settled her gaze upon the two men. Almost a full year had passed since she had last seen them, but that hadn't been nearly enough time in her mind. She didn't regret in the least that at their last confrontation her husband had taken Alistair up by the scruff of his neck and the seat of his pants and sailed him overboard into the Thames. She only wished Beau was here now, watching over her with his usual care.

Alistair appeared thinner than before, she surmised. Dark circles were evident beneath his eyes, and his clothes were ill fitting and rumpled, far different from what his appearance had been in London. The portly solicitor appeared equally disheveled, his bulbous nose perhaps even more unsightly with the netting of broken veins that crisscrossed it. His eyes were red and watery, as if he suffered some allergy or perhaps repercussions from liberally imbibing in strong spirits.

Cerynise reluctantly extended an invitation for them to take a seat across from her, making an earnest effort to appear cordial. Her only reason for permitting them into the house was to learn what they were up to, and the best way to hasten that information along was to convey a modicum of civility. "Do forgive my surprise, gentlemen. I'm sure you can believe that your visit here is most unexpected. In fact, you're the last people I anticipated seeing today."

Alistair's unwieldy lips slipped upward unctuously. "Oh, no doubt, my dear girl, and I apologize most sincerely for startling you. But having come so far to see you, we couldn't bear to wait a moment longer. Our ship docked only this morning, and we hastened here with all possible spee—"

Bridget entered, looking quite fetching in a neat black gown, a frilly white apron and a starched white cap adorned with lace. Though the maid met neither man's gaze, she sensed their acute surprise and a strong hint of distress on the part of the solicitor as she went to her mistress. Bearing a tray upon which resided a cup of tea and the usual pitcher of cream and bowl of sugar, she offered the small tea service to Cerynise, who added sugar and cream to her cup. After laying a napkin across her mistress's lap, Bridget took her leave with quiet aplomb, winning for herself an ever-so-brief smile of approval from Jasper, who was hovering near the door.

"You were saying that you came here from your ship," Cerynise reminded Alistair, noticing that he had not yet fully recovered from his astonishment at seeing Bridget in her house. "For what purpose?"

"To make amends, madam," Rudd interjected. He shot a quick glance toward Alistair, as if seeking approval for his statement. "That's it, isn't it? All the way here Mr. Winthrop talked of nothing else, how he had wronged you. The man has been tormented with remorse. If you would but hear him out, madam, I'm sure you won't regret it."

Alistair was still struggling with his irritation at finding not only Jasper in the Birmingham household, but Bridget as well. He indicated the indomitable butler with a jerk of his oil-slicked head as he broached the subject to Cerynise. "How many more servants came with him?"

"All of them," she answered forthrightly and was quick to note the darkening rage on her former tormentor's face. Taking a bit of revenge upon the man, she set the spur deeper. "My husband gave them enough funds to make the journey, but by then, they were already making plans to leave you."

Alistair jabbed a finger in a southerly direction. "Did they bring that painting across the hall with them?"

"Of course," she rejoined, feeling a keen sense of pleasure to assure the rascal of that fact. She further needled, "In fact, they brought all my paintings with them, five of which have already been sold for a considerable sum...twenty-six thousand dollars to be exact."

Rudd choked suddenly and coughed against the bile that promptly rose into his throat. "A glass of water," he begged the butler. "I need a glass of water."

Solicitously Cerynise inquired, "Are you all right?"

Rudd cleared his throat, managing to gasp, "Will be as soon as I get some water."

Alistair silently smoldered. It was obvious now that the enticement they had planned to use would have no effect since the paintings were already in her possession, but he couldn't help but think of all that money they could have had...if not for Jasper. He'd wring that confounded butler's neck yet!

The barrister clutched the glass of water which the servant brought back and gulped down half the contents to ease the acidic burning in his throat. The liquid only washed it down to his stomach, where the juices soon began to ferment and erupt upward again in small gaseous bubbles. Rudd knew the signs only too well, and his distress deepened.

Cerynise returned to the business at hand, briskly warning them, "My husband will be averse to you coming here in his absence. He has instructed Jasper to watch over me. Naturally anything you say will be witnessed by him."

Rudd cast a quick, wary glance behind him at the indomitable butler and tried to soothe the lady's fears. They would have to come up with another ploy very, very soon or his companion would resort to his usual heavy-handed tactics. "How can we assure you there's no need of such precautions, madam?"

"By stating your business and then leaving," Cerynise answered succinctly.

Rudd pressed his fingers to his lips to hide a burp. Then, clearing his throat, he lifted a hand to her in appeal. "Our business is most private, madam...."

"If you're suggesting that Jasper be excused, Mr. Rudd, then I'm afraid I won't be able to hear you out," she informed him bluntly. "My husband has instructed Jasper not to leave my side while there's some question of my safety. And as I distinctly remember, you both have proven quite untrustworthy in my presence."

"We need some papers signed," Alistair announced, as if it pained him to admit that fact.

Rudd shot him a look of surprise, received a warning frown in return, and then cleared his throat again sharply, trying to dislodge another belch. "Yes, of course." He lifted a hand to his companion, giving him the honors. "Mr. Winthrop would like to explain the necessity."

Alistair made an earnest effort to do such a thing. "Well...ah...on further evaluation of my aunt's will, Mr. Rudd, here, found a clause which decreed that I would have to show just cause for not taking on the responsibility of your wardship, requiring both a court appearance and a signed affidavit from you to serve as a release. Until those two events occur, I cannot claim my inheritance."

Howard Rudd breathed a sigh of relief at the plausibility of his companion's stratagem and eagerly nodded in agreement. "A bit awkward for Mr. Winthrop's creditors, having to wait so long....Why, just to ask your compliance, we had to scrape up the funds to sail here."

In some confusion, Cerynise peered at the lawyer. "Do you mean to say that I must appear before a judge and, in his presence, sign a document releasing you from all obligations as my guardian?"

"That's it exactly," Alistair affirmed in his companion's stead and shot a glance toward Jasper. The butler was staring off into space, but Alistair had no doubt that the man was closely attentive to what was being said.

"I see no difficulty in going before a judge here in Charleston and signing such a document, as long as my husband's lawyer has a chance to read it over first," Cerynise reasoned.

Alistair winced for her benefit. "But therein lies the difficulty, my dear. You must return to England to make such an appearance."

"That's absolutely out of the question." Cerynise waved a hand to dismiss the merest possibility that she would go to such lengths for them. "If the matter cannot be resolved here in Charleston, then it shan't be done at all, at least not until my husband and I return to England on another sea voyage, but that won't happen until early spring."

"And in the meantime, I'm bereft of funds." Alistair shook his head dolefully.

"I'm sorry, but I'm unable to relieve your plight." Cerynise was not at all sympathetic. Had Alistair asked for such a thing before their departure from England, then she'd have gladly gone with Beau to carry out the man's wishes, but Alistair had been far too adamant about taking possession of her.

Rudd snapped his fingers, as if an idea just came to him, and tested the notion out on Alistair. "You remember that judge who made the crossing with us, don't you?"

The thinner man inclined his head almost warily, following the solicitor's lead. "Of course."

"Well, he's a proper English magistrate. If she signs the papers in front of him, it would be the same as being in an English court of law."

"That's right," Alistair agreed, smiling at the idea. "All she'd have to do is accompany us to the inn where we've all taken rooms and have him witness the event. That would serve our purposes very nicely indeed."

Rudd seemed extremely pleased with himself for having thought of the ruse. "Would you allow us to take you to see the judge, madam?"

Cerynise scoffed at the idea. "Not without my husband." And for good measure she added, "And a good dozen of his men to make sure we're not waylaid."

Rudd's face fell forthwith. All their hopes to take possession of her peaceably seemed futile. What were they to do? It was obvious she was too well guarded in her home for them to expect to be able to escape with her with any degree of success. And, of course, there were the servants, who could identify them.

"Are you suggesting, madam, that we would resort to that kind of duplicity?" Alistair asked in growing outrage.

Cerynise smiled serenely. "Perhaps."

With a growl Alistair launched himself out

of his chair and was across the room in a thrice, snatching Cerynise out of hers. Jasper gave a warning cry and dashed forward to defend her, but he gave no heed to the danger of passing Rudd, who, upon seeing his approach, seized a bronze bookend from a nearby table. The weighty piece crashed down upon the butler's head, spilling him forward to the floor, where he lay unconscious at the lawyer's feet.

Cerynise's scream seized Philippe's heart in the kitchen. Snatching up a meat cleaver, he raced into the hall with Moon following rapidly behind. By then, Alistair had already tossed his captive over his shoulder and was striding into the foyer with Rudd advancing swiftly on his heels.

Philippe espied them as he raced from the hallway. "Put zee madame down!"

Alistair made the mistake of opening the front door, which the master of the house had just been about to push inward. Beau had been summoned home by Cooper and, upon his arrival, had heard screams from within. It was the sight of his wife lying over the sly weasel's shoulder that sent his temper soaring. Drawing up a knee, Beau slammed it with brutal force into Alistair's stomach, doubling the man over with a painful gurgle. Deftly whisking Cerynise off the crumpling one's shoulder, Beau swept her to her feet and then quickly drew back a fist to finish thrashing Alistair. In the next instant he found himself facing Howard Rudd, who had nervously snatched forth the pistol he had been carrying in his coat. Despite the fact that the solicitor's hands were shaking dangerously, he had cocked the weapon and had it aimed generally in the direction of the captain's irate frown.

"B-back away from the d-door!" Rudd stuttered and tossed a quick look behind him at the two men who were almost upon him. "S-stay back, or I w-will kill the captain! So help me I will."

In the face of such a threat, Philippe and Moon could do naught but stumble to a halt.

"D-drop the cleaver," Rudd ordered the chef, trying to keep the bore of the pistol centered between the sapphire eyes as he cast another worried glance toward the two. Carefully the cook laid his makeshift weapon down upon the floor.

"Now, C-Captain," the barrister urged, stepping past Alistair. "You and your wife m-move to the north end of the p-porch...very carefully now."

Beau complied, drawing Cerynise with him. She was clinging to him, trying to place herself in front of him as a shield, but he would have none of it. With an arm clasped about her waist, he held her firmly against his side.

Rudd caught Alistair's elbow and, hauling him upright, pulled him through the doorway. His companion was suffering too much to be of any help, and Rudd shoved him toward the front steps of the porch with a command. "Run to the horses."

"Get the girl," Alistair croaked weakly,

clasping his arms across his belly. His pain was so intense he feared his vitals had been ripped asunder.

Beau swept Cerynise behind him and glowered at the two. "Over my grave!"

Alistair feebly swept a hand to indicate the captain and rasped, "Shoot the bloody bastard!"

"Nooo!" Cerynise cried, trying to thrust herself forward in front of her husband, but he refused to comply with her efforts and held her behind him.

Rudd snorted, denying the wisdom of his companion's command. But then, it wasn't the first time he had mentally questioned the intelligence of Alistair Winthrop. "Aye, and let the rest of them kill us," he derided, and then snapped, "Get to the horses."

Alistair hobbled hurriedly toward the hitching post where the reins of their mounts had been secured. Snatching the lines free, he hauled himself astride with a painful grimace. "Come on, Rudd. Let's get out of here."

Now that he had some open space between himself and his horse, Howard Rudd could breathe a little easier, but he was still wary of the captain. A man with a fiery temper was not to be trusted. "T-try anything, C-Captain, and you or y-your wife will die, and if y-you die, your wife will be at our m-mercy. Th-that much I promise."

He backed down the path over which Alistair had recently trod and, swinging into the saddle, slammed his heels into the sides of the rented gelding. He lit out amid a noisy clatter of hooves, leaving Alistair struggling to catch up.

Beau ran to the street and watched the pair ride away. They made a turn, but it was not in the direction he had hoped. They were heading farther inland, possibly toward open country, away from the docks.

Cooper was just arriving from his trek to the shipping company. Having sped there by foot, the young man was clearly out of breath and energy from his race back, which his employer, being well rested and frantic for his wife's safety, had covered in half the time.

Philippe, Moon and some of the other servants had come out onto the porch. It was Moon to whom Beau gave an order. "Find the sheriff, tell him what the blackguards tried to do, and urge him to gather up a posse and go after those two. If he needs descriptions, he can stop by here on his way out. I'll gladly tell him what those frogs look like."

"Aye, Cap'n!" With a casual salute, Moon hurried off to fulfill his behest.

Beau climbed the porch steps, slipped an arm around his wife, and swept her into the house. In the parlor they found Bridget kneeling on the floor beside Jasper. The butler was sitting up, holding a wet compress against the back of his head while the maid was wrapping a strip of cloth around the pad to hold it securely in place.

"I'm afraid I let my guard down, sir," Jasper apologized, lifting a brief glance toward Beau.

"I understand it was you who sent Cooper to fetch me."

"Yes, sir. At least I had Monsieur Philippe send the young man to warn you that your wife had visitors. I'm extremely thankful that Cooper found you in time."

"I'm grateful for your quick thinking," Beau responded. Hunkering down on his haunches, he asked solicitously, "How do you feel?"

"Like my head is twice as large as normal," the butler answered dryly.

Beau chuckled. "It doesn't appear to be."

"Bridget told me that Mr. Winthrop and Mr. Rudd have managed to escape, sir."

"Aye, but I'll let the sheriff search for them."

Jasper thought that an especially prudent decision. "It's best not to leave the madam right now. They could come back, sir."

Marcus's outraged squalls could be heard coming closer, and Cerynise stepped from the parlor to find Vera hurrying down the hall from the kitchen. The girl was clearly relieved to see her mistress. "I've done e'erythin' I could ta quiet him, Miz Cerynise, but he's a-wantin' ta be fed."

"I'll take him, Vera." Holding out her arms to accept her son, Cerynise moved to meet the young woman. The baby's outraged cries quieted immediately in his mother's arms, and eagerly he started rooting at her breast. Cerynise took him to the study and, behind a closed door, hastily plucked open the buttons of her bodice as she sank to the cushions of the sofa. When the portal was swung open again, she glanced around as Beau entered. Securing their privacy, he pushed the door shut behind him and joined his wife on the sofa.

It amused Beau to see his son searching with birdlike fervor through the cloth of Cerynise's gown. When the babe found nothing to assuage him, disappointed wails erupted, evoking a chuckle from his father. Cerynise finally managed to bare her breast and settled the infant against it. That was all it took. The boy latched onto her nipple with the greed of a glutton.

Her eyes glowing with love, Cerynise caressed the small head and then glanced up at her smiling husband with that same adoring gaze. "I would have missed you both terribly if Alistair had succeeded in taking me away. I'd have pined my heart out."

"No less than I, madam, but I would have come after you," Beau murmured reassuringly, bestowing a kiss upon her temple as he laid an arm behind her on the back of the sofa. "Did that toad say why he wanted you?"

Cerynise repeated what the two men had told her and grew a bit incensed as she recalled their demands. "Alistair actually wanted me to travel all the way to England with them, but when Rudd suggested that I could sign the papers in front of an English magistrate who came over on the ship with them, I said I'd do so, but only with you and an escort to protect us. That was when Alistair became irate. Mr. Rudd hit Jasper when he tried to come to my aid. One thing led to another." She heaved a sigh, mentally rebuking herself. "I shouldn't have agreed to see them. Jasper was fearful of some trick, but I ignored his warning."

"Hopefully they'll be caught, my pet. If they are, then we won't have anything more to worry about."

"Do you suppose that Redmond Wilson was somehow in cahoots with them? But why would they kill him if he was working for them?" She frowned suddenly, remembering what they had said. "According to Alistair, their ship docked only this morning, so unless they lied, they wouldn't have been here at the time of his murder."

"Alistair may have just said that to lead us astray, but it seems unlikely that Wilson was killed by strangers. Considering the number of men I sent out to look for him, the culprit was probably someone he knew and trusted." Beau shrugged. "Who knows?"

Cerynise looked down again at Marcus who was still ravenously sating his hunger. She smiled impishly as she lifted her gaze again to her husband. "At times his voracity reminds me of when you made love to me and proved yourself just as starved for appeasement."

Beau looked appalled at the comparison. "To my knowledge, madam, I've always tried to be gentle with you. When have I ever suckled you so unmercifully?"

"When you were delirious, my love," she replied, rubbing his thigh. "My nipples were quite tender afterwards."

The dark brows flicked upward briefly, conveying his chagrin. "Forgive me, madam, but considering my growing desire to have my way with you, I'm sure I was out of my head with lust for you."

"And quite feverish, too. I thought I was dreaming until I felt the pain of your entry, but by then, I had become a willing participant in your marital initiation. Whether you know it or not, my love, you gave me pleasure even then, though you were so sick it might not have been your intent. Still, I felt somewhat slighted when I realized afterwards that you hadn't even kissed me."

Beau didn't care to explain that he had always been reluctant to kiss the harlots he had sought out to satisfy his manly cravings. It was not until he had kissed Cerynise on their wedding day that he had actually become appreciative of that delectable practice. "I, too, thought it was a dream, but I'm glad it wasn't." He reached up to slip a finger through the tiny hand that kneaded her breast. "If I hadn't been alerted to the fact that you were carrying my child, madam, I might never have realized that you needed or even wanted me. For a time I was convinced that I was the only one who felt like that."

"We made a beautiful son together," Cerynise replied, dropping her head briefly on her husband's shoulder. Reminded once again of what those two scoundrels had tried to do to her, she shivered. "Hold me close, Beau. I need to be reassured that I'm safe in your arms."

593

Beau willingly obliged her, pressing his lips to the nape of her neck before spreading more kisses over her cheek and moving on to her mouth. When at last he leaned his head near hers and gazed down with doting pride upon his nursing son, the baby cut his eyes to look up at him. For barely an instant, Marcus stopped feeding and gave his father a happy gurgle. Then, with renewed dedication, he returned to his feast.

Several days passed before Sheriff Gates dropped by the warehouse to inform Beau of his lack of success in capturing Alistair Winthrop and Howard Rudd. Though the lawman and his posse had scoured the countryside west of Charleston several times since the botched kidnapping, they had found no trace of the culprits. However, the sheriff had received reports that led him to believe that Alistair and Rudd might have fled back to England on the first ship available. Two men fitting the descriptions that Beau had supplied were seen boarding a ship which had set sail before his deputy could go and question its captain.

Beau sincerely hoped the two were gone, but he would need irrefutable proof that the scoundrels were still aboard the vessel when it set sail before he could feel assured of his wife's safety. Although he considered Alistair and Rudd rather thick-witted at times, they had spurts of shrewdness which left him little choice but to suspect that they were not above faking their flight by devious methods. After he had checked with the captains of several ships inbound from London, which had docked the same day Alistair and Rudd had supposedly disembarked, Beau had failed to find their names on the lists of passengers. Yet, when he had gone to other vessels that had entered the port as much as a week earlier, his suspicions had been confirmed. Their arrival had been well in advance of Wilson's murder. Having now become cognizant of the lie they had deliberately told for some unknown purpose, he was convinced that they were completely dedicated to creating any fabrication to achieve their own ends, perhaps even for the purpose of hiding a foul, murderous deed.

His mother and father came in to stay with them for a few days to get better acquainted with their grandson. It was gratifying for both Beau and Cerynise to see the older couple so engrossed in the little one, whose comical faces and bright-eyed cooing elicited their delighted laughter. To celebrate the new addition to the family, the four, bedecked in all their finery, went to the theater to watch the American actor, Edwin Forrest, in a production of *Othello*. Since it was the first evening that she and Beau had gone out in elegant garb since Marcus's birth, Cerynise wanted to look especially nice for her husband. Her cream-colored satin gown, which bared her shoulders sublimely, was bejeweled with tiny seed pearls and other diminutive beads that shimmered in the light. Her hair was dressed on top of her head, and a creamy plume curled coyly behind an ear. The cameo and pearl choker graced her throat, and pearl and diamond earrings glittered at her ears.

In all, Cerynise created a beautiful, radiant vision that drew more than a few admiring stares from other men. Germaine Hollingsworth's own newly acquired escort stared agog until the petite brunette jabbed him surreptitiously with her elbow, quickly drawing his attention back to her. Even so, during the performance, Germaine caught him avidly perusing her tawny-haired rival through her opera glasses, which he had apparently borrowed for such a purpose.

"If you can't keep your eyes off that little tart, Malcolm McFields, I'm going home!" she hissed in an huff. The actor's booming voice made it necessary for her to repeat her threat in a somewhat louder tone, but in an abrupt moment of silence that ensued in the play, her last words were loud enough to draw sharp gasps of astonishment from the theatergoers and startle the performers. Germaine froze in sudden humiliation as she felt nearly every eye upon her. She saw the Birminghams glance around briefly, but they seemed much more interested in the performance than with her. The play resumed, but Germaine's attention had now been ensnared by the four. It nettled her sorely when Beau pulled his wife's gloved hand within his lap. As much as the conjecture disturbed her, she just couldn't imagine him ogling another wench in Cerynise's presence or her absence, which made Malcolm's effrontery all the more angering. Germaine glared askance at her escort, but after suffering through such a painfully embarrassing ordeal, she was unwilling to issue another verbal reprimand lest she find herself completely flustered by a similar occurrence.

Reluctantly Malcolm handed the glasses back, but that didn't stop him from casting fleeting glances toward the tawny-haired goddess who sat close beside her husband in the Birminghams' box. His continuing fascination proved too much for Germaine to bear. Indeed, after her disappointment over losing Beau Birmingham to one whom she had once sneeringly called Sticks, she had little patience to contend with another smitten swain. The last act was barely underway when Germaine tried once again to claim Malcolm's attention and realized it was again centered on Cerynise. She promptly carried out her threat and left him to peruse the other woman as much as he desired.

CHAPTER 18

Rumbling thunder dragged Cerynise upward from a sound sleep, and even as she struggled to full awareness, lightning flickered beyond the bedroom windows, illuminating the interior and filling her with a deep-seated apprehension. In that brief, jagged streak of light, she caught sight of the clouds that were hovering threateningly over the house. They were as dark and ominous as the blackness that still held back the dawn. In another flash she noticed the larger branches of the live oak located just beyond the house swirling chaotically in the forceful winds that were sweeping inland. In spite of the years that had passed since her parents' deaths, Cerynise hadn't yet been able to conquer her fear of storms. Seeking comfort and reassurance in her husband's presence, she reached across to the pillow beside her own. Alas, she found only an indentation where his head had been.

"Beau?"

"In here," he answered from the dressing room.

Cerynise rolled onto her back and noticed a soft light streaming from the doorway of that area. "It's still dark outside," she announced sleepily. "Why are you up so early?"

"I promised Mr. Oaks that I'd be at the ship just after daybreak so we can secure the *Audacious*. If you haven't noticed it yet, madam, there's a storm heading our way."

"Oh, I've noticed all right." Worriedly Cerynise glanced beyond the windows again and cringed as another stroke of lightning swept across the dark shroud. "Is it going to be that bad?"

"Too soon to tell right now," he replied, leaving the dressing room. He came to the bed and leaned across to give her a long, loving kiss. When he pulled away slightly, his eyes reflected the light as he smiled down at her. "Good morning, my pet."

With a soft purr she looped her arms behind his neck and drew him down to her again. The fact that he was naked was an open invitation for her to run a hand admiringly over the muscular contour of his back. "I was just dreaming about you," she whispered beneath the kisses that lightly caressed her lips. "We were playing together again in the study, and you were doing all sorts of wonderful things."

Bracing up on an elbow, Beau grinned down at her as he searched her face in the meager light. "I thought I was the only one who had dreams like that."

"Oh no, sir." She moved her hands downward over the steely hardness of his buttocks. "In fact, if you have time, we could create more memories to recall."

As much as he yearned to fulfill her request, Beau had to decline. He did so with a muted groan of disappointment. "Your invitation is enough to make me want to forget about going to the ship at all, but Mr. Oaks will be expecting me." He pushed himself to his feet again. "I'll be sending most of the staff to Harthaven as soon as they do a few things around here just in case the storm becomes severe. I'd like for you to go with them when they leave."

"Without you?"

"I may not be back until about five or so this afternoon, and there's no telling what the storm will be doing by then."

"Oh, Beau, I couldn't bear not knowing if you're safe or not," his wife argued. "I'd like to wait for you."

"I'd feel a lot easier about the situation if you went out with the first vanguard of servants," he said, hoping to convince her. "Jasper and the rest of the men will be going out later, after they finish securing the house, but I really think that you and Marcus should go out as soon as possible."

"But I want to wait here at least until Jasper leaves," Cerynise stated stubbornly. "That's the earliest I will go unless you're here to take us."

Beau heaved a sigh. He had been afraid she'd say that. "I'll return as soon as I can, my love," he assured her, slipping into his underwear. "If the weather begins to look bad and I'm still not back, Jasper has strict orders to take you and Marcus to the plantation. I will brook no refusal from you then, madam. After Thomas takes me to the ship, he'll be returning here to await your departure."

"But how will you get back?"

"I'll have my rain gear from the *Audacious* by then, so I can walk home. Once here, I can hitch up the chaise and drive out to the plantation."

"But, Beau..."

He lifted a hand, halting her protests. "I insist that you leave before the winds get too strong, madam. I don't want to have to worry about you more than I do already." He fastened his trousers and cinched his belt. "I'll leave for Harthaven myself before the storm becomes too severe."

"Please don't wait too long," she begged.

He answered her through the light-knit sweater he was pulling over his head. "I won't, my love." Settling the garment in place, he blew her a kiss and stepped to the door. "I'm going down to grab something to eat and instruct the servants on what I want done in my absence. You might as well go back to sleep if you can. There's no sense in you getting up so early."

"Promise me you'll be careful," she called as he closed the door behind him.

"I promise."

Cerynise lay still, listening to the sound of his booted heels beating a rapid staccato down the curving length of stairs. Even when she could hear his approach or departure, his footfalls clearly conveyed the energy and vitality of the man.

Cerynise dallied in bed for a while longer, and then addressed herself to a morning grooming. She fed and bathed Marcus and finally went downstairs. By then, most of the wooden shutters had been closed over the windows, and with the heavy clouds looming close overhead, the interior was as gloomy as if nightfall had descended. Lamps had been lit, and it was by their light that she carried Marcus around to view the progress that had been made.

"You're going to experience your first real blow, young man," she cooed to the baby. "Yet I think you're just the sort to enjoy it. A bit like your papa, you are."

As if in full agreement with her statement, her son gurgled at her charmingly, lifting his fine eyebrows and pursing his lips. His mother could do nothing less than nuzzle him and bestow a motherly kiss upon his soft cheek.

Jasper had addressed himself to the matter of preserving the furnishings in case the house suffered extensive damage during their absence. He was both instructing and assisting the male servants in that ambitious endeavor. Since there was no guarantee that the exterior shutters could withstand a destructive gale or that a limb wouldn't snap and crash through a window, the precious Oriental rugs were rolled up and placed against the walls of the hallway upstairs. Treasured bric-a-brac also went into temporary storage on shelves in linen closets located on both levels in the middle of the house. The crystal chandeliers were carefully wrapped with sheets to assure that no prism would plummet to the floor should strong winds sweep inward through broken windows. Outside, the wrought iron furniture was taken from the garden and stored in the carriage house. Soon after his return from the docks, Thomas started his own project, making the conveyance as watertight as possible for the baby's sake. During all of this, Philippe cooked and packed up baskets of food, a few for those who'd be leaving earlier but mainly for the ones who would be staying until later on in the afternoon. In all, it was a tedious, time-consuming process, and midday had already passed when the first group of servants left the manor.

Only a few moments before the appointed time that he and the mate were to meet and begin battening down the hatches and readying the ship for the storm, Beau sprinted aboard the *Audacious* beneath the covering of a small tarp, which he held over himself. Stephen Oaks was living in the first mate's quarters aboard ship, and in recent days had been charting a course for the Caribbean islands, where, during the winter months, he would be sailing. While there, he'd be selling much needed goods to the merchants and collecting new cargo for the return trip. At the moment, however, there was no indication to assure Beau that the mate was moving about or, for that matter, even up.

The rain was increasing, laying a heavy haze over the city, and Beau immediately went down to the captain's cabin to fetch his rain gear. It was so dark beyond the stern windows that a lamp had to be lit and placed on the floor directly in front of the locker so he could see into it. While searching for the necessary items, he noticed a large white bundle that had been shoved all the way to the back of the cabinet. Bemused, he pulled it forth and shook it out. The main item he realized was a sheet from his own bunk. It was spotted with old stains, very much like dried blood. The second article was a woman's lace-trimmed nightgown, which he recognized as one that had once been his favorite among those belonging to his wife. He hadn't seen it since well before their return to Charleston and, on occasion, had wondered what had happened to it. The back of the gown also bore similar stains, but there were others of a yellowish hue that had become stiff with age.

It didn't take Beau more than a second to realize what he was staring at, and yet he was staggered by the evidence he had found. Here was solid proof that he had taken his wife's virginity while he was out of his head with fever, and yet she had been so caught up with the idea of not tying him down against his will that she had refused to present it to him. If not for the fact that he had had his own entangled memories of that deed, she would have taken herself...and their baby...out of his life forever, just for the sake of honor.

Beau's vision blurred with a light filming of tears as he thought of what that occurrence would have done to him. Except for the fear that someone, whether Alistair Winthrop, Howard Rudd or another villain, would harm or even kill her, he felt so completely blessed and favored by her presence in his life that he could only imagine the torment and anguish he would have suffered had they not resolved the matter of their marriage and her pregnancy.

He glanced toward his bunk, the place where he had stripped away her virginity. How he must have hurt her in his fevered delirium, he mused, and yet...how could he be sorry for having done the deed when Marcus was now the pride of his life and Cerynise his truest love? Suddenly his heart bubbled over with joy, and he felt a burning desire to return to them with all possible haste.

Slipping into his rain gear, he hurried down the hall to Mr. Oaks's quarters and beat a fist upon the portal. "Eh, my mate, are you alive in there?"

"Ah...Aye, Captain, I think so," came a groggy voice from within. "I must have worked too long into the morning and overslept."

"Well, get yourself up. Bridget is going out to Harthaven, and she fully expects you to join her out there as soon as we're done here. From the looks of things, we'll be busy until nightfall unless you hurry yourself along."

"I'm moving! I'm moving!" Stephen called back with more eagerness.

Cerynise made a concerted effort to keep her mind occupied. She had sent Vera to Harthaven with assurances that she would follow with the baby as soon as the captain returned. She nursed Marcus, talked to him about all sorts of things and, when he slept, tried without much success to read. As the afternoon waned, the fierce winds began to howl around the house. Listening to the eerie sounds heightened her trepidation, and she had to remind herself again and again that Beau would be home soon and that even with the fury that was being unleashed, she was secure. The walls around her were strong and sturdy. Yet, in spite of her efforts, she found little comfort. Only when she could feel her husband's arms around her again would she be content.

Concern for Beau began to weigh her spirit down, and she paced about restlessly, looking at the clock many times in the passage of a moment. It didn't matter how strong, capable or experienced her husband was, she still feared for his safety and wanted him close at hand. She needed him there to soothe and comfort her. He was so gentle and adept at doing so, just as he had always been and probably always would be.

Jasper came into the study to urge her to think about leaving pretty soon, and as much as she dreaded going without Beau, Cerynise realized that she couldn't refuse his plea and perchance be the cause of some harm coming to her son or to the men. She didn't want to countenance any responsibility in that area, for she knew the servants would feel obligated to stay with her if she refused to leave. The vivid reminder of the tree that had fallen and killed her parents during a storm gave her enough cause to acquiesce to the butler's suggestion. Even so, it was with a heavy heart that she climbed the stairs and went to fetch her son and the satchel that she had prepared for him.

Holding her son close, Cerynise lifted the bag with her free hand. The baby whimpered a little, and she paused to cradle him close to her. He fussed, nuzzling her breast as if he wanted to nurse. A few moments' delay wouldn't hinder their departure, she decided, and was just reaching up to unfasten her bodice when she heard the front door slam.

"Beau!" With a glad cry, she rushed from the nursery and crossed to the door of the master bedroom. Sweeping it open, she hurried to the landing and, from over the balustrade, searched the central hall for her husband, confident now that the fears and memories of her parents' death, which she had been struggling to hold at bay all day, wouldn't trouble her any longer now that Beau was home.

The relief that had momentarily filled her vanished abruptly when she glimpsed, not her husband, but Alistair Winthrop and Howard Rudd moving around in the front foyer. Worse yet, Jasper, who had apparently gone to answer the door, was sprawled unconscious on the floor near the central hall. It looked as if he had been dragged back from the entrance, and at the moment Alistair was smirking as he slowly squeezed the trigger of the pistol he was pointing at the butler's head. With a gasp Rudd bolted forward and knocked the gun aside.

"Are you so bent on killing that you can't even realize that by shooting Jasper you'll alert everyone in the house?" the solicitor hissed in a rage. "We'll lock him in the kitchen pantry. If he comes around, he won't be able to get out."

"How many servants do you think are here with the girl?"

"Can't be more than one in the house besides the girl with the chef gone and that old tar and the driver tied up and gagged in the carriage house. With everyone scurrying around all day, I lost track. Have to take care of Cooper once we let him out of the privy. He'll set up a row when he realizes we wedged that timber against the door and he can't get out. How many did you count off?"

"About the same." Alistair sounded more than a little smug as he continued. " 'Twas convenient of the neighbors to vacate their house so we could watch the captain's house from their bedroom upstairs. Still, I'd have preferred waiting until dark before venturing over here. Someone could've seen us come over and gone to warn the captain." The man rubbed a hand over the natural concavity between his bony hipbones. "I'm still tender from that hernia he gave me a week ago. The bastard nearly tore me insides apart."

"Couldn't wait. The servants were getting ready to leave with the girl," the solicitor argued none too patiently. "Besides, the longer we delayed, the more likely our chances of being caught by the captain. He'll likely kill us if he finds us here again, so I'd rather get this damn fool thing over with as soon as possible. So far, a third of your aunt's fortune has served as an excellent incentive, but if I'm dead, the whole of it wouldn't do me a bit of good."

"Too bad I can't gut the captain like I did that Wilson fellow," Alistair muttered sourly.

Upstairs, Cerynise bit into a knuckle to keep from moaning aloud. She had known the two men were evil, but she hadn't actually counted on them actually being capable of murder.

"That was a necessity," Rudd rejoined acidly. "If Wilson had killed the girl, then there wouldn't have been much for us to take back to England. The captain's death would only be a passing pleasure, but if we don't hurry, it may become a requirement, hopefully one we'll be able to perform with our skins still attached. There's no doubt about it. Abducting the girl will be a lot easier without having to confront that damned Yankee."

"Could've blown me away by sheer surprise when he went off to his ship this morning. Sure saved us a lot of worry trying to figure out how we'd slice his throat on the sly so we could seize the girl. It seems the brave and mighty captain is just as nervous about a little storm as the rest of the people living in this area. Frankly, I don't know why everyone is in such an uproar. If you want my opinion, they're a bunch of spineless cowards."

"Maybe they know something we don't," Rudd reasoned in a terse whisper. "But no matter. We'll hide out in the country just like the rest of them until our ship sets sail. That ol' tumbledown shack gives us a good view of the road, and so far, we've had plenty of time to skedaddle under the bridge whenever we've seen the sheriff coming. After we gave our clothes and a couple of coins to those two vagrants and told them to wander along the wharves and onto that ship bound for England, we haven't been bothered much. Perhaps our ploy actually worked to distract everyone. In any case, I don't expect there'll be too much chance of the sheriff finding us after we take the girl. He'll likely think it was someone else's doing. Carting her aboard the ship in a trunk will be easy enough once we render her unconscious."

"We're being put to a lot of bother to keep her alive." Alistair sighed heavily, deploring the trouble to which they were being put. "What I wouldn't give to be able to break her beautiful little neck right here and now. Perhaps Wilson had the right idea."

"Wasn't his idea, remember?" Rudd retorted impatiently. "Or are you forgetting what we overheard in our room that night? But that's neither here nor there. It's ridiculous to think of killing the girl before we're able to claim your aunt's wealth, so don't start getting any ideas in your head about how easy it would be to put her out of her misery. If you kill her now, nobody would be able to confirm her identity by the time we got her corpse back to England. Besides, we wouldn't be able to hide the stench overlong in the close quarters of a ship. The captain of the vessel would surely become suspicious and come searching."

"You know, Rudd, you've become quite accomplished in the field of murder since we've been together. Nowadays you no longer cringe when we talk about killing people."

"Aye," the barrister agreed derisively. "You've taught me well. I just hope I don't hang for it."

"Cheer up," Alistair implored with a soft chortle. "Once we snatch the girl, we'll be sailing home to a fortune. Then we can do away with her and have pleasure doing it."

Cerynise's skin crawled as they casually talked of her death. Slowly, carefully, she backed away from the balustrade, hoping Marcus wouldn't make a fuss. Somehow she'd have to free Cooper before he arrived at the same fate as the other three servants. But the longer she thought about that idea, rational reasoning seemed to argue against her risking exposure to let the servant out of the privy. It was she whom the two wanted, not Cooper, and if they saw her with him, they'd then have no further reason to be wary of gun-shots. They might even kill him. Better for all their sakes if she remained hidden with her baby.

Cerynise fled into her bedroom just as another bolt of lightning rent the sky and cast strange elongated streaks of light into the house through the slats of the shutters. She was caught in a nightmare, virtually alone except for a helpless baby, at the mercy of a storm and the demons that were intent upon destroying her and everyone she held dear. Somehow she had to do something to win the day for all concerned.

She acted on pure instinct, with her free hand turning down the wick in the lamp until the bedchamber was plunged into total darkness.

Only the lightning provided her glimpses of the interior. Without pause, she hefted the baby's satchel, dashed into the dark nursery and closed the door behind her as quietly as possible. She didn't pause but with thumping heart eased open the door leading into the central hall. The corridor ran the full length of the house and, about midway, passed the balustrade and the two short corridors encircling it, one of which led to the landing near the door of the master bedroom.

A pair of wall sconces had been lit at each end of the main hall, and after setting down the valise, Cerynise crept stealthily down the hall in both directions to snuff the lights. Retracing her steps, she picked up the satchel and slipped into the little cubicle that served as a connecting hallway between two adjoining bedrooms on the south side.

Blessing the knowledge she had of the house, Cerynise carefully opened the door of the large walk-in linen closet located against the back wall of that short passageway. Carefully she slipped the key from the latch, stepped within, closed the door behind her and quietly locked it. Alone with her baby in the darkness of the interior, she dragged several sheets off a shelf and made a bed of sorts on the floor for her son. Then she sat down beside it, realizing only then that her legs were shaking beneath her. For a panic-filled moment, the mere awareness of her fear threatened to collapse her self-control, but she pressed trembling fingers to her lips, resolving to overcome her trepidations by her own will and fortitude.

Marcus started fussing, and Cerynise immediately put him to her breast. Nursing him gave her time to put her thoughts into clear perspective, and she began to form a plan to thwart the villains' intentions, based upon the hope that Marcus would fall asleep soon after his feeding. Her husband might be arriving home anytime now, and those men would kill him if they could. For once, it was up to her to save him, and she prayed that she could do half as well as he had in the past whenever he had come to her rescue.

It was not long before Cerynise became aware of Alistair and Rudd wandering through the rooms upstairs. She could hear their cautious footsteps and, beneath the door of the closet, could see a thread of light from the hurricane lamps they carried. She held her breath when one of them paused near the closet door and mentally offered a prayer of thanksgiving when they moved on without testing the knob. After exploring the two bedrooms on either side of the closet, they finally went downstairs again to continue their search there.

When Marcus had finished feeding, Cerynise laid him over her shoulder and patted his tiny back until a soft burp came from him. Taking every precaution she could to make sure he wouldn't wake because of some discomfort, she changed his diaper, immensely thankful that in the dark closet she didn't have to worry about anything more than it being wet. Slowly she rocked him until he fell asleep. Dropping a loving kiss upon his silken head, she held him for a moment more, dearly hoping that it wouldn't be for the last time. She laid him upon the makeshift bed, covered him with a blanket and left her cubbyhole, taking care to lock it behind her. It was most convenient that her gown had deep, concealed pockets into which she could deposit the key. Not only did the key open all the linen closets in the house, but it also unlatched the pantry door, where the two villains had talked about hiding Jasper.

Cerynise entered her bedroom once again, removed the pistol from the drawer of Beau's bedside table, and slipped it into her right pocket. There was no need for her to check the loading. Since the appearance of the dog, her husband had gotten into the habit of examining the pistol almost nightly before turning out the light.

"Where's the bitch gone to?" Alistair muttered from the lower level as Cerynise crept cautiously from her bedroom. "She's not down here, and she doesn't appear to be upstairs. Her baby is gone. Do you suppose she could have left?"

"In this rain?" Rudd scoffed. "She wouldn't take a baby out in this weather unless it was by carriage, and that's still here. No, she's in this house all right, probably hiding from us."

Although many of the lower rooms were still lit, both men were holding lamps to aid in their hunt for her. They approached the stairs, and silently she flitted past the balustrade to the main hallway. Slipping into the bedroom that Beau's parents preferred to use when they came, she pushed the door almost closed behind her, leaving a slit wide enough to allow her to watch the entrance of the narrow cubicle behind which she had hidden her son.

Hardly breathing, Cerynise peered through the crack as the pair of miscreants reached the upper level. They went down the hall toward the nursery and then, to her horror, Alistair turned in the opposite direction, entered the corridor between the two bedrooms and rattled the doorknob of the closet.

"This door is locked," he hissed, tossing a glance toward Rudd.

"Perhaps she's in there," the lawyer suggested, joining him.

Immediately Cerynise flung open the door behind which she had been hiding, letting it slam against the wall to gain their attention as she raced around the nearest side of the balustrade. She amazed herself by her own swift descent and sprinted into the kitchen. Hearing the rapidly drumming footfalls of her adversaries following in pursuit, she unlocked the pantry door and yanked it open, hoping to find Jasper conscious and fully alert. The lanterns in the kitchen illumined the interior of the pantry clearly, and she almost groaned in despair, for there was now not only the butler lying crumpled in the narrow space, but

Cooper as well. Both men were unconscious and of no help to her.

Gingerly she closed the pantry door, afraid of making a sound, and then darkened the room. For barely an instant a stroke of lightning lit the kitchen with narrow slices of light cast through the shutters. As she paused near the dining room door, she caught the sound of footsteps advancing through the room. Stealthily she tiptoed to the far end of the kitchen and slipped past the swinging door into the hall. She flitted down its length, turning down the wicks in the wall sconces as she went until the corridor was nothing more than a dark tunnel. Upon reaching the main hall, she heard the men's voices drifting down from the kitchen.

"She's been here, all right," Alistair announced in an angry tone. "The lamps are out now when they weren't a moment ago. I bet the bitch went outside to the carriage house."

"I didn't hear the back door being opened, and the way the hinges squeak, I'm sure I would have noticed it," Rudd assured him. Then he thrust out an arm. "Look over there! There's another door! Come on!"

Cerynise dashed from the hallway and, once again, ascended to the second story. Even as she reached the long table standing against the wall near her bedroom door, she heard Rudd urging his companion.

"Got to hurry. The captain could return any second."

"Where the devil has she gone now?"

"Upstairs, I think. She's leading us on a wild-goose chase, and this time I think the goose is winning."

"She's only a woman," Alistair sneered, sprinting ahead of the lawyer. Reaching the stairs, he flung a question over his shoulder, "What can she do against the two of us?"

Rudd heard a sound directly above them and lifted his head in time to see a massive vase stuffed with fall flowers plummeting toward his confederate. "Look out!"

It was Alistair's folly that he had to see what was coming. He glanced up when the heavy urn was only a short distance above his head and tried to jerk aside, but he wasn't nimble enough. He felt the weighty porcelain painfully grazing his scalp. The bottom of one of the delicately decorated handles broke just as it hit the top of his head. In the next instant Alistair let out a fierce roar of pain as the upper portion of the broken handle gouged his scalp and, upon passing his ear, promptly sliced it off. A second later the vessel shattered on the stairs, sending shards of broken glass flying like needles into their legs.

"The bitch! I'll kill her!" Alistair cried at the top of his lungs, clasping a hand over the bloody stub of his ear. "She maimed me!"

After prying a piece of porcelain from his own calf, Rudd picked up the severed piece of flesh and solicitously passed it to his partner-in-crime. "Maybe you can have your ear sewn back on."

"So it can rot?" A snarl came from Alistair

617

as he rejected the notion. "So help me, when I catch the bitch, I'll rip hers off with a saw!" he threatened, his voice fraught with pain. The jagged piece of glass sticking into his shin came out with a small spurt of blood. It trickled down his leg, but he hardly felt it with the agony he was suffering otherwise.

"*If* we catch her," Rudd offered, beginning to doubt that they were the crafty ones in this cat-and-mouse game. In fact, the girl had seemed pretty confident of her aim when she had peered down over the railing. He was sure he had glimpsed an expression of gleeful anticipation on her beautiful face.

Compresses were applied to the ragged nubbin that remained of Alistair's ear. Then his head was swathed in a towel to hold them in place. In dire distress now, he had lost the verve for adventure in this chase which he had heretofore been enjoying. He was out to seize the wench, and with every word he muttered he made it clear that from the moment they caught her, her life would be a hellish, torturous torment until the day she died.

The two wandered through the upper rooms, looking into every nook and cranny. It seemed weird but in the midst of their lofty search, they heard a siren's faint, melodic call from the lower depths. After creeping downstairs, they stepped cautiously to the marble floor, trying to avoid the larger pieces of broken glass that threatened to pierce the soles of their shoes. Even so, Rudd had to pause and set his lantern down to pick out one such splinter.

618

The lamps in all of the rooms had now been snuffed, and though the two men peered into the surrounding darkness, seemingly from out of nowhere a white specter soared toward them, emitting a shriek that was definitely of a female origin. Warbling screams of fright erupted from the two men, and in goggle-eyed fear they retreated from the winged demon that flew at them from the darkness, stumbling over their own feet in their haste to scurry out of its way.

Having forayed through the kitchen while the men were searching upstairs, Cerynise had come away with a spool of stout twine, a heavy iron kettle and a large bag of flour with which to weight it. It had met her mood to drape a sheet over the kettle to make it appear ghostly. The twine she had cut to a length longer than she was tall. One end she fastened to the handle of the pot and the other end to one of the spindles of the balustrade. After wrapping another length of twine around the kettle, or rather the belly of her spook, she had clasped the opposite end and then retreated as far as she could go back into the shadows beneath the stairs. There she had waited, much like a spider for a fly, until her victims ventured into her trap.

This time it was Rudd who caught the brunt of Cerynise's attack. Her contraption nearly lifted him off his feet when it slammed into him. It certainly served to spill him backward to the floor where the glass had been liberally distributed. There he lay as if frozen, staring upward in a stunned daze while the ghostly pendulum swung tauntingly to and fro above him.

"Are you alive?" Alistair queried, seriously doubting the fact, for the lawyer was staring up the ceiling fixedly and really didn't appear to be breathing. Perhaps all these years his companion had been suffering from some unknown malady that, at the moment of impact or at sight of the ghostly apparition, had stripped away his life. He thumped a fist rather harshly into the rounded chest, trying to provoke some response, and with a loud wheezing intake, Rudd sucked air into his lungs once again.

"What hit me?" Rudd gasped, thankful he could breathe again.

"A ghost," Alistair retorted satirically. "Of Cerynise's making."

Rudd swallowed and tried to move, then, gingerly feeling the back of his head, realized there was now a huge knot where his noggin had bounced on the marble floor. That was not all. He could feel something sharp piercing both his shoulder and backside. Rolling over, he allowed Alistair the honors of prying the pieces of shattered porcelain out of his flesh.

"It was unwise of you to ever throw Cerynise out of your aunt's house," the solicitor reminisced morosely, as if he had just had an afterlife experience in the nether depths. "I don't think she has ever forgiven us."

"I've got a lot more to forgive her for," Alistair growled, peering into the shadows beneath the stairs. Holding his glass lamp

620

aloft, well above his right shoulder, he crept forward cautiously, certain that he had seen some movement in the darkness beyond its glow. "Are you hiding back there, Cerynise?"

The bronze bookend was like a bat flying out of hell. It crashed into the lamp, breaking the glass and spilling oil down the whole side of him. It quickly erupted in flames. Alistair shrieked in sudden anguish and terror as the fire rapidly fed into his clothing and began to sear his flesh. In a panic he whirled and raced past the stairs, frantically snatching at the burning bandages on his head. Rudd was just struggling to rise, but gasped in horror and ducked out of the way as the human fire-brand leapt over him. In another moment the front door was jerked open, and Alistair went screaming into the torrential downpour beyond the porch. Rudd staggered to his feet and, holding one hand to the back of his head and the other against his bleeding rump, limped to the front door where, far beyond the porch, his partner-in-crime was presently getting thoroughly drenched.

"I think we should leave before she kills us," Rudd called out to the suffering man above the roar of the storm. "I'm not sure we should rile her any more than she is."

"*I'll rile her!*" Alistair blared from the front lawn. "*I'll impale her on a pike and let her car-cass rot in the sun!*"

"What sun?"

Alistair sought to gnash his teeth at his cohort, but the pain evoked when he tried to draw his lips back made him immediately regret his effort. "Never mind, you dunderhead! Just help me get back into the house. I'm drowning out here."

"Well, at least you're no longer burning," Rudd reasoned mutedly. He hobbled down the front steps and solicitously served as a human crutch to the half-seared man. By the time the two got back inside, their clothes were soaked and pools of water collected around their sodden shoes and spread in ever-widening circles. Walking on the marble floor proved hazardous. They went slipping and sliding with arms flailing wildly in a concerted effort to balance themselves. Though Alistair's wobbly legs threatened to collapse beneath him before he ever got there, Alistair reached the nearest bench and lowered his skinny rear onto the seat. Rudd clumsily skated over to the table where he had left his lamp and brought the light back to inspect the other's burns. It was worse than he had first imagined, for the whole right side of Alistair's face had been cooked. Raw flesh oozed beneath thickly curling, blackened crisps that, a few moments ago, might have been an outer layer of skin. Rudd seriously doubted that his partner would have to shave that particular side of his face ever again.

Grimacing at the sight, Rudd drew a handkerchief from his coat pocket, squeezed the water out of it, and solicitously tried to wipe away the charred peelings, succeeding only in extracting a fierce yowl of pain.

"My face is burnt, dammit!" Alistair railed in torment. "That's what the little twit did to me, besides burning half my body!"

"At least your ear is no longer bleeding," the lawyer counseled, curling his lip in repugnance as he inspected the charred glob. When he looked at his companion in profile from the right angle, it was extremely difficult to determine if he was human.

Alistair choked in outrage. "I can't even feel it anymore with all the torment I'm in!"

Rudd stepped back to survey the whole man and saw that, along Alistair's right side, all that remained of his coat and shirt were blackened shreds adhering to his bony chest and arm, which were crisply burned. Most of the hair on his head and chest had been singed to the roots, and his eyebrows were completely gone. Just looking at him made the lawyer cringe.

"Are you sure you want to continue our efforts to catch the girl?"

"Go find something to dress my wounds!" Alistair muttered.

"The captain may come back any moment now," Rudd reasoned.

Alistair snorted. "He'll likely wait until the rain slackens."

"It doesn't appear likely that that will happen any time soon. I think we should leave while we still can."

"*No!*" Alistair roared. "If it's the last thing I do, I'm going to kill that bitch, even if it's with my dying breath."

"It may well be," the lawyer responded ruefully. "We've clearly been outwitted by her."

"*Never!*"

"I'll go see what I can find to tend your burns," Rudd offered submissively. Wary of his feet flying out from under him, he made his way with painstaking care down the corridor, leaving a watery trail behind him. Once he entered the kitchen, he lifted the lamp high to light the path around the table and squished his way carefully toward the pantry. It was a common practice for salves and such to be kept in a kitchen, where most burns occurred, and he expected that his search of the closet would prove successful. But first, he'd have to make sure the two men were still unconscious and wouldn't attack him once he opened the door. He didn't know if they could do any more damage to him than the girl had, but he wasn't willing to give them a chance.

He was just passing the dining room door when the rays cast from his lantern touched on something that made his nerves stand on end. With a startled gasp he glanced around, just in time to see Cerynise with an iron poker poised above her head. In the next instant the rod came swishing downward through the air. Rudd threw up an arm to protect himself, but too late. His cry of alarm dwindled to a mute groan as the poker struck his head. A fiery pain exploded in his brain, and he stumbled forward to his knees, still clasping the hurricane lamp in a desperate grip lest he, too, find himself set on fire by spilling oil. In a dazed stupor he grasped hold of the girl's skirt. The rod was lifted once again and brought down, darkening his awareness to a pinpoint of light as he toppled aside. Then that, too, was snuffed as a third blow was delivered.

"*Rudd!*" Alistair called in a tone of panic from the front of the house.

Almost calmly, Cerynise placed the poker beside the solicitor's still form and picked up the hurricane lamp that had settled rattlingly to the floor. Moving through the dining room at a leisured pace, she watched the radiance reach out beyond her, flowing through the doorway into the central hall.

Alistair heaved an audible sigh as he noticed the approaching light. "I thought something had happened to you. I heard you scream." Silence continued unswervingly, and the scorched man struggled upward from the bench in intensifying alarm. "Rudd? Is that you, Rudd? Why don't you answer me?"

"I'm afraid he can't, Alistair," Cerynise replied, moving like a wraith into the hall.

Alistair gasped and backed away. "What did you do to him?"

She smiled stiffly as she passed the stairs and set the lantern aside on a table. "Put him out of his misery, I would presume."

"You mean...you...you killed him?"

Though Cerynise couldn't tell much from his blistered face, his tone had certainly sounded incredulous. "Perhaps."

"How could you...?" Alistair began, and

then abruptly remembered what she had already done to them. Suddenly he was afraid, enough that the hairs on the back of his neck, at least the few that were left, stood on end. "Keep your distance, bitch! Stay where you are!"

Ignoring his ultimatum, she glided ever-nearer. "Why, Alistair, what could I possibly do to you that you haven't already threatened to do to me?"

His eyes widened until she could see the whites, a sharp contrast indeed against his scorched skin. A warbling wail of fright burst forth from his singed lips. He wouldn't put it past the wench to employ some of his own threats to do him in. "You're a fiend!"

Her poise amazed Cerynise. She had never dreamt that she could remain unruffled in the face of danger. She had always been afraid that she'd panic in a dangerous situation and be utterly useless to herself and everyone around her. Silently she thanked heaven for her aplomb.

"Now really, Alistair, what right has a kettle to besmirch the pot and call it black?" The incongruous humor of her statement drew a chuckle from her as she peered into his blackened face. She slipped a hand into her pocket, taking hold of the butt of the pistol, and shrugged casually. "I shouldn't make jests when you're obviously in pain, should I, Alistair?" She shook her head sadly, and then, without pause, changed the subject. "So! Would you like to take Rudd's advice now and give up the fight?"

"You slut!" the thin man bellowed. "What *more* could you do to me that you *haven't* done already?"

"Put you out of your misery," she offered.

Jerking forth a pistol from the left side of his coat, he smirked lopsidedly with a measure of triumph. "My turn, bitch!"

The hazel eyes reflected the light of the lantern as Cerynise flicked a glance toward his weapon. "Before you kill me, Alistair, would you mind telling me one thing? Why have you done this? Why did you journey all the way from England to create havoc in my life? Do you hate me so much?"

"Why?" The man scoffed at her lack of insight. "For money, of course. What else?"

"Money?" Cerynise's brows gathered in confusion. "But Lydia left you everything. Wasn't it enough?"

His laughter was short-lived and chilling. But then, he had always seemed more demon than man to her.

"You stupid, senseless twit!" he choked and then shuddered at the pain enveloping him. "Lydia left me nothing! She couldn't see anyone but you after you came to live with her. You turned her affections against me. She wrote a new will, leaving you everything. She couldn't even spare me a farthing."

His answer was almost more than Cerynise could comprehend. "But I saw the will," she reasoned. "You showed it to me. It declared you as her sole heir."

"That was the *old* will, one which Rudd

627

had drafted long before you became Lydia's ward. She went behind our backs, she did, and made a new one on the sly. But I wasn't cognizant of that fact, and I became desperate, you see. My creditors were harping at me day and night, threatening to imprison me. I held them off as long as possible, hoping Lydia would do me a favor and die, but the strain was too much, and I wanted to live." He shrugged one shoulder lamely. "Her last night on earth...I visited her and put hemlock in that foul-tasting tonic she always sipped in the evening."

Cerynise gasped. "You mean you...she didn't...?"

"No, she didn't die of natural causes," Alistair finished for her with a one-sided sneer. "I was tired of having to argue and beg for every farthing she threw me, so I took matters into my own hands and"—he chortled crazily—"put the old hag out of her misery. I doubt that she even knew what I had done. Certainly that stupid doctor of hers didn't."

"Oh, Alistair, how could you?" Cerynise moaned.

"Actually, it was all very easy," he replied smugly. "All I had to do was think how rich I would be once Lydia passed on. I thought everything would be wonderful then, until I found out what the old hag had done."

Cerynise's mind reeled. No wonder he had been in such a hurry to get her out of Lydia's house...at least until he realized there was a new will. "That's why you came to fetch me from the *Audacious*." She was just beginning to understand the reasoning behind his attempts to take her captive. "By that time, you had discovered the truth and had plans to kill me as soon as it became convenient."

Alistair tried to nod, but the agony that the movement caused made him tremble uncontrollably. Another moment passed before he could continue. "I wanted to kill you. It would have been nice and tidy before you married the captain. Without a legal heir to your name, all of Lydia's wealth would have come to me." He wheezed in pain. "When your husband waved those marriage papers in front of me, I thought all was lost. But I didn't give up, not me. I came after you. We were intending to take you back to England, ensconce you in Lydia's house and then, after assuming legal guardianship over you, render you feeble and incapable of communication with strong potions. Of course, we'd have forced you to sign a will which would have left me everything in the event of your death. Oh, we'd have allowed you to have visitors for a while, some of Lydia's friends who knew you.... We'd have even appointed a nurse to care for you so no one would have suspected that we were feeding you slow-acting poison. Then we'd have buried you."

"Don't you think my husband would have come after me?"

"Oh, we were willing to pay for his death, someone who'd have made it look like an accident before the bloody bastard set foot on

English soil. People wouldn't have grieved his passing overmuch."

"You planned it all," Cerynise mused aloud. "Yet, except for Lydia's death, none of it will ever come to pass now."

Alistair had already come to that conclusion himself, but he was not above smirking at the power he held over her now. "At least you'll be dead."

"Did Rudd help you kill Lydia?" she queried, realizing there might have been a viable reason for her not trusting the solicitor.

"He didn't know anything about that. In fact, he only became an accessory after I killed another. As yet, he isn't aware that I poisoned Lydia, but he had no choice but to help me when I offered him a third of the inheritance. You see, he needed the money as desperately as I did. He's quite partial to his brandy and other things that cost money. Or perhaps he was once. Do you really think you killed him?"

"He won't be helping you, if that's what you mean." Cerynise tilted her head curiously. "I heard you say that you had stabbed Wilson because he was trying to kill me. Was that really the reason?"

"A necessity, Rudd said," Alistair admitted. "The tar was being paid to kill you to seek revenge on your husband."

"You say he was being paid, yet Wilson might have thought that he had enough cause to retaliate on his own...without inducement."

Alistair grimaced again at the pain he was suffering and staggered slightly before he could manage to bring himself in line. "It's not unheard of for a man to kill for revenge, but in this case, he not only had an accomplice, but there was someone else who had funds enough to guarantee their enthusiasm for such a chore."

"Do you know their names?"

"The man I heard advising Wilson to lay low for a time was Frank Lester. It seemed they both came out here one night to do you in. Frank was boasting about throwing you down the stairs at your husband."

"But why would they have been so careless to talk where you could overhear?"

Alistair winced, wishing at the moment that he had a whole vat of brandy to drink. It would probably be the only thing that would ease his discomfort. "We had a room right next door to them at an inn, a shabby one at best, but the only one we could afford. We heard voices coming through a vent in the chimney in our room and paused to listen. Here I was, newly arrived in Charleston, and the first person I heard those two discussing was you. I thought for a moment my imagination was getting out of hand."

"I've heard it said that Wilson was wary of strangers since there were so many people looking for him. How did you manage to get close enough to knife him?"

His blistered lips moved minutely, trying to form a sneer. "He had seen us getting off a ship

631

from England, and when we asked him about an inn, he told us where he was staying. Of course, he was cautious of others seeing his face, so he kept to the shadows most of the time or hid out in his room. After we overheard him talking to Frank Lester, we approached him on the dock in the guise of needing more directions. By that time, he thought nothing of talking to us, since he knew we were Englishmen and had no dealings with the local inhabitants."

"Are you planning on murdering me by some other devious means or do you intend to kill me with that?" Cerynise asked, indicating the pistol he was holding.

"I guess it really doesn't matter now how I kill you. Considering my present condition and without Rudd to help me, taking you back to England seems rather farfetched. I can only hope that after killing you here, I'll be able to collect on some of the inheritance before your husband sends investigators to England to search me out."

Alistair winced and raised his weapon, aiming it toward her heart. "I can't say that it's been a pleasure knowing you."

Cerynise had already cocked the pistol in her pocket for the sake of safety some time ago, but she couldn't foresee having enough time to draw it forth from her skirt before she fired. Her finger tightened on the trigger, but in the next instant the front door was flung wide, and Beau swept in, clothed in rain gear. Alistair glanced around in sharp sur-

632

prise and immediately swept his own weapon around and centered its bore on the other man's chest.

"Nooo!" Cerynise shrieked, pulling back the firing mechanism in swift reaction. The recoil of the pistol knocked her backward, but in a quick, hazy glimpse she saw blood fly outward from Alistair's chest as the lead shot burrowed deep. He seemed to convulse forward, and a wry smile twisted across his scorched lips as he peered up at Beau, who, surprised by it all, could only look death in the face as the man centered the weapon on his chest.

Cerynise screamed again, her heart all but stopping. It was a fleeting moment of terrifying, wrenching suspense as the hammer fell. A deafening explosion of sound was fully expected by all three, but there was only a dull, rasping click of metal.

Alistair stared down in amazement at the pistol. "Should've known," he mumbled as the weapon toppled from his loosening fingers. "Got wet, it did." He slumped to his knees and stared down at his rapidly reddening chest. Then he canted his head toward Cerynise, and his unruly lips curved awkwardly. "Should've taken Rudd's advice and left before you kilt me....You were always far luckier than I...." He collapsed forward to the floor and, after a choked gasp, breathed his last.

Cerynise leapt across his still form and, despite her husband's sodden gear, threw herself into his opening arms, sobbing harshly in relief as he clasped her hard against him.

"Oh, Beau! I thought he was going to kill you! I didn't know his gun wouldn't fire!"

"Rest easy, madam," her husband gently soothed. "His intent was to kill me, and he paid for it with his life."

"He killed Wilson and Lydia...and others," she gasped through her sobs. "He told me so."

Beau drew back and searched her face. Noticing that her gown had become soaked by his rain gear, he began to shrug out of it. "Did he kill Wilson because he was afraid that the tar would talk?"

Cerynise shook her head, trying to wipe away her tears with the back of a hand. "No, not at all. As farfetched as it might seem, Alistair killed him because Wilson was trying to murder me. Wilson also had an accomplice-...that man whom you talked to Germaine about the night of Suzanne's engagement party...Frank Lester. He and Wilson were being paid to kill me for someone who wanted to exact revenge on you."

"Germaine," Beau muttered with sudden certainty. "She all but threatened us that night on the porch. I didn't take it much to heart at the time, but I might have underestimated her."

Cerynise glanced down at Alistair and shivered as she averted her face. "What are you going to do about her?"

"Leave her to the sheriff," Beau answered without pause, laying his raincoat over the dead man. "I don't ever want to see that bitch's face again."

He went back to close the front door and, taking Cerynise's hand, pulled her with him as he stepped around the body and moved into the central hall. The house was dark except for a hurricane lamp burning on a table, and though he glanced around and peered into the shadows beyond the meager light, he saw no evidence of any of the servants. "But what happened to the men? Did Alistair kill them, too?"

"No, thank heavens," Cerynise replied. "Moon and Thomas are presently locked up in the carriage house, and Jasper and Cooper are in the pantry...."

"In the pantry?" Beau queried in surprise, taking up the lamp. "Did Alistair put them in there?"

"Aye. Rudd helped him do it, but the last time I looked, Jasper and Cooper were both unconscious."

When they came to the remains of the vase and flowers scattered over the stairs and the marble floor, Beau paused, lifting the light higher. "But what happened here?"

Cerynise glanced around at the mess she had caused. "Well, I had to do something to thwart Alistair's devious plans."

Beau cocked his head as he awaited her answer. "What did you do *exactly*?"

She lifted her slender shoulders, only just now realizing how costly the container had been. Perhaps it, too, should have been put in the linen closet. "I dropped the vase down upon Alistair from above. It cut off his ear."

Beau chuckled in rueful amusement. "Cut off his ear?"

"Alistair was quite perturbed about it. Threatened to sever mine with a saw."

"Well, the way he looked when I came in, I thought he had already ventured into hell and somehow managed to come back," her husband remarked, unable to squelch a grin. "What else did you do to him? Roast him over an open fire?"

"I'm afraid I threw a bookend at the lamp he was carrying. It broke and the oil spilled over him and he caught fire. He ran outside to douse the flames, but he wasn't entirely the same when he came back. Neither was Rudd."

Beau could only stare at his wife in amazement. He hadn't known her capable of such tactics, but he was immensely relieved that she had had the grit and fortitude to prevent the culprits from doing their mischief and that she was now safe. "Where is Rudd?"

"He's in the kitchen." Cerynise bit her lip worriedly, fretting over what she had been forced to do. "I hope I didn't kill him, but I had to make sure that he'd remain unconscious while I dealt with Alistair."

Beau's amazement was advancing by leaps and bounds. "What did you do to Rudd?"

"I hit him with a poker."

"Good heavens, madam! Do you mean to say that you served those men their just due all by yourself?"

Cerynise shrugged her shoulders in a lame gesture of admittance. "I had to do something,

Beau. I overheard them making plans to kill you if you came back early. They were going to take me back to England where eventually they were going to murder me so Alistair could gain the inheritance...."

"But I thought he had already inherited everything...or was it true what he told you on his last visit?"

"He's been lying all along, at least since the day he learned that Lydia had changed her will, leaving everything to me." Cerynise leaned her head against her husband's shoulder as they moved past the stairs. "It must have come as a terrible shock to him after he threw me out of Lydia's house."

"So that's why he was so anxious to reclaim you as his ward."

"He wanted me to expire before witnesses in England so he could claim Lydia's fortune as her only living kin."

Beau paused as he caught sight of something that looked very much like a wraith hovering in the shadows beneath the spiraling staircase. He peered intently at the thing, trying to make it out. "What in heaven's name is that?"

"Oh, that's my friendly ghost," Cerynise announced, waving a hand toward it. "He helped me knock the wind out of Rudd."

Her husband looked at her, truly flabbergasted at her inventiveness. "But what is it?"

"A large kettle with a bag of flour in it and a sheet covering it all," she explained, rather proud of her creation. "I think Alistair and Rudd actually thought it was real for a moment. They screamed as if they thought the banshees of hell were coming after them."

Beau chortled. "Oh, my dear, dear wife. To think that I missed it all!"

"Are we going to leave Alistair in the house while we travel to Harthaven?" she queried worriedly, reverting back to her real concern.

"As a matter of fact, I don't think we'll have to go now," Beau replied. "The storm has changed course and is blowing out to sea. If it doesn't revert back, we'll be safe enough here."

Cerynise heaved a deep sigh in relief. "I wasn't looking forward to the long ride after what I've been through tonight. If not for the fact that I'm a nursing mother, I'd try some of that brandy of yours to calm myself." In some amazement she thrust out her hands to show him how much she was trembling now that he had come home.

"What did you do with our son while all of this was going on?" Beau queried.

"I locked him in the linen closet upstairs." She rose on tiptoes to bestow a kiss upon her husband's lips, and then stepped away. "I'll go and fetch him."

"You'd better wait until I can light a lamp for you. The rest of the house is as black as a bats' haven. I thought when I came home that you had already left because everything was so dark."

"I doused the lanterns so I'd know where those two brigands were. They couldn't get around the house without light, so it was easy for me to keep track of where they were."

Beau lit an oil lamp and handed it to her. "I'm truly amazed at your resourcefulness, madam. I'm also very proud of you for defending your family so well."

"Alistair and Rudd forced me into it." Cerynise accepted his offering with another sigh. "I could have done nothing less."

"Madam, from what you've told me, I can only imagine that you were superb. I'm just sorry I missed it all."

"If you had been here, you'd have taken care of those two in short order." She nodded as she came to a firm conclusion. "I think the next time you have to secure your ship before a storm, I'll either go with you or take your son to Harthaven at the first mention of bad weather. I don't believe I can stand another evening the likes of which I've just experienced."

Beau placed a doting kiss upon the top of her head. "If it will ease your mind, my pet, I'll make a point of staying close beside you whenever storms are approaching. Would you like that?"

"Oh, yes!" Cerynise smiled as she searched his face. "Then I can be assured you're safe, too. The fact that my parents were killed during a storm makes me worry about your safety when you're gone during bad weather."

"Don't fret yourself, madam," Beau urged his young wife. "I'm just as anxious to come home to you."

Cerynise released a long sigh of relief. "I know that, but I shall continue to pray and trust to the heavens to keep you safe for me and Marcus."

Beau grinned and swept his hand toward the stairs. "Go get our son, madam. I haven't seen him all day, and I'd like to bestow a little fatherly attention upon him."

"Yes, sir." She dipped her head in an eager nod and hurriedly picked a path through the broken glass on her way to the stairs.

When Cerynise unlocked the door of the linen closet upstairs, she found that her son had just begun to rouse from sleep. Gathering him close, she murmured loving words against his cheek. "Your papa is down below, my son, and he's wanting to see you."

Marcus blinked his eyes at the light she carried, as if he wasn't at all sure he liked being disturbed by such brightness. Still, he stretched in the curve of her arm and yawned, drawing a smile from his mother.

The kitchen was ablaze with light by the time she entered. Jasper and Cooper were sitting at the table, groggily submitting themselves to their employer, who was in the process of wrapping bandages around their heads. Moon and Thomas, who had been tied up and left in the carriage house, were otherwise unharmed. As for Rudd, he was still living, but no determination could be made as to his condition or if he would actually revive.

Moon and the servants sat around the kitchen table, listening intently as Beau told them what his wife had done. All of the men were clearly astounded by Cerynise's ingenuity and mettle to confront the two villains by herself. The fact that she had shot Alistair after he had tried to kill Beau was understandable in their minds, considering how much she adored her husband.

"It's been a very traumatic day," Cerynise declared, setting her mind to other matters. "And I'm hungry. Where is the food that Philippe packed for us before he left for Harthaven?"

Beau inclined his head toward a pair of baskets that had been left on a far worktable. "I think we could all use something to eat, my love." He glanced around at the men to see if they were in agreement. "Is that right?"

"Ye can bet yer bloomers on that, Cap'n," Moon rejoined jovially. "Me belly's gnawin' on me backbone, an' if'n ye don't mind, I'll have a pinch o' me own rum ta settle me hands." The tar stretched forth the knobby extremities and exaggerated their trembling for their benefit. "I ain't quite o'er that there Rudd fella thrustin' a pistol in me face. He was shakin' worse'n I was."

"I noticed he had some difficulty with that when he held the pistol on me," Beau rejoined with a chuckle. "I was more afraid of it going off by accident than I was of him pulling the trigger. And by all means, Moon, drink whatever you like. I'm sure you could use some strong libation after what you've gone through. In fact, men, feel free to indulge yourselves in something other than tea and coffee. My liquor cabinet is open in the parlor, so help yourselves."

"I wish I had something to comfort me," Cerynise sighed wistfully.

Her husband smiled at her above the houseman's head as he tied off the bandage. "The suggestion you made this morning might serve such a purpose, madam. Perhaps you'll have to try it later."

Cerynise's eyes glowed back at him and held a promise that readily communicated the fact that she was agreeable. "I definitely will, but as for now, I'm famished."

Beau took their son from her, allowing Cerynise to unpack the victuals. Soon a delectable supper was laid out for all of them, and as her husband pulled around a chair to sit beside her, he leaned across his son to pluck at the large hole in her pocket.

"You ruined your dress shooting Alistair."

Cerynise slipped a hand into her pocket and ruefully examined the rent as she thrust three fingers through the hole. "I really didn't expect it to cause so much damage."

Moon cackled in sudden amusement, feeling no pity for the men who had tried to kidnap her. "Jes' think o' what it did ta poor ol' Alistair Winthrop."

Cerynise realized she hadn't seen Alistair's body in the foyer when she came downstairs. "Where did you put him, anyway?"

"Moon and Thomas hauled his carcass out to the carriage house," Beau replied. "There was no sense in keeping it in the hall where we'd stumble over it. The last of the storm should be beyond us by morning. If so, Sheriff Gates can be fetched as soon as it's light.

He'll want to know about Frank Lester and my other suspicions."

If Germaine had truly connived to kill, Cerynise had no doubt that justice would have its day. A shiver was elicited from her as she began to think of the verdict a jury would arrive at and wondered if a woman had ever been hanged in Charleston. Whether for man or woman, it was a gruesome train of thought for her to dwell on. "Let's talk about something else right now."

Beau readily conceded to her wishes. "Mr. Oaks said this afternoon that he and Bridget have finally set a date for their wedding. 'Twill be the second week after he returns from the Caribbean."

"Oh, that's wonderful," Cerynise replied, but as she realized that she'd be losing Bridget, she grew suddenly glum. "But I shall miss her terribly."

"No need, madam," her husband reassured her. "Bridget will be staying on as your maid and, in that capacity, will be traveling with us on the next voyage, much to Mr. Oaks's delight. Of course, she'll have to content herself with sharing his cabin, for my parents are also talking about coming with us."

"Ye know, Cap'n," Moon interjected with a chortle, "maybe ye oughta think 'bout takin' on passengers on a regular basis. Ain't no ship finer 'an the *Audacious*."

Beau grinned and shook his head. "I rather enjoy searching out all that cargo I bring

643

back to the Carolinas and I don't think the passengers would be willing to pay fares that would equal the profits I now make."

"Well, then if'n ye won't consider that, maybe I can offer ye 'nother suggestion. I hears Billy Todd's been lookin' toward a naval career lately. If'n that be true, ye'll be needin' a cabin boy like meself ta see ta yer needs aboard that there fancy ship o' yers."

"That might be a possibility," Beau allowed and then chuckled. "But you know you'll have to tolerate Monsieur Philippe's cooking."

Moon drew his face up in a disgruntled frown. "Ye wouldn't want ta choose betwixt the two o' us, would ye, Cap'n?"

Beau shook his head as if sorely distressed by the choice presented him. "If I do, Moon, I'm afraid I won't be letting Philippe go. I've gotten quite fond of his cooking over the last few years."

Moon winced at the captain's decision and tentatively took another taste of the clam croquettes. He gummed the food for a long moment reflectively before heaving a laborious sigh. "I su'pose I could get used ta this here stuff if'n I had ta."

"I'm afraid you'll have to if you want to sail under me," Beau stated candidly.

Moon cocked a squint toward him and chided, "You drive a hard bargain, Cap'n."

Beau chuckled. "Aye, I do."

The worst of the storm had passed by the time morning arrived. By the ninth hour the authorities had already been out to the Birminghams' residence. When they left, they took Alistair's remains and the injured Rudd with them. The barrister's skull had been fractured, it was later determined, but he would likely recover. If he did, he'd probably spend the rest of his days in prison. There was, of course, a chance that he would hang, but that was for the jury to decide. The injured servants were far more fortunate, for Jasper and Cooper were already much improved and bent on restoring the house to its former splendor.

The following afternoon the sheriff came out to the house to inform Beau that Frank Lester had confessed that he had helped Wilson in an attempt on Cerynise's life and that Germaine Hollingsworth had talked him into doing it, claiming that Beau had offended her. Upon her arrest, the woman had screamed denials like a cornered shrew. Her father had been outraged that such slander could be cast against his precious daughter and had threatened to see the sheriff thrown out of office. But Sheriff Gates had stood his ground and had taken Germaine into custody.

"What a relief," Beau sighed after witnessing the sheriff's departure. "Now I can stop fretting for your safety."

Cerynise slipped her arms around his lean waist and rested a cheek against his broad chest. "Now I won't have to feel like a prisoner in my own home."

Beau leaned back to peruse her face. "What

would you like to do outside our home to celebrate your new freedom, madam? Go to the theater? Have dinner somewhere? Perhaps a visit to the couturier would suit your mood. Or would a carriage ride suffice?"

Cerynise tilted her head at a reflective angle. "Philippe is a much better chef than anyone in the city. I'm not particularly bent on going to Madame Feroux's and listening to her gibberish. There's not a performance at the theater that we haven't already seen. And I'm not interested right now in a carriage ride."

"So tell me, madam, what is your pleasure?"

The corners of her lips turned upward enticingly as she rose on tiptoes to whisper near his cheek, "Playing in the study would suit my pleasure just fine, sir. Would you be interested?"

Beau's eyes sparkled above a wide grin. "Absolutely, madam. It was just the very thing I was hoping you'd say."

With a debonair grin, he offered his arm and escorted her into the front room, where he locked the door securely behind them.

EPILOGUE

Charleston basked in the glory of a brilliantly clear autumn day. The leaves on the trees were turning, and there was a scent of the changing season in the air that was positively intoxicating. Fall flowers were in bloom in the garden around the Beau Birmingham house, and the distant neighing of horses could be heard from their paddocks down the street. Sitting in the backyard gazebo with her husband, Cerynise held her son in her arms and reflected on the fact that everything looked so wonderfully normal. There was no sign of damage from the storm of a fortnight ago.

A happy sigh escaped her, earning a smile from her husband, who sat in a chair beside her. "You sound content, madam."

"I *am* content. Wonderfully so."

Beau glanced around as the butler approached. "What is it, Jasper?"

"A gentleman from England is here, sir, wishing to speak with your wife...except that he called her by her maiden name."

Cerynise was reluctant to go inside and break the revelry of this moment that she was enjoying with her family. "Why don't you show the man back here, Jasper," she suggested. "I'm sure he'll be able to appreciate this fine weather we're having."

Jasper smiled and inclined his head. "As you wish, madam."

The visitor was promptly escorted to the backyard gazebo. He was a man of middling years with neatly trimmed gray hair. His dark trousers, unadorned waistcoat, and somber frock coat proclaimed him a serious sort. The questioning gaze he bent upon Cerynise was certainly most intent. "Miss Kendall? Miss Cerynise Edlyn Kendall?"

"Actually, it's Cerynise Birmingham now,

sir," she replied and swept a hand to indicate Beau. "This is my husband, Captain Birmingham. And you are...?"

"Mr. Thomas Ely, Miss Kendall...'' Hastily he corrected himself. "I mean, Mrs. Birmingham." He smiled. "It may take me a while to get used to your married name, after thinking of you for so long as Miss Kendall. Even after learning you had gotten married in England, I've still continued thinking of you as Miss Kendall, for which I must beg your pardon, madam. I shall endeavor henceforth to use your rightful name."

"Thank you, Mr. Ely."

He looked at her curiously. "May I ask if my name means anything to you, madam?"

Perplexed, Cerynise shook her head. "No, I'm afraid it doesn't."

Thomas Ely nodded as if her answer confirmed something that he had been mindful of for some time. "Before her death, Mrs. Winthrop had indicated that you didn't know anything about her intentions. She was afraid you would be burdened by them, and she loved you far too much to cause you any concern whatsoever."

"Her intentions?"

"To make you sole heir of her estate, apart from a few bequests to the servants, of course."

"But how would you know that?" Cerynise queried in bewilderment.

"Forgive me, Mrs. Birmingham. I should explain that I served as Mrs. Winthrop's solicitor."

"Mr. Rudd was her solicitor for a time," Beau interjected. "Are you aware of that?"

Mr. Ely frowned at the mention of the name. "Oh, indeed, sir. Mrs. Winthrop dismissed him several years ago after deciding that he wasn't to be trusted. She believed he was in league with her nephew, Mr. Alistair Winthrop." A momentary scowl passed across the lawyer's face, but banishing it, he hastened to explain, "Mrs. Winthrop engaged me soon after arriving at that decision. One of my first duties as her solicitor was to draw up a new will." Facing Cerynise again, he added, "The woman was very clearly dedicated in her intent to leave you virtually everything she owned. As it stands now, Mrs. Birmingham, you're a *very* wealthy woman."

Cerynise peered up at him with some perplexity still showing on her face. "May I ask how you found me after all this time, Mr. Ely?"

At Beau's invitation, the lawyer took a seat across from them as Bridget came out to serve them tea. When the maid left, the man took a sip from his brimming cup and sighed in pleasure at the flavor. It was more like the good English tea to which he had become accustomed. Thus far he had failed to find a favorable comparison in the Carolinas. Of course, the cream and sugar helped.

"I fear that my tardiness in finding you will take a bit of explaining, madam," the lawyer apologized at last. "My belated arrival must seem very strange to you, but unfortunately, I suffered an...incident...many months ago. I nearly died and was quite ill as a result, to the extent that for a time I was bereft of my memory. Even when it began to return, the events closest to the time of my... ah...disability...remained rather muddled. It has only been in recent months that I've been able to recall enough to resume my business and my search for you."

Thomas Ely sighed with genuine regret. "After recovering, I made the assumption that you were still in England and that your name was Kendall. When that availed me nothing, I despaired of ever finding you. But shortly thereafter, I realized that you might have married. I began searching through church registries and finally came across a record of your marriage to Captain Birmingham. From there, I spoke with the parson who married you and discovered that you might well be a resident of the Carolinas."

"I applaud your persistence," Beau responded politely. "But I must confess that I'm rather surprised that you came all this distance when you could have easily sent a missive to us."

"Ah, well, as to that..." A deep frown again gathered the man's brows. "I regret to inform you that Mrs. Birmingham may be in some danger. You see, the incident that resulted in my loss of memory was actually an attempt on my life. I was extremely fortunate to survive it. If not for the fact that someone caught sight of me and rescued me soon after I was thrown into the Thames, I wouldn't be here today. Under the circumstances, I thought it best to come posthaste to warn you."

"We appreciate your concern," Beau assured him. "I would presume the man who tried to kill you was Alistair Winthrop?"

The lawyer could not conceal his surprise. "Why, yes! But may I ask how you came by that knowledge?"

Briefly Beau told the lawyer what had happened, and at the conclusion of his story, he added, "It may sound callous to one who has never experienced the trauma of being in constant jeopardy, but I feel enormously relieved that Alistair Winthrop is now dead, and that my wife and I no longer have to live in dread."

A look of immense relief had also settled over Thomas Ely's face. "I cannot tell you what a worrisome weight this news lifts from my own mind, sir. The thought of that man still roaming free and able to strike me down again has dogged my every step since he tried to kill me. I informed the authorities, of course, as soon as my memory returned, but by then he had already disappeared from England, and there was little they could do."

Beau had some questions about the legal arrangements needed to secure Cerynise's property and invited Mr. Ely to spend the night so they could discuss the details further. The lawyer cheerfully accepted, for the first time in many months feeling as if he didn't have to glance over his shoulder to see if anyone was there.

651

Much later, when the couple were at last free to retire for the night, Beau drew his wife from her side of the bed and enfolded her within his arms. "Have you given any thought what you want to do with Lydia's estate?"

Cerynise nodded eagerly against his chest. "Actually, I've been giving careful consideration to that very matter and have come to some definite conclusions, of which I hope you'll approve. Since my paintings have begun to sell for sizable amounts and you're wealthy enough to support your family in a luxurious style...if that were at all our wont...I see no need in selfishly hoarding the bulk of Lydia's estate. So, I'd like to have a large fund set aside to help that nice Parson Carmichael administer to all those children he has taken under his wing and perhaps have an orphanage built for them where they could have beds aplenty. I think Mr. Ely would be willing to oversee the distribution of the necessary funds, don't you?"

"Oh, indeed, madam. If he put himself to so much trouble for the sake of Lydia Winthrop, I have no doubt that he'd be equally dedicated about bringing your desired wishes into fruition. Anything else?"

"Well, I've been thinking of endowing a school for artists where both women and men would be welcomed."

"To paint nudes?" her husband teased.

Cerynise giggled and playfully nipped his chest. "Now don't let your bawdy thoughts get out of hand, sir. There are many things artists can paint besides nudes."

Beau tried to appear saintly, but he failed by a wide margin. Leering at her, he asked, "Would you like to paint me in the nude?"

Cerynise sat back on her heels and, sweeping down the covers, looked his long muscular body over with a positively critical eye. He was certainly a beautiful subject, but his reaction was just as she had expected it would be. She shook her head, feigning exasperation. "How would I ever be able to keep my mind on painting you in the nude when you'd flaunt yourself like that every time I looked at you?"

"Flaunt myself?" Beau pretended a manly outrage, and then threatened, "I'll flaunt myself, madam. Just watch me."

Trying to curb a grin that proved unquenchable, Cerynise closely ogled his manly beauty. "I'm watching, sir. What do you want to show me?"

"This," he murmured huskily, sweeping her down beside him and kissing her with unrelenting passion.

When Beau finally lifted his head, his wife begged breathlessly, "Oh, don't stop. Do it again...over and over and over again...."